SUMMER OF LOVE
A *San Francisco Chronicle* Recommended Book
and a Philip K. Dick Award Finalist

"Just imagine the Terminator in love beads, set in the Haight-Ashbury 'hood of '67." —*Entertainment Weekly*

"Captures the moment perfectly and offers a tantalizing glimpse of its wonderful and terrible consequences."
—*San Francisco Chronicle*

"A fine novel packed with vivid detail, colorful characters, and genuine insight." —*The Washington Post Book World*

"Heartfelt but devoid of flower-child sentimentality, hard-nosed without being cynical, certainly not the last real word on the subject, but arguably the first." —Norman Spinrad

"Remarkable . . . the intellect on display within these psychedelically packaged pages is clear-sighted, witty, and wise."
—*Locus*

"[An] honest yet generous picture of an era slipping quickly into history." —*The Plain Dealer,* Cleveland

"A priority purchase." —*Library Journal*

PANGAEA

BOOK I: IMPERIUM WITHOUT END

LISA MASON

Drawings by
Tom Robinson

BANTAM BOOKS
New York Toronto London
Sydney Auckland

PANGAEA: BOOK I IMPERIUM WITHOUT END
A Bantam Spectra Book / May 1999

SPECTRA and the portrayal of a boxed "s" are trademarks of
Bantam Books, a division of Random House, Inc.

ISBN 0-553-57571-6

Published simultaneously in the United States and Canada

Bantam Books are published by Bantam Books, a division of Random
House, Inc. Its trademark, consisting of the words "Bantam Books" and
the portrayal of a rooster, is Registered in U.S. Patent and Trademark
Office and in other countries. Marca Registrada. Bantam Books, 1540
Broadway, New York, New York 10036.

PRINTED IN THE UNITED STATES OF AMERICA
OPM   10 9 8 7 6 5 4 3 2 1

CONTENTS

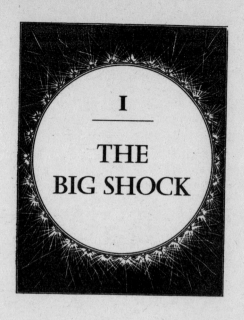

I

THE
BIG SHOCK

FACET 1

> Darkness: Nothing or all.
> Night endures till dawn breaks.
> The action is being.
> The forbearance is doing.
>
> **The Orb of Eternity**

Commentaries:

Councillor Sausal: Thus we commence with the pervasiveness of Pan and the illusion of duality. Before Pan there is Pan; after Pan there is Pan. Pan is All, even that which appears not to be Pan.

Yet this is a time when Pan does not appear to exist. The Eternal has chosen not to reveal Itself.

So, too, in times lost to antiquity, the Imperium was unformed. Yet the Imperium has always reigned, without beginning and without end.

Therefore the prudent person should remain still and await the proper direction.

Guttersage (usu. considered vulgar): Any fool can see that darkness is the beginning and the end, Pan but a fleeting flash of light.

But even a fool might as well stand still. If you stumble around in the dark, ten to one you'll break your neck.

Our City of Atlan, the crest of Prime Hill. Milord Lucyd's cloudscraper, the Villa de Reve:

Only three days had passed since Milady Danti had been murdered, and Our Sacred Imperium of Pangaea still grieved. No one needed more sorrow and confusion over the scandalous demise of the most beloved woman in the Mind of the World. Yet on the morning of the fourth day, by no volition of his own, Lucyd cast the first confounding dream of Danti.

Adamantine sunlight of Pangaean high summer shone through stained glass portals in the dreamchamber, illuminating curves of costly Cordilleran marble and an angel in a sarcophagus, dreaming.

He lay like one dead in an aetheric shell, a morpheus veil shrouding him head to toe. Yet his stillness was illusory, his quiescence deceptive. His Honorable Milord Lucyd Sol naitre Primus cast dreams in the Mind of the World, and when an aetherist of the angels dreamed, all Pangaea dreamed with him.

The shell hummed, a rhythm as steady and reassuring as Lucyd's heartbeat. No one could fabricate aetheric shells like this anymore. An ovoid the size and shape of a capacious coffin, wrought of a single piece of hand-hammered silver, the shell sported kaligraphs of the Omnipresence of Pan that shimmered into being and deliquesced into the argentine sheen. Ancient and elegant, the shell was a prized possession Lucyd had inherited from his mothers, handed down in his family from progeny to progeny since times lost to antiquity.

Hypnolia hung heavy in his senses, vapors scented of anisette and lemon verbena, with an intoxicating hint of raptureroot. Hypnolia once promised oblivion.

Promised sweet dreams.

But not for Lucyd. Not now. Perhaps never again.

Danti! My beloved Danti! How could this happen to you?

Morphic paralysis immobilized Lucyd's muscles. His blood cooled, slowed, lulled, stilled, pulsing to a languorous beat.

Down and down, deeper and deeper, dreaming and dreaming . . .

Platinum curls haloed Lucyd's high-domed forehead, a glabrous face that might have been sculpted of bone. Wide-set eyes—closed now—darted beneath albescent eyelids. An aquiline nose poised above white ribbons of lips, the acuminated jut of a chin. A bodysuit of silver sateen sheathed his long, slender limbs. Substantial diamonds in atlantium settings winked at his earlobes, throat, wrists. The wounds in his carpal bones ached. Bandages swathed his hands. His feet, etiolated and tender, remained bare, the toenails frivolously painted with silver polish. Milord Lucyd loathed any constriction of his feet while he lay in the aetheric shell, dreaming.

He dove deep into hypnogagia, deeper and deeper still, till his waking consciousness flickered and winked out. His dream-eye opened. The Mind of the World lay before him, an infinite glimmer. He sensed the susurration of two hundred million shareminds, avidly awaiting his dream.

Dear Pan, I serve again.

It was his Imperial duty as an aetherist.

His birthright as an angel.

His privilege. And his burden.

Even during this, the greatest sorrow of my life, I serve the Imperium.

He dreamed—

A limestone cliff.

A woman.

She strides along the lip of the cliff, a solitary figure in a windswept gown of Imperial purple silk. Her streaming hair forms a white-gold pennant against the waves of a great bay. A whisper of wind, the sigh of the sea, leaves rustling in a coppice of willows, the plucked strings of a cymbalon played by an unseen musician—these are the only sounds.

The woman halts, poised at the lip of the cliff, and gracefully turns toward the dream-eye.

"My love, how I cherish you," Milady Danti vows. Her

exquisite face glows. Her slanting sapphire eyes blaze like the inner core of a flame, the hottest part, lit by the passion and purity of a sacred sharer. "I will cherish and love you for Eternity."

Everyone dreaming Lucyd's dream instantaneously apprehended this: the supreme purity of Pannish love, love that only sharers in sacred sharelock could give and receive. Everyone also apprehended an extraordinary and gratifying truth: that every person of every pure and subpure in Pangaea, however high or low, could enter into sharelock and know the joys of Pannish love.

Danti smiles her enchanting smile, but abruptly she leans over the cliff. A heedless movement that might have unbalanced her, sending her plummeting to the rocks below.

Lucyd moaned, a ragged exhalation through dry lips. Milady Danti walked and talked in the Mind of the World only as a figment, a distillation. A construct of memories of the woman who once lived and now had vanished from the world of flesh and time.

Danti still appeared in every one of Lucyd's dreams, but Danti herself, Lucyd's sacred sharer of fifty years, amounted to no more than a meticulously preserved corpse reclining in an all too real sarcophagus. The embalmers had told him they'd stitched together what they could and reconstructed the rest of clarified beeswax, carved ivory, and gemstones. They had begged for his opinion of their craftwork.

"Her consecration to Eternity will be attended by thousands and dreamed by millions more," the chief embalmer had said anxiously, wringing her natron-scalded hands. "Please tell us, milord. How well did we capture her likeness?"

Lucyd could not bear to look upon the abomination. *Take it away. Take it out of my sight.* The embalmers had regretfully removed the translucent sarcophagus and taken it to the preservation vaults in the Pyramid of Perpetuities, pending the Imperial consecration.

What a mockery of the Eternal. A desecration of Pan. This corpse wasn't Danti. Not compassionate, lovely, generous, gentle Danti, who hadn't deserved to die the way she did. And die alone, without him, her sharer, at her side.

The agony had struck him first in the utter intimacy of sharer's sharemind. Her excruciating terror. Pain slicing through her knees, her belly, her breasts, her neck. Through her eyes. He'd known exactly when her Essence had fled the agony. And still he couldn't believe it, had hoped against hope it wasn't true. Had fallen to his knees and prayed to Pan like he hadn't prayed in years.

He'd collapsed when the crier had delivered the news, refused to apprehend the atrocity in the stylized gloss of the crier's Imperial sharemind. He'd sent for his house physician. The physician had prepared a potent anesthetic, wielded her scalpel, and cut out the sharelock chips from between the carpal bones of his hands. *Take them out, take them out. I never want to see them again.* Lucyd would permit no priestess-facilitators and their sacred surgeons to examine his bandages. To touch his angelic flesh. He'd refused to see them when they'd come to collect the chips.

Imperial Vigilance Authority had declared Danti's death an act of terrorism: the despicable work of the foes. The foes, always the foes, vicious thugs and terrorist clans of the impure, merciless criminals and mindless fanatics, everpresent and ever elusive. It was an inescapable fact of life and death in Pangaea. No one escaped the pestilential touch of the foes. Their bloody hands touched everyone.

Terrorism? Lucyd's mouth tasted of ashes. His heart clenched in his chest. Terrorism elevated Danti's death to some grand Imperial cause and, at the same time, reduced her tragedy to a political issue. No, her death had been nothing less than senseless, cold-blooded murder. He'd demanded that Vigilance and the High Council *do* something about it.

"It's not as simple as you think, milord," the Chief Commander of Vigilance had told him. "The foes are born among the impure like beasts in the field. But if we must concede the impure are still people, the foes are not." The commander had leaned closer, lowered her voice. "They are living agents of Inim, the Supreme Adversary. Milord, they possess devilish powers."

Lucyd had recoiled from the magister pure. Gigantic in stature, intimidating in demeanor, she smelled of a sour, salty scent. "And Pan defeats Inim as our sun defeats darkness every dawn," he had replied acidly. *What a fine excuse. Typical of a magister.* "Do you dare tell me Imperial Vigilance is blessed and powerful, and the impure despised and powerless, yet your vigiles can't seem to capture these foes whose only birthright is their impurity?"

"We try, milord," the Chief Commander had murmured. Her limpid blue eyes, at first sympathetic, had turned cold.

"Not nearly hard enough," he'd snapped back.

What monstrous incompetence had permitted armed terrorists to infiltrate the Hanging Gardens of Appalacia, where Danti and twenty of the highest angels had gone to view the blooming of the first white roses of summer? Lucyd remembered how she'd laced up her sandals, chosen her gown and her jewels, fastened her hair into a coil at the nape of her neck. How they'd quarreled over whether he'd escort her, and how he'd declined, because lately his head ached after he'd been casting dreams. How after she'd gone he'd administered a bit of nopaine and lain down for an afternoon nap.

Since that dreadful afternoon, Vigilance had posted extra walkabouts on Prime Hill. A maximum security windship circumnavigated Villa de Reve every hour. "I'd advise you to take your own precautions, milord," the Chief Commander had said as she took her leave. "Lest the same terrorists seek your life." Armed bodyguards now stood at every door and ground-floor window of the cloudscraper. To his grief and sorrow unassuaged by the nepenthe his physician had administered, Lucyd added the razor-edged indignity of fear.

Yet a thought, unbidden, occurred to him now: If Pannish love was the vitalizing force of life, the only significant state of the heart anyone could desire, the moral and spiritual bedrock that upheld the Imperium without end, the motivation of every human being, the power that compelled and sustained the generation of the family, the very perpetuation of the Imperium, then—

Then after fifty years of sacred sharelock, Lucyd might as well be dead, too.

Danti hesitates at the lip of the cliff, gazing down at the rocks below. A dead leviathan has washed up, its colossal grey-skinned corpse battered by the surf. Despair furrows Danti's brow as the leviathan's blood stains the rocks. Her eyes film with tears, her mouth grows taut. . . .

"No," Lucyd whispered. Death and ruin had no place in Lucyd's dreams. Nor had despair. No tears. No tears, ever! "This is *my* dream."

"Milord?"

The inquisitive whisper insinuated itself into his dream. *Another* acolyte-auditor? This was the third time in less than half a season that the magisters administering the Temple of the Mind of the World had dared send an acolyte-auditor to intrude upon his dream.

"Now what?" Lucyd snapped.

"Milord, you hesitate. Is anything wrong? May I assist you?"

"I hardly think so."

The absurdity would have provoked Lucyd's derisive laughter if he hadn't been deeply dreaming. An acolyte-auditor assist an aetherist of the angel pure? What a lunatic notion.

What was this person's subpure within the middle purities? Scribe or cleric? One who performed a mundane and technical task like auditing dreams could scarcely pretend to a higher subpure. Most likely his ancestors had for a millennium carved poets' kaligraphs on stone tablets. For the next millennium, they'd inked poets' verses on vellum or parchment. And finally this, auditing aetherists' dreams in the Mind of the World.

A necessary evil? Well, perhaps. Lucyd did not approve of the dreams of conquest and bloodlust other aetherists cast. Yet as long as there were aetherists who cast dark dreams, dreamers who desired to dream them, and—most importantly—Imperial approval, there would be ugly, violent dreams in the Mind of the World. Such dreams typically lacked any redeeming pedagogical value, however, and it was good and necessary that acolyte-auditors scrupulously audited them.

But auditing was strictly middle pure, removing things the main concern, and thus far removed from blessed proximity to Pan.

Whereas Lucyd cast dreams of everlasting beauty. Dreams upon which every pure and subpure could meditate and joyfully learn about Pannish love, the nature of Pan, and Imperial duty. Dreams preserved in the Mind of the World for all Eternity.

Lucyd stood next to the center of Pan, the highest subpure among the highest pure, supremely blessed.

Now the descendant of such a low pure and subpure asked an aetherist of the angels if he required assistance with a dream? What impudence!

What strange situations our new technologies have created.

Such liberties would never have been permitted in times lost to antiquity when the Ancient Ones shaped the Mind of the World, and no magisters or acolyte-auditors hindered them.

Lucyd could envision this particular acolyte-auditor only too well. Some pasty little person strapped in a smeary aetheric shell, Imperium issue, kept strictly under lock and key. He would recline right now in a daub-and-wattle cubicle in a cloudscraper downtown owned by the Temple of the Mind of the World. Reeking of cheap food and cheaper cologne, the acolyte-auditor would quaff caf, yearn for a quid of qut, and count the minutes till his workday was done. Then he'd catch the wagon to his leased villa in Pleasant Valley and forget the travail of auditing dreams. Till he woke next morning and started all over again.

The acolyte-auditor did not *cast* dreams, of course. The Imperial shell he employed permitted only limited access to auditing functions—monitoring, transcribing, rearranging, and, yes, censoring. These limitations were bound to foment resentments. Lucyd harbored a strong suspicion this particular acolyte-auditor didn't dream at all. From his rude voice and ruder manner, it was entirely possible the acolyte-auditor loathed auditing Lucyd's dreams. Acolyte-auditors were grievously underpaid, prone to brooding, and notoriously disenchanted with their subpure.

"Then pray continue, milord," the acolyte-auditor whispered.

Pray continue. Such arrogance! Since when had he ever *ceased* casting dreams for the edification of Our Sacred Imperium? And since when had the temple magisters decided that he, His Honorable Milord Lucyd, required this insulting and interminable auditing?

At any moment of the day or night, a million people on Pangaea dreamed Lucyd's dreams. Another ten thousand among the streetsweepers who unloaded offal on the moon, perhaps all twenty thousand atlantium miners who toiled on Sanguine. This acolyte-auditor wouldn't know of Lucyd's off-world dreamers or of the Doors that led to the other worlds. *The Imperium keeps its Secrets.* Only a few knew of the Doors. But no one could keep secrets from Lucyd. He possessed angel's sharemind, the most powerful of the purities, encompassing them all. Angels could know anything they wanted to. It was their prerogative.

Every pure and subpure was insatiable for dreams of love, and Lucyd could never dream enough of them.

Pray continue. . . .

How can I continue without you, Danti?

"Milord?" the acolyte-auditor whispered again. "We're waiting."

Still Lucyd hesitated, swallowing bitterness and grief.

"Do you wish to finish for today, milord?"

"I've not even begun," came his harsh reply.

"Then pray begin."

Danti sings in a lilting, sweet soprano:

> *I'll stand beside you through the night,*
> *And stand beside you in the dawn,*
> *Oh, sacred sharer.*
> *From life to life,*
> *From now till Eternity,*
> *I'll cherish you,*
> *Oh, sacred sharer!*

"That's more like it, milord," the acolyte-auditor whispered. Didn't even have the decency to keep irony out of his voice. "Give us more of that."

A mischievous quirk plays on Danti's full lips, and a little dimple in her left cheek deepens. A lascivious look slips into her eyes. She blushes, impishly averting her eyes in a mocking show of shame.

Everyone dreaming Lucyd's dream instantaneously apprehended this: that although the purity of Pannish love should never be sullied by the bestial urge, even an angel like Milady Danti sometimes stirred with the ancient shame. Everyone tingled with the sensation of lust aroused and lust consummated.

During fifty years of sacred sharelock, Lucyd and Danti must have visited eroticians fifty thousand times. Lately they'd patronized the Salon of Shame and a delightful person there named Tahliq. Afterward, when they'd taken their fill of Tahliq, they'd gossip endlessly over wine about the irrepressibility of shame, and laugh and laugh and laugh.

But Lucyd permitted no hint of their bawdy escapades in his dream. The shadow of Danti's smile, that was enough.

Swallows swoop across the horizon. Mourning doves warble their bittersweet birdsong. Danti turns away from the lip of the cliff the way she always turns, the way she's turned a hundred times in this dream.

"I must leave you, my beloved," she says.

And then she stumbles.

"No," Lucyd muttered. "No." Surefooted Danti never stumbled. No stumbling in his dreams. No stumbling, ever!

Danti regains her footing, and a furtive expression flits across her face, calculating, sly. Her eyes become veiled, the very irises change, sapphire deepening to the flat black opacity of roadpitch. Coarse vermilion streaks snake through her hair. Her angelic figure shrinks, shrivels, now as misshapen as an impure grotesque. Her gown flaps around scrawny limbs, now a tunic and leggings of black sacking. Danti—can this devilish strumpet be Danti?— stoops and gropes in a clump of ragged grass. Finds an object hidden there. Stands and tauntingly opens her hand.

With a flip of her wrist, she flings the object at the dream-eye.

"No!" Lucyd shouted. "Dear Pan, no."

"Milord?" said the acolyte-auditor, voice alarmed.

It's a jewel, a crystal, a faceted globe about the size of a pondplum. An orb fashioned of atlantium. Diamond-shaped facets reflect sparkles of light as the orb tumbles, inflating, burgeoning till it's gigantic, filling up the dream-eye. On it plunges, implacable, almost willful.

The orb comes at last to a shuddering stop.

A facet rolls into view.

"Don't do this to me, Danti," Lucyd pleaded. But of course she couldn't hear him. She was dead. "I am *not* casting this," he muttered to the acolyte-auditor. "This thing does *not* emanate from my consciousness."

"Then eliminate the foreign object at once, milord," the acolyte-auditor said coldly.

The facet expands till the image etched there overwhelms the dream-eye, obscuring the dream itself. Tiny glyphs shimmer, sinister and inexplicable. Demonic faces appear, whisper harsh incantations, disappear. Till at last there is only—

Darkness.

The dream winked out.

The acolyte-auditor fell silent.

And Lucyd found *himself* standing at the lip of the cliff, a solitary figure in a windswept gown of black sacking. The panorama vanished—cliff, bay, sky—everything, *everything* gone. The cymbalon plunged over the cliff, crashing on the bloodstained rocks below in a cacophony of discordant chords. The wind howled. Lucyd gazed down and an abyss yawned open at his feet. Stones tumbled into bottomless depths. Above the sky boiled away into black oblivion—starless, still, and dead.

Darkness. The province of Inim. The end of everything.

Pan, I wished for death.

Had his wish been granted?

But he wasn't dead. Not dead at all.

His first thought, *What a pity.*

Lucyd gasped for breath, tore the morpheus veil off his face and neck, and peeled it from his chest. Perspiration had pooled over his breastbone, staining his bodysuit. His clenched hands ached, the bandages sticky. He flung back the lid of the aetheric shell, dispersing the hypnolia vapors. He smelled the acrid salt of his own fear. He struggled to sit up.

What the devil was that?

He had *no* idea how the dream of love he'd cast a hundred times before had changed into this confounding thing. *No* idea what the tumbling carved jewel had been, or why the jewel had radiated such strange, disturbing power.

And the strumpet? She certainly wasn't Danti. No, not possible. He didn't know who she was, had never seen her before. How could Danti have changed into a grotesque strumpet? And how could the strumpet have intruded upon his dream?

Only angels possessed aetheric shells for casting dreams. Only the Temple of the World of the Mind possessed shells for auditing. All the rest of the pures enjoyed dreams by invoking Imperial sharemind with the Mind of the World, but they neither cast dreams nor audited them. They only dreamed.

He closed his eyes and shuddered, recalling the strumpet's grotesque face and figure.

Impure.

Was this an omen of his death, then? An impure foe *was* coming to assassinate him?

A shiver slithered down his spine.

In his fifty years of dreaming, he'd never cast a prescient dream before.

The Temple of the Mind of the World would be furious, of course. Lucyd could just hear the magisters' tiresome complaints. *We've trusted you, milord. We've counted on you to cast dreams of love in the Mind of the World. And your dreams have become the stuff of horrible fancies, heedless of your own command.*

Would the temple swear out a complaint and have Vigilance arrest him? Seize his aetheric shell? Flog him in the center of Marketplace for everyone to mock?

Suddenly someone stood over him, silent and purposeful.

Alarm burst in his heart. His eyes flew open. He flung out his hands, shielding his face—as if that would protect him from a death blow. "Who's there?"

"Milord?" It was only his handmaid who stood outside the aetheric shell, anxiously peering down at him. A barrel-shaped creature with an apple-cheeked face, Dote had brought a silver tray with a steaming pot of hazelnut caf, a celadon cup, a syringe and needle, and a vial of nopaine. The sweet scent of the caf wafted through the dreamchamber. "Milord, do you wake?"

"Yes, yes, Dote." Lucyd ran a hand through his platinum curls. His scalp was damp, sour-smelling. His pulse fluttered in his long, narrow wrists. The dream had thoroughly rattled him. "I wake."

Long ago he'd given the handmaid permission to speak first, since serving him often required that she rouse him from a somnolent state—as she did now. But his permission—kindly meant and practical at home—had so confused Dote in her protocol with higher pures outside Villa de Reve that the pious, mild-mannered drud had gotten herself arrested for a protocol violation when she'd offered to assist a blind magister across Allpure Square. "*You* retrain her," Danti had snapped after they'd gone to Quintus Jail, paid the stiff penalty for a protocol violation, and escorted a weeping Dote home. He'd regretfully withdrawn his permission to speak first and reinstated traditional purity protocol.

Now, unwittingly, he hurled his angel's sharemind at the hapless handmaid, who cringed as if he'd whipped her and fell to her knees without dropping the tray.

"Milord," she cried. "Have I offended thee?"

"No, no. Dear Dote, I'm sorry." He'd never required sharemind to command the handmaid. He had no desire to enter into mutual consciousness with her now. With her drud sharemind, she could apprehend perhaps a tenth of his consciousness. The tenth that dominated her. "Do stand."

He turned away as she struggled to her feet, ashamed of the heedless imposition of his Pan-given sharemind upon such a trusting heart. He gazed out a portal, inhaled deeply of the sultry summer air—and coughed. The septic stench of the Bog infused the atmosphere all the way up here, on Prime Hill. It was worse than ever this summer, the reek of that melancholy, forsaken place. The wilderness—banned, sequestered from Our Sacred City, and yet asserting its presence by an inescapable scent. He should take comfort in that—even the Bog withstood oblivion. He inhaled deeply again. Perhaps after all his costly perfumes, hypnolia vapors, and the scent of hazelnut caf, this reek of the lost world within his world was the true smell of Pangaea.

"Dote, tell my majordomo I'm not receiving anyone this morning," he told the trembling handmaid. He could just see the entourage of temple magisters climbing up the hill with the offensive acolyte-auditor in tow. Even the Cardinal herself might attend. *We demand an explanation, milord. We demand your assurance this won't happen again.* And he could satisfy neither demand. "I don't wish to be disturbed till after my midday meal. Bring me my sphinxes."

Dote flung the tray down with a crash and stumbled off to find Lucyd's pets. He clucked his tongue, but forgave her clumsiness. Dote's comforting face, broad strong hands, complete devotion, and grasp of every detail of his personal needs were typical of the handmaid subpure, especially Dote's family. Dote and her ancestors had served Lucyd and his ancestors since the third War of the Rebellion, when Lucyd's family had freed them under the repeal of the mandate of indenture. They'd stayed on out of loyalty and been paid fair wages ever since.

He looked forward to the sphinxes. His sphinxes always inspired his smile and coaxed him into a semblance of cheer.

He sat up in the aetheric shell, disoriented still, and massaged his eyes with gentle fingertips. "Weird things, Danti," he muttered. "I've dreamed weird things I've never *seen* before. And for the whole Mind of the World to dream. The beastly magisters will demand I recant, I know it, I *know* it. And I'm not even sure what I'm recanting *from*. My head is *throbbing*. Danti, are you listening?"

Out of long habit he flung a hand onto the pillow next to him where his codreamer had always lain, caressed the coverlet the way he had for fifty years. He could cast dreams alone, if he wanted to, and had from time to time. But what comfort, what assurance, she'd always given him during the arduous, lonely task of dreaming. Where were the soft curves of Danti's hips, the tiny white teeth flashing between rosy lips, her bell-like laughter?

No one lay next to him. No codreamer shared the shell. He was alone, of course. He ground his teeth till his jaw ached. Infuriated tears stung his eyes. "Damn it, Danti, it's too hard. I *need* you now."

Had he truly lost command of his dreams?

And if that was so, who in all Pangaea could help him, now that Danti was gone?

"Here we are, milord." The handmaid returned with the two sphinxes, one tucked under each stout arm. She released the pets, curtsied, and closed the dreamchamber door.

Lucyd climbed out of the shell. "Come, come, Sitla, Arvel. Come to me." The sphinxes wound around his ankles, mewing sulky protestations. "My pretty pets," he crooned as they gazed up at him with their big, dark, thick-lashed eyes. Their plump little faces grew taut with anxiety at Lucyd's distress. Sitla wrapped her arms around his knee, pressed her face against his calf muscles.

In his time Lucyd had owned eight generations of sphinxes, but these two were the most sensitive. "Your mood muses," Danti had teased him. They entered effortlessly into sharemind with him on the most primitive level, in the inarticulate sanctuary of his Essence, in his heart. He found their simple apprehension comforting, far more soothing than his physician's nepenthe. The sphinxes loosened the knot of pain and grief inside his chest, if only for a moment.

The soft yellow fur on Sitla's arms, high little breasts, groin, and fat calves had been combed and perfumed. The pet fussed with her coiffure. The bangs had been cut straight over her forehead and the rest fell over her shoulders in a wavy golden mass, everything kept in place by a headband of woven copper. Arvel matched her well with his tawny fur, a deeper gold with glints of russet. His tiny biceps and thigh muscles were delightful to behold. He too wore a headband, a necklace, bracelets, and anklets of fine silver chain.

Except for the jewelry, Lucyd's sphinxes ran about naked. Lucyd wondered if he should furnish them with loincloths, perhaps a brassiere for Sitla. But, no, he liked their furry bestiality. In any case, they'd grown accustomed to it. Unlike the handmaid, drud subpures as severely shaped as sphinxes possessed no moral conscience of their own. They observed purity protocol only out of the blindest instinct and lived happily as their master instructed them.

"Now, Sitla, my darling. Easy does it, Arvel," Lucyd murmured as they mewed and pressed against his ankles. "Your master cast a bad dream, that's all. That's why he needs to see you smile." He spoke to them as if they could actually understand. Well, that's what pets were for. Perhaps sometimes they did. Lucyd found a piece of honeycomb on the tray Dote had brought. He broke off a corner. "Beg, Sitla. Beg for me, darling."

Sitla knelt and stretched out her tiny hands in a fetching pose of supplication. He teased her for a moment, dangling the treat up and down while she mewed and grasped at it in frustration. At last he lowered the treat, and she snatched it, stuffing the honeycomb in her mouth. When she finished chewing, she carefully licked her fingers clean, then commenced vigorously biting her fingernails. "Tah, tah," Lucyd scolded her. The sphinx's cuticles were bloody and raw despite Lucyd's efforts to break the pet's bad habit. Perhaps the recent earthshock activity, Lucyd thought, had disturbed the poor little thing.

Arvel playfully seized Sitla's hand and stole a kiss on her downy cheek. Lucyd lightly slapped Arvel's wrist, but he had to smile. He spied the pet's tiny erect member through the fur of his belly. *That's* why he didn't clothe them; they were much too entertaining this way. "Stop flirting, Arvel, or I'll have to put you outside. And Sitla, little darling, *please* stop biting your nails."

Bong! Bong! Bong! Bong! Bong!

They flinched, all of them, master and pets, as the Harbinger commenced tolling.

The gigantic gong's basso tones reverberated across the megalopolis of Atlan, sending a palpable quiver through the sultry air. A five-mag earthshock was about to strike, that's what the tolling signaled. Lucyd dashed to the water clock, carefully counted the measured drips. Each drip a second, each second signaling a minute of warning. Thirty drips and then—

Bong! Bong! Bong! Bong! Bong!

He tore open the dreamchamber door and shouted to his staff, "Prepare the house. We've got thirty minutes."

How could one properly prepare an entire cloudscraper for an earthshock in thirty minutes? Lucyd fumed. Our Imperial Bureau of Ground Control really ought to do better at predicting than that. And what about the promises of preventing earthshocks? Preventing them, once and for all? Instead there had been more earthshocks than ever in recent years, more shocks and stronger ones than Lucyd could recall in his sixty-seven years. A four-mag shock just last week had dislodged the mortar of five million chimneys in Central Atlan and rent a nasty crack through the foundation of Villa de Reve.

A breach of promise, that's what it was. A failure of Imperial duty. Perhaps even a sin against the perpetuity of the Imperium. *He,* Milord Lucyd, was expected to continue casting dreams despite the most devastating loss of his life, yet the smug magisters administering Ground Control permitted another earthshock? And not just a trembler. Five mags!

"Peace and calm, my pets," Lucyd murmured to the frightened sphinxes as Villa de Reve commenced battening down. The cloudscraper was quite intelligent, more intelligent than most angels' houses. He couldn't imagine how the lower pures fared, with no intelligence in their dwellings at all. The furnaces shut off, the shutters clapped shut, the basement reservoir filled to capacity from Lucyd's private water table and sealed itself shut. His handmaids scurried about, latching closets and cupboards. The housemaids secured the crystal and the rare ceramics. The cooks doused the cookstones in the ovens. The majordomo barked orders to the beck-and-call men, who secured the grounds and regarded the hired bodyguards with undisguised suspicion.

Bong! Bong! Bong! Bong! Bong! Bong!

Six mags?

Alarm jangled through Lucyd's nerves.

The floor shuddered, just the slightest tremble, as if the cloudscraper had drawn a tremulous breath and released it again. Lucyd's own breath caught in his chest. Sitla squealed, her fur raised in alarm. Arvel's eyes widened, his pupils huge. *It's going to be the Big Shock,* Lucyd knew with sudden certainty.

Is that what the dream signified?

The Darkness was an omen that the Big Shock has come?

Villa de Reve had stood for centuries. He'd expected it to stand for centuries to come. The cloudscraper had been superbly constructed and securely bolted to the solid bedrock of Prime Hill. Lucyd inspected and improved the foundation once a year. He'd commissioned builders to repair the crack from the four-mag but—they hadn't yet started the assignment.

A six-mag?

He feverishly recollected what a magnitude meant. *Ten times the force.* Then a five-mag would be ten times more destructive than the four-mag, and a six-mag would be ten times again more destructive than a five.

Would the ancient prophecies of the Apocalyptists be fulfilled at last?

Lucyd ran to a portal, released the shutter and the stained glass pane, and peered out, desperate to gaze at his spectacular view.

Will this be the last time?

The blue haze of Sausal Bay extended to the northern

and eastern horizons. A charming assemblage of ships and
piers and waterfront establishments rimmed the boardwalk.

There, directly above the Sacred Center of Marketplace,
hovered the Pagoda of Pan, a massive stabile of Imperial
purple and dazzling gold, the upturned eaves and floating
rafters every Pangaean knew.

Directly below, the Obelisk of Eternity thrust up from
the dazzling white flagstones of Allpure Square. Symbolic
of the ascension of the material plane to the aetheric—and
upward, to all Eternity.

Lucyd shifted his gaze. On the northeast promontory of
Imperial Hill, the stupendous pink-granite edifice of Our
Supreme Temple of Sacred Sharelock commanded a fine
view of its own.

Antiquity Park and Allpure Library lay between the temple and the hustle-bustle of Central Atlan. The gentle lawns
and crumbling fountains yielded to north Marketplace, the
serv quadrant to the northeast, the drud quadrant to the
northwest. Along the periphery of these quadrants stood
the Imperial Natalries and Natalry Bank, hulking storehouses taking up six tremendous municipal blocks. Lucyd
approved of the natalries' location. It was true every unborn
pure grew there, and thousands of priests, priestesses, and
physicians of the middle purities staffed them. It was also
true thousands more serv and drud subpures staffed the
natalries, midwives and orderlies who carried out the filthy
labor of growing unborns. Lucyd sniffed. Better, then, for
such vital but repellent establishments to abut the low-pu-
rity quadrants, as the low pures themselves were vital but
often repellent.

The cluster of commercial cloudscrapers jutting up like
silver teeth along southeast Marketplace housed Vigilance
Authority, the Security Number Administration, the Temple
of the Mind of the World, and an Imperial treasury. Also
good. Middle-purity bureaus ought to stand proximate to
the middle-purity quadrant, though Lucyd disapproved of
how the temple abutted the periphery of the magisters'

quadrant to the southwest. One of the temple's rafters nearly touched the floor of the angels' mezzanine floating overhead.

Lucyd shifted his gaze further southwest, to the Pyramid of Perpetuities. There, the Imperial consecration of Danti would take place after the official mourning period.

He could not bear to look at the pyramid. Could not bear to think of Danti, lying in the frozen darkness of the preservation vaults. *Where are you now, my beloved? The Supreme Memorializer says there is no death, that with proper consecration, you will enter the Eternal and wait for me. But what does that really mean?*

He swept his eyes to northwest Marketplace. Rancid Flats began abruptly at the edge of the drud quadrant. Shabby shops and saloons and eroticians' salons led to the promiscuous mix of daub-and-wattle hovels of drud pures and impoverished serv subpures. The black-thatched rooftops stretched to the horizon.

Lucyd squinted. Above the flats rose the glittering brass plate of the gong and its tripod set upon the sharp incline of Harbinger Hill. And far beyond the flats, punctuating the horizon with its turrets and machiolations, rose the Great Wall separating Our Sacred City from the Bog.

So familiar. So enduring. Beloved Atlan.

Fifteen minutes, and counting. His pulse palpitated with anxiety. Was that another tremble beneath his feet?

A majestic windship sailed overhead, its silver sails billowing. Bright blue kaligraphs skimmed across its hull, depicting the Verses of Ecstatic Obedience to Pan. A Vigilance craft, surveilling the streets.

Such lovely, everlasting streets. Even Rancid Flats struck him as a vision of changeless stability. Lucyd watched a gaggle of clovens, identical slender brown-haired children perhaps ten years old, as they were shepherded across Panthalassa Boulevard by two sturdy caretakers, protocol chips blazing like little yellow suns in their foreheads. Middle pure clovens, from their modest stature and green-and-bronze-striped cloaks, heading for an earthshock shelter in southeast Marketplace.

Or so Lucyd hoped. He wanted to shout out the portal, *Hurry!*

He gasped instead. Two dark furtive figures stole across the boulevard behind the clovens. Two silver slivers gleamed in the summer sunlight. *Daggers?* The furtive figures fell upon the cloven children, stabbing, swiping at bookbags, food sacks, purses. Reedy little cries split the air.

Foes! Hateful, pestilential foes.

The audacity! In the midst of an earthshock warning. And for what? A sack of flatbreads? Lucyd leaned out the portal, strained his eyes. *Is that blood? The blood of pure little children?*

The Vigilance windship abruptly swiveled.

"It's about time!" Lucyd shouted out the portal. "*Get them!*"

Two vigiles stepped out onto a side deck of the windship, one with a crossbow, the other a firebolt. They trained their weapons, fired. Iron darts and bursts of flame rained down upon the furtive figures.

The foes sprinted down the boulevard, dark cloaks rippling behind them.

The windship soared after the fugitives.

But if Lucyd's eyes weren't deceiving him, the foes abruptly vanished.

Living agents of Inim.

Did he believe the Chief Commander now?

He wasn't certain what to think. Only that he'd seen the furtive figures vanish.

The weeping caretakers knelt beside their terrified charges, embracing the wounded. A siren ululated, threading through the clang of the Harbinger. A Tertius infirmary ambulance clattered up, followed closely by a squad of walkabout vigiles. The caretakers loaded the children onto the wagon.

Wagon and vigiles sped toward southeast Marketplace.

Seven minutes, and counting.

Fury choked him. *Why does Vigilance permit these abominations?* And a needle of fear. *Why were two foes lurking about the base of Prime Hill?*

Below in the walled garden surrounding Villa de Reve, a flock of startled ornises flew up into a pital tree. The ornises' twittering grew louder, harsh and frenzied, as if the birds had spied a serpent or a cat. A guttural roar drifted into Lucyd's ears from over a great distance. The beasts in the Bog were trumpeting and howling.

Suddenly lightning crackled over the bay, though Lucyd could see no storm clouds. A powerful metallic stench infused the air. The wind lifted in an eerie keen. Waterspouts spun up out of the waves offshore, whipping the bay into frenzied whirlpools. He could see gigantic waves rearing, crashing over the Sausal Boardwalk, ripping ships from their moorings, smashing hulls against piers, smashing the piers themselves. Shopfronts and saloons and Imperial Fire & Shock crews disappeared beneath the deluge.

The Harbinger reverberated ceaselessly now, the tones assaulting Lucyd's ears and nerves. With the keen of the wind came the keening of people.

And then:

A booming rose out of the morning, growing louder, and louder still, the way thunder rumbled when a summer storm blew in. But this thunder resounded from deep below the ground.

The shock struck.

Our Sacred City quaked, the quaking motion changing into a violent swivel. Great temples and cloudscrapers pitched back and forth, not huge blocks of granite and tremendous lattices of metal anymore, but a child's toys of straw and stuffing.

The Shrine to the Unknown Ancestor in Antiquity Park toppled with a roar, geysering chunks of mortar and petrified wood. Eruptions of dust churned up throughout the megalopolis as structures shook apart and collapsed.

A fissure split open down the center of Panthalassa Boulevard. A wagon and team plunged into the newly carved chasm. Anguished bellows of the driver and drayers rang out.

Fires flared in the flats as spilled cookstones ignited the parched daub-and-wattle hovels, commencing a deadly dance over thatched rooftops.

Villa de Reve shuddered, a turbulent, jagged motion. The breakfast tray went flying, hot caf gushing out of its pot and purling across the floor. Lucyd staggered, fell to his knees. Pain exploded through his right kneecap where he'd had surgery last year to remove torn cartilage. Another jolt flung him clear across the marble floor.

The sphinxes loped away, yelping. Lucyd shouted after them, "Sitla? Arvel? You stay!" But they were gone. After the four-mag shock, he'd found the pets huddled in the linen closet, nestled in a mound of flannel sheets. How he'd wished he could have joined them.

Lucyd crawled on his bandaged hands and aching knees, seeking refuge next to the aetheric shell. On and on the shock rocked. *Will the whole world shatter? Sheets of ocean, slabs of cities, flung into the void, leaving nothing but a dead cinder spinning in space?*

Nothing but Darkness?

"It *is* the Big Shock. Damn you, Pan." Lucyd shook his fist. "Make it stop!"

As if, so commanded, Pan would reach out and hold Pangaea fast, as the Imperium had held fast since times lost to antiquity.

But the shock didn't stop.

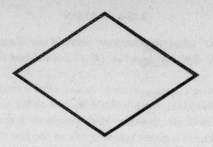

FACET 2

> Light: All or nothing.
> The day shines till twilight covers it.
> The action is doing
> The forbearance is being.
>
> **The Orb of Eternity**

Commentaries:

Councillor Sausal: Thus we proceed to Pan revealed in full glory and the manifestation of all things of the world in degrees of proximity to Pan. This is an auspicious time when beginnings succeed, progress advances, and completions end well.

So, too, the Imperium reigns in full glory and resists all impurity, chaos, and darkness.

Therefore the prudent person should enthusiastically commence new undertakings, diligently pursue undertakings in progress, and expeditiously complete undertakings nearly finished.

But beware. Without constant vigilance, impurity corrupts purity, chaos defeats order, darkness overcomes light.

Guttersage (usu. considered vulgar): A builder constructs the magister's house in the day, but neglects to install a lock on the back door.

A foe enters the back door at night, murders the magister, and steals his jewels.

Northwest Atlan, five leagues beneath the Sausal Coast.
Appalacia Rift, the Imperial Observation Chamber:

The massive chasm convulsed before Plaia's terrified eyes,
and she shrieked, though she'd trained at the academy to
observe landmass bounce. Had witnessed a dozen nasty
earthshocks in a dozen unstable rifts in the past season and
a half alone. Had known, as a mastery student in resonance
theory and application, more or less what to expect.

Not this time.

The observation chamber vibrated with bone-crushing
force. Choppy images oscillated before her eyes—the
rough-hewn rock, jags of lamplight, the resonance team
huddled against the wall. Carved in the southern periphery
of Appalacia Rift out of superhard basement granite, girded
with stupendous metal struts arching across the curved
walls and domed ceiling, the chamber had been designed to
withstand earthshocks of nine mags or more—theoretically.
Now *every*thing shuddered as if solid stone—the whole
world!—had transformed into gossamer before the onslaught of a tempest.

The side of the rift wasn't just bouncing. It was . . .
Plaia didn't know *what* the hell it was doing. She'd never
felt a rift move like this before. If gravity had suddenly
loosened its grip upon the planet, and they'd all been
scooped off the floor and smashed against the ceiling, she
could not have been more astounded.

"Damn you, Gunther," she shouted, sincerely loathing
her bedmate of the moment. Who cared if he was also her
proctor at the academy and super of the resonance team?
"It's the Big Shock, we're too *late*—"

—realization like a punch in the face—

"—and we're all gonna fucking *die*!"

Gunther mouthed a reply, but she couldn't hear a word.
Panicked, couldn't even *try* entering into sharemind with
him or her teammates. Or maybe their mutual conscious-

ness *was* this paralyzing panic, the last state of consciousness she'd ever know.

She clung to the safety harness binding her to the chamber wall, alternately cursing and praying, for all the good
either did. She ground her jaw, tried desperately not to bite
off her tongue. Her fingernails gouged bloody crescent
moons into the palms of her hands.

Six mags, hell. Who knew how much planetary force
bucked beneath her feet?

It's the demons Pan cast out of Eternity, her gentle second father had told her after she'd been flung from her bed
by the five-point-seven centered directly below Pleasant
Valley. She'd been four years old, it had been twenty-six
years ago, but she never forgot that terrifying night. The
fearsome clanging of the Harbinger. The roar of the shock.
The violent shaking. Things whizzing over her head in the
dark. The north wing of her fathers' villa had sunk into
sandy soil churned into quicksand by the vibrations. The
house next door had collapsed. Two villas down the block
had caught fire and burned to the ground. She and her
sisters had wept, convinced the stories children told each
other about the end of the world had come true. *Demons of
Inim, trying to shake Pangaea apart from hell. But they
can't, our daughters,* gentle Trenton had assured them. *Pan
and the Imperium won't let them.*

Some fable for babes! The monstrous shaking was nothing *less* than demonic. The Imperial Bureau of Ground
Control, in all its idiocy, was right about one thing: Earthshocks were increasing, in frequency and intensity, in every
known rift in the world archipelago. The shocks threatened
the very bedrock of Pangaea.

Threatened the perpetuity of the Imperium.

Who knew what might happen if the shocks went on?

The end of the world.

And now before Pan and the Imperium, the resonance
team had failed. *Why didn't Ground Control send us down
here sooner, when we might have done some fucking good?*

But a little *shaking* wasn't all they were in for, oh no. Plaia tightened the strap of her safety helmet and braced herself. Fissures shot through the northern facade of the rift, crackling through the solid granite wall like cheap glaze on pit-fired pottery. With an earsplitting roar, the facade collapsed. A layer of schist as thick as her two outspread arms sheared off, flinging an avalanche of gravel into the chasm.

Flinging gravel *across* the chasm, too. Rock cascaded upon the place where she, Gunther, and the resonance team crouched, clutching their harnesses and musical instruments in trembling fists.

She hunched down, tightened her shoulders and neck.

Bang! on the crown of her helmet. And *bang . . . bang, bang, bang bang bang bang bang.*

Sickening, rotten-egg reek of sulfur fumes. She spied fiery sprays of magma gouting deep in the rift. There'd been magma eruptions at Andea Rift, unexpected eruptions of tremendous force and volume. Some of the finest minds the academy had ever seen had died in the Andean observation chamber.

Including Tivern.

Brilliant, beloved Tivern. The notion of Tiv in agony, consumed in a blast of magma, grieved Plaia beyond tears. And terrified the piss out of her now.

Aboveground the five predictors of a major earthshock at Appalacia Rift—subterranean fumes, well water shifts, salinity shifts, foreshocks, animal perturbations—had been crystal clear. An impassive crier from Ground Control had descended the well shaft to the chamber at Cordilleran Rift where, after the four-mag, the resonance team had been working for days, up at dawn till late into the night, patiently conducting postshock observation and resonance application. The crier had summoned them, posthaste, to the Sausal Coast. Plaia hadn't even had time to dream. The Harbinger had reverberated in her ears as the team sped down the shaft to the chamber. The gongmaster—and the bureau—had dallied *way* too long.

The floor of the observation chamber abruptly sank beneath her feet, undulated, swiveled.

The landmass of the whole world *swiveled?*

She glared at Gunther. *They* had no time to dally! Surely he would signal the team to evacuate the chamber, at once, under extreme emergency.

He did no such thing.

What was their esteemed super doing?

As usual, Gunther was shouting frenzied commands, slapping at his forehead with the palm of his hand, agonizing over the magnetometer, the magnitudometer, the salinometer with its irritating *drip-drip-drip*. All the while flipping his dull yellow quiff over the pink dome of his skull, dodging gravel, frantically waving his conductor's wand around.

As if the team could possibly take scientific measurements, let alone produce resonance when they were all going to fucking die.

He was such a fussy flibbertigibbet conscientious académé, oblivious of everything save the task at hand, oblivious of everyone save himself, it made Plaia want to puke. They'd be crushed by rock, incinerated by magma, and he'd still be worrying about recording the data and losing his hair.

And this man—a *man* no less—wanted to enter into sharelock with her for Eternity? Mistress Plaia Triadana (also known as the Plaything in certain circles) naitre Tertius? Oh, académe men were appetizing and amusing and definitely her predilection in bed. But such unreliable and tempestuous creatures that she had to wonder if entering into sacred sharelock with one was such a good idea.

Gunther had badgered her night and day with the big question since they'd embarked on the riftsite expedition. Sometimes she suspected he'd arranged the whole thing—luring her with ten credits toward her mastery—just to keep her away from her chums. Who naturally exhorted her to dump the silly bore and go tavern-hopping with them again.

Now the rain of rock eased to a drizzle. If they managed to flee the chamber alive, Plaia and her teammates would suffer half deafness for days, would have to sign and mime for a shot of teq at Abandon All Hope Saloon on the Sausal Boardwalk.

If anything was left of Abandon All Hope.

Or the Boardwalk.

Or Atlan.

"Play, damn you all," Gunther shouted. "Don't curse at me. Do you believe in resonance? Yeah? You do? Then play, damn you all, play."

Her teammates released their grip on their harnesses and withdrew their musical instruments from where they'd been sheltering them, cradled against breasts, tucked between knees. Ribba fingered her flute, Donson struck a chord on his zitar, Paven pattered on his drums. Plaia seized her cymbals and gently touched them together, rubbing the brass edges in a circular motion, producing a sound like a gentle sea.

Miraculously, they began to play. The beautiful resonance soared down through the expansive brass mouths of the amplifiers, reverberating deep into the rift.

And then, and then—like a sorcery, the flute's lilting notes, the zitar's harmonious chords, the measured drums, the whispering cymbals echoed up and down in the rift. The bucking of the rock eased to a nerve-wracking roll. The deafening roar died away to a reproachful grumble.

Plaia glanced into the wide eyes of her teammates, their irises obliterated by dilated pupils, their pale faces stricken. Human stinks of urine, vomit, and excrement cut through the rift's mephitic haze. Here and there, someone bent over, overcome by sickness.

Their sharemind was excruciating.

Never seen anything like it—the Big Shock—is it really?—couldn't be the Big Shock, we're still here. Yeah, it

was the Big Shock, and we're still here. Or are we dead?
Yeah, we're dead, we just don't know it yet. See? Crushed
skulls, fresh brains, greyish and terra-cotta-colored, intesti-
nal-looking. Dislodged eyes splattered on the floor, optic
nerves trailing, fibrous stalks—

How rude! Who envisioned such morbid fancies?
Enough! Plaia abruptly withdrew her consciousness. No
one among the team could compel her into sharemind, except perhaps Gunther flexing his super's prerogative, the
furrow between his brows glinting with the academy's tiny
protocol chip. And then only as to matters pertaining to the
team.

She frowned. Actually, Gunther *could* compel her into
sharemind through purity protocol. As the slightly higher
subpure between the two of them, his sharemind was
slightly more powerful. Plus, as the higher subpure, he held
the prerogative.

His academe subpure had been elevated by the wild
streak of an inventor. Some rambunctious ancestor had designed a crank for an Imperial thresher—still in use—af-
fording all the descendant families preferred status in
engineering and scientific academies. Whereas Plaia's ancestors had plodded along, dutiful proctors in science masteries with strains of librarian, categorizing and arranging
the knowledge of the world.

He wouldn't dare bully me.

She loathed the notion that he *could.*

Even Paven, whose ancestor had been an eminent geo-
physical theorist, but whose immediate family had lost their
money in unlucky investments, wasn't a bully. As for the
scope and power of anyone's sharemind, it was one's birthright, according to pure and subpure. But you initiated or
entered into mutual consciousness according to tempera-
ment. All young scientist-musicians of the academe subpure, her teammates were a sensitive lot. Highly educated
like everyone of the middle purities, order and information
the predilection of their subpures, more or less well-bred, of

modest stature yet nicely shaped, they were neither magister perpetrators of derring-do and domination nor drud ductdiggers with the sensibilities of a stone.

Why the *hell* hadn't Ground Control ordered them down here sooner?

Gunther's commands grew more audible, his nasal tenor hoarse, cracking with strain. "Reset the magnetometer. Julretta, get a reading off the magnitudometer, *now*. Paven, *beat* those bloody drums. You want to restore harmony? You believe in resonance? Then play, damn you all, play. Plaia, get your sweet ass over here and bang those cymbals before I bang you."

The scientist-musicians paused, astonished that Gunther actually intended to stay. *Stage a mutiny,* crackled through their sharemind—Plaia's outraged contribution—followed by enthusiastic affirmations. *That's what we've got to do. Pummel Gunther into a bloody pulp, work the pulley in the well shaft, and get the hell out of here.*

But Plaia couldn't summon the energy to spearhead a mutiny just now, lovely though it would have been to punch Gunther right in the teeth. No one else stepped forward to claim the honor. His super's sting buzzed through their sharemind. To Gunther's humiliatingly explicit command, Plaia tossed her curls, pulled her leggings a little tighter around her sweet ass, and told him, "Bog off, chum."

Yet play they did, and quite well, too, producing some of the most beautiful resonance Plaia had ever heard from their ensemble. Gunther had chosen the symphony of the Fires of Longnight, simple soothing tunes every caretaker had sung to every babe of every pure in all Pangaea—maybe even babes of the impure, too—since times lost to antiquity.

They could all thank Tiv for their present predicament.

Plaia had studied under Tivern's proctorship at Sausal Academy after she'd changed her mastery for the fourth time. The proctorship had been brief, lasting a mere season. Yet in that season Tivern, the eminent resonance theorist who played a dazzling flute, had been an inspiration. Someone Plaia could finally respect and admire—and emulate. Resonance theory was an exciting new direction in earth-shock prevention. Not to mention a respectable calling for any academe, almost guaranteed to secure funding and out-placement with Ground Control.

Plaia had regretfully discovered she didn't possess much talent with flute or cymbalon or zitar—and only a little more with drums. But she was very good with cymbals, attentive and passionate, never missing her cue. She'd felt happier than she'd been in all her years of fumbling around at the academy, combining her new mastery in resonance with the ecstatic clashing of brass.

"We hope you can stay with this mastery long enough to graduate before you're thirty," her fathers had admonished her.

She'd been dining with them at the Feast of Darkmoon, and they'd loudly proclaimed this fine, sarcastic speech in front of her sisters, their sharers, their families, and four other families of their subpure. She'd sprung to her feet, flung her napkin into her plate of noodles, and stalked out of the feasthall, aflame with indignation and shame.

She *was* sincere about resonance. She *believed* that resonance would ameliorate, maybe even prevent, earth-shocks and preserve the everlasting peace of Our Sacred Imperium.

And then Tivern had died at Andea before spring had turned to high summer, and Gunther had assumed her proc-torship.

Ground Control had downplayed the catastrophe. The criers announced that Tivern had perished of a wasting dis-ease and one of the angels, Milady Esobel, cast a slick dream of the academe's life in the Mind of the World. Plaia happened to know Tivern *had* smoked too much bacco and drunk too much skee for far too many seasons. It was a plausible explanation, and sufficiently tragic. Tivern's family had consecrated her Essence to Eternity in a private ceremony. Plaia hadn't been invited.

But rumor had its own sly ways. The Imperium, the Mind of the World, the angels and their dreams, the priests and priestesses and acolyte-auditors, the magisters administering Our Sacred City, the vigiles patrolling the streets—none of them, not all of them put together could suppress the sheer exuberance of rumor. "To rumor!" Plaia and her chums proclaimed over shots of teq at Abandon All Hope Saloon.

And rumor whispered a magma eruption in that faraway riftsite had taken Tivern's life. An eruption where no known magma chamber had ever been charted before. What did *that* signify for landmass bounce?

Tivern had predicted bounce, the capricious upward and downward movements of the shell of rock upon which the whole world perched. Bounce occurred in zones where the basement rock hadn't yet cooled and remained unstable, creating rifts—gaps and cracks in the cooler upper strata. The reverberations of bounce in an unstable zone caused the shocks that disrupted the entire shell.

Tivern had installed observation chambers deep within each major rift to study the nature of bounce. After several riftsite expeditions, she'd discovered another startling fact. Each rift produced its own distinctive vibration—a resonance, a chord. Subsequent intensive riftsite expeditions garnered yet another provocative observation. When the five predictors showed up, the distinctive vibration within a rift became discordant, and earthshocks occurred.

Tivern—ever the iconoclast, a reputation that drew rebellious academes like Plaia as surely as feltwings flew to a flame—had declared that the world was a living being. A *listening* being. Ground Control had never fully endorsed her view. But if Ground Control had mastered shock prediction, the bureau had failed miserably at prevention. And Tivern had developed a tantalizing application based on her theory: resonance. When the five predictors indicated disharmony was mounting in a rift, the projection of beautiful music, of resonance, deep into the chasm would soothe the restless rocks.

Restore harmony.

Ease the earthshock.

Sometimes it did.

But resonance was just a theory.

Perhaps an impossible dream.

"Oh, daar-aar-kest night," Plaia sang softly. "Holy night. All is calm. All is right. 'Round yon natalry, sharers with child. Holy infant, so pure and so mild—"

"Beautiful. That's beautiful," Gunther shouted. He'd stripped off his cloak, tunic, undershirt, and all his soft sweaty flesh jiggled, rather like he jiggled during fucking. Plaia envisioned him now, lying beneath her in his bedroll while she writhed astride him, seeking her shameful release.

He had his virtues.

Like what?

First, he *was* a man. She liked fucking him, he adored fucking her, and he sincerely tried his best to please her. Every now and then, he did. But that was only the bestial urge, the shame remaining from the barbaric times when men and women were compelled to bed each other just to generate a family.

Was *that* any reason to enter into sacred sharelock?

Hardly. No one needed to copulate just to generate a family anymore.

Come, now. Surely he's got other virtues.

All right.

Second, he held a proctorship at Sausal Academy and a temporary consultancy at Ground Control. Gunther was an up-and-comer. He'd believed in Tivern, in resonance application. As her proctor he believed in Plaia, despite her uneven transcript.

A much better reason.

Third, of course, he was an equal academe middle pure, his subpure slightly higher, her intelligence slightly higher. All things considered, well matched.

Yes, but that amounted merely to a convenience in meeting Imperial sharelock requirements. Matching that way wasn't *always* the answer to a sound sharelock.

Fourth, he'd inherited from one of his mothers a modest but comfortable villa and a small pondplum paddy that he leased to a family of hardworking druds.

She would inherit a tidy fund and an interest in her fathers' villa one day, but that didn't help her standing in their protocol right now. Right now all she possessed was her family stipend, which would be paid over to Gunther as the superior sharer and disbursed by him to her at his discretion.

If they entered into sharelock.

Fifth . . .

No, no, *no*.

She couldn't go on. Maybe Gunther didn't compel her, but he always spoke first. Touched her first. Entered into sharemind first. Paid for everything whenever they went out, stipulated where and when they'd go, and what they'd eat and drink. As was his prerogative as the higher subpure.

How she resented his prerogative!

And if she was suspicious of his prerogative now, of the slightly stronger and broader sharemind that was his birthright, how would she feel when they became sharelocked? When their intimacy became complete? What if he compelled her into a sharers' sharemind that frustrated and demeaned her?

Entering into sharelock was the most momentous decision anyone ever made, second only to one's duty to sustain the Imperium through destined labor. Or perhaps *not* second. Perhaps the duties of labor and sharelock were one and the same. Perhaps one duty stood at the right hand of Pan, the other at the left.

Sharelock with Gunther for Eternity?

No. Impossible.

She didn't feel Pannish love for him. And that was that.

In any case, Plaia liked being shareless. She could fuck whomever she pleased within her pure. There were plenty of attractive shareless bedmates in proximity to her subpure.

Why *should* she enter into sharelock?

Imperial duty made her blood run cold.

"Exquisite, people," Gunther shouted. "Superb! And now, gently, gently, Plaia, build up to your crescendo like you always do, my pretty pet."

She winced at his incessant public announcements that they were bedding. *That's it. Break it off as soon as this tiresome expedition is over. I'll hold my own at the academy. I don't need his proctorship.*

Julretta, bent over the mag meters, winced, too. A doleful young woman with the lank brown hair, somber brown eyes, squat little pear-hipped figure, and perpetual scowl of so many female middle pures who staffed the academies and offices of the Imperium, Julretta had been one of the younger students Plaia counseled over the last season. Plaia had led Julretta, as Tivern had once led her, into resonance theory and application. They'd quickly fallen into a complex and ardent companionship.

How unlike uncouth Gunther Julretta was. The young woman had often told Plaia—quietly, in private—how much she adored Plaia's passionate spirit and restless, quick mind. And her unusual reddish gold curls, her odd golden green eyes, her curved cheekbones, her luxurious mouth. Her high breasts an erotician wouldn't have been ashamed of. The involuted waist above slim, athletic hips with the nice surprise of slutty buttocks.

Plaia had been told she was beautiful since she'd emerged, variant from her pure and subpure. Such declarations neither surprised nor particularly flattered her. Ever since she could remember she'd been adored and despised, envied and disparaged, held up as proof of Tertius Natalry's incompetence, and proof of Pan's infinite creativity because of her variance.

What she'd appreciated in Julretta was the meticulous, methodical ways the young woman possessed, a characteristic academe subpures were renowned for and which Plaia lamentably lacked. Their mutual affection had become so profound, Plaia had thought she might love Julretta in the Pannish way: love that endured, love that generated and sustained a family. The Eternal Ideal, free of the jealousies and territorialities and estrangements that plagued mere bedmates of the moment. The Ideal Ecstasy, untainted by the bestial urge.

Should they, could they enter into sharelock? Tentatively, they'd discussed the big question. Julretta had declared her Pannish love straightaway, her commitment to bring a family into the world with Plaia and serve the Imperium.

But Plaia's fathers had been dead set against their daughter's alliance with the young woman, who was of cleric and librarian subpures. Not disreputable, certainly, but not nearly as high in the academe purity as Plaia's subpure. Endless arguments later, Plaia had reluctantly conceded that perhaps someone of a slightly higher subpure was in order.

Had she been wrong to give Julretta up?

Maybe not. Every time Plaia had lain with Gunther, she'd glimpsed Julretta's scowl, her angry eyes. And every time Plaia had been preoccupied with setting up camp, polishing her cymbals, or measuring the Tivern grooves—her one exacting field task and one that always gave her a blinding headache—she'd return to Gunther's bedroll and find Julretta there, laughing, flirting, sharing a jar of beer.

"Mags coming down on all meters, people," Julretta called out now. Excitement percolated through her customarily controlled contralto. "Magnetics decreasing point-oh-five attractions to the northeast."

"Excellent," Gunther shouted. "Keep it up, Jul."

Julretta's dark eyes flashed coyly at him, then darted to Plaia.

No, with her jealousy and covetousness, Julretta might have been a difficult sharer. To make matters worse, they'd tried pleasuring each other once, and Plaia had reluctantly discovered she didn't desire to bed a woman, not even Julretta. If she and Julretta had entered into sharelock, Plaia would surely have found herself satisfying the shameful urge with the purchased embraces of a licensed erotician.

Pannish love for all Eternity. Her privilege. Her Imperial duty.

But what did it really mean?

Plaia admired Milord Lucyd's dreams, and dreamed them every chance she got. She hummed Milady Danti's theme, "I cherish you, oh, sacred sharer." She, Julretta, and Ribba had wept all day when a crier had descended into Cordilleran Rift with the news of Danti's death. They'd devoted the next two days to scandalized discussion of the tragedy. A clan of foes had ruthlessly engineered Danti's death, and the deaths of twenty other angels.

Who in the Imperium was safe if impure foes could breach the vigilance surrounding the highest angels?

"Honey, they're agents of Inim," Ribba had whispered. "They're responsible for the abductions, too."

"And the tortures and the mutilations," Julretta had grimly added. "My half sister-in-lock? Foes abducted her right out of her fundamental school playground when she was seven. Left her three days later on her mothers' doorstep—minus an eye."

The three colleagues had shivered. If physical perfection suited to one's pure was guaranteed by the Imperium, mutilation and mayhem was nothing less than evil.

Milady Danti's murder had left Plaia deeply uneasy. She'd been unable to sleep or eat well these three days.

Even Gunther, who ridiculed Milord Lucyd's dreams and crooned Danti's theme in a mocking falsetto, had permitted the team their three days of grief and dedicated a moment of silence to the most beloved woman in the Mind of the World.

Now Julretta announced, "Bounce is stabilizing. Magnitude minus point-two strengths and falling in the rift."

Ribba shouted, "Thank Pan!"

"I'll thank you to blow that flute, Rib," Gunther said in such a suggestive tone that the whole team tittered.

"I cherish you, oh, sacred sharer," Plaia sang softly. Couldn't get the tune out of her head. She should desire Pannish love. Should desire to enter into sharelock with someone suitable.

Why did her fancies constantly wander from should?

Like the trespasser she'd glimpsed during the Festival of Spring Moontide. The memory teased her halfway to madness. Southeast Marketplace, Tythys Street. The north perimeter where the quadrant for middle pures met the servs'. Book merchants, caf vendors, priestess-facilitators from Our Temple of Sacred Sharelock distributing their pamphlets did a brisk business among the festival crowd. "Hai, Dubban," his companions had called to him, a swarthy brute of a boy.

Raven-black eyes flashed above jutting cheekbones. A thong bound his raven-black hair into a tail that trailed down his sinewy back. His sleeveless tunic, the copper-orange of a serv, bared the gleaming copper curves of his biceps. She could see his hands were clean and finely made. His subpure would be skilled handworkers, then, in the crafts perhaps. He'd glanced at her, she'd glanced back, and shame had shivered through her so intense it had frightened her.

Bad boys, she'd thought with a smile. *Not where you're supposed to be.* Lower pures ought to stick with lower pures, but proximity could be so vexing.

The border monitors had begun to shriek, their huge red mouths poised open in a ululation. Vigiles had charged upon the trespassing servs, swinging security clubs. Vigilance sharemind had crackled through everyone in the quadrant. An old man had swooned. Plaia had glimpsed bloodstains on the servs' orange tunics.

A vigile had swished her dagger, nearly lopping off the bold boy's hand.

The servs hadn't stolen anything or begged for money. They'd strayed only a moment or two. *Stop it!* had risen in her throat. But she'd bitten her lip, bitten back her shout.

Plaia had breathed easier when she'd seen he'd been too quick for the vigile. He'd stridden down the boulevard to the northeast quadrant, slapping shoulders with his bloodied but defiant companions, casting contemptuous glances at the cowering middle pures.

And then he'd glanced back again. She'd met his eyes for the second time. Pain and longing had spasmed across his bold features. How candid he'd been with his shame. How unlike manipulative, repressed Gunther. For a moment, she'd thought *she'd* swoon.

Serv pure. Lower. Inferior.

Contaminated. Tainted. Filthy, even, before her gaze.

Forbidden.

Julretta announced, "Salinity in the substream is decreasing by one-point-three solutions." She plunged the salinometer's slender needle into a small waterflow gushing out of a pipe extruding from the side of the observation chamber. The waterflow originated in a deep tidal streambed on the north side of the rift. "The sea's out of the bedrock above us."

"We did it, people," Gunther shouted.

Plaia set down her cymbals and embraced Donson, the pair of them grappled Ribba, and the trio careened across the observation chamber in a rollicking jig. Gleeful yelps and shouts of the team echoed, rivaling the earthshock's grumble.

Then a terrible foreboding seized Plaia. She looked up, Julretta glanced back, Ribba, Donson, Paven, even Gunther—all met eyes. With a flash of sharemind, they simultaneously apprehended, *Could our shouts disturb the resonance we just produced?*

But chaotic little human voices shouting at random

couldn't override carefully orchestrated resonance focused and amplified into the rift—could they? Tiv's modulated voice rang in Plaia's memory: *No decibel is inconsequential. Observe how the great soprano's vibrato shatters the crystal goblet.*

And as if to prove Tiv had always been right, the observation chamber suddenly shuddered in a tremendous aftershock. Four and a half mags or more! More powerful than the shock at Cordilleran Rift. The team's shrieks of glee turned to muffled gasps of horror. The scientist-musicians, caught in mid-embrace, abandoned their merriment, ran for their harnesses, strapped in. Seized their instruments.

And fell silent, barely daring to breathe, while the rocks complained of their disharmony.

"Play," Gunther whispered urgently. "Gently, gently, people, play!"

They took up flute, zitar, drums, cymbals, and they played the lullabies of the Fires of Longnight as if their lives—as if the world—depended on it.

Blue-green flames of an oilwood campfire flickered in the observation chamber. Smoke trailed up in a twisting plume, vanishing into the vent vaulting above. Several teammates had lit cheroots, adding the astringent scent of bacco to the pungency of oilwood smoke.

Only midmorning aboveground, and the summer sun would be hot, the sky grey with dust, the air sultry and choked with the smell of ashes. Plaia shivered in the unrelenting chill and darkness belowground. "Why can't we just *go*?"

"Because we can't. In any case, this is the safest place to be right now," Gunther said. Rather unconvincingly, she thought. She reconsidered her plan of mutiny.

Moments ago, two solemn criers had descended into the well shaft with Imperial sharemind of the shock's aftermath. Plaia glimpsed collapsed bridges, demolished houses, toppled storehouses half-sunk into sandy soil. Slabs of stone tilted at crazy angles in a devastated waterduct, precious fresh water spewing into sewage. Fissures and fisticuffs plagued the shattered waterfront. Ships and shopfronts were reduced to matchsticks tossing in the turbulent surf.

Twenty thousand people missing, believed to be swept out into Sausal Bay by the giant waves just prior to the shock.

To the north, in the Hercynian Sea, ten thousand tourists vacationing at the famous Floating Towers witnessed a tremendous expulsion of magma from the vent in the seabed. Now *that* had been pretty.

Plaia recoiled from the criers' stylized sharemind. The giant waves now pummeling the Sausal Coast had given back what they'd taken away, flinging debris, dead fish, and human corpses into waterfront alleys.

But there was good news, too.

Atlan residents, to the credit of all their pures and subpures, had long anticipated and prepared for earthshocks, and especially the Big Shock. Structures known to be at risk had been evacuated when the Harbinger had sounded. Cookstones doused, furnaces tamped down, water supplies secured, shelter sought. Ambulances and emergency wagons of every purity clattered throughout the megalopolis, dispensing aid. Neighbors exchanged food, medicine, the care of children and the elderly. Sophisticated Atlaneans had always been generous in earthshock emergencies, even if such generosity was not so forthcoming when the ground was quiescent.

What would anyone expect? The purities are the purities, always were and always will be. We do what we're destined to do, no less and no more.

Usually the plodding predictability of the middle purity annoyed Plaia. But now she sighed with gratitude that no deaths had been reported in Pleasant Valley.

"Our Sacred City has survived the Big Shock," the criers had assured everyone. "As Pan survives. As Our Imperium survives forever and ever, without end."

"I'm tired of observing," Plaia grumbled. "I want to breathe fresh air. I want to see the sun. I'm *cold*. I want to go home and see if my fathers are all right."

"We're to stay till the morrow. Or till the aftershocks ease to less than a mag," came Gunther's weary answer. The man could barely force a croak from his throat. Plaia might have felt pity and compassion for her bedmate of the moment if she wasn't so aggravated with him.

They sat together on his bedroll laid out on the cold stone floor, Plaia reclining between Gunther's thighs while he kneaded her aching shoulders and neck. She felt as if she'd been pummeled by an unforgiving fist.

All right. Fifth, he's a decent masseur.

"The expedition has been a disaster," she said, unappeased by his skillful hands, though his fingers unraveled a painful knot in her right shoulder. As usual, he'd directed that she sit. That she submit. She refused to take pleasure in his ministrations.

"Now, my pretty wise-ass, don't sulk, however much it becomes you. I think the expedition has gone well."

"Gone *well*? In what way?"

"In every way, my darling."

"I don't think so."

"We've survived. It's not the end of the world."

"What if this *isn't* the Big Shock?"

"What in hell do you mean?"

"What if this is just the *beginning*? Why did Ground Control stall?" He started to interrupt, but she preempted him. "We had the predictors well in hand, and we arrived too late at Cordilleran to do any good. We were far too late here. The timing has all been off." She twisted around to look at him. "And another thing. When I measured the Tivern grooves?" These were the markers Tivern's teams had carved ten seasons ago into opposite sides of every major rift at the observation level. Plaia brandished her databoard. "The south side of Appalacia Rift isn't bouncing, Gunther. It's sunk. It's sunk by two lengths. And it's moved. Moved northwest by four whole lengths, as a matter of fact."

"Moved northwest!" He guffawed. "My pet, the shell bounces up and down like a great big featherbed made of rock. Farber and Helden proved this after your beloved Tivern proposed the theory." He tapped the tip of her nose with his forefinger. "It doesn't move. It *can't* move. Think, my pet. Where can it move *to*?"

"But the south side did. Didn't you feel that swivel?"

He shook his head. "The rift is like an unstable spring in the featherbed. A crack in the world shell. A big crack, to be sure, and a crack to be reckoned with if the whole shell were to destabilize and collapse—"

"Gunther. The rift didn't bounce *or* collapse. It moved laterally."

"You're talking about the landmass of the world, Plaia."

"I measured the grooves three times."

"You must have mismeasured."

"That is *just* like you. Blame *me* when you don't like what I have to say."

"Pet, you're just not very careful. We've had this problem before."

"I was *very* careful this time. The south grooves sank by two lengths and moved northwest by four."

"Shh, shh, now." His fingers found another knot in the nape of her neck. "Look, it doesn't really matter. The main thing is we've harmonized the rift's vibration."

"I don't think so," she said again. "Our proof is going to be shit."

"Our proof is going to be just fine. Julretta's done her usual excellent job reading and recording the meters. We've got all we need to persuade Ground Control to continue—"

"To continue *your* funding," she finished for him. "We're supposed to stabilize the bounce, isn't that what the Imperial directive to Ground Control mandates?"

"We *are* stabilizing the bounce."

"No, we're not."

"We are or the entire shell would have collapsed into the magmatic core and I wouldn't be massaging your beautiful neck."

"Maybe the shell isn't going to collapse like everyone thinks—"

"Precisely. The worst has come and gone."

"How can you be so sure? The magma eruption at Andea suggests—"

"Suggests nothing. There was no magma eruption at Andea. Tivern drank herself to death."

His disingenuousness stunned her into silence. They'd heard the first terrible rumors of Tiv's death together as they'd conferred in his chambers at the academy. She'd climbed onto his lap and wept. Soon she'd discovered something else in his lap besides the comfort of his arms. Sorrow had led, in the way sorrow sometimes will, to indulgence in the ancient shame.

His falsehood infuriated her, tainted her bittersweet memory of their first time together. "That's a lie, and you know it," she said in a harsh whisper.

"The Imperium announced—"

"The Imperium lied."

"Hush!" He clapped his hand over her mouth.

She pushed his hand away. "Are the ears of the Imperium so sharp the High Council can hear me way down here? Or have they posted spies among us?"

"*I* can hear you. I won't tolerate such heresy from you, Plaia."

"I will say what I please."

"You will obey your team super and hold your tongue."

"Are you so frightened of a few little words, Gunther?"

"I'm frightened for the soundness of your little mind."

She struggled up from his hands, but he slid his fingers from her collarbone to the tops of her breasts and then to her nipples, twisting them painfully. She felt the edge of his teeth on the nape of her neck, the flick of his tongue prob-ing the bruise he'd made. "Woman, how you excite me. You're the most exciting bedmate I've ever had. I love your variance. Our children will surely have your hair, your eyes."

"Oh, my variance! So *that's* what you love."

"Don't be absurd, Plaia. I enjoy our conversations, ex-cept maybe this one. Your subpure is fine, too. I don't mind if you're a little lower. I like your fathers, really I do. And your sisters aren't so bad except for Tania, but we don't have to live with her, do we? Oh, Plaia, let's tie the knot when we return to Atlan." He was pleading. "Enough of this vacillation. Listen to me. Pass no more rumors, they cannot possibly profit you. And resist me no longer. Your coy ways won't profit you, either, my pet."

"I'll resist you, or anyone else, as long as I please." She wanted to strike him, and not for the first time today. She couldn't bear his touch one moment longer. "Never call me your pet again. Or refer to my ass in front of my teammates. I'm no sphinx, to be bought and sold on the shadow market by unscrupulous rich angels. I'm an academe, the same as you, Gunther, my pure is equal to yours, and I'm mistress of my own destiny. And my variance."

"You've got only one destiny, Plaia, like every Pan-gaean. I've spoken with your fathers. They agree with me it's time you faced your duty of sharelock and generate a family."

"I can wait till I'm seventy to generate a family, if I want to. I can wait till I've fulfilled my Imperial duty of labor. Maybe your career is well in hand, Gunther, but I haven't even begun mine."

"You'll be too tired to care for children when you're seventy."

"I'll be able to afford a caretaker by then. What makes you think," she said, shoving him away, "that *I* want to care for children?"

"I've seen you with your nieces and nephews. You're more patient than I could ever be."

"Oh, am I? I've reached the end of my patience with you, Gunther. So that's why you're chasing after a lower subpure. You want a caretaker for your children without having to pay for one."

He seized her shoulders. "That's not true, Plaia."

"No? Then why don't you propose sharelock to Chief Proctor Witkin? Rumor says she's desperate to generate a family. She's only sixty and of a much higher subpure than you. Then *you* can care for *her* children."

"I don't feel Pannish love for Chief Proctor Witkin."

"I don't feel Pannish love for you."

"You will when the temple installs the sharelock chips." He scowled as she vehemently shook her head. "There are other ways, Plaia, to compel you to fulfill your duty."

"*Compel?* There you go again, Gun. I've no duty to you. Or anyone else."

Tie the knot with him? Not in five thousand years! She sprang to her feet and left him gaping at her. She strode across the observation chamber, her eyes seeking out Julretta in the flickering gloom.

The young woman crouched unhappily with their teammates by the campfire. A pot of crab chowder had been hung over the flames, and a pot of caf. The delicious homey scents filled Plaia with profound gratitude that she and her teammates had survived the earthshock. Ribba and Donson had laid out wineskins and beer jars on a burlap throwcloth, platters of flatbreads and fried eggs, baskets of pondplums and the first seaberries of the season. At least the academy hadn't been stingy with their provisions.

Julretta's jealousy, her protectiveness—"Gunther is a beast," she'd advised Plaia before the expedition—the young woman's own flirtatious interest in Gunther, suddenly struck Plaia as exceedingly interesting.

She sat beside the young woman, picked up a wineskin, and squeezed a warm sour stream into her mouth. They'd abandoned protocol during their erstwhile companionship, but now Julretta sat silently, waiting for Plaia to exercise her prerogative and speak first.

She swallowed the wine and grimaced. "What a fright. I thought for certain we were on our way to Eternity. How are you faring, my little Julree?"

The young woman blushed at the old affectionate nickname. Even if Plaia hadn't desired her in bed, they'd been close. Closer than bedmates, as close as sisters. They'd spent many languid nights together talking about their families, their bedmates, their hopes, their dreams. Plaia might have shared her body with Gunther, but she'd shared her Essence with Julretta.

Their separation now struck Plaia keenly.

"Not half so well, apparently, as you, Plaia," the young woman answered tartly. "Isn't it a bit early for wine?"

"Not for me, child. Anyway, who can tell if it's morning or night in this gloomy place?"

"I see it's not too early in the morning for pleasuring, either."

"Ah, Julree, it's finished between Gun and me. He thought this expedition, being thrown together day and night, would persuade me to tie the knot with him."

"And you're not persuaded?"

"He's persuaded me quite convincingly to finish it."

Julretta reached for a flatbread, nibbled it. "Does Gun know it's finished?" She averted her eyes, feigned a casual tone, but Plaia wasn't fooled. Julretta always had been transparent.

"Not yet. He won't take it well. Frankly, I can't tolerate any more of his tantrums while we're stuck in this damn rift."

Julretta nodded. "Perhaps he'll permit us to evacuate by midday."

"Not till the aftershocks ease to less than a mag. That's what he told me."

"Oh, dear. We'll be down here for days."

"Perhaps, Julree," Plaia said slyly, "you could persuade him otherwise. You're so good with the data."

Julretta glanced up, her plain features drawn with contrition. "Oh, Plaia, I didn't mean to imply—"

"It's all right, child. Truly, you'd be doing me a favor."

"He'd never touch me. I could never compete with you for his affections."

"You most certainly could, you pretty thing."

The young woman blushed again. "Everyone knows how much he adores you." At Plaia's shrug, Julretta continued to regard her with a pained expression, filled with tenderness. "Your fathers will be disappointed, Plaia."

"Yes, well. My fathers are forever disappointed in me. I would never tie the knot with someone I don't feel Pannish love for just to please them."

"They didn't much approve of me, did they?"

Plaia squeezed out more wine. "I allowed them to disapprove of you. It hardly seems fair. My second father's subpure is much lower than my first father's. Yet their own mothers and fathers permitted their sharelock, and they've generated a fine family. Yet they denied me you."

Julretta's dark little eyes shone ardently. "Perhaps it's best we each enter into sharelock with a man. It will make bedding an easier pursuit."

"Naughty child. Sharelock has nothing whatsoever to do with bedding."

Julretta giggled. "All right, then. It will save on the cost of hiring handsome eroticians."

"Which in my case would spend up my stipend *and* what'll be left of my inheritance after the tax collectors."

"For shame!"

They both guffawed and took each other's hands. How sweet to joke and laugh with Julretta again. Plaia bit back her regret and aimed her stream of wine into the young woman's mouth. She sputtered, wine spattering down her chin. Plaia reached over with a handcloth and gently blotted her face.

"Damn you, Plaia. It's only midmorning." Julretta's voice fairly melted with affection. "You know I would never have begrudged you anything you desired," she declared so earnestly that Plaia's heart stirred.

Plaia wanted to chastise the young woman that her jealousy would have led to considerable begrudging. But she kept silent, unwilling to taint the tender interlude. "Well," she whispered, "I don't begrudge you bedding Gun, if that's what you desire. Go to him with my blessing."

"Say, you two," called out Donson. "Are you gossiping or cosseting?"

"Bog off, Donson," Plaia said, her voice good-natured but slightly acid. "I was Julretta's counselor last season. We're sisters."

"Then bring your sister and your wineskin over here and gamble a while with us," Donson said. "I got my hands on an orb." He was a short, dark, slender fellow, as spare of flesh as Gunther was ample, and his proctor subpure was equal to Plaia's. Donson was not at all unpleasant to look at. Or gamble with. Or sit next to and speak with freely.

"Come, let's play," Plaia said with a laugh and stood. She took Julretta's hand, hoisted the young woman to her feet. "I've got exactly twenty-three ores and five bits in my pocket. The only other thing of any consequence that I can lose this morning is my tunic."

"Which I shall be delighted to claim," Donson said, waggling his eyebrows up and down.

The teammates catcalled and hooted and described other items of Plaia's apparel on which they'd like to place wagers.

The two women joined the gambling ring in high good spirits. Gunther had, Plaia was relieved to see, bundled up in his bedroll and was restlessly napping, an angry mound of injured pride. The man was exhausted. He'd worked harder than any of them on the riftsite expedition. He was sure to win a promotion to senior proctor, maybe even a permanent consultancy with Ground Control. There was no telling how much power he'd garner if he secured Imperial favor. With the eminence of his family, he could claw his way to the top of the academe subpure. *He'll make a very fine sharer . . . for someone.* She could practically feel him silently berating her across the chamber. When his sharemind nipped at her, she resolutely refused any mutual consciousness.

She sat cross-legged on the burlap throwcloth, seized a fresh wineskin, and guzzled the thick golden flow. "All right, Donson, tell me. What is this thing?" She plucked the glittering object from his hand.

"That, my sweet, is an Orb of Eternity."

About the size of a pondplum, the orb filled the palm of her hand, an iridescent pale purple crystal. The curvature had been skillfully shaped and carved with precise diamond-shaped facets—she counted thirty. Each facet bore a kaligraph surrounded by tiny strange glyphs.

"Is this really atlantium?" She felt a trembling, the slightest irregular vibration emanating from the thing. An eerie aura clung to it. She recalled the impure fetish she and her sisters had found in their fathers' back acre when they were children. A desiccated dead turtle bound to a cruciform, two clusters of ornise feathers impaling its eye sockets, the fetish—a gruesome product of someone's nasty imagination—had sent a palpable chill through her.

Like this orb.

Only the orb wasn't gruesome. It was stunning. Hypnotically beautiful.

She felt a sting, nearly dropped the thing.

"Sure, it's atlantium." Donson grinned. "Weird piece of work, isn't it? *The* genuine article. Banned by the High Council three seasons ago."

Plaia had never seen him touch anything so carefully, not even his beloved zitar. Atlantium. Genuine atlantium. She'd only seen chips and slivers in her fathers' jewelry. Never a whole intact crystal as huge as this. "Why was it banned?"

"The druds and servs believe the orb foretells the future,'' Donson said. ''The High Council *hates* that idea. Only the Imperium can foretell the future, y'know.''

''And predict earthshocks and the weather and the movement of the stars and eclipses of the sun and moon and, honey, whether I'll find a new bedmate next week,'' Ribba said.

The circle laughed and hooted.

''Watch out, Donson. Vigilance will arrest you if you're caught with that thing,'' Paven slurred. He grinned devilishly, his disheveled mop of sable curls haloing his head, and playfully tickled Julretta's ribs.

Julretta angrily shoved him away.

''They'll do more than that,'' Donson said. ''Summary flogging and five seasons' hard labor. *And* the Temple of the Mind of the World'll strip away your sharemind.''

Now a chorus of disbelieving groans resounded.

''Nobody can strip away your sharemind.''

''Impossible!''

''The Imperium can't do that.''

''That's what I heard,'' Donson said darkly. ''The Imperium knows how.''

''Oh hell, Donson. Just like the Imperium knows how to go to the moon and Sanguine,'' Paven said skeptically. ''Vigilance can barely keep its windships afloat. Don't believe everything you hear.''

''Now that *is* true,'' Donson said. ''The Imperium *does* know how to go to the moon and Sanguine. All you need is a good farglass, and you can *see* the factories on the moon. And on Sanguine.'' To another round of disbelieving protests, ''I swear! There's this huge monument on Sanguine. I've seen it!''

''But is it true the orb can foretell the future,'' Plaia said. ''That's what *I* want to know.''

''I've got a friend who rolled the orb in a gambling ring,'' Donson said. ''She wagered on the Wheel. It turned out to be the ruling facet. The next day she was struck by a transport wagon. The wheel smashed her knee to smithereens. They had to amputate her leg.''

Everyone groaned again. Plaia shivered.

"Then put it away, Donson," she said, laying her hand over the orb. That sting again. Anxiety jittered across her skin. "Maybe we shouldn't do this."

"Don't be a scaredy rabbit," Ribba said, lit a raptureroot and handed it to Plaia. Sweet narcotic smoke drifted over the campfire. "The orbroll is my favorite gambling game."

"But if it's illegal—"

"The cults are illegal, too, but that doesn't stop anyone from going to cult raves."

"Cults?" Plaia pulled on the raptureroot, let loose a cloud of smoke. She feigned the wide-eyed, slack-jawed astonishment of an innocent. "Do you mean to tell me there are *cults* in Our Sacred Imperium?"

"Oh, just a few," Ribba said dryly. "The Serpent Sect, the Millipedes, the Flesh Eaters, the Unborn Dead, the Tah Tah Heads, the Plasma Worms, the Bog Pissers, the Hundred Agonists, the Pure Impurities, the Impure Purities, the Bogbeasts. Hai! Shall I go on?"

"Cults are for druds and servs," Julretta said. "They're stupid and low."

"Don't be such a Pannish stick, Julretta," Ribba said. "Me and my last bedmate went to a Bogbeast rave. Honey, it was up*lift*ing."

"Yeah, Julretta. Who wants to meditate on dreary old Pan all the time," Donson said. "Go rave."

"And get flogged *and* thrown in the clang *and* lose your mastery."

"Vigilance needs to catch the damn foes, not chase after mastery students," said Ribba. "Let's go! Roll that orb."

"You're right, Rib," Plaia said with a laugh. "No one will threaten our masteries down here. Who cares?"

"Maybe you should care, Plaia," Julretta slurred. "You don't give a shit about much of anything else."

Plaia turned to her colleague, taken aback. Genteel, soft-spoken Julretta, using foul language? The young woman was drunk after one mouthful of wine. Plaia, none too clearheaded herself, hazily recalled Julretta never drank. Her sobriety was one more attribute, and a very laudable attribute, too, to recommend the young woman for sharelock. *Some*one among sacred sharers ought to remain sober. At least most of the time.

Everyone in the gambling ring teased Julretta, and Plaia abruptly became aware that her teammates had consumed great quantities of beer and wine in the aftermath of the shock. Along with the raptureroot, a jug of teq surreptitiously made the rounds, hand to covert hand. Gunther would not have tolerated raptureroot or teq on an academy expedition, but Gunther—tired man, happy fortune!—was snoring away in his bedroll. Ribba never went without her roots, and some roustabout like Paven had thoughtfully smuggled in the jug.

A thrill of arousal nibbled down Plaia's belly, thrust deep between her thighs. Donson, throwing his head back, his mouth gaping with hilarity, suddenly struck her as the most inviting male creature she'd ever laid eyes on. Or had laid eyes on within the last ten days while she'd been relegated to a bedroll with good ol' Gunther.

"How do we do it, then?" she implored Donson, the feigned innocence she did so well. Thirty going on thirteen, Gunther had said of her flirting. Or had that been the bedmate before Gunther?

"You roll the thing like a knucklebone. When the orb comes to rest, one facet tops it off. That's the ruling facet. You can wager on the ruling facet if you want to. The gamemaster, that's *me,* child," he said with a wicked grin, "will also accept odds on the proximity of other facets to the ruling facet. Understand?"

"It's a game for simpletons," Julretta announced, sharp belligerence emerging from her inebriation. "You can hardly call it a game at all. There's no bloody skill to it whatsoever."

Ribba said briskly, "Quick odds-making is a skill, Jul. Pooling wagers may pay off very well."

"Let's have at it, then," Plaia cried gleefully.

"Gently, now." Donson handed the orb back to her. "That's solid atlantium, remember. Worth a bloody fortune. I'm in hock up to my eyeballs to a foe marketeer."

"That alone'll get you thrown in the clang, Donson," someone called out.

"And flogged."

"And stripped of your stipend."

"Two to one says the Spider is within two facets of the ruling facet," someone else said.

"Thirty to one the Lake is the ruling facet, three to one the Lake is within three facets, ten to one the Lake opposes the ruling facet," Ribba said shrewdly.

Donson slung his arm around Plaia's shoulders in a comradely embrace. His hand, lying loosely down her arm, brushed against the swell of her breast. She arched into the casual fondle. He whispered, "What's your wager, my sweet?" and she felt the tip of his tongue searching her ear.

Excitement defeated the anxiety in her blood. She shrugged away from Donson's mouth. There were other places she wanted that tongue to travel. "I don't know. I don't know what all the facets are." The bold, swarthy serv boy abruptly loomed in her memory, stirring her into a frenzy. *Why do my fancies constantly wander from should?* How she resented proximity! She nestled closer to Donson, imagining so vividly he was that bold boy that the groin of her leggings felt suddenly damp. How she wanted to be touched. By that boy? *Forbidden.* But lacking him, by someone proximate, by anyone, anyone more or less equal. "Is there a facet for stormy weather?"

"There's one for Clouds," Ribba offered.

"Clouds it is. Twenty ores on Clouds, thirty to one, dead on as the ruling facet."

"Thirty to one," Donson said. "Dead on! Are you sure? You can wager on proximity."

"I don't give a damn about proximity. All or nothing. You know," she whispered in his ear, "I'm going to lose everything this morning, anyway."

"Thirty to one on Clouds." Donson laid down her challenge.

"I'm in," Ribba crowed, and the other teammates shouted their wagers, flinging down a clatter of ores and bits.

Plaia grinned and winked at Julretta, but the young woman gazed back solemnly, her face pinched, her eyes darting.

Julretta, jealous again. Did she covet Donson, too? Whatever Plaia desired, Julretta desired? Plaia shrugged. Oh hell, what could she do about Julretta's heart? Or anyone's heart? She'd given up, long ago, trying to change anyone. No one changed. *She* didn't change. The purities were the purities. She'd never see her beautiful bold boy again. Maybe she'd never enter into sharelock with anyone.

And the Imperium lasted without end.

She shook the orb in her two cupped hands, flung it across the throwcloth.

And the thing spun, leapt, tumbled across the cloth, dancing and whirling as if it possessed a strange animation of its own. The orb spiraled round the ring of gamblers, once, twice. Impossibly thrice. And came to rest precisely in front of Plaia again.

"How did you do that?" she demanded of Donson, who only shook his head and guffawed till tears sprang to his eyes.

"You think I've got a string attached to it? Or a lodestone?"

"*Do* you?"

He squeezed her breast roughly. No more pretense of happenstance that his hand had found itself in an opportune spot. "I swear to you, I've never seen anything like it."

"Clouds," Ribba declared as she peered at the ruling facet. "Dear Pan, it's Clouds."

"No, really?"

"It's Clouds, I tell you. Thirty to one."

"You fixed it, Donson," came a chorus of accusations.

"Never! Never in five thousand years," Donson protested and wrestled Plaia tightly into his embrace.

"She cheated."

"She's robbed us all."

"Fuck you, Plaia."

"That's the gamemaster's prerogative," Donson called out.

"This facet is considered evil. It signifies uncertainty," Julretta sternly announced above their teammates' shouts and incredulous laughter. "She's entitled to two more rolls."

"I thought you didn't believe in low things, Jul," Ribba taunted her.

"I took the last class in orb studies at the academy before the Imperial ban," Julretta said indignantly. "And I'm telling you the oracle entitles Plaia to two more rolls. Two more chances to determine her destiny."

"You roll the orb again for me, my little Julree," Plaia said, helpless with laughter. "I give you my two chances at determining destiny. I don't need them."

"Everyone needs extra chances at destiny."

"Not me, child. I'll stay shareless. I'll inherit from my fathers. I'll make a fine career for myself at the academy. My destiny is assured."

"Oh, Plaia, don't be so sure," Julretta said in such a tone of alarm that Plaia glanced up.

A crown of clouds descended over her head, diminutive thunderheads flitting with tiny images: Gunther's frown, her fathers' distraught faces, a fiery spray of magma. A tiny sphinx, blinking enigmatically and drawing a silver handcomb through her wispy white hair.

Ribba was counting out the money, Donson kissing Plaia's neck, Paven guzzling teq. The gambling circle was grumbling, chuckling, gossiping.

Only Julretta gazed up, openmouthed.

Sharemind is playing tricks on us.

The clouds dissipated.

Plaia laughed uneasily. "Don't look at me like that, Julretta. You're getting wrinkles in your forehead."

And she lay back in Donson's arms, closed her eyes, and surrendered to his caresses. She forgot him completely as she invoked Imperial sharemind and entered the Mind of the World. Where she dreamed of a sacred sharer who could make her feel the way she'd always wanted to feel.

FACET 3

> Point: Central or static.
> The rock endures in the restless river.
> The action is concentration.
> The forbearance is scattering.
>
> **The Orb of Eternity**

Commentaries:

Councillor Sausal: Pan is the sacred center from which all things of the world issue forth, the great stillness from which all manifestation ensues. Yet the things of the world would not issue forth and manifestation would not ensue without the ceaselessly emerging movement of Pan.

So, too, the Imperium observes the law of proximity among the purities but permits the subpures to mingle among themselves and rise or fall according to their divinity, function, acquisitions, and attributes.

Therefore the prudent person who undertakes the great task must devote all thoughts and actions to that task. But beware of stillness that stagnates.

Guttersage (usu. considered vulgar): A fool who always stays in one place never sees the world.

A fool who always travels never has a place to stay.

Our City of Atlan, the periphery of northeast Marketplace. The Imperial Natalries, Quartius Natalry:

Dubban crouched, dazed and shaking, against the inner strongwall on the seventh floor when the aftershocks finally subsided. Fear wouldn't stop hammering in his chest. Acute frustration assailed him: There was nothing he could do. Nowhere to run.

When the Big Shock comes, it'll annihilate the Imperium. Pangaea will shatter into a million pieces and plummet into the center of the world. And every pure who has observed the law of proximity, fulfilled his Imperial duties, loved and respected Pan will ascend into Eternal Bliss. And Inim will rise from the flames and seize the impure, seize all who have permitted impurity to taint them, and fling them into Eternal Torment.

Dubban had had night terrors over Apocalyptist prophecies since he'd been a babe two decades ago in the Far Reaches. Now, two decades later, would Inim seize him and fling him into Eternal Torment? He'd observed proximity and purity protocol like a good serv. He'd fulfilled his Imperial duty of labor well enough. But not his duty of sharelock.

Was he tainted?

What had he made of his pathetic midwife's life?

And why did he harbor so many impure thoughts? Would impure thoughts condemn him to Eternal Torment? Would he be denied Eternal Life after this ephemeral life?

Someone was sobbing, ''Forgive me, Pan, please, please.''

Someone else whispered, ''Shut *up!*''

When the Harbinger had sounded, the orderlies and custodians had sealed the windows with canvas swaths to keep out the dust. The heat in the ges tank chamber, never less than unbearable, had become so intense Dubban thought he'd collapse. Sweat gushed from his pores till he was stewed. His tongue had plastered itself to the roof of his mouth. His thirst was overwhelming. A guttering magmalamp lit the semidarkness now and then, illuminating in hellish tableaus the gigantic chamber, the rows of gestation tanks, the terrified faces of his fellow midwife-natalists.

This is it. I've died and gone to Eternal Torment.

They'd been on ges tank duty. They couldn't do a damn thing when the Big Shock struck. The amniotic fluid sloshed wildly, tiny tidal waves smashing five thousand unborn against the smeary sides of their tanks. And that had been just on the seventh floor of Quartius Natalry. What about the other tanks, the other floors, the other natalries?

What about Natalry Bank? If the bank collapsed . . . His mind balked at the notion. Ninety percent of Atlan, maybe half of all Pangaea, generations upon generations wiped out. . . .

What a disaster!

He blinked back angry tears. The physician-natalists— hell, the Superior Mothers and Superior Fathers—had promised the midwives and orderlies and custodians, had promised *him,* Dubban Quartermain naitre Quartius, this could never happen. An earthshock—*any* earthshock, even the Big Shock—disrupt the natalries?

No, never. Not in five thousand years.

The natalries had stood in the heart of Central Atlan since times lost to antiquity. The most secure bedrock in the megalopolis. The most advanced building construction in the world. Some portion of the foundation refurbished and bolstered on a daily basis, construction workers constantly underfoot.

Where else would the Prefecture of Atlan and the High Council of Pangaea situate the most massive generative facilities in the world? Facilities containing every unborn of every pure and subpure in Our Sacred City, not to mention countless unborns from the provinces beyond?

Even unborn angels.

The Imperium had declared that the Apocalyptists preached a false and impure prophecy. These days the Imperium could predict earthshocks. And the Imperium would overcome earthshocks, just as Pan overcame Inim. Neither Pangaea nor the Imperium would ever end.

Did the Imperium lie?

The natalry trembled again, and an entire row of ges tanks against the west wall swayed and lurched. With a *screech!* the tanks broke free of their security bolts, skidding helter-skelter to the edge of the tables. Dubban could not believe his eyes. The tanks teetered back and forth, as if they couldn't decide their destiny, and then they toppled off the edge, shattering on the floor.

A crash assailed his ears. He cringed.

"Oh, shit!" someone screamed. Maybe Waldo, his super. A super's rage lashed through the midwives' sharemind. A sharemind that suddenly yawned open and sucked him in.

Dubban hated sharemind like that. Hated sharemind compelled not just by a higher pure's prerogative, but by the communal whining and backbiting of proximate subpures. He resisted it, reviled it, shut out the sharemind with his own rage. *Back off, and leave me alone.*

Amniotic fluid gushed out of the tanks, purling across the floor in viscous ripples. Fragile birthsacks splattered, the translucent tissue shredding on juts of broken plasmaglass. The unborn—little question marks of slick pink flesh—wriggled and convulsed. The amniotic fluid coagulated the way blood did, in thick, sticky pools.

Dubban glimpsed the chips containing their security numbers, like a little blue mole, on each unborn's fragile shoulder. A reddish aureole of inflammation still surrounded each one. Inductor-surgeons from the Security Number Administration had installed the security numbers in these unborns just yesterday. A loutish trio brandishing scalpels in their long thin hands, the inductors had been in such a hurry to finish their task they'd dropped a trayful of chips, which had scattered across the floor. They'd ordered Dubban down on his hands and knees. Given permission to

speak, he'd asked, "How will you know which security
number belongs to which unborn?"

"Shut your trap and pick 'em up, midwife," one induc-
tor had snapped.

Dubban had been scarcely able to sleep since. The inductors *didn't* know. They didn't care. It was horrifying. And
nothing less than eye-opening. How many other trays of
security number chips had ever been dropped by loutish
inductors? *The security number identifies the unborn, its
purity, subpure, and lineage, and reserves its account at
Natalry Bank.* That had been his first lesson as a midwife-
natalist. Security numbers were essential. How could the
inductors be so careless?

Dubban wondered if the tiny stout arms of these steve-
dore subpures would be damaged by the unborns' terrible
plunge, then realized that was the least of his worries. Hun-
dreds of yolk stalks had torn loose from the Feed. The
sickening smell of brine and blood rose up in the sweltering
heat.

"Dubban, you gimpy lug!" shouted Waldo. Yeah, that
was Waldo, all right. "You piece of shit! You lamebrained
nitwit! I thought I told you to check the bolts on those
tanks!"

"I checked them," Dubban muttered.

"I told you to double-check!"

"I did double-check."

"You couldn't have! Look at this fucking mess. You
fool! You idiot! You must have forgot. This is the last time,
Dubban. I swear to Pan I'll cut you loose. You must be
qutted out again."

Glowering silence. *Yeah, so what?*

He knuckled his eyes and kneaded his forehead, attempting, futilely, to persuade a trickle of circulation into his
aching brain. He knew he shouldn't have chewed that last
quid of qut. But he had anyway, gazing out his window at
the last dawn stars and wondering what his life would ever

amount to. And that had been *before* he thought the world was coming to an end.

What a lousy night.

He'd decided to leave the Serpent Sect, once and for all, and Romana, willful wench that she was, had decided to leave him. Well, good riddance. She would never have entered into sharelock with him, she'd made that clear right from the start. "You should know. I don't much like men," she'd said. He would never have entered into sharelock with her, either, not in five thousand years. No, not till the Imperium ended.

They were both serv pures, their subpures more or less equal. With her skillful hands, Romana cleaned vegetables of bitter outer leaves, filthy roots, and inedible stems for the chefs who conceived and prepared the dishes. With his skillful hands, Dubban cleaned unborns of contaminated fluids, unwanted threads, and disposable yolk stalks for the physician-natalists who assisted the unborns' emergence from their ges tanks.

Under proximity and purity protocol, they ought to have been very happy.

Now Dubban wondered how he ever could have wanted to fuck her in the first place. Romana was as dim-witted as an ox and not nearly as shapely. Her thin black braids crawled down the slab of her back. Her face was a lump of dough. She was loud and crude and lazy, always reeking of beer, flinging her cheroot butts on his floor, begging him to buy her something delicious or pretty. And he had, plenty of times.

What a fool.

Then why had he been shaken and saddened when she'd left? She'd risen off his pallet, flown into a fit when he'd told her he didn't think he wanted to go to Serpent Sect raves with her anymore. "Then we got nothin' more to share, chum," she'd declared. Her tunic swirling in fury, she'd slammed his door behind her with a resounding *bang*.

And left him in his solitary daub-and-wattle hovel on

Misty Alley. Alone again, her scent lingering in the straw, and an incomprehensible ache in his chest.

Waldo shouted, "You, Garth." This was Dubban's shiftmate. "Are we dead? No. Are we still standin'? Yes. Then get them buckets, get fresh amnio. You, Dubban. Get these unborns back in fluid. We'll rehook 'em to the Feed later. Get back to work, you idiots, before they all die on us."

"They'll be better off than me," Dubban muttered. But he scrambled to find a bucket, a jug of amnio. Found a bowl of tepid wash-up in the supply room, dumped water over his face, down his throat.

He'd never fulfill his Imperial duty of sharelock, not with a serv pure like Romana.

That was why his chest ached. His heart. He had a problem with his heart.

He blamed his mother.

Eight years ago his mother had taken him aside before he'd been harvested by the Quartius Natalry in the Far Reaches. He'd been at the age of ripeness, a difficult and confusing time. At that momentous occasion, she'd told him what she'd told each of her twenty-one sons: "Entering into sharelock can be a difficult thing."

Bandular, a striking raven-haired woman with raven eyes to match, had become such a deft and popular midwife in the Far Reaches that she'd essentially commanded her own purity's natalry. Dubban's father Kendi had taken care of him and his brothers while his mother had battled with addle-headed physician-natalists and supercilious priest-natalists. For the first ten years of their sharelock, Bandular and Kendi had generated two unborns a year. All had turned out to be sons. In the eleventh year, Dubban had been the last.

Dubban had always wondered if his mother had hoped for a daughter. She'd never made him feel anything less than wanted, but at moments like last night, after Romana had walked out, he'd always felt remorseful, as if he'd failed her.

"Generation of the family is vital to the Imperium. That's why sharelock is one's Imperial duty," Bandular had told him in her solemn way. "It's also an Imperial pain in the neck. Especially when parents can't afford to hire a caretaker subpure. Oh, don't worry," she'd said with one of her rare grins at his wince of distress. "I love all my sons. Especially you, Dubban. Selfish to say, but you're the one most like me." She'd traced the curve of his cheekbone with her worn fingertips. "Know this, my son. Sharelock may truly become the state of joy the angels dream of when you share everything with your sharer. Including," she'd said with a wink, "your bed. *Especially* your bed. And I don't mean just for the warmth."

"But," Dubban had protested, shocked, embarrassed, and confused, "doesn't the bestial urge sully the purity of Pannish love? Shouldn't sacred sharers—"

Bandular had laid her forefinger across his lips. "Never mind what sharers should. The Imperium tells you these things because the Imperium fears the urge."

"But why should the Imperium fear the urge? If the urge is bestial and shameful, and sharelock is contaminated by it—"

She'd pressed her finger again. "You'll find out. I'm a midwife-natalist, my son. And a woman. No one believes in the natalries, and the labor we perform to ensure each new generation, more than I. Someday when you're older I'll tell you about the way things were before the natalries. The way," she'd said with a dark, enigmatic look, "things still are for some poor sufferers. For now I'm telling you the best way, the joyful way to enter into sharelock is with someone of your purity, equal to your subpure, or nearly so, whom you also desire. Believe me, Dubban," she'd said with another smile that made him blush, "it's not bestial or shameful when you're with a sharer like that. And the natalries will *still* do their best to generate your family for you and your sharer, whoever he or she is.''

No one else, including his father, had ever spoken so frankly with him about sharelock or bedding. His mother's words blazed to this day in his memory. Yet when he'd secured an Imperial work permit and journeyed to Atlan as a boy of sixteen to work in the great natalries of Our Sacred City, he'd begun meeting the easy shareless men and women of his pure who swarmed the megalopolis in every subpure one could imagine.

And he *hadn't* discovered what his mother had boldly hinted at. Instead he'd discovered that every terrible thing people said about the bestial urge was true. It had nothing to do with sharelock, one could contract disease if careless, and the laws of proximity and purity protocol could drive one mad. Oh, he'd sorted out his predilections. He'd discovered he desired only women, though three of his closest brothers desired men and two desired men and women, and of those five, four brothers had entered into sharelock with men, and the fifth remained shareless. What he'd found was that fucking bedmates of the moment like Romana left him feeling bereft, empty, and sorrowful.

He'd never find Pannish love. Let alone fulfill his Imperial duty of sharelock with the sort of sharer Bandular had chuckled about. Never find a sharer who would be to him as Milady Danti had been to Milord Lucyd. And now even she, *everyone's* beloved sharer in dreams, was dead.

Never find a woman of his pure, let alone his subpure, like the lovely woman he'd traded glances with during the Festival of Spring Moontide. He'd barely escaped southeast Marketplace with his hand intact and his back unbloodied.

The purities are the purities, and the Imperium lasts without end.

She was a higher pure.

It was hopeless.

So Dubban had chewed one last quid, a greasy little bundle of the bitter herb that had been his only pleasure since he'd come to Atlan. The quid had stung the inside of his cheek. Steeped in cheap skee most likely, to conceal its inferior quality.

Damn Horan Zehar. The qut purveyor had charged him top ore, added his latest purchase to the impossible debt Dubban already owed, and, to beat it all, cheated him. He risked the summary removal of his thumbs if he were caught conducting commerce with an impure, and the purveyor *cheated* him. And not for the first time. Dubban had planted his fist in the hovel's wattle wall, kicked in his door.

Then the qut had kicked *him* in, an explosion of mind-numbing oblivion.

And he forgot his sorrows, his rage, his hopelessness—for a few empty hours. The cold fist of qut squeezed his Essence into darkness.

He woke this morning, qutted out, his knuckles skinned, his doorlock requiring repair, and sincerely regretted his habit. What would Bandular think if she knew?

Now Dubban fell to his knees in the viscous pools of amnio, scooped up an unborn, and cradled the pathetic creature in the palm of his hand. Bulbous bald head, miniature hands on immature stumpy arms, fingers tightly curled, it was on its way to Eternity, suffocating and starving without the Feed. The sliver of a mouth gaped open in a tiny desperate gulp. But this unborn couldn't save itself by breathing. Its lungs weren't ready for emergence from watery ges tank to airy creche.

Garth and the other midwives handed buckets of amniotic fluid into the ges tank chamber like firefighters dousing a blaze. Dubban gently slid the unborn into a bucket, but it was already dead.

A grim priestess-natalist darted among the buckets. She stopped before Dubban, made the sign of the Imperial star over the little corpse, and muttered, "From the bosom of Pan to the bosom of Pan."

"Superior Mother, is this unborn's Essence going to live

in Eternity?'' Dubban asked, his skinned knuckles stinging in the fluid.''

''Of course.''

''But it was never really alive in the first place.''

''Of course it was alive,'' she snapped. ''It just didn't emerge.''

''Then does it live as an unemerged unborn for Eternity? Are there ges tanks in Eternity? Ges tanks for each purity?'' Dubban furrowed his brow. ''Or does it simply live in a sea of amnio? Are there different seas for each of the purities? Or do they all swim in one sea?'' He brightened. ''Like fish? Minnows and leviathans all swim together, don't they?''

The priestess-natalist glared at him. ''Pan loves each unborn according to its purity,'' she said. ''You ask too many questions, midwife.'' And darted away.

Ha! She doesn't really know.

''Get to work, you poxy servs,'' Waldo shouted. ''The Big Shock has come and gone, and we're still standin', ain't we?''

What can you do, Dubban thought, *where can you run, when the Imperium goes on without end?*

''Say, Dub. We're roundin' up an orbroll,'' Garth said to him as the midwife-natalists stood, stoop-shouldered, in the brightly lit laboratory. ''After all this excitement, we and the shiftmates want a bit of action. Want to go in halves with me on a spread of six facets? What do you say to that?''

''I say bugger off, Garth.''

Each midwife stood before a high pristine platform, peering down through a viewglass. Dubban carefully touched the knobs, readjusting the focus. The viewglasses in the Atlanean natalries were far superior to the glasses his mother employed in the Far Reaches. He still regarded the instrument with respectful awe. A column of thick crystal set at each end with crystal lenses, suspended in a metal frame with knobs to adjust the view, the viewglass permitted Dubban to glimpse a part of the world so far beyond the capabilities of anyone's sight, so infinitely tiny, that it was invisible without the viewglass.

A world within the world.

What Dubban peered at now in that tiny, invisible world was a birthpod.

Physician-natalists employed all sorts of technical terms for female pods and male seeds. Dubban usually just referred to pods and seeds, which reminded him pleasantly of vegetables. In polite company, everyone referred to their "Imperial materia."

The term sprang from more than mere modesty.

Pods and seeds harvested by the pure's natalry when a girl or boy reached the age of ripeness at twelve years were stored in Natalry Bank in one's account and identified by one's security number. Dubban, or any pure, possessed the privilege to direct his account as he saw fit under purity protocol. But if he died, became incompetent, or "failed in his Imperial duties"—a vague term with which families liked to threaten rebellious progeny—his parents or heirs succeeded to the privilege of directing his account. And since natalry banks were supported by the public fisc and benefited from Imperial technology, the Imperium held the ultimate right of seisin in every citizen's account. The Imperium could legally seize an account and direct the materia as it saw fit.

Dubban often found himself having to explain this legal tangle to puzzled friends. You were harvested, your materia went into your account, you owned it, but sometimes you didn't—actually, in the end you didn't. Dubban didn't personally know anyone whose account had been seized by the Imperium. But then he didn't associate with that sort of person.

Insolent midwives had all manner of obscene names for Imperial materia. Dubban refused to use them. When he'd been eight Bandular had beaten him with a flyswatter for teasing a girl-cousin about her rotten eggs. He'd never made that mistake again.

The birthpod Dubban was examining now had been seeded in the Rite of Begetting. The seeded pod was growing just fine, and it was time to remove the bad threads inside it. He refocused the viewglass again and blinked back the ache behind his eyes. Pruning was hard work, the hardest and last task of the miserable morning before his midday break.

Midwives didn't participate in the Rite of Begetting. The mere touch or presence of a low serv subpure like a midwife might contaminate the sacred rite and impede the generative power of Pan. The rite was the province of priests, priestesses, and physicians. And sharers, of course.

Some devout Pannists disputed the wisdom of including sharers if they were of a low purity. Dubban recalled his parents' heated arguments. "People need ritual," Kendi had argued. "People need to *feel* the connection. Sometimes sharelock isn't enough, even with the chips." Ever the conservative, Bandular had countered, "But sharers don't *need* to attend the rite. Who knows if the presence of low-pure sharers increases the risk of contamination? Look at the high mortality rate for serv unborns."

Dubban had wanted to remind his mother that *she* was serv pure. She may have directed the Far Reaches natalries after decades of dedicated service, yet she was forbidden to attend the most sacred ceremony of her own institution—except when she'd attended her own Rite of Begetting as a sharer. Didn't she feel humiliated?

But he'd said nothing. He hadn't wanted to feel the slap of her flyswatter again.

Pruning the birthpods—now *that* was the province of midwives. Dubban squinted through the viewglass at the bad threads that needed pruning. At first the threads had all looked the same to him. But after four years of pruning, he'd learned to distinguish them. And he'd noticed the threads to be pruned were different, depending upon which pure or subpure he happened to be working on. Sometimes he wondered why, since the physician-natalists said the bad threads were pretty much the same from pure to pure. The bad threads contained diseases and all manner of physical abnormalities, weaknesses, deformities, and impurities that would disable the unborn who would grow from the birthpod. Impurities like palsy, moron's curse, splintered blood, pustules, and the like.

Then why were the threads different? *You ask too many questions.* Still, Dubban couldn't help but wonder. How did the different threads affect each unborn, then, and in what way, from pure to pure, subpure to subpure? Did the physicians claim the bad threads were all the same so the midwives wouldn't feel they violated protocol when they pruned?

Just what was he pruning, anyway?

Why do I have so many impure thoughts?

The midwives, naturally, joked unceasingly and blasphemously about this unpleasant and exacting task.

"Whoops," Garth said now, jostling his arm, "there goes that tadpole's left eye. Whoa! There goes her left tit."

"Back off," Dubban warned, wresting his arm away. He always pruned as meticulously as he could, even when he was qutted out. If midwife his subpure always had been and midwife he always would be, at least he'd fulfill his Imperial duty of labor. Pruning was a challenge.

He'd suffered side by side with Garth for four wearisome years since he'd come to Atlan. He'd come to detest the jug-eared twit even more than the day they'd first met. Maybe more than he detested Waldo or the other supers.

"Come now, Dub ol' mug," Garth continued, grinning. "I came out only five ores behind after the last roll. I can pick 'em, I tell ye."

Dubban carefully set down the hand-levers. The levers directed the miniscule pruners down in the tiny world beneath his viewglass, pruners with which he snipped the threads so carefully. "Garth. Have I, in all the time we've worked here, have I ever, *ever,* wagered on a roll of the orb?"

"Maybe there's a first time. Don't shake yer head like that, why not? This is a particularly fine orb, too, I've seen it meself. Got me a fine, fair feelin' about this orb. I can *see* just how she'll roll, I tell ye. This'll be a winner, Dub, I just know it—"

"That's what everybody says, Garth. And the orb never rolls like you think it will. It's a waste of good money. Not to mention time. Not to mention it's illegal, or have you forgotten? Can't you get it through that thick bone of a skull? The orb is impure witchery."

Garth sniggered. "'Tis no witchery. 'Tis a game, chum. A rousin' good game."

"A game that will ruin your life if you get caught. Besides, the orb hexes things."

"I'll say. The tax collectors can't grab their pound of fat outta all the money that changes hands on orbrolls. 'Tis a hex upon the Imperial Treasury, I'm sure. *That's* why the High Council outlawed 'em."

Dubban resumed his grip on the hand-levers and glared at the twit. "Didn't you dream Milord Lucyd's dream this morning? Didn't you dream of the orb? Didn't you see how the orb changed Milady Danti into a monster?" Dubban shivered. He'd awakened with a start. He'd always averted his eyes whenever someone tried to show him an orb because he'd heard just one glance could bring bad luck. Now an orb had filled his dream-eye as if someone had shoved it in his face. The dream had frightened him badly. "If that's not witchery and a hex, I don't know what is."

Garth's tiny brown eyes sparkled with nasty mischief. "Nah, I don't dream them love dreams," he said sarcastically. "Maybe it was the qut that changed Milady Danti into a monster, eh, ol' mug?"

Dubban whipped around and seized the twit's collar in his fist, brandished the other fist in Garth's pudding face.

"Hai, you rowdies," Waldo shouted. "I warn you, Dubban, this is the last time you're causin' trouble. I'll have to dock your wage if you don't cut it out, chum."

Dubban released Garth's collar, pushed him away. "Shut your trap and leave me alone."

"No harm done, Dub," Garth said. But he wouldn't stop grinning.

The easy sharemind among the midwives crackled with derisive amusement.

Dubban returned, disgusted, to his task. Sweat beaded his brow. He blotted his face with a clean cloth. Tangled translucent knobs connected in long, looping strands each to another, the threads coiled in a serpentine mass within the birthpod. His eyes blurred and teared at the strain of peering through the viewglass.

He didn't choose which threads to prune. The physician-natalists did that, designating the threads with tiny colored markers. The physician-natalists couldn't perform the actual pruning, though. The pruned threads were discarded, they were waste and filth, ephemeral, far removed from proximity to Pan. Physician-natalists couldn't touch the pruned threads any more than the botanist-poet who'd planned the Hanging Gardens of Appalacia could touch the dead branches, weeds, and wilted blossoms pruned by her gardeners. Physician and botanist subpures were too close to Pan to touch ephemeral filth.

Gardener of the Imperium, that's me. Morose thought. In the story, the Gardener angered Pan by allowing lower purities to devour the fruit of a Sacred Tree consecrated to the angels. In some versions, the Gardener even encouraged the despoil, since the fruit was nourishing and the people were starving in a drought. In every version, the Gardener was cast out of the Sacred Garden and condemned to wander Pangaea, alone and in shame.

Dubban hated that story. It didn't seem fair to punish what he thought was a good deed. An act of compassion. But his mother, devout Pannist that she was, had said, "The

moral is, my son, you must never mingle things meant for
one purity with those of another.''

Yet as far from proximity to the Eternal as pruning was,
still pruning was essential to ensure the health and integrity
of each birthpod. That had been Dubban's second lesson as
a midwife-natalist. As Dubban's skill with the hand-levers
had grown over the years and he'd become more accurate at
pruning, he'd found himself in great demand in the laboratories at all the natalries.

Garth's voice grated in his ear. ''Say, Dub. Is it true
you've broken off bedding Romana?''

Dubban glared again, surprise and a twist of regret pierc-
ing his chest. Just last *night*. . . . ''And who told you
that?''

Garth shrugged. That maddening grin played across his
mouth.

Dubban dropped the levers and seized Garth's collar
again. ''I said who?''

''Resa.''

Garth cocked his head at another midwife two rows
down, poised before a viewglass. A dark-haired dumpling
of a wench, Resa had bedded Dubban the night after his
first day at the natalry. He'd been flattered by her attentions
and astonished at how quickly a young man could find a
bedmate of a similar subpure in Our Sacred City. But she'd
clung to him too tightly after that, and he'd decided to leave
her alone. He didn't *love* her, never would *love* her.

''Resa and me, we had a bit of caf this morning before
the earthshock,'' Garth said. ''You know how she likes to
talk.''

He lifted the twit like a rat by the neck and shook him.
''And how does Resa know?''

''Dubban!'' Waldo's shout rang out. ''I warned you!
You're docked, you rowdy!''

''*How?*''

''She and Romana share a bed sometimes. Guess they
shared one late last night. Romana tells her everything.

Resa says now that Romana is through with you, they're talking about entering into sharelock. They both want to generate a family pretty bad. Now that the Big Shock has come and gone, I bet they'll tie the knot.''

And he didn't want to, in the middle of the laboratory, in front of all these midwives and physicians and priest-esses—

—but Dubban began to weep.

Deep fissures gaped among the cobblestones of northeast Marketplace and fingered up every temple, pyramid, and pagoda Dubban laid his eyes on. The wreckage was terrible to behold as he strode out of Quartius Natalry for his mid-day break, fists clenched, teeth grinding. Waldo had finally let him go after a round of reprimands and humiliation, culminating with threats of decreasing his hours *and* dock-ing his wage.

Maybe it's too bad the end of the world hasn't come. Maybe Eternal Torment would be better than the Imperium without end.

Still, the whole world hadn't cracked apart and fallen into the flames of Inim. The damage was bad, but not as bad as everyone had always feared.

We're still standing, ain't we?

Sheer relief percolated through him, and he found him-self chuckling at the wreckage with the giddy humor of a survivor. There, a duct geysered sewage-strewn water. Im-pure children with little deformed hands picked through shattered cookpots and crushed databoards till a security monitor chased them out of the quadrant. Seawater ran an-kle-deep in the streets. He'd have to dry out his clogs over cookstones tonight. Vendors' carts and concessions lay in absurdly snarled ruins. Colorful trinkets and spilled food had been scattered about like spoiled festival confections. Three vendors had come to blows over a crumpled, water-logged box kite.

But we're still standing.

He strode up to a cod vendor's wagon beneath a multicolored sunshade. "Fifty bits for a carton of cod?" He surveyed the grill. Gravel clung to the breaded fillets. The vendor must have plucked them from where they'd been flung on the ground and deposited them back on the grill. "That's robbery!"

"That's our price, my chum," said the cod vendor, a tiny, white-haired serv no taller than a magister's child.

"Since when? It was twenty bits yesterday. And look at this filth." He flicked away a chunk of gravel.

"Since the Big Shock, my chum. Yesterday food weren't likely to be scarce. Today it's fifty bits, filth or no. Step aside if ye ain't hungry."

"I'm hungry, I'm hungry."

Dubban doled out this extortion for a carton of fried cod and fried tato slices, ten bits extra for a dollop of pickled cream sauce, another ore for a jar of beer. He wasn't a tall man, but he was powerfully built, more robust than most of his subpure. He attended gamefields and wrestling rings as often as he could, after the sedentary labor of midwifery. Hard muscles curved in his arms and thighs. An uncontainable nervous energy coursed through him, requiring considerable amounts of fuel to stoke the engine of his taut body.

He strode to Allpure Square and found a vacant bench, miraculously unscathed amid the rubble. He sat and gazed up at the Pagoda of Pan floating overhead. Before him the Obelisk of Eternity canted alarmingly to one side. The marble base had ripped right out of the white flagstones. The obelisk wouldn't last for any Eternity if the Imperial monument builders didn't get off their lazy duffs pretty damn soon. The obelisk would topple as surely as the cod vendor's wagon.

Dubban made the sign of the Imperial star at his impure thought, picked gravel off his cod and tatos, and devoured them, avidly licking salty grease and sauce off his fingers. Vendors' food always tasted wonderful in the open air but invariably his stomach gurgled for the rest of the day. Usually he brought a sack of flatbreads and a pot of curd cheese from his hovel.

A Vigilance windship sailed overhead, scarlet kaligraphs depicting the Story of the Faithful Handmaid winking around its hull. In the story, the handmaid amputated her own hand just because her employer, a magister, ordered her to in a fit of pique. The magister then arranged for her sharelock to a kindly beck-and-call man, who pampered her for the rest of her life.

Dubban hated that story, too. The magister was a cruel beast, the handmaid a fool. If the handmaid's Imperial duty of labor was to serve with her hands, wasn't fulfillment of that duty a higher obligation than the magister's irrational order? Shouldn't she have refused, or run away? But Bandular had said, "Serve higher pures, subpures, and your superiors and you'll be rewarded, my son."

He glimpsed vigiles peering down at him from the windship. Handmaids were drud subpures. Why depict a drud's homily over the serv quadrant? He suppressed a curse. It was insulting. He wished he could shake his fist at them, but didn't dare.

How was it that magister subpures could ride in the sky? They weren't angels. What would it be like, riding in a windship? Dubban couldn't imagine. Most likely, he'd never see for himself. Servs didn't ride in windships. The highest purity that could ride in windships—and the shabby public windships at that—were middle pures.

Like her. Like the woman at the Festival of Spring Moontide.

I could have lost my hand to a vigile's dagger, just for looking at her.

"Peace and calm," declared a vigile patrolling the quadrant. A tall, broad-shouldered woman with badges of rank pinned to the shoulders of her blue-and-silver uniform, the vigile presided over the chaos with an expression that managed to be both commanding and compassionate at the same time. She brandished an enormous crossbow loaded with a vicious-looking arrow. A firebolt and a dagger dangled from her belt. "Peace and calm, if you please."

Vigilance sharemind shot through the quadrant, subduing everyone. A chill shivered down Dubban's spine as vigilance sharemind curled around his consciousness and he acknowledged his submission to the vigile's authority.

"What if the earthshocks don't stop, eh?" shouted the scrawny trinket vendor, her wild grey hair framing a face deeply grooved by weather and time. Her tiny deft hands lingered over her trinkets.

"The Imperium will not permit any more earthshocks, dame," the vigile said. "Peace and calm, I say."

"And what if more shocks shake yer arse even worse 'n' this 'un, eh? What then?"

The crowd gasped and muttered. Everyone might whisper them, but no one spoke such Apocalyptist rumors aloud.

"The Imperium will not permit more shocks." The vigile signaled to an underling, another strapping vigile with a manly face as impassive as a marble wall. The underling seized the trinket vendor by her arm, quietly asked to see her security number, and escorted her away from Allpure Square. "The Imperium will not permit worse shocks."

Three vigiles surrounded the vendor in the alley behind the cod vendor's wagon. Her voice shrilled, then stilled.

Dubban cringed and turned away, unwilling to witness the vigiles slicing off a piece of her tongue. He guzzled his beer. So he wasn't the only one with impure thoughts. The trinket vendor had impure thoughts, too, and the courage— or foolishness—to voice them. Ground Control couldn't really stop the shocks, could it? If the bureau could, why did the shock occur today?

The High Council had proclaimed Ground Control *would* stop the shocks. The High Council had also proclaimed that Vigilance would capture every foe in Pangaea and imprison or execute the criminals according to the severity of their crimes. And the foes and their vicious clans would never kill or torture any pure ever again.

But look at what had happened to Milady Danti. An angel!

The thought of Danti, her terrible death, abruptly saddened and sobered him. He wiped beer foam off his lips with a handcloth and flung it in a public wastebin with his empty carton. Flung the beer jar in, too, so violently the jar shattered in the bottom of the bin. What a tragedy for Milord Lucyd. Losing a sharer like Milady Danti, a sharer of fifty years? If only Dubban could find a sharer of his own pure like—

—like the woman he'd glimpsed at the Festival of Spring Moontide. The curve of her cheekbones, shadows pooling beneath them when the sunlight beat down on her face. Gold-green gleamed in her eyes, the wavy mass of her hair the startling red-gold color of breadfruit leaves turning in autumn. So beautiful, so voluptuous, she'd taken his breath away.

She was too sensual to be an angel, too petite to be a magister, too fine and finely dressed for serv or drud, too delicate to be an erotician. Within her middle purity, she must have been a very high subpure; look at her remarkable variance. He wouldn't have been surprised to discover she was a sacred surgeon at the Temple of Sharelock, from the fineness of her small hands.

He'd never know.

No, he and Soral and Natch had no right to roam that particular section of Tythys Street, gawking at the festival crowd and hoping to buy an expensive brand of skee they could never find in Rancid Flats. But *she'd* had no right to look at him with such sweet promise, such longing. Such quick, flirtatious intelligence in her eyes. The way a woman looks at a man when she wants to bed him. The way Milady Danti had looked at every dreamer in Milord Lucyd's dream this morning.

But she had. She'd looked twice.

Dubban ground his teeth. Sweet promises that could never be fulfilled.

He'd turned away from her, dismayed at her audacity. Disgusted with himself.

And he'd wept in front of everyone at the laboratory, not for Romana, but for her. The impossibly lovely woman forever beyond his grasp.

No one had jeered at his rage and sorrow, not even Garth or Waldo. The midwives had returned to their tasks before the viewglasses, somber and silent. Even Resa, who'd had nothing but scowls for him since they briefly bedded, had given him a small squeeze on his shoulder.

He would have cursed his mother, if he could. Bandular's advice and her teachings were like two sharp, curved horns, charging at him, threatening to impale him. *Enter into your duty of sharelock with the purity of Pannish love, but also enter with desire, with no fear of the bestial urge.* And, *Never mingle what belongs to one purity with another.*

But he couldn't possibly curse his mother. Instead he cursed the angels. *Damn them for taunting us with their dreams.*

Garth was right. Dreaming Milord Lucyd's dreams of love was stupid and wasteful. When he lay down, closed his eyes, and invoked Imperial sharemind, and the paths of the Mind of the World presented themselves to his dream-eye, he should choose the dreams of bloody battles and conquest cast by Milady Faro. Even the dreams of depravity and torture cast by the popular Milord Sting. At least dreams of torture wouldn't torture his heart.

Perhaps he'd go to another rave of the Serpent Sect, after all. Amid the cultists' frenzy and the pounding drums, he could forget what could never be, if only for a little while.

A group of harried tourists wandered past him, Far Reaches men and women from the look of their rustic hide leggings, laced tunics, and peaked caps far too hot for summer in Atlan. They turned to him with wide, frightened eyes and spoke to him in Far, with a drud accent. He could barely understand them, it had been so long since he'd spoken any Far dialect.

Dubban liked tourists, especially those from the Far Reaches. He delighted in their reverence for the megalopolis, their awed eyes and open mouths before the great temples, pyramids, and pagodas they'd only heard about in songs or dreamed in angels' dreams. They were charming, usually polite, and a bit clumsy. They reminded him of himself four years ago as a boy of sixteen. He enjoyed pointing out the sights and watching their dazzled expressions.

"Does Our Sacred City shake so violently all the time?" they asked.

Dubban reassured them this morning's earthshock was the Big Shock, and now it was over. "The Imperium won't let it happen again," he said loud enough for a passing vigile to overhear him. The tourists tipped him an ore for his time and his talk, which he declined at first, then accepted.

He directed them to the northwest quadrant, where they could locate a licensed tour that took drud pures to the Pyramid of Perpetuities, the Temple of Sharelock, and other points of interest. He urged them to hurry, before the security monitors spied them and they got into trouble for proximity violations. He sought out the iced fruit vendor for himself. He was standing over the vendor's cart, contemplating, *Shall I have the pondplum or the cream with crushed seaberries?,* when he felt the claw of a hand clasping his shoulder, digging fingernails like talons through his work shirt into his skin.

"So, my fine Dubban. How go your labors at the natalry this excellent day, hm?"

Dubban knew that hand, those talons. He turned to face the qut purveyor. "Horan Zehar."

Impure.

Dubban recoiled. Even the lowest drud, however severely

shaped, could boast of symmetry, solidity, a certain beauty and strength suited to pure and subpure, superb health and soundness of body. All the purities could thank the Imperium and the natalries for that—for the blessings of the Superior Mother and the Superior Father, the wisdom of the physicians, the diligent labor Dubban and the midwives performed to ensure the health and integrity of every seeded birthpod. This was the fundamental security, the great gift the Imperium had given to its people by the grace of Pan.

Horan Zehar—all the unfortunates of the impure—was horrible to behold. No one of the purities suffered the drooping of one eye, the flare of one nostril, the constriction of the other. The twitch at one corner of twisted lips, the sallow complexion bearing pockmarks and scrofulous blemishes. The ridged and swollen dome of a skull beneath thin greying hair dusted with dandruff. The palsied trembling of a hand carried at a mangled angle on an emaciated arm, while the other lurched forward, a claw with broken yellow fingernails. The frail stoop in a body broken by impure birth and wretched circumstance.

The qut purveyor raised a filthy rag to his nose and expelled a quantity of phlegm. Dubban flinched. Diseases still plagued the purities, just as foes stalked amid the Imperium. Diseases still killed and maimed, just like foes killed and maimed. But those of the purities withstood many diseases and were immune to others. Just as Imperial vigiles protected citizens from the foes. Or were supposed to.

No wonder the impure lived below and beyond all the purities, lived in their own bleak world apart from Our Sacred Imperium. They couldn't even dream the angels' dreams in the Mind of the World.

How could he have ever allowed Garth to persuade him to try qut when he'd been depressed and lonely four years ago? How could he have ever allowed himself to become tangled up with an impure criminal like this qut purveyor?

Too easily, that's how.

"Over here," Dubban whispered harshly and ducked in the alley behind the cod vendor's wagon. A splattering of blood stained the cobblestones where the vigiles had taken the trinket vendor. He didn't want to look at it.

Horan smiled, gaping, black-toothed, witless—apparently. Dubban knew by now never to assume the qut purveyor was too stupid to exact promises he didn't intend to enforce, or too feeble to inflict injury for promises broken. He carried weapons beneath his black cloak, a strange garment that covered him neck to toe and always seemed to stir around him even when there wasn't a breeze. The trembling idiot's face belied ferocious strength and formidable guile. Dubban still ached from the time the irate qut purveyor had flung him to the ground and soundly kicked him in the buttocks. And he was hardly a frail man.

"You didn't answer me, my fine Dubban."

He snorted. "The Big Shock has destroyed Atlan, the last quid you sold me reeked, my super's docking my wages at the natalry, and I haven't got a bit to my name. Milord."

"Dear me. Let me consider your answer, point by point." The purveyor extended his bony forefinger. "First, that was hardly the Big Shock. No, no. When the Big Shock strikes Atlan, *nothing* of Our Sacred City will remain."

"The Apocalyptists have been saying that for years. If today is any indication, the Imperium will last forever. Ground Control will never allow—"

"Ground Control is a sham perpetrated upon the purities. Ground Control secures fine stipends for its academe toadies paid out of the outrageous taxes extracted from your humble wage. You know that. I've thought many things of you, my fine Dubban, but I never thought you were stupid."

Dubban thrust a finger in the collar of his work shirt, loosened the constriction around his neck. He suddenly found it hard to breathe. "You haven't sought me out in northeast Marketplace to discuss taxes, have you, Horan Zehar?"

"There, you see? You're not stupid." The qut purveyor

grinned, rolled his bulging misshapen eyes, and counted point two on his knobby finger. "I'm shocked, *shocked,* to hear you disparage the quality of my wares. You mean to tell me you were dissatisfied with the quid?"

"The quid was soaked in skee. The quid put a nice pustule on the inside of my cheek. And you still squeezed twenty ores out of me. Twenty ores I haven't got."

"On top of the two hundred you already owe me, hm?"

"I haven't kept track."

"Oh, but I have. My fine Dubban, I'll need repayment out of you, and soon."

"Like I said, I haven't got it, and my supe docked me."

"I'm sorry," the qut purveyor said with feigned solicitude while he glanced warily at the vigiles who swarmed throughout the quadrant, bearing firebolts, crossbows, and daggers. "Then you'll have to do something else. You'll have to find another way."

"What else can I do? I never wager on orbrolls or athletes. I'm the youngest of twenty-one sons, and my family hasn't got two bits to rub together. My subpure is midwifenatalist, I'll never be anything else. I haven't got a bedmate who would be willing to add her wage to mine. I'll never enter into sharelock with a sharer possessing assets who would share her bounty with me. Go ahead and squeeze me, Horan. You can't squeeze blood from dust."

In less than an eyeblink, the qut purveyor lashed out and commenced viciously striking Dubban all over his body. Struck over and over, with deft razor strokes of his thin, deformed hands, till Dubban's flesh stung and throbbed.

The foes were renowned for their skill at maiming and killing with their bare hands.

And in broad daylight, in northeast Marketplace, with sharp-eyed vigiles patrolling everywhere and Vigilance craft flying overhead, the impure monster managed to assault him unseen, unheard. The impact of Horan's hands promised more punishment if one cry escaped Dubban's lips.

And if the vigiles observed him transacting illegal commerce with the impure purveyor, the Imperium promised punishment, too. He'd be finished as a midwife-natalist if he lost his thumbs to a Vigilance interrogator.

What can I do?

Dubban fell to his knees, crashing against the backdrop of a concession hawking children's hand puppets. He swallowed his cry of pain.

"Get up, you're not a weakling," Horan Zehar snapped. He slipped his torturer's hand beneath Dubban's elbow and single-handedly hoisted him to his feet. "Don't let the fucking vigiles see you."

"No, I won't." Dubban choked down terror and rage. If he'd fought back, would he have found himself lacking an eye, teeth, several fingers? Now he truly had no notion how powerful Horan Zehar might be. How badly the purveyor could hurt him.

He said between clenched teeth, "What do you expect me to do, Horan Zehar?"

"I expect, my fine Dubban," the purveyor said mildly, "that you'll do whatever I say."

FACET 4

Line: Guidance or division.
A stone wall surrounds the magister's house.
The action is inclusion.
The forbearance is separation.

The Orb of Eternity

Commentaries:

Councillor Sausal: After all things of the world issue forth, they manifest in proximity to Pan in the degree to which they resemble the divine. Further, things gather with others according to their proximity to Pan. Higher gathers with higher; lower with lower.

So, too, the purities manifest in proximity to Pan in the degree to which their functions resemble the divine. That which is created by the mind, unique, and eternal, is close to Pan. That which is served by the body, anonymous, and ephemeral is far from Pan.

Therefore the prudent person must act in relation to one's pure, one's subpure, and one's family. Honor and obey higher pures, subpures, and superiors. Protect and guide lower pures, subpures, and inferiors.

Guttersage (usu. considered vulgar): Magisters drink with magisters because they don't want to get sloshed in the company of fools.

Fools drink with fools because no one else will get sloshed with them.

*Our City of Atlan, the periphery of Northwest Marketplace,
Rancid Flats. Jugglers Lane, the Salon of Shame:*

Something else would happen. Tahliq didn't know what,
exactly. What more could possibly happen after the Big
Shock?

Anything, of course.

Perhaps the end of the world has a beginning.

The conflagration across the lane, for instance. Like
tongues they were, coruscating tongues of yellow and orange, the flames leaping from the rooftop of the Bawdy
Harridan Saloon. How they intrigued Tahliq with their deft
licking strokes, their swift power to annihilate. She studied
the conflagration from the second-story window of her dallying chamber. Could she learn a new technique?

Down in the lane, amid the spilled jigsaw puzzle of
wreckage, a costermonger wept over her two young children. A toppled lamppost lay across their small crushed
skulls. No one could help them now. As she wailed, bending over the little corpses, two impure boys in black sacking, their faces brightly blotched and misshapen, crept up to
the costermonger's wagon. Hands darted. The costermonger's cash sack vanished, and the boys did, too, before Tahliq could shout a warning out her window.

They'll be full-fledged foes only too soon.

She shrugged and returned to her contemplation of the
flames. A new technique was just what Tahliq needed to
please Lieutenant Regim Deuceman this afternoon. Where
was her fine, strapping vigile? How had her beloved fared?

For a moment she envisioned his splendid body sprawled
in a fissure, broken and bloody.

No! Not my Regim.

She dismissed the bloody vision, determined to weather
the shock's aftermath with her customary insouciance. No
disaster would ever halt her commerce, except perhaps the
end of the world.

Yet she could not dispel the apprehension beating deep in her breast. *Something else will happen.*

What a dreadful spectacle. Fires everywhere, fallen walls, scattered chimney bricks, shattered glass. Blood. And the impressive crevice that had cracked open in the middle of the cobblestones? Wouldn't *that* be a hazard for passing travelers when night descended. Besotted councillors and drayers alike would find themselves top over toes and wondering—if they didn't split open their skulls first— where all the solid ground had gone to.

And there she'd be with a sympathetic word and a helping hand, no matter who staggered up out of the crevice. She'd offer her shoulder to lean on, and then she'd ask, *Do you have the urge tonight? Permit me to serve you.*

Every sharer and shareless, on one night or another, journeyed down to Jugglers Lane and entered the rose-pink door of the Salon of Shame. Every pure and subpure, in one weak moment or another, risked life and limb for the privilege of abandoning purity protocol. Of yielding to the ancient shame and Tahliq's skillful ministrations.

For a price.

It was her Imperial duty as a licensed erotician. Her birthright as a drud. Her burden. Sometimes her privilege, too.

Her privilege especially when she lay with Lieutenant Regim Deuceman. If it weren't for her Imperial duty, a drud like her would never know the joys of touching a glorious magister subpure like him.

The Big Shock, my, my. So the world hasn't ended like the frightmongers said. Too bad; the Imperium goes on without end. And the damnable purities and their damnable protocol. Who among them will need someone to make the earth shatter again tonight?

Tahliq smiled at the flames.

The saloonkeep of the Bawdy Harridan shouted for help. She'd always been fond of Ergeo, but she didn't move a muscle. How often she'd warned the silly sod that when the

Big Shock struck—as it surely would one day, and sooner than anyone cared to speculate—Ergeo would find his saloon aflame if he didn't secure the great cookstones over which he roasted luscious flanks of meat. She'd pointed, *here and here, my darling. Hire a smithy to pound bolts into the wall. If the world ends, whoever survives will need to eat and drink.*

But Ergeo was a typical saloonkeep, bit-pinching and sticky-fingered, as arrogant a proximicist as the highest angel. Part company with ten whole ores for a smithy to bolt his kitchen grills to the wall? Ten whole ores for a catastrophe that might or might not occur some fine day? *His* ten ores jingling in the pocket of a low serv subpure like the smithy, who took her jar of ale to the back of the saloon and arm-wrestled with the likes of roadbuilders?

Would Ergeo listen to Tahliq Jahn Pentaput naitre Quintus, however wise and practical her words might be? Ha, and ha! He'd parted with plenty of ores for her company on the pleasure couch whenever his sharer went to Marketplace. But he took her advice with a grain of grit.

Now poor old Ergeo had paid the price. The Harbinger hadn't given him nearly enough warning to secure the stones. Tahliq's smile deepened as she watched Ergeo and his sharer desperately hurling cookpots of beer on the implacable blaze. Naturally the earthshock had shattered the waterducts servicing Jugglers Lane, and no one had running water. She might be a drud and a licensed erotician, of the lowest pure and most despised subpure in all Pangaea, but Tahliq adored it when time and consequences proved she'd always been right.

Her hand flickered over her breast in the hexagram of Afrodite, She who ruled the moon, the tides, and women's fertility. "Mout? Mout!" she shouted to her handmaid. Sacred gestures might protect one's Essence from evil spirits, but they didn't protect one's rooftop from a conflagration. "Where the devil are you, girl? Get your buttocks in here."

The Harbinger *had* given Tahliq and her handmaid plenty

of warning to thrust stout oak sticks through the handles of the cupboards in the kitchen and the feasthall. They'd doused their cookstones and filled Tahliq's bathtub to the brim with fresh water. Tahliq had tossed pillows beneath her massive feast table and taken up camp. *If the world collapses into the flames of Inim, I might as well be comfortable before I die.* She'd reclined on the pillows with her favorite forbidden book, a wineskin, and a raptureroot.

At first the fury of the shaking had terrified her. When the Salon of Shame had commenced pitching, Mout had bolted for the laundry chamber and burrowed into the mound of soiled linens, believing if she didn't see the shuddering roof, no beams would fall on her. At the worst of it, Tahliq had seized a leg of the table and slid back and forth across the floor with it. Her prized chandelier had crashed upon the tabletop, crystal shards impaling the ironwood. She'd congratulated herself for deciding to lie beneath such a fine piece of furniture.

But when the ground didn't crack open and deliver her to Eternal Torment, she'd lain back and enjoyed the rollicking ride. Tahliq had prepared for the Big Shock all her thirty-five years.

Naturally the megalopolis would be devastated. She laughed and whooped. The construction workers would be as busy as a hillful of ants, mopping up. Then they'd come to her, exhausted and disgruntled, smelling of sweat and mud, desperate for a shot of skee and a tussle on her pleasure couch. She adored construction workers, their brawny bodies and gratitude and generous tips. The women liked to give her little gifts.

She would earn enough funds to commission a new chandelier—something bigger and fancier—in no time at all.

Ergeo glanced up as she sat smiling in her window. Sweat had plowed pale rivulets down his ash-stained face, his eyes blazed like a madman's, and she realized why she was fond of him. Away from his odious little sharer, he was a passionate brute.

She waved gaily to him.

She couldn't hear his voice above the crackling of the flames as he swore violently, spat, and finally mouthed and mimed, *Got any water?*

She shook her head, shrugged, *Sorry.* Who knew how long it would be before the ductdiggers repaired the water supply to Jugglers Lane? She had her own uses for her bathtub filled with fresh water.

What a pity. The Bawdy Harridan would burn to the ground before Imperial Fire & Shock crews arrived with their slow-as-mud wagons, sweaty vats of tepid water, incontinent pumps, and absurd dirigible nozzles. This was Rancid Flats. At the moment Fire & Shock crews were stumbling around on Prime Hill, all over Marketplace, in Pleasant Valley, along the Sausal Boardwalk, at the Great Wall. They'd be preoccupied many long hours in more important places inhabited by higher pures before forging on to Rancid Flats, where servs and druds lived and died beneath the shadow of the Harbinger.

"Mout," she shouted again.

"Here be I, my dame."

The handmaid shambled into the dallying chamber, a she-bear of a girl with big-knuckled hands useful for punching insolent patrons in the nose and heaving rowdies out the door. She wrung those big hands now, trembling as violently as an epileptic, tears cascading down her broad, furry cheeks.

"Now, my little Mout. What's the trouble?"

"I's scart, my dame."

"Everything will be all right. The earthshock is over."

"B-b-b-but . . . what if a shock come again, my dame?"

"If it does, we'll just lie beneath the feast table again. But I don't think it will."

"Is this the Big Shock, my dame?"

"Maybe." More firmly, convincing herself too, "Yes. And you see? We're fine. For a while, anyway."

Tahliq gazed at the drud girl, an odd concoction of compassion and contempt roiling in her heart. The handmaid was as handsome as an old boot, vibrant as caf grounds in the bottom of Tahliq's cup, intelligent as a potato, lively as overcooked rice, cheerful as an Imperial embalmer. How strange that Tahliq—who possessed considerable charms, beauty, and wit—shared the same purity as Mout. Both druds, but of vastly different subpures, Mout's more respectable than Tahliq's. Their sharemind encompassed complete mutual consciousness, but their intelligence was so wildly divergent Tahliq avoided sharemind with Mout whenever she could. It was just too frustrating and exhausting to enter into sharemind with a simpleton.

The purities were the purities—but sometimes, Tahliq thought, they weren't so pure. A blasphemous thought? A traitorous thought? Ha, and ha! She wasn't a Pannist. She despised the laws of proximity, purity protocol, the sharemind with which every pure emerged, according to birthright. Tahliq revered Afrodite, She who gave life and took life away, the sacred leveler of all living beings. And when it came to pures and subpures, protocol and proximity, Tahliq had seen just about everything.

"Fetch a broom and a bucket of water, and go up on our roof, Mout."

"Yes, my dame. Uh." The handmaid knit her low furry brow. "What shall I do up on our roof, my dame?"

"You shall make certain we don't catch on fire, my little Mout." Tahliq checked her temper. No one could blame the drud girl for her attributes. Slowly, carefully, "If you see cinders or hot ashes blown over by the wind, you must sweep them off with the broom. Yes? And if you see flames leaping over from the Harridan, you must douse our shingles with water." Tahliq thought again. "And summon me at once."

The handmaid knit her brow in concentration, nodding slowly as she took in each of Tahliq's instructions.

"Do you understand, my little Mout?"

The handmaid's opaque yellow eyes flew up at her, glistening with comprehension. "Yes, my dame!"

"Very good. Go now. And tell Dori"—this was one of Mout's thirty sisters, cut of the same canvas as Mout—"to bring me my schedule of patrons for the evening. Tell her to be quick about it."

"Yes, my dame."

The handmaid shuffled out, and Tahliq returned to her meditation of the flames. She mimicked the thrusting movements with her tongue, imagining all the tender places on a human body where such devoted ministrations would be appreciated. The motions felt sweet. Would feel sweet to whoever received them.

Tahliq knew this absolutely—the pleasure her patron would feel—through her gift of allpure sharemind. Her allpure sharemind apprehended a patron's consciousness in all its fullness—fancies, intelligence, memories, passion, sensations. The very Essence of a man or woman.

What a shock it had been to discover, as a young apprentice, that she could enter into sharemind with any person of any purity who lay with her on her pleasure couch and share total mutual consciousness.

But only then—only on the couch, while she performed her Imperial duty.

A strange gift. It wasn't at all like Imperial sharemind that permitted every dreamer to enter the Mind of the World. Nothing like sharemind between unequal pures or higher and lower subpures—the protocol made her teeth ache. Or within a purity, among equal subpures—discrepancies in intelligence could be worse than protocol. Not even like the utter intimacy between sharers that sharelock chips conferred, though Tahliq couldn't be certain of that. She'd never entered into sharelock or worn sharelock chips.

When she didn't lie with a patron on her pleasure couch

Tahliq entered into sharemind with other pures and sub-pures in the usual way. With her limited drud sharemind she could apprehend only a small portion of a higher pure's consciousness, while offering the full delight of her wit to any pure whose apprehension was broader and more power-ful.

She'd kept her silence about her strange sharemind ever since she'd discovered she possessed it. She trusted no one, not even her mothers. Licensed eroticians themselves, her mothers had never breathed one word that a drud subpure like her could possess allpure sharemind—the highest sharemind possible. The sharemind of an angel.

Variance. Deviation. Impurity.

A trick of Quintus Natalry while she was an unborn? Some bumbler's mistake? A secret Imperial experiment?

She'd given up wondering why.

Still wondered how.

It was the puzzlement of her life, this aberrant sharemind. Not that she didn't appreciate a gift so useful for her gainful undertakings. But who knew what the Impe-rium would do to her if the inspectors discovered she pos-sessed sharemind forbidden to her purity?

She'd heard the rumors all her life that the Imperium could take away one's sharemind. She didn't know how.

She didn't *want* to know how.

Tahliq disliked puzzlements. Puzzlements were of little use to her. She didn't linger long on them. Puzzlements were for higher pures, for acolyte-auditors, justices, and academes. For those who labored long and painfully with their thoughts.

Tahliq labored long and exquisitely with her body, the same sort of severely shaped body her mothers and their mothers had possessed. Huge eyes, the irises ebony-black, an afterthought of a nose in a flawless copper-colored com-plexion, plum-red lips, thick and pliant. Sometimes she coiled her bronze-colored hair around her head. Other times she spilled abundant braids down her back to her waist. Her second mother's brother, who'd given his seed to generate her, had been blessed with extraordinarily long, thick hair.

Tahliq's gigantic breasts pained her if she didn't bind them up in a corset of intricate leather straps. The scarlet nipples protruded like the thumbs of a freerider begging passage at the side of a road. These—the breasts, the nipples—resembled food and reminded patrons of the savage time when women fed their babes with their own bodies.

Tahliq's tiny waist? A pretty thing that yielded to the swells of her belly and massive hips, the astounding hillocks of her buttocks. These swells and mounds also recalled the savage time when, amid suffering and the threat of death, women grew the unborn inside their bodies. The unborn struggled free when it could no longer breathe blood. Once Tahliq's wide hipbones meant there would be less pain and danger in that struggle for her, the trapper, and the unborn, the entrapped.

A living embodiment of the ancient shame, that's what you are, Tahliq's mothers had taught her. *That's why we're the most despised subpure in Pangaea.*

The flames' crackling subsided, and she heard Ergeo's curses, his sharer's wailing, the costermonger's weeping, the randy howl of a wild sphinx in the alley behind the Salon of Shame. Two Fire & Shock crews arrived, after all, clattering up in their wagons, lathered drayers snorting.

Tahliq avidly leaned forward. Such enormous, handsome drayers. They'd glossed their bronze skin with costly oils. Bright red tattoos encircled their tremendous biceps and thighs—the proud mark of gladiator subpures. When they weren't pulling Fire & Shock wagons, these drayers fought on the Imperial gamefields.

But the drayers didn't pick the fight that followed.

Scrappy little firefighters leapt out of the wagons and swaggered to the blaze, whereupon the two subpures commenced a lively shouting match. This quickly escalated into a shoving match and then fisticuffs over who would win the fee for quenching Ergeo's fire.

"I beg you, I *beg* you," Ergeo cried, pulling out hanks of his hair. "Meat and drink for your subpure and all your families. For two whole seasons."

"Make it three seasons, chum," said the swarthy super of one subpure, grinning through her silver-tipped teeth. "And the blaze is out, just like *that*." The super snapped her fingers in poor Ergeo's face.

"We'll take two and a half seasons," said the other super.

Whereupon the first planted a fist in her face, and the two supers went down, rolling and punching in the dust.

"I beg you, I *beg* you—"

The saloonkeep's predicament no longer amused Tahliq. The turbulent light from the conflagration flickered strangely. The red-lacquered walls of her dallying chamber shimmered with unsettling shadows, shadows that seemed to come and go regardless of the light.

Something will happen. . . .

Tahliq turned away from the window and stood before her cheval glass, fussing with her gown of Imperial purple silk. She'd worn this, Regim's favorite, with her amethyst cabochons set in atlantium. She always wore her finest for Regim.

Regim, where are you, my beloved?

His splendid body, broken and bloody—

No!

A snarl suddenly curled in her ear. "So you smile at the saloonkeep's catastrophe, hm? Perhaps one day you'll long for a little more sympathy when catastrophe strikes *you*, lovely dame."

Impure.

She whirled away from the cheval glass, loath to face the qut purveyor, more loath to stand with her back to him. She made the sign of the Imperial star, her smile sardonic. "You know very well catastrophe will never strike me, Horan Zehar. I'm blessed by Pan and revered by the Imperium without end."

"You're the most despised subpure in all Pangaea."

"And you're impure, despised beyond despising."

"Precisely. I know where I stand—*beyond* the Imperium." The purveyor returned a mocking version of the Imperial star.

"I know where I stand, too. I'm not impure."

He twisted his face in a horrible grin. The strange black cloak he always wore shivered around his shoulders. "Ah, but you revile the Imperium every bit as much as I do. I must say, you look especially beautiful on this excellent day. Everyone in Atlan is weeping and moaning about the Big Shock, and here you are, laughing in Imperial colors."

She casually backed away from him and reached for the sharp little crescent blade she used for opening sacks and missives. She'd heard about or known herself nearly every way a patron could threaten or harm an erotician. Thirty-five years at the salon—first as her mothers' babe, then their wine-girl, then an erotician in her own right—had taught her that. She twirled the blade through her dextrous fingers.

"And here you are, filled with idle compliments," she countered. Mildly, belying the fear stinging her throat, "How did you enter my dallying chamber without being announced?"

"Have I startled you, lovely dame?" The qut purveyor bowed deeply with sardonic obeisance and proffered a large bale neatly wrapped in burlap, the squarish package of one fullweight of qut. Where had he concealed it? She'd seen no bulge beneath his cloak. "Surely you wish no one to see an impure purveyor seeking your company. You'd lose your license, not to mention several seasons of your freedom and a few lovely appendages."

She brandished the knife and dropped her smile. "Tell me, Horan Zehar, and be quick about it."

"Dame Tahliq, I knocked on your door and was not received. It seems both your handmaids are scurrying about on your rooftop with brooms and buckets of water. Such foresight. Such enterprise. Most commendable.''

Horan knew very well her handmaids possessed the foresight of a gnat and the enterprise of a sloth. ''*No* one enters my dallying chamber unannounced, unscheduled, and unbidden. Do you understand me?''

''I sincerely apologize. I only wanted to deliver your qut.'' His misshapen, mismatched eyes darted around the chamber. ''I know you never indulge in the wasteful vice, but I wouldn't want your patrons to be kept waiting for theirs.''

How did he get in here without me seeing?

Tahliq didn't despise the impure, like most pures did. She pitied them, refusing to condemn the unfortunate creatures whose ancestors had refused the benefits of the natalries and whose progeny were so plagued with ills and deformities it was a wonder they managed to survive as a people.

Still, the impure were the breeding ground of the foes.

And she might not have despised all the impure, but Horan Zehar disgusted and terrified her. He was a foe, of course, only a fool couldn't see, with his stealthiness and the weapons he casually flashed now and then. Which meant he might be only a qut purveyor, an illegal calling in itself. Or he might be one of the thugs who committed atrocities against the Imperium, against innocent people without reason, mercy, or purpose. Her beloved Regim had told her all about the massacre of Milady Danti, how the angels had been hacked to pieces by vicious foe weapons known as devil stars.

Who knew what Horan Zehar was capable of?

Dread pounded through her blood. She seized the cash sack she'd set aside for him, tossed it in his hands. ''Take your payment, Horan Zehar, and get out.''

With growing alarm, she followed the qut purveyor's glances about her dallying chamber. Suspicion snapped at her. Had she neglected to dispose of a patron's personal effect? Left some revealing clue about her trade that Horan might use for his own purposes? It was difficult enough to evade the prying eyes of the Imperial inspectors who came every new moon to review her license.

"What more do you want?" she said coldly. "I said get out."

His eyes slid back to her and lingered. As if he was considering whether to overpower her, and how, and if she'd cry out or cut him with her absurd little knife. Another chill, deeper and icier, shivered through her.

"Beautiful erotician," Horan said, his grating voice suddenly unctuous, wheedling. He took a step closer. "As it turns out, there *is* something else besides money I want from you today—"

His suggestion was only too plain. Lie with *him* on her pleasure couch? Her stomach clenched at the thought of an impure lying with her. Could she apprehend his consciousness with her allpure sharemind? Was her strange gift so powerful she'd enter into mutual consciousness with an impure?

What atrocities would she witness there?

"No," she shouted.

"But I haven't said—"

"And I said no. Never!"

The purveyor brandished the cash sack and shook it, jingling the ores. "My grateful thanks for your payment," he said with a smirk. "But what I want from you is this, Dame Tahliq. I want you to cast the Orb of Eternity for me."

"Cast the orb! But I haven't got an orb." She knew very well the penalties for possessing an orb. She quickly amended, "I don't know what you mean. What is an orb?"

Horan grinned, black-toothed and lopsided. "Now, now. I've heard on good authority that you're a superior orbcaster, Tahliq. Don't bother to deny it." A beseeching look softened his terrible face. "Please cast the orb for me. I have need of an oracle just now." The lopsided smirk returned. "No one will ever hear about it from me. I'll pay you, of course.'' He jingled the sack again. ''Half of this. Will that do?''

''Five hundred ores for one casting?''

''Does that seem fair?''

''Fair?'' Tahliq burst into disbelieving laughter, then caught herself and glared at the purveyor. She'd never cast the orb for more than a tenth that sum, and felt herself well compensated at that. She usually cast the orb without payment at all, cast it only when she was moved by the force of the orb itself. She'd cast the orb since she was a little girl playing with the weird shiny bauble at her mothers' feet. Had witnessed more than a few strange things the orb could do.

And kept her silence.

Was this a trap? Would a foe spy upon a pure for Vigilance? She'd met every requirement of her Imperial license her entire life, as had her mothers and their mothers before them. And she'd honored every obligation to Horan Zehar, at considerable risk to herself and her livelihood. Why would he wish to ruin a reliable buyer of his wares?

It didn't seem likely.

Then again, when it came to likely and unlikely, Tahliq had seen just about everything, too. *Damn the Imperium for forcing me to wonder if this thug would report me as a practicing orbcaster.*

The qut purveyor continued to grin at her, good-natured now.

She shrugged. ''It doesn't matter how much you propose to pay. I haven't got an orb.'' After the High Council had enacted the ban, she'd carefully, lovingly hidden her orb in a little cask stashed under the floorboards beneath the massive bed in her sleeping chamber.

''But I do.'' Like a conjurer, Horan proffered a magnificent orb on the long bony palm of his hand. Now he towered over Tahliq, as if he'd suddenly grown taller. It wasn't the first time the qut purveyor seemed to change shape before her eyes, his black cloak stirring and shivering around him.

She recoiled, but the orb drew her like a magnet. Light sparkled in the facets, purple scintillations shooting off the polished atlantium. The kaligraphs shimmered, the tiny glyphs surrounding them twinkling like minute stars.

She reached out and gently took the orb from him. Rolled the orb between the palms of her hands, feeling its throb of power. Yes. A genuine orb.

She had absolutely no reason to trust him.

She stared squarely into the qut purveyor's horrible eyes, searching for betrayal there. And glimpsed the depths of depravity, the gaze of a predator. The zeal of a foe of the Imperium. For once, she felt reassured. He would sooner offer his own hide to the Chief Commander of Vigilance than betray her.

She smiled, at last, and nodded. "I would be privileged to cast the orb for you."

She ushered him into her library, a windowless inner sanctum softly lit by magmalamps. Huge settees upholstered in brown oxhide surrounded the circular casting carpet set in the center of the floor.

Walls floor to ceiling were lined with books. Some of the books were permitted, but most were forbidden by Atlanean regulation, Pangaean decree, or both. Tahliq and her mothers and their mothers had diverted considerable amounts of shadow sector tips into acquiring the books on the shadow market and keeping them safe. "Preserve the old knowledge," one of her grandmothers had said. "Or we'll forget important things." Tahliq owned the classic volume of the Orb of Eternity with the facets, the oracles, and scholarly and vulgar commentaries. Since the ban, she'd removed the volume from the library and placed it with the orb beneath her bed.

"Sit," she bid Horan. He crumpled into a cross-legged

heap before her on the carpet. She rearranged her gown and sat opposite him, demurely composing her limbs.

She rolled the orb in her palms, sensing the power of the Ancient One who'd crafted the foretelling device in times lost to antiquity. Images flashed before her and flickered out—

A face, huge almond-shaped eyes, silvery blue skin.

The vastness of space, glimmering galaxies, roar of cataractic stars.

Ancient oceans, waves crashing over the world, leviathans rising from the depths, gasping for air.

Primordial jungles, beasts stalking amid vine and leaf to grapple and struggle, to copulate or kill.

A thousand other images flickered before her eyes, hovered, and faded away.

And she sensed her connection with all things of the world that ever had been, were now, and ever will be.

She flung the orb onto the center of the carpet where the labyrinthine design of foretelling had been woven. The orb rolled along one length of the labyrinth, abruptly changed direction, took another course. She smiled with satisfaction when Horan's eyes widened, filled with awe and respect at the sight of the orb tumbling.

"Done is done," she whispered.

The ruling facet came to rest before her.

Her eyes skimmed, then plunged into the facet.

And she found herself peering down into an abyss. Stones tumbled into bottomless depths. She peered up at the sky, an oblivion rendered starless, still, and dead.

"Darkness," she whispered. "Darkness is a difficult oracle. One of the evil ones." She shifted uncomfortably on the casting carpet. "Darkness. That which was before the beginning of the world. That which will be after the end of the world. All that remains hidden, unknown and ever unknowable."

"Darkness," Horan whispered. "Ah. Then Darkness it will be." He stared pensively at the facet as if the orb had revealed an oracle he'd anticipated—and deeply regretted. "Fascinating. You know, of course, this is the facet that appeared in Milord Lucyd's dream this morning before the earthshock."

Tahliq regarded him coldly. "How do you know what appeared in an angel's dream, Horan? The impure don't possess Imperial sharemind, do they?"

He grinned slyly. "Alas, we do not. Only the purities possess sharemind, Imperial and otherwise."

"And you never dream the angels' dreams in the Mind of the World."

"Very true. At least not through Imperial sharemind," he replied enigmatically. "How clever of you, Dame Tahliq, to have cast the same facet that appeared in Milord Lucyd's dream."

"I have no power over the orb to cast this facet or that. And I don't dream Milord Lucyd's dreams of Pannish love, this morning or any other morning," Tahliq added acidly.

"No, beautiful erotician?" Horan said. "You who profit so handsomely from the institution of sacred sharelock and all that it lacks?"

"*I* profit? Pannish love and the angels' dreams profit the Imperium."

"Such blasphemy! I thought Pannish love was the highest state of grace any pure could aspire to."

"So the Imperium is furnished with new laborers, each properly generated within his or her purity." All her rage at the purities and protocol blazed forth. "And sacred sharers possess the honor of being locked together in the common cause of caring for the little laborers till they're old enough to assume their Imperial duty and care for themselves."

"Such a cynical view of the joys of family life, Dame Tahliq. But surely you believe in Pannish love?"

"Pannish love is deplorable and contrary to the truth of who and what humanity is."

Now Horan Zehar feigned shock. "And what is the truth of humanity?"

"That Ideal Love and the ancient shame arise from the same source. Or *used* to, till the angels' dreams persuaded the purities to relinquish their nature in deference to their Imperial duty."

"Ssh, I implore you." Horan pressed a finger to his lips. "Such traitorous words."

"Ha! and ha! Milord Lucyd and his lady themselves patronized my salon. You'll never guess what they wanted to do."

"Do tell."

"Never in five thousand years," she said with a toss of her head.

Horan chuckled. "That's all right. I'll amuse myself by guessing." He grew somber again and studied the facet, his hideous face twisted in a perplexed expression that was almost childlike. "What do *you* think this oracle portends, orbcaster?"

Tahliq drew a breath, touched the facet with her fingertip. "The orb may portend. And the orb may . . . create what it portends." The power of the orb surged through her again. "It means," she declared in a ringing voice, "that something significant and terrible will transpire this night when darkness comes. Not another earthshock, I think. This Darkness"—she studied the glittering facet before her—"is a darkness of the heart. A darkness of humanity's deeds."

Horan nodded slowly. "Darkness of the heart and dark deeds at the darkness of this day. So it will be done. You've been most helpful, Tahliq. I thank you and gladly tender your fee." He spilled out a quantity of money from the sack.

Suddenly the qut purveyor sat up on the casting carpet, caution twisting his face. He leapt to his feet, a sharp sniff whistling through his misshapen nose. "I smell a magister," he said. "A vigile is here."

Tahliq scrambled to her feet, alarmed. It wasn't time for

her assignation with her beloved Regim. Had Horan somehow signaled Vigilance, after all, and now a vigile had
come to arrest her? She glanced around the library, searching for what devious means the qut purveyor might have
employed. But the library had no windows. There was no
one else within besides her and Horan Zehar.

"What the devil are you chattering about now, Horan?"
The pitalwood door was firmly shut. "There's no one—"

Tahliq glanced back at the casting carpet.

Horan Zehar had vanished.

The rap on the pitalwood door came half a moment later.
Tahliq gathered up her gown, hurried to open the door.
"Mout, you goose. You nearly made me jump out of my
skin. Is everything—"

The tall, powerfully built young vigile strode through the
door, his dagger, crossbow, and firebolt dangling from his
belt.

"Regim, my sweet," she blurted out, forgetting in her
astonishment that he insisted on protocol up till the moment
they entered the dallying chamber. Only then he abandoned
himself.

"Your neighbor's fire has made the looters and ravishers
bold," he said with the frown that always made her smile,
the gravely downturned lips of a displeased boy. "I'm early
for our assignation, I know, but the walkabouts summoned
me to Rancid Flats." Lieutenant Regim Deuceman grimaced. His expression of disgust couldn't mar his breath-
taking beauty, the golden glow of his massive face, the
chiseled lines of his cheeks and chin. The blue of his
vigile's uniform reflected in his large clear eyes, bluer eyes
than any sapphires Tahliq had ever seen. Fine golden curls
fell across his forehead, behind his ears, and down to the
high, starched collar of his jacket. "I know the area. I patrolled here when I was a walkabout two seasons ago."

"How well I remember, my sweet. That's when we met." She glowed at the memory. A gang of stone carvers—clovens with a mean streak—had become too rowdy for Mout and Dori to handle. She'd summoned Vigilance, according to her citizen's prerogative, and Regim had marched through her rose-pink door. She'd never seen such an impossibly handsome man. He'd arrested the clovens, summoned a Vigilance windship, dispatched them to Quartius Jail. And stayed with her for the rest of the night and most of the next morning, though he knew he'd be reprimanded by his commanding officer for tardiness.

He met her reminiscing glow with another frown. "Yes. Well. The damage here isn't half so bad as the boardwalk, but much worse than in Marketplace or Pleasant Valley."

"In Rancid Flats we sleep and eat upon one great marsh."

"So you do." His stern look abruptly softened. He regarded her anxiously. "You don't mind that I'm early?"

"Never, never, my sweet."

Regim glanced sharply at the casting carpet, his eyes glinting with suspicion. "What were you doing, Tahliq?"

She followed his gaze. The orb still lay in the center of the carpet, together with a scattering of ores.

Illegal, outlawed, forbidden!

"I was dallying about on the floor, thinking of you." Tahliq stood on tiptoe, threw her arms around his neck, and covered his face with the openmouthed kisses that always dazed him. Inspired, she employed the movements of the flames she'd just mastered.

A small curious smile curved his lips in spite of his somber mood. *What is this new kiss?* Desire glittered instantly in those blue eyes. She glimpsed his tumescence in his leggings and reached for him.

How fine! Her allpure sharemind opened like a flower in the sun. He easily entered into mutual consciousness with her. She didn't probe. She kept her presence very still and quiet, so quiet he never suspected they had entered into a forbidden sharemind. He only apprehended the glow of unity he always felt with her, bound together in trust and sensual ecstasy.

Not like sharers, locked in their Imperial duty.

He was enjoying her haste, her flame kisses. She reveled in his response. *Not what they taught you at Vigilance Academy, my sweet. Not what you dream of.* Usually, when Regim came to her, they would sit and sip wine in her reception chamber, carefully observing proper purity protocol. He'd speak first at length about his duties and troubles, only able to relax after he'd unburdened himself. She'd ask his permission to remove her garments, which he would give, and then she would slowly and formally remove his. Whereupon he'd seize her and carry her upstairs to her dallying chamber and her pleasure couch.

Haste did have its virtues.

She knew how to play his passions so well! If only he would unlock his heart the way he unlocked his shame. Look past protocol and Imperial duty and acknowledge the truth of what they shared. They didn't require sharelock chips to enforce their bond. Through her allpure sharemind, when they lay together on her couch, she knew she aroused him in ways that he could not comprehend. Aroused his tenderness, too, if he would only permit himself to feel it.

She also knew a conservative Pannist and ambitious vigile like him would never understand how she possessed her allpure sharemind, even less that she should be permitted to keep it. No, she'd decided he must come to her first, out of understanding and acknowledged love, before she could ever reveal this aberrant, deviant gift of hers.

The orb! She swiftly turned, silk aswirl, and flung herself on the carpet. She rolled the orb behind her, tucked it into the small of her back. She tore off her gown, ripping a seam as she did, and heaped it on the floor.

Regim's eyes held, riveted by her nakedness. *Living embodiment of the ancient shame.* In another swift movement, she rolled the orb beneath her crumpled gown, scooped the ores aside, and stretched out her arms. "My beloved vigile, come. I've been longing for you all day. Even the Big Shock couldn't distract me from thoughts of you."

He unbuckled his belt, tore off his weapons. He knelt before her, spread her knees, and took his fill of kissing her till she cried out, "Ah, you're the best, Regim. The best ever." With trembling fingers she unbuttoned the multitude of fastenings on his uniform, pulled off his boots, his leggings, his stockings.

His face grew fierce, unsmiling. She apprehended how the strictures of proximity, his abhorrence of the vast distance between their purities, warred with his desire. But desire won. They grappled on the carpet as violently as wrestlers and cried out together when rapture surged through them at the same time.

"How I love you, Regim," Tahliq whispered. "Dear Afrodite, how I do love you." In a low, husky contralto, she sang Milady Danti's theme, echoes of which she'd heard in their mutual consciousness at the moment of rapture. Her Regim dreamed Milord Lucyd's dreams, then. "From now till Eternity, I'll cherish you, oh, sacred sharer."

"Stop it, Tahliq." Regim withdrew from her angrily, rolled away. The allpure sharemind vanished, the sights and sounds and sensations of his consciousness wrenched away, locked back inside him. He seized her gown, roughly blotting his thighs and belly on the fine silk.

Rubbing off your shame, Tahliq thought bitterly, spiraling down into the darkness of solitude. *But you can't, my sweet.*

"Stop it now." He grimaced, revulsion plain on his face. "Here, here are your hundred ores. Listen to me, there's something important I must tell you. It's the real reason I came here early today."

"Yes?" She trembled at his ominous tone, his revulsion, the aftermath of their violent coupling.

Something else will happen.
Something terrible.

And as if possessed by its own volition, the Orb of Eternity clattered across the library floor. Forbidden fruit, shiny-bright and tempting.

FACET 5

Circle: Distinction or confinement.
The magister selects a sacred sharer.
The action is choice.
The forbearance is constriction.

The Orb of Eternity

Commentaries:
Councillor Sausal: Like the circle, the center of Pan perfectly encloses all that is sacred and excludes all that is profane.

So, too, entering into sacred sharelock is a solemn commitment of the highest order, not merely to one's sharer and family, but to the Imperium and Pan. Sharelock is the most respected, favored, and blessed achievement every pure and subpure may attain in a lifetime, and the cornerstone upon which the Imperium rests.

Therefore the prudent person who enters into sharelock forsakes all others, devotes all effort to the family, and delights in all the rewards sharelock brings.

Guttersage (usu. considered vulgar): No fool who enters into sharelock has ever been happy.

No fool who hasn't entered into sharelock has ever been happy.

Northeast Sausal Coast, Imperial Hill. Our Supreme Temple of Sacred Sharelock, the west wing, a preparatory chamber:

Regim should have arrested her. It was his Imperial duty as a vigile. His birthright as a magister. Privileges and burdens meant nothing. He'd failed his duty on this, the most momentous day of his life.

Tahliq was trafficking in contraband, in impure witchery subject to criminal prosecution. She had possession of an orb, and she couldn't claim ignorance of the law. She'd attempted to conceal the filthy thing.

Regim Landom Deuceman naitre Secundus methodically unbuttoned his jacket, pulled off his tunic and shirt, and stuffed the soiled garments into a laundry sack.

The preparatory chamber at early evening, in the undamaged west wing of the temple, was hushed, cool, furnished in scarlet and gilt, lit by flickering magmalamps. The scents of cinnabar and lemon glory wafted through the chamber. A musician sequestered in a service booth out of Regim's sight plucked slow notes on a cymbalon. Aftershocks stirred the chamber now and then—or was it just his nerves?

This evening would change his life.

Disquietude descended upon him.

Tahliq must have hidden the orb on the floor beneath her clothes, the silky purple gown she'd stripped off with such stunning abandon. Regim stilled the smile on his lips, the stirring in his loins at the recollection of the erotician's latest and most memorable performance. He must have disturbed the orb when he picked up her gown to blot away the taint of the bestial act. Removing the gown must have set the thing rolling, though the orb had—he recalled with a shudder—actually *hopped* across the hardwood floor.

The thing had sped beneath a formidable leather settee and lodged itself deep underneath like a feral creature eluding a hunter. He'd glimpsed its amethyst-colored gleam.

But when he went to reach for the thing, he'd found nothing at all beneath the settee.

He'd never seen an orb before outside of Vigilance custody. In the wild, so to speak. He'd read and heard about this weird phenomenon, though he'd never actually witnessed it till this day. The things seemed to move of their own volition. Certainly the orbs that had been seized and sequestered in Vigilance custody never hopped and rolled around on their own. They lay quite still, as stones and dead things ought to.

She must have been gambling with the thing. Worse, she might have been orbcasting. Drud pures like Tahliq were notoriously superstitious. Regim had always thought drud superstitions pathetic, but more or less harmless.

Till three seasons ago, when the High Council had enacted Imperial Law Section 616.1 under Title 13, Impure Activities. The new law banned orbs, orbrolls, and orbcasting, with stiff penalties—corporal punishment, imprisonment, hard labor—for a variety of violations. Every vigile from the Chief Commander on down had been reeducated about the Orb of Eternity.

Impure origin. Source of contaminated thoughts. Fomenter of confusion about Pan and the Imperium. May cause protocol violations. Contributes to the shadow market via contraband smuggling, gambling, and tax evasion. Rumored to possess the power to foretell the future. Rumored to cause accidents. Arrest all violators.

But whether Tahliq possessed an orb, whether she'd been gambling or orbcasting, wasn't all that troubled him.

Someone had been with her in her library. The presence of another had been unmistakable. A stirring in the air, a foreign scent, a rumple in the garish rug on the floor. A half-glimpsed shadow, the trail of a cloak. Regim prided himself on his ability to observe, his training in discerning details. The successful performance of his Imperial duty mandated his constant vigilance.

Someone had been there.

Yet this unknown person had vanished by the time Regim had finished shutting the door. The door was the only entrance to Tahliq's library he knew of. He frowned. Had the erotician installed a trapdoor or a secret panel among her forbidden books? Why had this person wished to escape, undetected? Why not simply take one's leave, after a proper introduction?

Suspicions sprang to his mind. *Is this person subject to a detainment warrant? Suspected of subversive activities? Wanted for a crime?* Would Regim have recognized Tahliq's visitor from Imperial wanted posters? His frown deepened. Did this person know *him*?

He should have arrested the erotician for *that,* for colluding in the surreptitious exit of an unknown person reluctant to encounter an Imperial vigile.

Then there were her forbidden books in the library, texts filled with repellent obscenities. Drawings and descriptions of the bestial act that were meant to be artistic, from the several books he'd glanced at once or twice—perhaps thrice—when he'd come to see her.

How long had he known the erotician? Misgivings tightened his chest. He'd engaged in assignations with the creature over eight seasons—or was it nine? He calculated painfully. He'd visited the Salon of Shame every three or four days, and had grown older, he realized with a flinch, by two years.

And all to sate the bestial urge, which the erotician both provoked and quenched with her dreadful body. For she was only that, of course: a body, severely shaped, of the lowest drud subpure, which he both loathed and lusted for at the same time. A body from which he apparently, regrettably, could not stay away.

A body, he reminded himself, *with scarcely more intelligence or higher emotions than a beast.* That was the proper way to regard an erotician. The proper way to behave? One paid an erotician for the bestial act, then took one's leave.

He earned a respectable wage as an Imperial vigile. He'd

squandered a disrespectfully large portion of it on Tahliq. The folly of youth? He wasn't so young anymore. He was approaching five-and-twenty years. In any case, youth didn't excuse his behavior. He hadn't exercised the discipline and rigor noteworthy of magister pures. He who could lift a fiftyweight in each hand, sprint full speed four leagues without faltering, raise his chin to crossbar a hundred times, had not mastered his shame.

Pan, who has granted me such great good fortune, guide me to conquer this darkness within me.

A sharp knock came at the door of the preparatory chamber, startling him. "Milord?" The obsequious voice of a beck-and-call man. "Are you ready for your gown?"

"No," Regim snapped. "I haven't bathed in the cleansing waters." *And need to. How I need to cleanse myself.*

"Do you desire assistance with your bath, milord?"

"No! Leave me alone."

Regim's father and his two mothers had all been vigile subpures since times lost to antiquity. Their sprawling, brawling household of three dozen children spanning several generations of ages had been kept by a series of long-suffering caretakers who'd barely managed to maintain internal peace and calm and cook regular meals. No one had ever tendered niceties like scrubbing Regim's back in the bath. Ever since he could walk, he'd managed his own baths and clothes and progress through Vigilance Academy.

He wasn't accustomed to beck-and-call men or handmaids or isolate musicians, though he knew he'd have to become accustomed to them and manage staffs in his new life.

But this wasn't quite the time for radical adjustments. He was acutely aware he was still beholden to no one but his father and mothers, and then to himself. He wished to savor the last remnants of his privacy.

"Are you sure, milord?" the beck-and-call man called anxiously, still waiting outside the door. Most likely the drud was as unaccustomed to magisters refusing his assistance as Regim was to receiving it.

Regim softened his tone. "No, thank you. I . . . I am meditating on Pan. I wish to be alone."

"Whatever you desire, milord."

"Is there still time for me to bathe?"

"Plenty of time, milord. The ceremony won't begin for another hour. The custodians are clearing away the last of the damage. A bit of slab from the entablatures came off. It wasn't so bad, after all, was it, milord? The Big Shock, I mean. Certainly not what everyone has always feared."

Everyone was ready to proceed, despite the Big Shock. Two thousand guests had confirmed. The temple staff had prepared the Sanctum, even as aftershocks rumbled through the megalopolis. The families had clamored that the ceremony must go on. *We've survived the Big Shock. Nothing will ever destroy Pangaea. Nothing will threaten the Imperium without end.*

Disquietude stung him again as the beck-and-call man chattered on. Regim wasn't so certain nothing would ever threaten the Imperium. Threats abounded this night. The guests and the families hadn't witnessed the fires, the broken buildings, the newly rent chasms churning with raw sewage, the terror and chaos on the streets. Riots and looting among the druds in Gondwana Valley had worsened with nightfall. Even complacent, law-abiding academes and clerics had savaged the wreckage of saloons and hotels on the Sausal Boardwalk. Thievery and ravishment, it seemed, had become the local sport.

And here he stood, about to step into a perfumed bath while his squad patrolled the streets, securing peace and calm for the Imperium. Wasn't he shirking his Imperial duty in the worst crisis the Imperium had ever seen?

Can't this wait?

But when Councillor Claren Twine naitre Secundus, newly appointed Chief Advisor on Impure Activities to the High Council, had sent *his* declaration, "The ceremony will proceed tonight, Lieutenant Deuceman,'' Regim had gone to the temple without further protest.

''Will everything be ready?'' he said now through the chamber door to the beck-and-call man, unable to conceal the throb of anxiety in his voice.

''Never fear, my milord. Everything is always ready for the Twine family.''

The cymbalon player commenced a new melody in a minor key, slow and heart-wrenching. Regim disliked sentimentality, disliked manipulation, and he knew Tahliq was supremely skilled at both. He should have arrested her this afternoon, should have taken her into custody. It was his Imperial duty.

Why hadn't he?

Awkward silence had ensued after the orb rolled across the floor and lodged itself out of his grasp. Tahliq had leapt to her feet, found a decanter of d'ka. She'd poured a snifter for him and helped him dress, chattering about the Big Shock, the fire across the lane, how she'd warned the saloonkeep to secure his cookstones.

It was then, after he'd dressed, that Regim had informed her he was entering into sacred sharelock this evening with Dame Clere Twine, a high magister subpure, Adjunct Prefect of Atlan, the daughter of High Councillor Claren Twine, and heiress to the Twine family fortune. That the affection she harbored for him, poignant though it was, was misplaced, ill conceived, and hopeless. The vast difference in their pures meant they could never enter into the utter intimacy of sharers' sharemind, not even with sharelock chips. *That's not true,* she'd cried, but he didn't want to hear her lies and manipulations. They could never share any commonality of interests, assets, or pursuits. The very notion of wearing sharelock chips with a drud nauseated and frightened him, no matter how clever she appeared to be. He would never have known her, spoken with her, *touched* her if she hadn't been a licensed erotician, and he a slave to his bestial urge. She'd only touched *him* beyond the strictures of purity protocol because he paid her.

She was impossibly his inferior.

And he had no feelings for her.

Regim had rehearsed this parting speech before he'd gone to the Salon of Shame, an hour early for their assignation. When he'd recovered his senses after their dizzying bout of pleasure, he'd found himself in a severe and skeptical mood. What if a Vigilance squad had come to secure the salon from looting and found him there with her? What if the squad had seen her forbidden books? What if the squad had found the orb?

He might have found *himself* in Imperial custody.

The erotician could have jeopardized him, jeopardized his career, his family. Especially his impending sharelock and his family-in-lock to be.

He should have arrested her, *would* have arrested her—
But he hadn't.

Because Tahliq had wept.

Regim stripped off his leggings fouled by the afternoon's assignation and stood, pensive and naked, about to stuff the filthy garment into the laundry sack. She'd wept wildly and, oddly, his chest had clenched at her tears. He'd kissed her again—actually, he'd succumbed to the bestial urge again—before taking his leave.

Another rap at the door startled him.

"Oh, my cherished one." Clere burst in the door. "Tonight, my sacred love! For today only proves how fragile and precarious life can be. Let us not delay joining the two of us as one for all Eternity."

"What . . . what are you doing here?"

"The beck-and-call man told me you needed help."

"What?" he said again stupidly. Anxiety assailed him. *What did she want?* He suddenly felt as if he were being spied upon. He quelled his annoyance. *She's about to become your sharer.* Was he truly that anxious about relinquishing his life as a shareless man? Wasn't this the highest honor, the most beautiful state of being, that anyone in Pangaea could ever hope for?

Why do I feel someone is spying on me?

"Silly boy. I've come to help you bathe and dress, my Regim."

Before he could protest, she seized sack and leggings from his hands and clutched them to her breast as if his soiled laundry were a precious prize. She pranced around the preparatory chamber dressed in her ceremonial gown of Imperial purple sateen, a crown of atlantium and amethysts set upon her wispy grey curls.

Regim smiled at her charming antics. Mistress Clere Twine naitre Secundus, at age fifty-seven, stood nearly as tall as Regim, as lean as an athlete on the gamefield. Magister pure. She was so pure! The long-jawed face, thin as a whip. The pale blue eyes, slightly crossed as all Twine eyes were. The distinguished nose exactly like her father's prominent proboscis. The distinctive thin lips destined to issue commands.

Clere's years of service to Our Sacred City as the Adjunct Prefect of Atlan and to the Imperium as her eminent father's protégé and most promising successor, might have taken a toll upon her noble features. But her fine blond hair threaded with grey didn't trouble Regim, any more than her lined complexion or angular physique.

Did her greater years and experience affect his desire to enter into sharelock with her? Generate a family with her? Of course! She was the only person he'd ever felt Pannish love for. Did it matter she was thirty-two years older? Absolutely not. This was the great gift of the Imperium. Her Imperial materia, harvested decades ago and stored in her account at Natalry Bank, remained as fresh as her vanished youth. Her self-sacrifice, her political experience, her exten-

sive connections inspired Regim's respect and reverence
more than youth and physical beauty ever could.

Elegant, commanding Clere.

She'd needed a Vigilance escort to tour Al-Muud, a drud
village near the eastern periphery of the Great Wall.
There'd been some danger. The village was known to harbor a large population of the impure. Regim had just been
promoted from walkabout to lieutenant and given permission to deploy a windship. The Chief Commander had ordered all lieutenants into formation in front of the Vigilance
Authority cloudscraper. Clad in a smart bodysuit of indigo
flax, Clere had strolled among the ranks of vigiles standing
at attention.

"Her, her, and him," she'd said. Pointed last at Regim.
"And him. Definitely him."

He'd been honored, flattered, nothing less than awed
when she'd smiled at him. She'd taken the seat next to him
in the windship, and, after a few formal courtesies and
awkward protocol, they'd talked and talked and talked.

The politics of the purities?

"But intermingling is inevitable," he'd argued. "The
purities' functions are, after all, interdependent, especially
in a city the size of Atlan. The natalries alone employ thousands of people from four purities and twenty subpures, and
they all have to work together, or the unborn would suffer.
A family household like yours, prefect, must employ people
from at least two purities and four or five subpures."

"My household employs all five purities, lieutenant,"
she'd said tartly. "On holy days, we commission an angel
to dream for our subpure. And they're all kept in their
place, even the angel. The purities are the purities, and
ought to remain so. Intermingling has become indecently
promiscuous. Marketplace is a disgrace. Imperial Fire &
Shock ought to let Rancid Flats burn to the ground and
rebuild serv and drud sectors."

"Does Our Sacred City have funds to rebuild?" he'd asked with circumspection. Tahliq and her rose-pink door flashed in his memory. He swiftly thrust the image away.

"No, of course not," she'd replied with an even look. "We'll conscript the servs and druds to rebuild their own neighborhoods. That would be the proper way. It's high time proximity was respected again. As Prefect of Our Sacred City, I'm calling for stricter penalties for protocol violations."

That had been an eye-opener. And only the beginning of what Clere Twine had to say.

She'd confided in him. She was adamant about her plans to exterminate the foes, eliminate their criminal activities, and segregate the impure, at least within Central Atlan.

"Devilish powers, pox," she'd said with a toss of her grey curls. "The Chief Commander of Vigilance needs to be hauled before the Chamber of Justice and interrogated. She's gone soft on the impure." She'd leaned close and whispered in his ear, her breath hot on his cheek. "Tell no one you heard me say this, lieutenant, and it will surely profit you in the future. Understand?"

"Of course, my prefect," he'd whispered back. He'd long suspected the Chief Commander of softness, too. Had never dared speak of it. And had kept his silence—was she testing him?

Instead he'd asked, "And what of earthshocks, prefect? Is Ground Control developing technology to prevent them?"

"Ground Control, ha! Ground Control is a gang of cowards, afraid to offend the High Council with bad news and afraid to take firm and decisive action. I'll be the first one to say it—the shocks are worse than ever! And I'm no Apocalyptist. The shocks, my dear Regim"—she'd taken his hand in her fervor—"truly are evil. They wreak millions of ores' worth of damage. Cause tens of thousands of deaths. They change the very face of Our Sacred City and our Pangaea, and not by Imperial planning and foresight, from the wise and considered direction of magisters. By catastrophe. By chaos.''

"The shocks weaken the faith of the purities in Pan and the Imperium,'' he'd offered softly. It was her prerogative to touch him as the higher subpure, of course, but he'd found himself light-headed at her warm familiarity. "They insult the perpetuity of Pan and all we've inherited as the beneficiaries of the Imperium.''

"Yes! Well said.'' She'd actually squeezed his hand. "Did you know that Ground Control relies on the opinions of academes? At Sausal Academy. Do you know this academy? A hotbed of shareless young dissidents who shamelessly copulate among high and low subpures with no regard for protocol.'' She'd whispered in his ear again. "It's disgusting.''

He'd nodded, unnerved. He'd never known an academe except perhaps as a walkabout casting his vigilance sharemind over a middle-pure crowd.

"Do you think, my prefect,'' he'd asked cautiously, "the cults should be actively suppressed or covertly encouraged?''

She'd beamed at him. "Another excellent question. Do you believe in Pan, my dear Regim?''

"Of course''—he'd caught his breath, taken a huge chance—"my dear Clere.''

"Splendid.'' She'd given no indication she'd noticed *his* familiarity—which was good. She hadn't been offended. "But do the lower purities believe like they should? Believe in Pan and Inim? I fear their belief isn't as steadfast as it once was. Our Sacred City is an exciting place to live. No one wants to stay home at night anymore, studying the Word, the Commentaries, the Homilies, the Stories, when one could be out dancing.''

"The sacred teachings do amount to twenty volumes.''

"So they do. So let them dance at their raves. The cults excite the lower purities and engage their interest in spiritual matters. With their vulgar rites and local godlings, the cults stir the flames of faith. I think, my dear Regim, the cults may prove a useful tool for the Imperium. Declare them illegal, but permit them to conduct their rites. Encourage them to inculcate faith, and suppress them to impress fear. Randomly, as part of the same Imperial policy. Keep them on their guard and therefore compliant. And never a significant challenge to faith in Pan."

Another mind-boggling lesson in statecraft. Regim had become aware of an overwhelming desire to protect and serve her.

"The Orb of Eternity, on the other hand, is an entirely different matter than the cults. Are you familiar with the ban?"

"Of course. Through Vigilance." He'd become aware of her intent gaze on his face, registering his reaction.

"The orb is of impure origin. The Committee on Impure Activities itself has established that. This impure thing has stirred too much interest among the purities. It was time to suppress the orb. And Sausal."

He'd ventured, "We all read Councillor Sausal in fundamental school. Not with the oracles of the orb, of course. I suppose those were expunged in the school texts. But I'd always thought his commentaries were insightful about Pan, the governance of the Imperium, one's duties—" His voice had trailed away as her infuriated eyes silenced him.

"Councillor Sausal was relieved of his duties as Chief Advisor on Impure Activities specifically because of his ill-advised fascination with this impure witchery. The Orb of Eternity encourages illogic, weakness. Confusion about Pan, Inim, and the Imperium. It's unfortunate Sausal chose to discover meaning where no meaning exists. There are those on the High Council, of course," she'd added, "who wish to rehabilitate the purest of Sausal's commentaries. Councillor Sausal is, after all, from one of the First Families of Atlan. The family name"—a contemptuous tone—"is splattered all over Our Sacred City."

He'd worried about her mounting vehemence, steered the conversation to less controversial issues.

Their favorite dreams in the Mind of the World? "Lucyd's dreams of love, of course!" she'd exclaimed and clapped her hands.

"My favorite, too."

"Milady Danti is so beautiful and graceful, isn't she?"

"Well, yes," he'd said carefully. "But nothing can compare to the beauty and grace of a magister woman."

And finally, tentatively, sacred sharelock.

"What a joy that must be!" she'd said, her pale blue eyes filming with unexpected tears. "To enter into sharelock. To generate one's family, my dear Regim, by the grace of the Imperium. I've wanted that my whole life."

"I've always wanted that, too. My dear Clere."

They'd agreed about nearly everything, and the remaining points of disagreement had only led to more spirited mental sparring.

She was the most brilliant, accomplished, ambitious, insightful, pious, devoted person he'd ever met. Certainly she was the most powerful person who had ever smiled at him. He'd hardly realized they'd entered into deep sharemind till an escort had tapped him on the shoulder and said, "We've arrived at the Wall, lieutenant. We'll be entering Al-Muud in ten minutes."

And he'd known, in a dazzling instant, he'd found Pannish love.

But she was so much higher, of councillor and prefect subpures. Her father was one of the most powerful people in all Pangaea, she herself with her own considerable status in Atlan. Her mother, a direct descendent of the First Council, now embalmed, gazed down from a translucent sarcophagus in the magister tier at the Pyramid of Perpetuities. And of course the Twine family was unimaginably wealthy.

And he a mere vigile, his father and mothers vigiles, his whole family vigiles. Nothing but vigiles. He'd thought of his family's household with shame. Anguished, he'd gone home that night to his rented quarters off southwest Marketplace, lain down on his solitary bed, and entered into Imperial sharemind. The vast glimmer of the aether had appeared before him, the paths leading to angels' dreams. He'd almost chosen Milady Faro's latest dream of conquest.

Instead, he'd chosen Milord Lucyd's path of love.

And he'd dreamed of a lower subpure who met a higher subpure. Milady Danti had worn the costume of a priestess, Milord Lucyd of an illustrious physician. After arduous intricacies of proper purity protocol, they'd entered joyfully into sharemind and realized Pannish love.

It had been a dream aimed at the middle purities, of course, who were burdened with so many disparate subpures. But when Clere Twine had stopped by Vigilance the next morning and asked him to dinner, he'd boldly entered into sharemind with her and declared himself.

She hadn't rejected him.

She'd said yes.

"My beloved, what a surprise," he said and covered his nakedness with his hands. He laughed uneasily, unable to dispel the sensation of being spied upon. He was still soiled from Tahliq. "You're much too early, my love. I haven't bathed in the cleansing waters."

The magnificent steaming bath at the back of the preparatory chamber, fragrant with cinnabar and lemon glory, stood ready for his ritual cleansing.

"But I told you. I'm here to help you bathe, my cherished one," Clere said. A peculiar grin Regim had never seen spread across her thin, wrinkled face. She set down the laundry sack and leggings, took his shielding hands in hers, and slowly, deliberately examined him. "Permit me to serve you."

He shrank from her avid gaze. The physical body was of

no consequence between him and Clere. Their Imperial materia was all that mattered.

"You needn't serve me in any way, my beloved," he said anxiously. How he wanted her to revere him one-tenth as much as he revered her! "You look feverish. That will never do. Please, cherished one, I can bathe myself. Go and dress yourself."

"But I *am* dressed, Regim, as you can plainly see. What I really want to do is *un*dress."

She giggled, high and giddy. So unlike his calm, sophisticated Clere. Had she lost her reason? Should he summon the beck-and-call man, procure a soporific for her? He hesitated, unwilling to offend her in any way.

"I *want* to serve you," she said brightly. "I want to know *all* of you, now that we'll live as sharer and sharer." She picked up his leggings again. "I know your face and your views well enough. Now I want to know your scent." She crushed the leggings to her face and sniffed deeply.

A long silence. A jumble of expressions across her pinched features—astonishment, recognition, horror, outrage, injured pride. He didn't know what to do.

"What's this smell?"

"My cherished one, do not—"

"You engaged in the bestial act, didn't you, Regim? On this day, the day we're to enter into sacred sharelock?"

"My love, it was nothing. Less than nothing. It passes into nothing—"

"With whom?"

"Just an erotician. For a pittance."

"Was it a male or a female?" She pressed his leggings to her face again, regarding him with blazing eyes. "A female, wasn't it?"

"A female, yes."

"What's her name?"

"She has no name. I don't know her name." Regim averted his eyes, hoping she couldn't see the lie. How could he remedy this terrible blunder?

"That's your predilection, then? When it comes to the bestial urge? Women?"

"Well, yes," he said cautiously.

"Only women?"

"I've never had any shameful interest in men."

"Splendid. One never knows." She studied him. "Naturally, I'd hoped as much."

"My dear love," he said desperately, "please don't concern yourself over a carnal act I bought from an erotician."

She tucked the leggings into the laundry sack, brooding. "You know, Regim, all my life I've dedicated myself to Pan. To the Imperium, to Our Sacred City, to my parents' family. The bestial urge has never been of any importance to me."

"How fortunate for you, my love. I'm glad you've been spared. The bestial urge is a curse."

"And of no significance to Pannish love?"

"Precisely! My dearest Clere, we always think alike." He chuckled with relief. "I do apologize for my urges. I sincerely hope you don't think less of me. They're easily satisfied and easily forgotten."

"You're about to become my sharer for all Eternity. Your urges are of utmost importance to me, however bestial the priests and priestesses say they are. Nothing? Less than nothing? I hardly think so."

She gazed at him as if she would devour him whole. What was this madness? What had possessed her? The shadows in the preparatory chamber shimmered strangely around her.

"For the first time in my life," she whispered fiercely, "another has aroused the bestial urge in *me.* Surely you're aware," she said, reaching out and touching the hard, flat muscles of his belly, "how beautiful you are, my dear Regim." She touched his shameful member, which sprang up, tumescent in spite of his will.

He recoiled from her touch. This was *not* the dignified Clere he knew and adored. "My beloved, the impending ceremony has unsettled you," he said reasonably. "You don't know what you're saying. You don't know what you're doing."

"Don't I? Has this erotician taught you many skills?"

Tahliq, and all she'd taught him, the way her luxurious skin shone like burnished copper, the astonishing swells and involutions of her body, the cries she made, the way she tasted . . .

Regim's face felt on fire.

"How can I make you understand?" he tried again. "My cherished Clere, you take great and well-deserved pride in the feasts you serve, isn't that true? Would you become resentful if I came home to you with the scent of crab chowder on my breath at the hands of a skillful chef? Feasting at another's table amounts to a greater offense to your honor than purchasing a bestial act on an erotician's couch. An act, my darling Clere," he pleaded, "with which you need not soil yourself. With which I would never seek to defile you or stain the purity of our Pannish love."

She smiled skeptically. "I'm stipulating as a condition of our sharelock that you cease carnal relations of any kind with all other persons of whatever pure or subpure."

Anger squeezed his throat. She'd never made such a stipulation during their courtship or negotiations, and she knew it. But he stilled the protest on his tongue. This sharelock would catapult him out of his humble vigile subpure to the top of the magister pure, and Clere knew that, too. She could've had her choice of anyone of their pure, man or woman, younger or older, beautiful or plain. One sharer, or two or three, or more. The Twine family was *very* rich.

She'd chosen him.

He eyed her cautiously. Perhaps this mania would pass, her stipulation be forgotten. "My Clere, you are as pure to me as Milady Danti. The dreams of Pannish love between her and Milord Lucyd have always been my dreams, too. They were ideal sharers."

She threw back her head and guffawed. "Do you really

believe that in fifty years of sharelock Lucyd and Danti resorted only to eroticians? That in fifty years they never fucked?''

He gasped at her slur. "Yes!"

"Really, Regim. That's pathetic. Why would an aetherist in sharelock with a beautiful woman of his own exalted subpure expose his angelic body to a drud scarcely higher than a beast?"

Hanging in the air between them, *Why would you?*

Clere removed her atlantium crown and carelessly discarded it on a side table, drew off her finger rings, the pendant from her neck. She began unlacing the bodice of her gown.

"I've never been touched, Regim. Oh, I've been harvested, but I still have my courses. It's a tradition among my subpure that our women retain custody of some of the Imperial materia till we enter into sharelock. So we may physically know begetting one time."

He stared at her, horrified. "If the urge . . . stirs in you, my Clere, I will be happy to find you an erotician." He clawed at the laundry sack, scrambling for his filthy clothes. "I'll find one at once, my love."

"Oh, no, my beloved Regim," Clere said, slipping off her gown and slipping into his arms. "I want only you."

Twenty phalanxes of vigiles in full-dress uniform and prefects in Imperial regalia flanked the processional hall of Our Supreme Temple of Sacred Sharelock. Crowned councillors sat in the balconies above. Regim, stepping into the Portico of Initiation, nearly burst with pride to witness every subpure of his purity honoring him and Clere.

He moved awkwardly in the gown of Imperial purple sateen. The atlantium crown lay heavily on his golden curls. Clad in traditional black, his father and his mothers solemnly approached him. They all linked arms and promenaded down the aisle.

"Good-bye, my son," his father said, tears glinting in his bright blue eyes. "You've done better than we ever could have hoped. And we've always hoped the best for you."

"Thank you, my father."

"We're so proud of you, our little Reg," his first mother whispered.

His second mother, walking behind the trio, wept into her black veil.

Regim caught his breath. He'd seen the Sacred Sanctum before when he'd served as honor guard at the sharelock ceremony of another vigile in his squad. Still, the sanctum awed him anew. The caryatids with carved marble gowns, the entablatures bearing flickering kaligraphs of the Story of Pan and the Sacred Sharer. Two thousand guests had comfortably gathered there. Sizzling magmalamps lit the sanctum with an ethereal golden glow, enhancing the flushed and painted faces of celebrants and temple staff, the magnificence of their costumes and uniforms, the solemnity and joy of the celebration.

Clere, gowned and crowned, marched down the aisle, escorted by her eminent father and the embalmed body of her mother in a translucent sarcophagus borne by handmaids.

The priestess-facilitators of the temple had arranged colossi before the Exalted Altar. At the ceremony of the vigile in Regim's squad, the priestess-facilitators had placed three colossi before the altar, two in Male regalia, one in Female regalia. The vigile had entered into sharelock with a man and a woman.

Regim gazed up at the two colossi of carved white shellstone specially arrayed for him and Clere.

One colossus bore traditional accoutrements and regalia of the Male: a beard, a dagger, a staff, an ear of corn.

The second colossus bore traditional accoutrements and regalia of the Female: breasts, a shield, a distaff, an apple branch.

Two dozen cymbalon players struck a resounding chord, commencing the magnificent Processional.

As Regim strode regally up the aisle with his father and mothers, the image of Clere stripping off her gown, standing before him gaunt and naked, haunted him.

He'd tried everything to dissuade her.

"It's a tradition of *my* subpure that our men retain custody of the Imperial materia until *we* enter sharelock," he'd warned her.

Her pale blue eyes had glittered. "I know."

"But if you still have your courses—"

"My love, you worry about the wrong things. If this union bears the holy fruit, I'll have it harvested and properly grown at the natalry. I'll be in no danger. I'll get on with my work."

He'd dutifully performed the bestial act as best he could, though the shame had been overwhelming. He'd been appalled to see a pool of her blood on the couch in the preparatory chamber.

"My cherished one, I didn't mean to hurt you. Or defile you."

"You haven't hurt me or defiled me. You've given me joy."

Now he met Clere's eyes across the aisle, blue to blue, and his joy overwhelmed the disquiet she'd left him with. How he cherished her. Beloved, exalted Clere. She'd been like a young girl in his arms, and it was terrible, terrible what he'd done. Once they tied the knot, he vowed he would never defile her again. If the bestial urge troubled her, he would insist on an erotician and pay the male himself.

He knelt next to her and thrust the disturbing matter from his mind. The Supreme Facilitator descended from the Exalted Altar and stood, bearing the Chalice of Sacramental Wine and the Wand of Life in her hands.

"Will you, Clere Twine naitre Secundus, take this man to be your sacred sharer, to keep and to cherish, to generate a family, and fulfill your Imperial duty from now till Eternity?''

"I will."

The Supreme Facilitator dipped the Wand into the Chalice, traced the Imperial star on Clere's forehead, and offered her a sip of wine.

"Will you," the Supreme Facilitator intoned, "Regim Deuceman naitre Secundus, take this woman to be your sacred sharer, to keep and to cherish, to generate a family, and fulfill your Imperial duty from now till Eternity?''

"I will."

The Supreme Facilitator traced the Imperial star, tipped the Chalice. Regim greedily gulped the thick red wine. The beck-and-call man had told him the wine contained an anodyne.

"In the name of Pan, I pronounce you sharer and sharer."

Now a sacred surgeon in her bloodred robes approached him. Regim placed his hands on the Tablet of Lock borne by the surgeon's assistant. With a flick of her scalpel the surgeon cut an incision and slid a diamond-shaped sharelock chip through his skin into the carpal bones of Regim's right hand. The surgeon deftly performed the same operation on his left hand. The beck-and-call man had warned Regim that he might feel a sting and a bit of vertigo when the chip activated, but between the sacramental wine and his elation he felt nothing. There was surprisingly little blood. The sacramental wine must have also contained a stanching herb.

And then the chips locked, and ecstasy exploded through him, *Clere, Clere, Clere!*

Surgeon and assistant turned to Clere, and installed the sharelock chips in her hands. Threads of blood trickled from her knuckles. Regim watched, awed and delighted, as Clere squeezed her eyes shut, tilted her head back, and moaned with her own ecstasy.

A shout rose from all throats, "To Pan! To Eternity! To sacred sharelock! To the Imperium without end!"

Regim seized Clere's hand, raised their clenched hands above their heads in the Salute of Victory. They turned and marched back down the aisle as drummers pounded out the Tattoo of Honor. The assembled families and pures flung handfuls of apple seeds over the newly locked sharers.

Regim walked hand in hand with his sharer as if in a dream, the dream of a lifetime. No angel's dream in the Mind of the World could rival this splendor, this joy.

And then something caught his eye—a movement among the attendants, some peculiarity of light and shadows. The shimmer that had disturbed him in the preparatory chamber before. He turned toward Clere, alarmed.

He felt a terrible stinging in his left thigh. Stunned, he glanced down. There, impaling his gown, penetrating clear through his thigh muscle, quivered a silver stiletto. His blood began to spurt all over the gown, the purple sateen blossoming with black stains. The stiletto abruptly unfolded into a six-pointed star, which commenced circling his thigh. Each point lacerated him by turns, shredding the gown, slicing skin and muscle, as the weapon whirled, faster and faster.

A devil star?

A devil star!

Pain plummeted through him. He nearly swooned.

Then terror and outrage surged through his blood, reviving him into a frenzy.

"It's foes!" he shouted. He seized Clere, pushed her to the floor, and flung himself on top of her, shielding her with his body.

Screams reverberated in the sanctum. People ran, panicked, shoving and ducking for refuge. The silver slivers of folded devil stars whizzed across the sanctum, deadly shimmers barely glimpsed before they struck flesh and commenced their deadly dance.

Someone seized Regim by the shoulders, yanked him to

his feet. His captain stood before him, quivering with rage. "It's not just foes, it's the fucking Heaven's Devils. Seal off the Portico, lieutenant. I'll hang myself before I let them get away with this again." The captain strode on.

Clere knelt at his feet, seized the devil star with her bare hands, and plucked it from his thigh with a furious, inarticulate scream. She smashed the fluttering weapon on the floor, striking it precisely in the middle. The devil star cracked and lay still.

"That's the only way," she gasped, "to disarm them." The palms of her hands oozed blood. She kissed his knee. "We've got to get you to a doctor at once, my darling love. It's poisoned."

"How do you know that?" he demanded.

"Oh, my Regim," she said, sobbing, "I know far too many secrets about the Heaven's Devils. They've come to murder me, at last."

"Hush, cherished one." He briefly cupped her cheek. "No one will murder you. I won't let them. I promise."

Regim glanced back at the Exalted Altar, searching frantically for his father and mothers. He couldn't see them. He searched again for Claren Twine, saw no sign of his distinguished father-in-lock. *His bodyguards have taken him away, I only hope.* When he glanced down at his feet again, Clere was gone.

Gone.

"*Damn* it," he bellowed and drew the ceremonial dagger from his belt. It was better than nothing. "They've seized her. They've taken Clere!"

"Where are they, lieutenant?" a vigile shouted and drew her crossbow.

He examined the aisle jammed with frenzied people, the portico leading out of the temple. "I don't know. I can't see them."

A chill crawled down his spine as a woman sang in a ragged soprano—

> *Farewell, sighs and sorrow,*
> *Farewell, tears and grief,*
> *Welcome, blood and death!*
> *Welcome, Heaven's Devils*
> *Who wreak wrack and ruin*
> *On the Imperium!*

A man shouted, "Death to the Imperium! Death to magisters!"

Regim dropped to his hands and knees. Clere's kidnappers wouldn't have taken her out the front entrance, where heavy security had been posted. They would have to be more devious than that. He crawled to the front of the sanctum. The Supreme Facilitator must have kept chambers behind the Exalted Altar, maintained a private exit for security purposes.

Would the foes know that, too?

Regim crawled, ignoring the anguished entreaties of guests and attendants. He found his father huddling behind the Exalted Altar.

"They dragged her that way," his father said, sobbing. "Two of the scum." A devil star spun up and down and around his arm, the startips carving out chunks of his flesh.

Regim seized the devil star, ripped it out of his father's flesh, smashed it in half on the floor the way Clere had done.

Then he scrambled to his feet, sprang up the altar steps. Yes! A panel, ajar, slid open at his touch, revealing a waterduct angling away beneath the temple.

They hadn't gone far. His beloved Clere had seen to that.

He glimpsed her flailing at her captors. The desire to protect and preserve her gripped him so violently he thought he might swoon again. Two Devils grappled with her. He smiled grimly. Powerful Clere! They could barely restrain her fury.

The hideously misshapen man flipped back a flowing black cloak as he seized and bound Clere's arms behind her back. Everything mismatched about him: his eyes, ears, nostrils, one side of his face from the other. His body was humpbacked, one arm far longer than the other, his hands like claws. His spindly legs appeared as if they could scarcely carry him. Yet carry him they did, and swiftly, bearing Clere down the shadowed passageway.

Regim's rage blazed. He knew this abomination, this notorious trash. Horan Zehar. Detainment warrants outstanding in every province of Pangaea.

But what did the Heaven's Devil want with his beloved Clere? Why disrupt this, their sharelock ceremony, the most sacred of days?

Oh, my Regim, I know far too many secrets about Heaven's Devils.

Come to murder his beloved? Over his dead body.

He wanted to sprint down the passageway, behead the impure beasts with one stroke of his ceremonial dagger.

He did not. Heaven's Devils were the most dangerous clan of all the foes, and he faced two against one till he freed Clere of her bonds. And the dagger was flimsy. He slipped into the shadows and swiftly followed them.

Water purled beneath his feet, growing deeper and deeper. The earthshock had severely damaged Atlan's system of waterducts. Water leaked everywhere. He cautiously shuffled his boots against the flat of the floor, kicking aside the spikes the Devils had strewn behind them. Caltrops— that's what the spikes were called—little odd-shaped knobs of metal bristling with needles as long as a man's finger that could impale an oxhide boot and the foot within it.

He knew a few Devils' secrets himself.

Closer now, he could see Clere splashing in the filthy water as the second Devil struggled with her. The Devil brandished a gag, stuffed it in Clere's mouth, but Clere lunged, trying to bite. The Devil backed away into the glare of a magmalight, and Regim got a good look.

A female. A very young female from her slight figure and brightly blemished cheeks, more misshapen and grotesque than Horan. Mismatched eyes the flat black opacity of roadpitch, coarse vermilion streaks snaking through tangled white-gold hair. Tunic and leggings of black sacking clung to her scrawny limbs.

She smirked. The sly, calculating grin of a devilish strumpet.

Suddenly Regim knew where he'd seen the wench before.

This morning, in Milord Lucyd's dream.

FACET 6

Spiral: Infinity or repetition.
The magister reviews the law and repeals the mandate of indenture.*
The action is evolution.
The forbearance is extinction.

The Orb of Eternity

Commentaries:

Councillor Sausal: Pan manifests in each moment and for all Eternity. Yet Pan also may take a direction, forward or backward, and may assume a path, ascending or descending.

So, too, the Imperium enacts laws that benefit the purities and repeals laws that cause discord and confusion.

Therefore the prudent person should respect purity protocol, obey Imperial law, and observe decorum within the family.

Historical Note: Under the mandate of indenture, serv and drud purities were considered "property" and subject to the will of angel and magister purities. The lower purities protested the mandate, leading to the First–Third Wars of the Rebellion, which caused much grief, bloodshed, and destruction of property. The High Council repealed the mandate and indenture is, to this day, strictly illegal.

Guttersage (usu. considered vulgar): The sage climbs the staircase to the top of the tower.

The fool treads around the base of the tower and never goes anywhere at all.

West Atlan, Imperial Hill. The waterduct beneath Our Supreme Temple of Sacred Sharelock:

"Watch out, my father!" Salit Zehar shouted as the monstrous vigile lunged at them from out of the shadows. A blade glinted in the vigile's hand. Ho! The puny dagger he'd worn for their wretched sharelock ceremony. Well, she supposed it was sharp enough. *Beware of **any** object wielded as a weapon,* Horan Zehar had taught her, *it will kill you just the same.* The vigile swung viciously at her father. "He's got a knife!"

Salit seized the frantic Twine she-butcher by her bound wrists and awkwardly grappled her. Horan parried, refusing to defer to the frenzied vigile, and grinned, taunting the vigile with his nerveless mastery. Admiration and love for her father flooded Salit's heart. And keen respect. She had sparred with Horan, knew more than a little of his combat-craft.

The vigile paused, studying them with contemptuous eyes. Salit assessed him in turn. He was huge, even bigger than the Twine she-butcher, standing head and shoulders above her father and nearly twice her height. Well-endowed and highly developed muscles bulged beneath the gaudy ceremonial gown. But the gown rendered him clumsy, fumble-handed and slug-footed. *If he were any kind of a real warrior, he'd strip.* She smirked at the notion. She'd savor seeing this abominable magister buck naked and trembling before Horan Zehar shredded him into food for sphinxes.

A blooding! It was going to be a real blooding. Her lessons tumbled through her head.

Manifesto of the Apocalypse, Edict One: Destroy the purities.

"*You* watch out, my daughter," Horan said mildly in the dialect Heaven's Devils employed. His chameleon cloak swirled around him. "You haven't got a cloak, my darling."

"Ho! And who's forbidding me a cloak?"

"The Dark Ones. I happen to concur."

Salit pouted. "You could convince the Dark Ones otherwise if you really wanted to."

"I don't want to."

Salit stamped her foot, soaking her leggings with a splash of filthy ductwater. "Why? Why won't you give me a cloak?"

"You're too impetuous, my daughter. You lack the warrior's maturity and clarity of judgment. The cloak is a powerful tool. We fear you'd abuse its powers. *I* fear it, too."

"Oh, I see. I'm permitted my first blooding at sixteen, I smoke bacco and drink beer, but I can't have my own chameleon cloak till I'm a crone of eighteen?"

"You see? This is just what I mean, Salit. Stop whining and watch your back."

The Twine she-butcher wrenched out of Salit's grasp and kicked, catching Salit in the knees with the pointed toe of her fancy shoe.

"And secure our prisoner," Horan snapped. "The object of terror is terror."

"All right, all right." Her father was forever lecturing her. The Twine she-butcher was no warrior, but the kick stung. Enraged, Salit thrust her fist into the she-butcher's gut, punching again and again. The she-butcher doubled over. Salit shoved her to her knees.

"My father, I slew two vigiles all by myself in the Sacred Sanctum just now." Petulant, unwilling to let the matter rest. "*And* I infiltrated the Hanging Gardens with you *and* I ignited the inferno bolts so you and Seth and Maw and the Alchemist could execute Milady Danti and the angels. Why can't I have my own cloak?"

"Don't argue with me, girl." The vigile feinted again,

and her father leapt nimbly out of reach of his dagger. Horan cocked his head to one side the way he always did when he meant to steal the thoughts of a pure.

Imperial sharemind furthers the propaganda of the Imperium, her father had taught her. *Sharemind among the purities is mutual oppression. And sharers' sharemind locks one person into the prison of another's thoughts. We of the impure possess no sharemind with sharers, among ourselves, or with the Mind of the World. But don't despair. We may be all alone, each within his or her own mind but, my daughter, we are free.*

And the conclusion of that particular lesson—

When you steal into someone's thoughts, never give away your own.

"This one knows us," Horan whispered. "He knows of me, well, he's a vigile. No doubt he's seen one or two of my detainment warrants."

"No doubt he's drafted one or two of your detainment warrants."

"No doubt." Horan chuckled at his daughter's cheek, then swiftly grew somber. "But, my darling, observe how he watches you. Observe how he registers you, over and over. I think he's seen your lovely face somewhere, as well."

"Yes, I've seen her ugly face," the vigile shouted, startling them both. This vigile understood Devil dialect? *He's more dangerous than we know.* "This morning before the Big Shock. I saw her, together with that other impure contamination, the Orb of Eternity."

"What in hell is he spouting about, my father?" Salit whispered.

Her father ignored her. "And where, I implore you, did you see these terrible things, milord?" That voice, both wheedling and derisive. How Horan managed to persuade the enemy to talk, time and again, with that voice!

"In the Mind of the World," the vigile blurted out. "I warn you, Horan Zehar—"

"Me?" Salit squeaked. *"I'm* in the Mind of the World? My father—"

Still he ignored her. "Fascinating. So our brave vigile dreams Milord Lucyd's dreams of love, hm? The handmaids and beer jerks have chattered about nothing else all day."

The vigile narrowed his eyes. "If you had anything to do with contaminating the Mind of the World, Horan Zehar, I'll have you flayed alive."

"But first you'll have to figure out how contamination infiltrated the Mind of the World," Horan said mildly. "Do you suppose the famous angel Lucyd is a friend of the impure?"

The vigile flinched so violently Salit thought he might collapse of an apoplexy. Salit trembled herself. Could her father's accusation be true? Or had he flung it out for the outrage, the way he always did? The Twine she-butcher moaned through her gag, violently shook her head.

The vigile ignored his sacred sharer. "Is he?"

"Surely not." Horan grinned.

Manifesto of the Apocalypse, Edict Two: Infiltrate the Mind of the World.

Exhilaration sang in Salit's blood. Horan was up to something, something new and phenomenal. Something he hadn't confided in her. What, *what*? How her father enjoyed outwitting the purities, always one step ahead of everyone, even the High Council.

Even the Heaven's Devils. Even her.

Suspiciously, "My father, how could *I* possibly appear in a famous angel's dream? Milord Lucyd doesn't know me. He's never seen my face."

"This is talk better left to another time, my darling." Horan whirled, sending the vigile whirling, too, searching for his elusive target.

"Tell me how *you* know this," Salit shouted and stamped her foot again, drenching herself. Impetuous? The impure possessed no Imperial sharemind. How did her father know of this angel's dream and what had appeared in it? Didn't she have the right to know? "Tell me now!"

"Hold your tongue, girl, and we'll talk later," Horan said sternly. "He understands us, don't you see?" Her father winked at the vigile. "We'll discuss the matter further when we take the Twine she-butcher to her Reckoning before the Dark Ones."

"Impure. Bastard." The vigile sliced the air with the dagger, didn't even come close to her father. Sliced again.

How her father enjoyed tormenting his enemies! He'd taunted the bodyguards who'd tried to save Milady Danti, reminding them of their grievous failure as they'd stared, horrified, at the bloody tidbits of her corpse. "Look," he'd said, "look well how you've failed the Imperium," just before he'd slashed their throats.

And *she* was impetuous and self-indulgent? Now, there was an issue to raise at their next lesson: *Is it effective, my father, to taunt your prey, and what strategic benefits do you gain?*

"I'll never forget your ugly face," the vigile declared, staring at her with eyes like two spots of blue fire. He advanced on her and their captive, swinging his toy of a knife, but she seized the Twine she-butcher and easily evaded him. What a bumbler the vigile was. "You'll never escape Imperial Vigilance, impure wench."

"But first, milord, you'll have to catch her," Horan said in his mocking singsong.

Suddenly self-conscious, Salit rearranged the three Orbs of Eternity she wore on a leather cord strung around her neck. *Always carry contraband on your person,* Horan had taught her, *you never know when you'll require a bribe or a bounty.* Finger-combed her hair. What had she looked like, there, in the Mind of the World? Did that mean all the purities in all Pangaea knew her face? Was she . . . famous? Or was it infamous?

"Gah, my father. Will I need to disguise myself?"

"Most likely, my darling." Horan gestured slightly with

his chin, indicating where he wanted her and their captive to go. "Enough talk. Get behind me."

Salit moved. Why hadn't they seen or heard or smelled this vigile till he was almost up their arses? Too busy splashing in filthy ductwater with the Twine she-butcher. Too filled with her magister stink. Well, that was another lesson. At the cusp of sixteen, Salit was learning her lessons fast and furiously.

Her father and the Dark Ones had carefully planned the abduction, torture, and execution of Dame Clere Twine naitre Secundus. Since Horan had first heard the rumor Clere Twine was entering into sharelock, they'd thought of nothing else. The ceremony was to be held in the main sharelock temple in Atlan, a place that had been riddled with ducts and secret passages since times lost to antiquity. They would impale her head and the quarters of her body on five consecrated posts, tattoo the five edicts of the Manifesto of the Apocalypse on each of her body parts, and plant the posts around the Obelisk of Eternity in Allpure Square first thing in the morning.

Manifesto of the Apocalypse, Edict Three: Annihilate the High Council.

Where had Horan heard the rumor? Salit wasn't entirely sure how her father collected his intelligence. He'd always been secretive, even with her. His depth and range and accuracy were astonishing. She'd concluded long ago that qut purveyancing must have had much to do with Horan's success.

Qut wasn't illegal, but taxed to the skies. Proffering a quid with the Imperial purple wax seal unbroken may have been a symbol of status among wealthy angels, but most qut addicts among the purities bought their quids on the shadow market at a tenth the cost through impure purveyors like Horan Zehar.

Who in turn acquired his wares from foe clans that specialized in relieving Imperial qut wagons and taxhouses of their wares. The Dark Ones, who among other things controlled all impure dealings with the purities, had granted her father the purveyance after lengthy negotiations.

Horan's routes took him from Prime Hill to Jugglers Lane, from Central Atlan to Gondwana Valley, from angels' cloudscrapers to eroticians' salons, and every place in between where an addict couldn't pass the day without a quid. Horan's ability to move invisibly among the purities—at their invitation, at their insistence, despite the risk of Imperial prosecution—surely accounted for his remarkable inventory of intelligence.

This afternoon he'd said in his mild way, "It's confirmed. The Twine she-butcher will enter into sharelock at the big public temple tonight despite the earthshock."

"How do you know?"

"I overheard the vigile while he ravished his erotician."

And Salit had marveled. Truly, Horan Zehar was the master of dark things. The prospect of the blooding had sent her into a frenzy of anticipation.

Now she thrust her bony knee between their captive's shoulder blades, shoved Clere Twine facedown in the water, and planted her bootheel on the she-butcher's neck. Held her there while she gurgled and flailed. What a pity Salit couldn't drown her. But Horan had specifically commanded her not to steal the she-butcher's life.

Pox! Salit could only torment her a little while, stuff the urine-soaked ball-gag into the she-butcher's mouth. The mouth that had over three decades commanded the harassment and torture of Salit's people—little children, the sick, the lame, gravid women, the elderly. The mouth that was about to order extermination of the impure, if Horan's intelligence proved right about that, too.

All the impure despised Clere Twine. Yet the she-butcher's father, Councillor Claren Twine, newly appointed by the High Council as the Imperial Advisor on Impure Activities, was far more powerful. And far more dangerous. He'd been given license to harass and spy upon her people. Why didn't they seize him, too? She and Horan could have circumvented his bodyguards as easily as they'd slipped past the temple sentries. Yet when she'd asked Horan, he'd only said, "The Dark Ones have their uses for Councillor Twine. Do as you're told."

A *real* blow against the Imperium, that's what Salit craved. The execution of Milady Danti had been too swift, too perfunctory. The most beloved woman in the Mind of the World had been as beautiful as rumor said, as pale and slender as the first white roses of summer she'd come to view. But Danti up close and in the flesh had been shriveled and ancient to Salit's eyes, shockingly a crone, her nacreous skin as delicate as wrapping tissue. Danti had succumbed to the cherry laurel vapors released by the Alchemist from the inferno bolts long before the devil stars had carved her into a thousand pieces. She'd suffered little pain and no more than a tremor of terror.

Salit had no passions about the famous angel one way or the other, but she'd craved a *real* atrocity for her first blooding. Yet the Dark Ones hadn't despised Milady Danti the way they despised Clere, the Twine she-butcher, and all Clere's purity.

Manifesto of the Apocalypse, Edict Four: Eliminate security numbers and sharelock chips.

Why? Salit had asked about Edict Four. *The impure possess neither security numbers nor sharelock chips, have access to neither. Exactly,* her father had said, enjoying her bafflement. And had refused to explain.

Now the vigile lunged at Salit, and she leapt away, dread jolting her heart. Her hands seeped sweat. Her knees knocked. Fear shivered through her belly, loosening her bowels. She gripped her hands beneath her scrawny rib cage and vigorously pulled up in the fear-conquering technique Horan had taught her.

Horan snapped, "Get the Twine she-butcher on her feet and hold fast to her." He turned deliberately to the vigile, spoke in perfect Atlanean-accented Pangaean. "We'll cut out her eyes and her tongue later.'' Taunting, circling round the vigile. In Devil dialect, ''It's time to go, my darling.''

''Yes, my father.'' Salit jerked their captive, choking and gasping, to her feet. Disgusting to seize the she-butcher, embrace her as close and vigorously as a bedmate. But she did as her father bid.

The vigile stumbled and grimaced, and Salit saw blotches of blood crisscrossing his ceremonial gown in the wound pattern wrought by a well-flung devil star.

One of hers? Ho!

''He's hurt, my father!'' Salit smirked. As always, they'd coated the razor-sharp startips with poisons and fecal matter. The smallest puncture could cause blood poisoning, necrosis of the flesh, and death—before the victim even knew how badly he or she had been wounded.

''A wounded beast is all the more dangerous,'' Horan said in his lecturing tone. Her father's voice softened into an ominous whisper, the way he spoke whenever he sensed the whip of destiny. Whenever a foretelling came upon him. ''If this bumbling vigile should capture me, my daughter, you must take the Twine she-butcher to the Dark Ones at once. Habash Qaled and Asif and the other clanfolk of the Devils and Hell's Teeth will be looking for you. Do you understand?''

''Yes, my father.''

''Take Crescent Causeway to the cove and then again through the Deep Tunnel. Habash Qaled will take you to the Cavern of Reckoning and the Dark Ones. She alone knows the way. The causeway is flooded from the earth-shock and severely damaged at the Remote End, but still passable as far as the tunnel. Don't go near Blackblood Cavern or our tentsite. Understood?''

''Understood.''

The vigile shouted, ''I vow I'll see you both flogged in Allpure Square for all the purities to witness!''

''But first you'll have to catch us, milord,'' Horan said in his mocking singsong and slashed at the vigile with his left hand. His bony fingers curved over his handpiece of long metal claws, raking rows of blood down the vigile's broad chest. With a firmer grip on the metal claws, Horan could rip the chest muscles right off a man, pluck out his heart, gut his bowels.

Why didn't he?

Salit's heart pounded. *What* was her father planning? Could they seize the vigile, too? Display him and flay him before the Dark Ones? What a glory! Salit yanked a devil star from her belt, taking care not to touch the startips, and pressed the weapon hard against the flanks of the Twine she-beast.

She glanced over the vigile's shoulder. A squad of temple sentries marched through the panel behind the Sacred Altar. They caught sight of the altercation and sprinted down the duct, only a few hundred paces away, and closing *fast*.

"Sentries come, my father," she called out. "More vigiles, too."

"Then let's be done," Horan said mildly and moved in for the kill.

They wouldn't take the vigile prisoner, after all. Salit prepared herself for the vigile's execution.

Horan raked the metal claws again, forcefully this time, drawing four deep grooves in the vigile's chest, catching, nearly pulling loose his pectoral muscles.

But the vigile abruptly feinted with his fist, struck with the puny dagger. A move so skillful Salit could not help but admire him—even as she despised him. His long arms outreached Horan's claws. The dagger found its target, carving viciously across Horan's belly.

Salit shrieked, "My father, my father, my father!"

Horan groaned, seized the last star from his belt, flung it at the vigile's wounded leg.

The vigile shouted in agony and seized the star before it could commence its whirl of pain. He smashed the weapon against the wall, aiming for the weakness at the star's center.

Salit stared, astonished, as the devil star cracked in the vigile's hand and fell powerless. She met her father's horrified eyes. *Much more dangerous than we know.*

"Ah, Darkness," Horan whispered. "Truly the erotician orbcaster *can* foretell. Darkness for the world, darkness for magisters, darkness for Devils. Darkness of the heart. Darkness for me. My daughter," he said, "don't forget your lessons." He shrugged out of his chameleon cloak and grasped the writhing garment in his fist.

And a wizened little man with silvery blue skin crouched before Salit, clutching his belly, blood leaking through his fingers. Salit examined him carefully. In her whole life she had never seen her father uncloaked. *This is the first time. This is the last time.* He was far older than she'd ever realized and not nearly as misshapen. He was distinguished-looking, almost handsome. Superbly handsome, to her eyes.

"Dada," she whispered, reduced to a child.

"Do as I've taught you, my daughter."

The vigile pounced on him like a hunting beast, bent over him, plunged the dagger to the hilt into Horan's neck just below his ear. Grunting, perspiring, the vigile methodically worked the blade in jagged strokes across Horan's throat to the other ear.

Even after the mastering of nerve and mind, the training with slaughtering beasts and wild drud subpures, her witnessing of the execution of Milady Danti, her assassinations in the Sacred Sanctum—still Salit felt anguish and repugnance seize her heart like a fist.

My father.
The last time.
The last time I will ever feel this way.
Farewell, tears and grief!

"Magister butcher," she screamed as she watched her father dying. She breathed deeply and focused her will, momentarily releasing rage and grief the way Horan had taught her in the presence of a blooding. "Death to the Imperium! The Apocalypse is here!"

She thrust her fingers through the aperture in the center of her last devil star. Whirled it, plunging the tip into the she-butcher's back, and released the weapon to do its lethal busywork. The star spun in a tight circle, gouging deeply. The she-butcher shrieked through her gag as a startip punctured her lung, her liver, her kidney.

"My darling daughter," Horan slurred, blood gurgling in his throat. "What have you done?"

"My duty to the Dark Ones."

"You know too little of your duty, Salit. Well, done is done. Be sure to cut out her belly, too. I witnessed their rutting in the vigile's preparatory chamber. She's probably fruitful with his child." He flung his bloodied cloak at her. "Take it. Never let it fall into Imperial hands. Don't fail me, my daughter, even after Darkness takes me."

"I'll never fail you, my father."

Horan Zehar lay back, then, and quietly died.

Salit quelled the trembling in her heart, blinked back tears. Breathed the terrible stench of blood and excrement. She seized the devil star, yanked it out of the Twine's back, and aimed now for the she-butcher's belly. The star flew, struck, scooped out the Twine's intestines, her kidneys, her birth chamber. With a heavy splash the she-butcher crumpled to the floor, the ropes of her entrails sweeping away in the surging water.

"You monster!" the vigile cried. Perhaps the vigile already felt the poison in the startips. Perhaps his injuries compelled his trembling. For tremble he did, violently, and tears drenched his face as he knelt beside the writhing she-butcher. He held her hands while she thrashed in her death throes. "Clere, ah! my beloved Clere." He tore the gag from her mouth and, to Salit's astonishment, kissed her deeply. Vigiles and prefects touched mouths in affection? Unheard of!

"I will love you forever, my sacred sharer," he whispered. "I will avenge this atrocity, I swear it."

The Twine she-butcher shrieked, a terrible ululation that went on and on, and then she surrendered her Essence to Eternity and fled the ephemeral world.

Salit awkwardly pulled her father's bloody cloak around her shoulders and backed away from the grieving vigile, his gutted sharer lying limp in his arms.

The vigile gazed up at Salit with his blue-fire eyes, brimming with incalculable rage. He clutched his chest, his bleeding thigh, struggling to stay conscious despite blood loss, poison, and grief. "I will hunt you down from now till Eternity, ugly girl."

"You slew my father, my closest kin in all the world," she spat back. "I'll hunt and torment *you,* foul vigile."

"Arrogant strumpet. *You're* the hunted one. I heard you speak with your father. I heard and understood. He was right about you. You're no warrior."

"Ho! Heaven's Devils have infiltrated the pleasure gardens of the angels, we've bloodied your highest shrines, and now we infiltrate the Mind of the World. You will fall, vigile. The Imperium will end!"

The vigile rose, shaking, to his feet. "I promise I will cut you slowly into a thousand pieces. I will vivisect you with my own hands. All our Sacred Imperium of Pangaea will mock your misery and applaud your shame. I'll never rest till I see you dead."

In the same mocking singsong Horan Zehar had always employed she quavered, "But first you'll have to catch me, milord."

She stepped into the shadows.

And vanished.

"Salit," came the whisper. "Are you here, my comrade?"

She still stood, trembling, five paces away from her father's stiffening corpse, pressed against the wall of the waterduct. The chameleon cloak had wrapped itself tightly around her, head to toe, with only a slit left open for her eyes. Every muscle ached.

She tried to speak. Could not.

The vigile, the temple sentries bearing the corpse of the Twine she-butcher—all had gone hours ago. Salit hadn't tried to run. She couldn't possibly have outrun the vigile, his stride nearly twice the length of hers.

And so she'd stood these three hours, tightly pressed against the wall, her feet soaked to the ankle and freezing by degrees in the cold water. Every time another squad of temple sentries and vigiles had marched down the duct, their boots raising a wake in the water, she had prayed none would glance at the place where she stood and notice how the water eddied around her invisible ankles. She'd prayed no one would suddenly take a sword, slash the blade across the wall.

And slice her in two at the waist.

Ho! They weren't so clever, after all, these Imperial vigiles. None had possessed the wit to discover her. None had known the secrets of chameleon cloaks. Well, that was another lesson. Since she hadn't possessed one yet, her father hadn't taught her much about the cloak. *Hadn't wanted to whet my appetite any keener than it already was.* What she knew about cloaks—that Horan appeared to change shape and sometimes vanished before her eyes—she knew mostly from her own observation.

And after he'd shed the cloak for the last time, his strange transformation? She wasn't yet sure *what* to make of that revelation.

Beneath the tight sheath of the cloak, the orbs she'd strung on the thong around her neck sizzled like glowing cookstones against her breast.

Manifesto of the Apocalypse, Edict Five: Preserve all chameleon cloaks and Orbs of Eternity and conceal them from the Imperium.

Why? she'd also asked about Edict Five. *Because cloaks*

and orbs originate with our people, Horan had said, *and our people have remained untouched by the Imperium since times lost to antiquity. Thus, orbs and cloaks must stay with our people, as long as our people survive.*

How her father had liked games! His reply had been both more provocative and more inconclusive than most of his answers. Salit had always wondered about Edict Five.

Now she coaxed her voice into a stunned whisper, "Asif, my comrade? Is it you?"

"Yeah, it's me." A lanky beanpole of a young man disengaged himself from the shadows and groped toward her. He swiveled his head this way and that, searching for her and plainly not seeing her. "Where the hell are you?"

Ho, she'd employed the cloak well for her first camouflaging. Even a Heaven's Devil assassin, highly trained at twenty, couldn't detect her. *Beware of your triumphs,* Horan had said. *Believe you've reached your highest skill, and next time you'll die.*

She glanced behind her, assessing the surroundings.

The cloak had easily simulated the pale, pebbled wall of the duct. She hadn't done much to will it—to hold the vision of her environment within her mind and command the cloak to mimic what she saw. From the scraps of information her father had tossed her, she understood that was the way one directed the cloak. Her father's accusation—*impetuous*—stung in her memory anew. Maybe it was true. She wasn't very good at holding a thought for long in her mind. How would she fare one day when the blue-eyed vigile charged at her in the middle of Marketplace, his dagger drawn, and she needed to command the cloak?

She drew a ragged breath, released it, and watched Asif swing around toward the sound. His gnarled wrists protruded from the cuffs of his tunic. His leggings of black sacking barely reached his ankles above the black slippers covering his enormous feet. Her comrade would require a new set of clothes before the end of the season. Nearly as tall as a vigile, Asif cut a fine figure, never mind the scarlet blotches on his golden brown complexion, the mismatched features, the twisted limbs. *Impure.* Yes, he was, and proudly so. Three devil stars, a battle hammer, and a lance dangled from his belt.

Salit had never seen such a beautiful sight. She flung open the chameleon cloak, dispersing the camouflage. "Asif, oh, Asif, my father . . ."

Asif started. "*There* you are, Salit! Gah, so I see." He bent over the corpse, making the triangular sign of Darkness over Horan's death grimace. "We feared as much. We feared for *you,* my little comrade."

Asif folded her into a loose-limbed embrace, awkwardly stroking her hair, the nape of her neck. His fingertips felt like sand on her skin. Like Salit, he'd cut grooves in them and doused them in corrosives to obscure the impressions that fingertips left after a touch upon a surface. Imperial Vigilance knew techniques of discerning these impressions. No one of the impure, of the foes—especially of the Heaven's Devils—left fingertips untampered.

"*I* feared for you, my Salit."

Gratitude, sorrow, longing, and a surprising tingle of lust surged in Salit's blood. She knew—from Horan again—her intense feelings were the aftermath of combat madness, blood shock, and grief. Yet she'd often surreptitiously watched Asif. They each wore the clan band of Heaven's Devils pierced through the skin over their hearts. They were clan-bonded, then. But she'd often wondered if her tall vigorous comrade could ever consider her for his own bonded one.

She bit back her unruly sentiments. "The Twine she-butcher is dead."

"We know that, too. We saw them remove her corpse at the end of the duct. Her new-made sharer, the vigile, is wild with grief."

She smiled grimly. "Asif, I gutted the Twine she-butcher with my own hand." Added a small lie, "As my father commanded me." Of course Horan had done no such thing.

Asif gasped and glanced at her in amazement. His voice took on a new tone. "You did well, Salit." He pressed his lips against the furrow between her brows. "Wrap the body in your cloak. I'll carry him. Wait a moment." He unsheathed his lance. "Come here, I'll shave your head. The sentries know all about your colorful hair."

Salit stood stock-still as Asif hacked off her vermilion-and-white tresses and carefully gave them to her. Vigilance would return to examine the scene of Clere Twine's murder, but Vigilance would also know by now that Horan Zehar's daughter had been here. *Leave evidence where no evidence is required.* She flung the hair into the water at her feet.

"Is there still danger?" she said.

"Temple security has been tripled. They know we know about this passage, of course. Crescent Causeway is filthy with vigiles. And forget the tunnel." He grinned at her as he teased the blade over the swells and ridges of her skull, shaving her bald. "There you go. You're beautiful. We'll take the pipeline instead. Habash Qaled will be waiting for us. Many are moving their tentsites out of Blackblood Cavern till the wrath of Vigilance cools. Are you thirsty?" He held out a wineskin.

"Parched!" She suddenly realized she was perishing of thirst and badly needed to urinate. She took the skin, drained it, returned it to Asif. Touched her shaved scalp. Her skin felt stubbled and scraped raw and cold. But what a liberation, to be free of hair! "Asif, the vigile killed my father and has sworn he'll kill me. I swear to you I'm going to torment him all his days till the day I decide to kill him."

She wanted him to smile and nod, but Asif frowned. "Salit, Salit, don't talk that way. We do as the Dark Ones bid us. No less, but certainly no more."

"I'll petition the Dark Ones. I'll plead my cause. My father was one of our finest warriors of the shadow sector, and a master at acquiring intelligence about the pures."

"I know, Salit, but—"

"Don't you think the Dark Ones will seek revenge upon his killer?"

"Don't presume to know what the Dark Ones will seek."

That silenced her. Asif was right, of course, but she despised the fact that he was right. She ground her teeth, flung the cloak over Horan's body. The chameleon cloak clung to its dead master as if the spirit within it grieved. Salit knelt and rearranged the cold, unyielding limbs as best she could.

She blinked back tears again. She'd prepared other corpses for burial, clanfolk and tentsite neighbors. But this was her father. Her teacher, her closest kin in all the world. She made the sign of Darkness and whispered, "Good-bye, Horan Zehar. I swear to *you* I'll torment your murderer till the day I die."

Asif hoisted the corpse over his shoulder. "Quickly, my little comrade." He set off into the shadows.

Salit sighed and followed him, weary to the marrow of her bones. All her life she'd known what to do: listen and learn from her father. Despite her rebellion and her sassing, she'd always listened. She'd always done as Horan Zehar had bid. Now her destiny spiraled away from her, speeding into shadows lost to the future.

II

SUMMER
RAIN

FACET 7

Square: Order or rigidity.
The aetherist enters into sacred sharelock with a barren
    mathematician who proposes a great theorem.
The action is perfection.
The forbearance is sterility.

The Orb of Eternity

Commentaries:

Councillor Sausal: Pan is eternal perfection and stability. The four-sided equilateral polyhedron is a perfect and stable form and thus granite squares are
chosen as the foundation of the temple.

So, too, a sharer must be chosen so that sacred
sharelock becomes a stable relationship in which to
generate the family. Sharelock, as an Imperial duty
and a joy, is the foundation upon which the Imperium
is built.

Therefore the prudent person should seek order in
daily life, regulate things great and small, and apply
exactitude when embarking upon any significant task.

Guttersage (usu. considered vulgar): Perfection has
its flaws.

*Central Atlan, the Pyramid of Perpetuities, before the en-
trance to the Venerated Vestibule:*

"There's no danger, Milord Lucyd," the vigile said, wiping raindrops off his face. "Vigilance Authority promises—"

"Vigilance Authority cannot even protect its own subpure," Lucyd said to the insolent creature. "I have no intention of relying on Vigilance Authority's promises."

Lightning forked through the roiling thunderheads. A huge *boom* reverberated in the soaked summer air as if Pan was announcing to the world that Milady Danti was to be consecrated to Eternity.

Lucyd's private windship hovered a handbreadth above the tessellated granite pavement. Angels and magisters thronging the vestibule within their purity cordons politely ignored him according to traditional mourning protocol. No one came forward to embrace him or offer condolences. He was much too high a pure and subpure to be spoken to or touched without his permission, and he had no wish to exercise his prerogative. *Strangers, nothing but strangers to me.* He could feel the intrusion of their inquisitive eyes. Hear their murmurs, some sympathetic, some snide.

He turned his gaze away and studied the soaring granite slopes of this tribute to humanity's survival for Eternity. Once he'd admired the classic architecture, the precious marbles. The friezes depicting myriad grinning skulls, the frescoes illustrating Eternal Bliss and Eternal Torment. The kaligraphs crafted in times lost to antiquity exhorting Faith and Trust in Pan.

This morning the pyramid filled him with nothing finer than anger and melancholy. How could he have ever delighted in skulls, in torment? *My beloved Danti, they say your love is with me for Eternity. But all I feel is emptiness.*

The tiny windship, a teardrop topped by a crown of multicolored wings, enveloped him in its translucent blue embrace, conforming to his slender physique. The hull was sentient and perfectly malleable, as hulls on private windships of this vintage usually were. Another priceless heirloom from his mothers, irreplaceable and rare, the windship gently accommodated Lucyd's slightest movement, his slightest whim, almost before he had even conceived of it.

Which was more than Lucyd could say for the gigantic golden-haired vigile, one Lieutenant Regim Deuceman according to the badge pinned to the shoulder of his uniform. The vigile had confronted him before the vestibule and impeded his entrance into the pyramid. The protocol was inexcusable, should have provoked the wrath of Vigilance—but this creature *was* Vigilance.

"For the last time, please disembark from your ship, milord."

"No." Lucyd leaned toward the speaker in the windship's exit portal, though he was loath to come one hair closer to the vigile. "My ship shields me."

"We've posted ten times the usual guard. The pyramid has quadrupled its staff. There's no danger." The lout loomed over Lucyd's windship, promising his own danger.

The arrogance of this magister creature!

"You don't understand. I never go out into your . . . mundanity." Lucyd coughed delicately. "I haven't gone out of my house in over a season. I haven't attended a public function in decades. I . . . I cannot bear sunlight."

Which was true enough. Lucyd pressed fingernails lacquered silver into the hollow of his throat. Couldn't bear the light and the heat and the mud and the rain and the air tainted with the breaths of other pures and subpures.

The air . . . Suddenly he couldn't breathe.

And what about air poisoned by cherry laurel vapors, air rife with weapons flung by terrorists?

Who could trust Imperial Vigilance after the atrocity committed by Heaven's Devils on the night of the Big Shock? At a sacred sharelock ceremony in Our Supreme Temple, no less, attended by two thousand vigiles, prefects, and councillors. Villa de Reve might have suffered severe cracks through its ancient foundation that terrible day, but Prefect Clere Twine had lost her life.

As Danti had lost her life. To the foes. To—the criers

now depicted in their Imperial sharemind—an especially vicious clan called the Heaven's Devils.

Is this progress, then? Progress toward the solution of a heinous crime? Vigilance now knows the name of the clan who cut my Danti into a thousand pieces? Then where are these Devils? Why aren't their heads impaled on posts in Allpure Square?

Lucyd had no intention of disembarking from his windship.

The summer storm pummeled Our Sacred City with hot rain. The rain was hotter, it seemed to Lucyd, the lightning deadlier, the winds fiercer, than they'd ever been before. Gales tore at buildings and roads damaged by the Big Shock and still only half-repaired. Construction crews cursed. The Imperial Bureau of Weather Control cringed at its ineptitude in shaping the winds. And those left without homes huddled in temporary shelters and prayed to Pan or a thousand other local godlings less stern. Or more likely guzzled teq and beer and gambled the drenched days away.

Does anyone believe in Pan anymore? Or is that only the doubt in my own heart?

The Harbinger had been sheathed in heavy canvas, the tripod bundled with haybales, but the gong gave off muffled bongs when the storm struck at it, moaning ceaselessly like a great foghorn. In the tumult en route to the pyramid, despite the Imperial escort, his diminutive windship had nearly capsized thrice. Lucyd, as he tumbled and lurched and struggled to right the battered little ship, thought of Danti.

How I love the summer rains, she would say, her enchanting smile curving her lips. *How I love the moan of the Harbinger when the wind tears at it. I feel safe, my beloved, tucked away in Villa de Reve with you. Cherished one, let's never leave.*

But you left, Danti. You left.

The escort of massive Imperial Vigilance craft surrounding and shielding the angel's windship couldn't prevent the rough-and-tumble, but the escort had prevented ship and angel from being swept away, plucked from Our Sacred City, flung across the Panthalassa Ocean, and hurled, headlong, into the barren torrents on the other side of the world.

If only they had let him go.

It hadn't escaped him that the escort amounted to more than mere courtesy. More than protection against the elements, even more than a defense against an attack by the foes.

He *despised* being here.

Danti, my revered Danti! How can I look at your dead body?

He'd begged the Supreme Memorializer—as much as an angel could ever beg an Imperial functionary—to be released of his obligation to attend the consecration and stand before her displayed corpse. "Permit me my grief in privacy. Hasn't she given the Imperium enough of herself? Why do you insist on this public spectacle?"

The functionary had visited Villa de Reve to make the final arrangements. "Surely milord knows an Imperial consecration cannot proceed without her Everlasting Presence," the Supreme Memorializer had said in an impatient and patronizing tone. "It's vital that the lower purities see her actual body that they may know in their hearts she lives forever. That they may know they too will live forever if they obey Pan."

"Dispense with the consecration, then. I don't care about formalities and traditions anymore. She belongs to me, and me alone. *I* will consecrate her to the Eternal in my dream for all the world to see."

In fact, Lucyd had received a commission from the Temple of the World of the Mind to dream of Danti's consecration. The usual impersonal contract written in triplicate requested his signature and thumbprint pressed in hot wax. But he didn't require memories of an actual event to dream. He could simply envision the pyramid, her sarcophagus, as he lay within the aetheric shell. The shell would project his

vision into the Mind of the World. And all who invoked
Imperial sharemind could choose his dream and know her
consecration had been consummated.

"On the contrary, milord," the Supreme Memorializer
had said, scandalized. "Our Sacred Imperium of Pangaea
will never forget Milady Danti. She was the most beloved
woman in the Mind of the World. She belongs to *us*. Naturally," the Supreme Memorializer had added acidly,
"you'll want to join her forever when you leave this
ephemeral world and enter the Eternal yourself. May I remind you, milord, you may only do that if you and she are
properly consecrated."

Lucyd had not bothered to suppress a skeptical snort.
"And if I refuse to attend?"

"I trust, milord, you don't wish Vigilance to ruin your
lovely front door."

The Supreme Memorializer had taken her leave, and Lucyd had summoned Dote to bring him a tall carafe of kapfo
wine. Hours had passed before he could calm his shaking
hands. The reddish diamond-shaped scars where the
sharelock chips had been removed had ached the way they
always did these days whenever distress assailed him. *What
is the world coming to, when temple flunkies can threaten
an angel?* After his outrage, a sharp prick of fear. *Would
they actually break down my door? Force me to appear at
their horrid ceremony?*

All that nonsense about the Eternal. Did Lucyd believe
it? Once he had, fervently, unconditionally. *Pan is the Everlasting Essence, each person a manifestation of that Essence. Essence is never lost, it only changes form. As above,
so below. As Eternity lasts forever, so lasts the Imperium.
So lasts every purity and every pure, forever and ever.*

Once he and Danti had sworn their belief in the Everlasting Essence in an especially beautiful dream. He'd dreamed
of her death—a whimsical, gentle death from advanced
age—and his ardent pursuit of her throughout time and
space.

What a farce, he thought now. *A sham, a dreadful delusion.* The truth was she was gone forever, and they'd never meet again. The truth was there was no Eternity. Only darkness. Darkness! The cursed oracle he'd dreamed of in the cursed dream. *That's* what it had portended. The death, not of his body, but of his faith.

"Sunlight?" The golden-haired vigile tapped on the exit portal. The windship shrank from his monstrous knuckles. "Milord Lucyd, there's no sunlight today. Those thunderclouds above us are thick as mud."

Thick as his vigile's skull. "There's always sunlight in the day, lieutenant," Lucyd replied primly. "The sun's Essence penetrates the clouds, however thick, just as Pan penetrates to the core of the world and to the innermost chambers of one's heart."

The vigile scowled. "That's true about Pan, of course. But there are no windows and no sunlight in the Memoriam. The pyramid is entirely lit by magmalamps." The vigile tugged at the exit portal. "Disembark, milord."

How dare he touch my ship. The protocol had gotten completely out of control. *I shall report him to his superior and get him sacked this afternoon.*

Lucyd swiveled the windship away from the brutish vigile. He found himself facing a barbarous, shrieking horde that had congregated outside the cordon surrounding the pyramid.

"Angel, angel, angel!" Ten times the usual security? Quadruple the Pyramid staff? The horde shouted, pointed, "It's Milord Lucyd! Hai, Lucyd! Hai, Lucyd! Look over here, milord! Over here!"

Two dozen heavily shaped female buckwheat threshers swooned dead away, were piled onto wagonbeds by gloved walkabouts, and carted off. Fisticuffs broke out among a gang of brawny roadbuilders. Howls of rage rose. Lucyd squeezed his eyes shut against the bloodied faces, fiery eyes, dislodged teeth.

Dear Pan! He swiveled the windship back, pressed a tissue to his lips. He was going to be ill, he was going to faint, he knew it, he *knew* it. Perspiration misted his pale forehead, his upper lip. His formal bodysuit of atlantium sateen clung to his underarms, the small of his back. His breath caught in his throat despite the cool, hypnolia-scented atmosphere with which the windship considerately had surrounded him. His eyes were so sore and red from weeping he couldn't blink without the sensation of passing his eyelids over sandpaper. He raised a pince-nez comprised of blue-stained lenses and glared at the waiting vigile. "I cannot bear light from magmalamps, either, sir."

The vigile snorted with exasperation. *Too bloody bad,* Lucyd thought. Thank Pan this magister creature possessed less powerful sharemind than he. Thank Pan even vigilance sharemind couldn't compel an angel, but only Vigilance security clubs, beating down his door. What would the vigile do now, smash open his exit portal?

How dare this low magister creature use a warning tone with him. Warning *him,* an angel!

"Milord, the Supreme Memorializer has requested—no, she's *demanded*—that you stand next to the Highest Councillor for all the pures and subpures to witness. She *demands* that you stand with your family for all the families of Pangaea to witness. You were milady's sacred sharer. You are"—an irritated pause while the dolt marshaled whatever thoughts he managed to keep in his brutish brain—"the most revered and popular aetherist in all Pangaea. We cannot proceed with the consecration without you, milord. No. We *won't* proceed. And that's that."

"I will hover beside the Highest Councillor in my windship, lieutenant. Everyone can plainly see who I am. My windship displays me well for your beastly consecration." Sarcastically, "Translucent blue harmonizes well with my coloring, don't you think?"

"Milord—"

"Lieutenant. I do not expose myself to your mundanity. Anytime, anywhere, for *any* reason. Milady Danti always concurred with my predilections. She would concur with me now, were she blessedly alive, no thanks to *you* and Imperial *Vigilance*. And *that's* that.'' Lucyd drew himself up. He'd never been robust, but he possessed considerable charisma and the undeniable charm of an angel. The windship conformed to his newly assumed stature, elongating and aggrandizing itself. ''Now step aside, lieutenant.''

The vigile, huge beast that he was, blocked the windship's path, seized the teardrop in his formidable arms, pressed his face against the translucent hull, and glared directly into Lucyd's eyes.

Lucyd gasped at the outrageous impropriety. He should have flown away while he had the chance. What could he do? He peered at the vigile's enormous face—golden slashes of eyebrows framing cavernous eye sockets, craggy cheekbones, an imperious snout over the hard-lipped commanding mouth, the squared-off chin. The face of a magister expecting rulership as his birthright, demanding domination, even though he was only a vigile—the lowest of magisters—keeping order on the streets.

A menacing face. So unlike Lucyd's delicate features, the pale angelic features of an aetherist who dreamed of universal beauty for all Eternity. The vigile was very ugly, Lucyd decided, more sinister with his chiseled countenance than a savage drud from the Far Reaches.

The vigile's lip twitched. Sweat trickled down his broad brow. Lucyd suddenly noticed the vigile's brilliant blue eyes were cloudy with pain. The vigile leaned laboriously on a sturdy metal body support strapped around his barrel chest and girding his massive left leg. His voice, so ripe with arrogance, so assured of his birthright to command and to be obeyed, cracked with some terrible inner strain.

''You,'' the vigile whispered through the windship's hull. ''I want to know why you didn't escort Danti to the gardens the day she was killed.''

How dare—? Rage shook Lucyd, sickness choked in his throat, and a perplexing needle of alarm pierced him. The windship infused its atmosphere with rich perfume as he struggled for breath. He felt perilously close to stammering. "Sir. Casting dreams has begun to take a toll on me, after fifty years. I was ill that dreadful day. To my everlasting regret. I've told Vigilance that. I would gladly have died in her place. I would have gladly died *with* her, if the Hand of Pan rendered her death inevitable. I've nothing more to tell you, lieutenant. *Now get out of my way.*"

The vigile staggered against the sudden propulsion of the windship, but regained his balance and easily restrained the tiny craft despite his disability and obvious pain. "I want to know who you know among the impure, Milord Lucyd."

Lucyd gasped again. The vigile's tone had become malevolent. He backed the windship out of the vigile's grasp. "What the devil do you mean?"

"Answer the question."

"Why . . . no one, of course! I only know angels. And only the highest angels. Aetherists. And only aetherists of the highest quality, not lovers of blood like Milady Faro and Milord Sting." At the vigile's peculiar leer, Lucyd swallowed hard. "What is the meaning of this rude interrogation? Are you after my assets? Is this an extortion? An impugning of my character? I warn you, lieutenant, I have the favor of the High Council myself. You'll never get away with—"

"I want to know why you dreamed of impure abominations. I want to know why you dreamed about the Orb of Eternity and a strumpet who happens to be a Heaven's Devil and an assassin."

The dream. Again, the detestable dream.

The enigma—the way his own vision had *changed*—had so haunted and frightened him, he hadn't dared cast a dream in the Mind of the World since that morning. *Have I truly lost command of my dreams?* Not alone, without Danti, without the reassuring presence of his codreamer reclining beside him within the aetheric shell.

Lucyd had expected a confrontation with the Cardinal of

the Mind of the World, not this sweat-dripping, battle-racked vigile. Since the dream he'd waited every moment for the Cardinal to ascend Prime Hill, together with five ranks of temple magisters and acolyte-auditors. With mounting anxiety, he'd prepared as best he could for an accounting, perhaps even a minor inquisition.

But the dreaded entourage had never arrived, and he'd received no message, not a word, not even a sharemind from the Cardinal. Every day that ensued with no contact whatsoever had only increased his anxiety.

And he hadn't dared initiate his powerful angel's sharemind to force a confrontation with the Mind of the World, as was his prerogative and his privilege. What if he'd stumbled across the intrusive acolyte-auditor who'd harassed him?

An angel—afraid of an acolyte-auditor?

An angel—whose prerogative it was to know anything about the world he chose to know—not knowing?

He still had only one explanation to give.

He tendered it now, regretfully, to the obnoxious vigile.

"I haven't got the slightest idea."

The vigile gave a bark of disbelieving laughter. "You have no idea how impurities contaminated your own dream?"

"No! I don't."

"You don't own an orb?"

"What, pray tell, is 'an orb'?"

More disbelieving laughter. "The impure thing in your dream, milord. The Orb of Eternity. Made of atlantium, a desecration of our Imperial gemstone. Impure conjurers have worked trickeries with the device since times lost to antiquity. Its oracles are filled with contaminated thoughts. The High Council banned the orb three seasons ago and banished Councillor Sausal." In a suspicious tone, "Surely milord has heard of the ban and the banishment."

The criers' refrain reverberated in Lucyd's memory. The great Sausal, pedagogue to every purity for nearly as many decades as Lucyd had seen life, exposed as a traitor to the Imperium. Lucyd paid scant attention to the news of the day, tiresome as news typically was. The incessant hysteria of the High Council over impure influences, the common-place concerns of the lower purities, affected him not at all. But he'd briefly looked up from his hazelnut caf in aston-ishment at the announcement of Sausal's banishment and felt pity for the beleaguered councillor. How powerful Sausal had been, a fountain endlessly spouting aphorisms about proximity and protocol. Sausal's commentaries were taught in every academy, cited in every text on Pannist philosophy.

This powerful and universally esteemed magister, ban-ished by his own purity? Lucyd shivered with foreboding. What *was* the Imperium coming to?

"Yes, actually, I do recall hearing about Sausal. But, lieutenant, I study only the classic texts about purity. Arista, Canto, the Ancient Ones. Councillor Sausal, yes, but the Sausal of a millennium ago. Not this late-coming progeny with his ceaseless, vulgar nitpicking over every pure's Imperial duties." Lucyd frowned. His Imperial duty had begun to weigh heavily upon him. "In any case, what does Sausal have to do with my dream, lieutenant?"

"Perhaps, milord, you've become beguiled of the impure abomination, as Councillor Sausal had."

"No, no, no! I am beguiled by no such thing. I have no use for the High Council's intrigues. And I've never seen that orb, or whatever it is, in my life. Except in my dream."

"And you don't know an impure girl named Salit Zehar?"

"Certainly not."

The vigile stared at him, skeptically searching his face.

Such unforgivable insolence! But the vigile disturbed him. No, more than that. The vigile frightened him. Lucyd swallowed his anger and said evenly, "Perhaps, *you*, lieu-tenant, may enlighten *me*. I'm eager, no, I'm frantic to know how impurities contaminated my own dream."

"Splendid. Then I want to talk to you." The vigile glanced around at the unruly crowd, the curious glances of the angels and councillors in the vestibule. The wrathful glances of his own squad. "Not here."

"I have no interest in a private tête-à-tête with you or any other vigile, lieutenant. You may send a crier with a sharemind of your inquiries or a messenger with a written list of your questions. I'll respond by my proxy as best I can. Good day, and Pan preserve you."

"No, I don't think so."

"I trust, sir, you don't forget your place—"

"And I trust you won't force me to bring my accusations before Vigilance Authority, the High Council, and the Temple of the Mind of the World before I've heard what you have to say and thought about your answers. Even angels aren't immune from the long reach of Vigilance. Especially when matters of impurity are in question."

"Are you threatening me, lieutenant?"

"I'm giving you a chance to clear yourself. Milord."

Lucyd averted his gaze. The vigile's blue eyes blazed with an unhealthy and repellent zeal. What *did* he want? But Lucyd had nothing to hide. He would not be intimidated by some vigile obsessed by his Imperial duty.

"Very well. You may meet me at Villa de Reve after the consecration. It's at Number Five Prime Hill. And now I believe I'll fly into the temple with my windship. You see, lieutenant, I cannot bear sunlight or lamplight or the breaths of other pures. Step aside."

Scarlet-clad carolers blared, their enormous petal-lips gaping, all mouth in tiny atrophied faces. "To the Eternal! To the Eternal! We consecrate Milady Danti to the Eternal! She lives foreeeeever!"

Cavorters capered among the memorializers, their long, slender limbs whirling, capes of gold velvet twirling. For drud subpures in constant demand for the sheer sight of their remarkable bodies, the cavorters were very beautiful, Lucyd had to admit. A particularly graceful fair-haired cavorter twirled by.

Lucyd reluctantly raised his eyes to gaze at Danti, the pale luminous cabochon of her face as exquisite in death as she had always been in life. As she still was in all his dreams. The embalmers had replaced the slanting eyes with ivory spheres set with sapphires. Lucyd's heart lurched at her sightless stare. Mockery! Desecration! He averted his eyes, tears stinging his eyelids anew.

I'm glad I never looked at her when they brought her to Villa de Reve. I would have taken my life then and there. I would have.

The pyramid staff had displayed her translucent sarcophagus atop the marble apex of the Perpetual Peak, a replication of the Pyramid of Perpetuities only slightly less grand than the Pyramid itself. *Symbolic of the ascension of the material plane into Pan. As above, so below.* Lucyd concentrated on the sacred teachings as longing for Danti clenched his breast like an invisible wrestler. The throng of memorializers gathered around the Peak, laughing and gossiping, drinking carbonated wine, costumed in feathered headdresses and festive gowns. Bearing that most ephemeral of the world's beauties—fresh flowers.

The windship beeped softly, alerting him to the presence of another. Lucyd nodded, signaling permission to speak.

"You must be so happy, Milord Lucyd," the magister whispered through the speaker in the exit portal. If she was annoyed Lucyd had insisted upon hovering beside her inside his windship, the Highest Councillor of Our Sacred Imperium betrayed no unseemly emotions. A colossal woman nearly as robust and chiseled as the wretched vigile, the Highest Councillor smiled, her practiced expression of kindness and radiant joy almost credible. "The consecration of your sacred sharer to the Eternal is an unforgettable event. We're so glad to see you here."

"Where else could I possibly be?" he replied sarcastically. The Supreme Memorializer must have informed the Highest Councillor of his objections, his reluctance to attend. A chill crept through his blood. Imperial functionaries reported to each other about an angel's behavior? Outrageous, insolent, inexcusable—but to whom could he protest?

"How delighted you must be that you'll join her in Eternity one day." She boldly patted the windship's hull as if it were Lucyd's shoulder.

"Delighted." Lucyd shuddered. The windship swelled, compelling a cushion of air beneath the councillor's hand, sparing him the pressure of her touch. If he hadn't refused to disembark from the windship, the magister would have actually *touched* him. Lucyd sniffed imperiously. He gave not one whit if she was the most powerful person politically in all Pangaea. Councillors mingling with aetherists in the Pyramid of Perpetuities at the consecration of an angel to the Eternal? The Ancient Ones would never have permitted it.

What strange situations our new politics have created.

Lucyd shook his head grimly. He and Danti had discussed the matter on the morning . . . the morning she'd gone to the Hanging Gardens. The number of angels had dwindled in the span of Lucyd's lifetime while magisters and prefects had flourished. Why? Perhaps the Imperial materia of angels had become less fruitful. Perhaps angels had shown less interest in generating the huge families common among magister subpures. And aetherists who cast dreams in the Mind of the World had diminished in power and influence while brutish vigiles rattled their swords at him and acolyte-auditors dared interrupt his dreams.

"Beg pardon, milord, but I must deliver the Imperial Panegyric." The Highest Councillor stepped forward and joined the Supreme Memorializer. Together the two massive magister pures ascended the steps of the Perpetual Peak, flanked the sarcophagus, and commenced their scripted praises.

"Milady Danti," cried the Highest Councillor, "we thank you for your beauty in our dreams—"

"—for your grace and kindness and Pannish love," intoned the Supreme Memorializer.

"—for your everlasting contribution to our comprehension of sacred sharelock and Eternal Pan!" said the Highest Councillor.

Danti's mouth moved and the Voice of her Spirit answered, "You're welcome, Our Sacred Imperium. I am eternally grateful to have served you."

The embalmers had wired her jaw, of course. A mimicker hid behind the sarcophagus, manipulated the wire, and spoke into an amplifier, imitating Danti's voice. Rather poorly, too. On and on this ludicrous exchange droned till Lucyd thought he'd go mad. The Supreme Memorializer had asked him to join them at the Peak and sing his own praises of Danti, but he'd declined and would not be persuaded otherwise. He cast his most intimate visions into the Mind of the World. He would give the Imperium no more of himself than that.

Lucyd swiveled the windship around and prepared to depart. He'd made his appearance, the memorializers had all witnessed his presence. What more could the Imperium ask—

The windship signaled again. He apprehended a sharemind hovering at the edge of his consciousness. A vast sharemind, an angel sharemind—but deferent, awaiting his initiation of mutual consciousness. He whipped around.

"Milord, may we express our congratulations at Milady Danti's consecration to the Eternal. And our condolences for your temporary loss of her presence."

Formal words, carefully spoken in perfectly accented high Pangaean. A tall, slender person of fifty years stood before the hovering windship. Platinum curls haloed a high-domed forehead, a glabrous face that might have been sculpted of bone. A gracious brow, wide-set eyes, an aquiline nose, white ribbons of lips above the acuminated jut of a chin.

"Good to see you, Tonel."

"Is it?" Mouth and eyes exceedingly somber.

"Of course." The heat of abashment rose to Lucyd's face.

"After all these years, I'm not certain."

Lucyd frowned, grateful again for the carapace of his windship shielding him from the mundanity. How vulnerable this slender person appeared, ground-bound, like a grub on seabent grass. A grub one could crush with a bootheel . . . *No, no, this is wrong. That's something Danti might say, only half in jest. I should not feel this way.* The windship filled its atmosphere with hypnolia vapors and the scent of fresh roses, and Lucyd felt a grudgingly fond smile slowly spread across his mouth. *That's better.*

"Tonel, my . . . son."

Lucyd flinched. All his progeny had assembled behind Tonel. Ten tall slim angels, each barely distinguishable from the next to Lucyd's eyes, so seldom had he seen them. Platinum curls haloed sculpted faces graced with the distinctive brow and nose and chin. Only a blind person wouldn't see the stern gleam of accusation in their eyes. Especially in the eyes of Tonel, the eldest by seven hours.

And their sharemind? Lucyd declined to enter.

That had been Danti's idea—to generate their first progeny with a round of ten. She'd overflowed with extravagant fancies at the age of fifteen. Lucyd, himself only seventeen, had loved indulging her. Why not? They were angels, perfectly matched subpures, beautiful and rich. He'd just started dreaming of her in the Mind of the World.

"How wonderful to see all my . . . sons."

"And I, milord," said their elderly caretaker, her silver hair braided and wound around her ears. The bright yellow protocol chip winking between her brows had permitted her to assert proper discipline over the angels when they were

young. The squat drud creature stood respectfully to one
side as befitted her pure and subpure.

"Gingi," Lucyd said fondly. "You've done well. Milady
Danti would be proud of you."

"A pity she didn't see more of us, milord." The unspo-
ken rebuke, *And you, too.* Her tiny black eyes glimmered
reproachfully. Her protocol chip blazed so fiercely she
winced in pain. Then the glimmer winked out, the chip
dimmed, and the dull sheen of dutiful subservience required of a caretaker returned to her.

"You all came," Lucyd said, astonished.

"Doesn't the Imperium expect, milord," Tonel said
evenly, "that the family attend the consecration of our father's sacred sharer and pay our respects? Didn't *you* expect us?"

"I'd hoped, naturally," Lucyd murmured. "But would
never demand." He kneaded his forehead with a trembling
hand.

Danti had been barren.

Her Imperial materia, harvested from her when she was a
girl at the age of ripeness, would not bind with Lucyd's
materia during the Rite of Begetting. The Superior Mother
and Superior Father had quietly explained that sometimes
Pan declined to bless a seeding because of a hidden impurity.

Danti had wept for days.

But the natalists *could* generate a family. Primus Natalry
had sparked her barren birthpods so they would receive and
hold his seed and had grown this brood of cloven sons.

He and Danti had taken custody of the infants when
they'd emerged from the ges tanks, a clutch of clovens who
completely resembled Lucyd but were bereft of any heredi-
tary influence from Danti. He and Danti had promptly
shipped the clovens off to Lucyd's villa in North Siluria,
where Gingi had raised them.

And he and Danti had returned to their idyllic life together of dreaming.

After fifty years, Lucyd was still trying to understand why Danti had hated his sons. And why he'd assumed her hatred as his own.

Now, so many decades later, none of his sons had entered into sacred sharelock. None had generated his own family. *Well, they're still young,* Lucyd thought. But as he gazed at their faces, he glimpsed the lines of age and sorrow etched in complexions as ivory-pale as his own. *Perhaps not so young anymore.*

"Well, then, good-bye, milord." They turned as if one, his sad-faced sons, and walked away.

"Wait! Where are you . . . where are you all staying in Atlan, Tonel?"

Tonel stopped, only half turned back. "Tythys Inn. The rooms are reasonable, the food passable, the wine robust."

"Well, cancel your rooms. Yes, yes. You'll stay at Villa de Reve."

"Oh, no, milord—"

"My son, you may address me as your father. I won't have my family staying at a cut-rate resort in southwest Marketplace. All those brutish magisters."

"Milord . . . my father, we all know how you felt about Milady Danti. This cannot be an easy time for you, despite the consecration." Impassively, "I've never much believed in the Eternal. Only in this transient life."

"Hush, Tonel. Not in the pyramid." But Lucyd smiled at this irreverent child he'd never known. Longing and regret for all that had been lost between them clenched at his heart. Odd fancies formed in his mind, a fancy of the eleven of them lounging in the south dining hall over platters of food and jugs of wine, discussing Pannish philosophy the way he and Danti used to do. Why not? Why couldn't he reclaim his family? He hadn't been cruel to them. He'd always supplied their every need, and generously, too. "I insist."

Tonel shrugged. "We wouldn't think of imposing on you."

" 'Tis no imposition. I've ten rooms on the second story just waiting for you this very moment." It felt pleasant, this parental protectiveness, this expansive hospitality toward strangers he hadn't seen in years. Strangers who also happened to be generated of his Imperial materia. "My staff will be delighted to serve you," he babbled on. The devastation of his grief perceptibly lightened. He felt he was made of air. "I not only insist, Tonel, I demand it as your . . . father."

His sons murmured among themselves and conferred earnestly with Tonel. How polite they were, how dignified. How solemn and reticent, surprise and pleasure tugging at their mirror-image faces.

"Of course, milord, my . . . father. As you wish and demand. May I ask something more?"

"You may, my son."

"If it's all right with you, there's someone else I'd like to bring with me."

A slim figure slipped out of the crowd from behind Lucyd's eldest son. Her white-gold hair formed a shining helmet around the luminous cabochon of her face, a youthful face of no more than twenty years. Slanting sapphire eyes gazed into his, not dead orbs of bone and gemstones, but real eyes.

Living eyes.

Vertigo seized Lucyd and spun him around. Darkness filled his consciousness. Falling, he was falling down a well of memory, into the abyss of grief. If it weren't for the windship, he would have crumpled, senseless, to the floor.

The young woman curtsied, whispered in the familiar beloved voice, "Milord."

"My beloved Danti," Lucyd whispered, the name tearing at his throat, the girl standing before him rending his heart. But of course she wasn't Danti. The corpse of Danti sightlessly stared down at the memorializers below her, celebrating her Eternal Essence with increasing drunkenness and abandon. "Who is this?"

"Milord, my . . . father, this is my colleague, Danatia." Tonel smiled at last, a sardonic smile, cold and tinged with guile. "We're thinking of entering into sharelock."

FACET 8

Triangle: Ascent or descent.
The ax splits a log.
The action is construction.
The forbearance is destruction.

The Orb of Eternity

Commentaries:

Councillor Sausal: All energy originates in Pan and, although Pan is the Highest Ideal, the energy is neither good nor evil, but dynamic. Good and evil emerge when energy manifests in the world and is directed by humanity's will, motives, and circumstances.

So, too, the Imperium commands the resources of the world and applies them for the benefit of the purities. But the Imperium's application of resources must proceed with caution and the observation of consequences, good or ill.

Therefore, the prudent person must carefully consider how any form of dynamic energy is to be applied, for such energy may uplift or degrade.

Guttersage (usu. considered vulgar): A fool wields an ax to split a log when constructing a house.

A fool wields an ax to split a log when destroying a house.

Our City of Atlan, the crest of Prime Hill. Milord Lucyd's cloudscraper, the Villa de Reve:

Traitor. Regim crouched behind the garden wall of the aetherist's cloudscraper and watched him approach. The private windship bobbed gaily up the hill, the decadent plaything of a parasite living off the sorrows and tribulations of the world. To think he, Regim, could have ever dreamed Milord Lucyd's dreams, could have respected him, admired him, revered him.

Puny, parlous angel Look at him, just look at him. All filled with himself, with his ludicrous dreams of Pannish love. This person is the abomination that dreams the Mind of the World?

Yes, the aetherist was a traitor. Or on the verge of treachery, and too stupid to know it. The longer Regim gazed at Milord Lucyd, regal and remote in the luxurious windship, the more he saw a lawless, heartless stooge. Why else would the most notorious Heaven's Devil in all Pangaea suggest the aetherist was a friend of the impure?

How many other angels were friends of the impure? Secure in their cloudscrapers, revered by every purity, dominating every sharemind, initiating every protocol—no wonder the angels had become heedless of Imperial concerns. *They didn't give a damn about the rest of the purities.*

An escort of Vigilance surveillance craft flanked the windship, sheltering the tiny craft from the summer deluge. Rain pattered on Regim's helmet and soaked the shoulders of his raincloak, dripping down his neck and into his collar, sliding down his skin thick and hot as blood.

Hiding behind his pure and subpure like a child clutching at a caretaker's ankles.

Fresh fingers of pain clawed through the wounds in Regim's thigh, jittered down the deep jags carved in his chest. He gnashed his teeth. His gut rumbled, hollow and sick. He was ravenous but hadn't been able to eat because

of the ache in his teeth. He clenched them every time the
pain throbbed. The soporifics the idiot physicians at
Secundus Infirmary had given him didn't touch it, and their
medicines had done nothing to stave off the infection.

He'd taken to medicating himself with liberal doses of
skee. *Do angels receive better medical care than magis-*
ters? Are prefects treated better than vigiles? You'd better
fucking believe it. A high pure and subpure always buys
more of anything. Of everything.

He slipped the flask of skee out of his pocket now, took a
long swallow of the liquor. *Fucking angels.* It had always
been his Imperial duty to protect the angels, the angels first
and foremost. But what had angels ever given him?
Dreams? Their dreams hadn't shielded Clere from a devil
star.

Collaborator, a lousy traitorous collaborator. What
depths of depravity had Milord Lucyd sunk to? How could
he do it? How could he collaborate with Heaven's Devils,
when his own sharer, his own Pannish love, had been cruelly slain by the vermin?

He got fifty years of Danti. I got less than an hour of my
beloved Clere.

Memories of Clere haunted him. How they'd coupled on
the couch before entering into sacred sharelock. Bestial?
Shameful? Never! How sweet and eager she'd been, like a
girl of seventeen, not a woman of fifty-seven. Like a virgin.
She *had* been a virgin. He would never forget the shocking
sight of her blood pooled on the couch where they'd lain
for the first time. What delights they might have shared as
bedmates. What ecstasies he might have given her, and
taken in his turn.

Hire an erotician to satisfy Clere's urge? What could he
have been thinking? Never! Hire an erotician for himself?
No, he would have given up Tahliq in an eyeblink. Clere
had been right, as she'd been right about most things in life.
How could he have permitted the lowest pure and most
despised subpure to touch his fine vigile's body when his

own sharer, a magister and a beautiful sensuous woman, had desired him, and him alone?

How complete sharelock would have been for them— Pannish love, the utter intimacy of sharers' sharemind, *and* sensual satiation of the body. Her burgeoning power would have belonged to him, as well. His own career would have soared. What partners they would have become, reinforcing the Imperium's might with her visionary policies, eliminating impurity and restoring proximity to its rightful place.

He wept to think of all he'd lost.

The sharelock chips ached in his hands. A priestess-facilitator from the Temple of Sharelock had called upon him, informing him he could have the chips removed. "But your sharelock does last for all Eternity, lieutenant. If you think you may want to generate a family with Clere someday, you should leave them in." A doe-eyed woman with a cap of white hair, she'd patted his hand sympathetically. "It will be difficult at first. Your sharemind will reach out for her, and she won't be there. But," she'd added, "every now and then a sharer *does* enter into sharemind with a deceased beloved one. Oh, it's a miracle. The Essence is Eternal, you know."

What if their coupling that night had generated the child Clere had desired? He'd been denied the chance ever to find out. *Curse the Heaven's Devil to hell!* If the Devil girl hadn't shredded Clere's womb, the natalry might at least have been able to harvest the holy fruit, had there been one. At least he would have had the comfort of their first and most special child.

For the five thousandth time, Regim envisioned exactly what he'd do to the Devil girl when he captured her. All the ways he'd prolong her agony and humiliation for days and days.

And he *would* capture her. He would hunt her down like the vicious beast she was till the day he—

"What are you doing in my garden, lieutenant?"

He leapt to attention, knocking his kneecaps against the

wall as he whirled around. Excruciating pain careened up
his thighs. He cursed, ground his teeth. The aetherist
hovered before him in the decadent windship, flanked by
two rows of baleful angels who, from the gloomy, uniform
look of them, must have been Lucyd's clovens.

*Then I was right about one thing, my Clere, and you were
wrong. Milady and milord never did lie together. Or mingle
their materia. They'd sparked clovens. Clovens of milord,
and a pack of weaklings, from the look of them. No wonder
the angels as a purity are dying out.*

"You consented to an interview, milord," Regim managed to gasp after the pain subsided. "Remember?"

"Of course I remember." This, in a supercilious tone, as
if Regim were no more than a beck-and-call man. "I did
not consent to your trespass upon my property."

"Your majordomo admitted me." In fact Regim had lied
to the sniveling drud and cast vigilance sharemind over
him, insisting he had an official warrant to enter.

"Then my majordomo will be whipped. You may come
this way."

The aetherist beckoned to the Vigilance craft hovering
above them, regally signaling the craft to be gone. The craft
hesitated, the crew observing as if he, a vigile—one of
them—posed a security threat to the angels. Regim stared at
the lead craft, running his eyes over its hull. The numbers,
what were the bloody Imperial tracking numbers? Excre-
ment-eating dolts. He would have a harsh word with the
pilots just as soon as he finished his interrogation of Milord
Lucyd. The craft lifted, lumbering away into the wind and
rain, Discourses of Pan and the Roadbuilder flickering
across their hulls in luminous orange kaligraphs.

You may come this way. Scowling, Regim dutifully
trailed after the tiny windship and its effete escorts through
a fabulous garden. Cobblestone paths wound amid exotic
palms, manicured pital and peyr trees, ponds overflowing
with waterplums, fountains gurgling in the rain. The sort of
garden he'd only seen in dreams. In fact he *had* dreamed of

this garden in one of Lucyd's dreams. The notion dazzled
and awed him, the familiarity of this place he'd never seen
before but had only seen in a dream.

Then his wounds throbbed, his rage blazed, and the knot
of resentment tightened around his heart. *Such an indulgence, this garden.* Another notion occurred to him, a notion that had gnawed around the edges of his consciousness
since the consecration, had gnawed and now bit: *This angel
possesses too much. All the angels possess too much. And
what have they done for the Imperium? Plague the purities
with dreams of sumptuous gardens they'll never own.*

The entourage entered the cloudscraper, a slender soaring tower wrought of Tythys marble of such a dazzling
white the sight nearly blinded him. In the vaulted portico
twined with rare ivies and blooming creepers, two ranks of
severely shaped handmaids and beck-and-call men genuflected.

They entered, and Regim found himself in luxurious
multicolored shadows. Cordilleran marble as ink-black as
the exterior marble was bright bedecked curved walls and
expansive floors. Intricate rosette portals set with panes of
stained glass permitted only delicate tinted mists of storm-
soaked light.

The aetherist favored hypnolia vapors. Favored? Regim
could have cleaved the air with his dagger. Cloying scent
clung in his lungs, nearly choking him. Drowsiness drifted
through his consciousness. No! He vigorously shook his
head. He would not succumb to the aetherist's stupefying
vapors.

Lucyd conferred with his clovens, especially the tallest
and weariest among them who held the hand of a slender
feminine figure cloaked and hooded in scarlet velvet. A
dozen deferent handmaids led the clovens up a spiral staircase, disappearing into the heights of the cloudscraper. The
aetherist led Regim into a vast reception chamber cordoned
off into cubicles of varying decor, from luxurious to plain.

The aetherist ushered Regim into a respectable magister cubicle and gestured to a couch upholstered in blue leather.

So. The aetherist grants private audiences even to servs and druds. What would Clere think of that? *Such promiscuous courtesy in such a high pure suggests a consciousness degraded enough to permit contact even with the impure.* Yes. Regim was beginning to understand Clere's frustration with the laxity among the purities.

"You may sit before me, lieutenant." Lucyd spoke a command to the windship. The exit portal flapped open, the ship extruded three trembling exit steps, and at last the aetherist daintily descended, emerging from his translucent blue cocoon. The steps instantly merged with the hull as soon as the aetherist completed his descent. The windship bobbed out of the reception chamber as if the thing were alive and knew exactly what to do.

Regim shivered at this gratuitous display of angel technology and quelled the urge to query: *What is that thing, anyway? Is it sentient? Where did you get it? What fuels it? Does it have a name?*

Disgorged from his fancy little ship, the aetherist stood unsteadily, a wavering stalk of living ivory, the famous face hollow beneath every angle and streaked with tears. He collapsed wearily into a brocaded chair set on a raised dais before Regim.

Regim's heart stirred in sympathy as he arduously lowered himself onto the couch, bending the hinges on his body support at the hip and stretching his girded leg straight before him. This man had lost his sharer of fifty years. . . .

You may sit. Oh, indeed? The purities were the purities, the angels were the angels, but magisters and prefects and vigiles ruled the Imperium these days. Magisters and prefects and vigiles kept the streets safe for all the pures and subpures. Perhaps it was time to reassess the true proximity of the upper purities to Pan. Who had said dreams in the Mind of the World were more dear to Pan than the perpetuity of the Imperium? *The angels, that's who.*

One day the Imperium would prosper and expand into the torrents on the other side of the world, to the moon, to Sanguine, and beyond to other worlds, as the High Council had always promised. Who knew how far the Imperium might reach?

And if that was so, perhaps it was time to reassess the order of the world. Perhaps it was time for a new order. An order ensuring the Imperium without end with firebolts and daggers.

Not dreams.

A battle-ax gleamed for a moment in Regim's consciousness.

The angel glanced at him askance and graciously said, "Would you care for some caf or chai? Perhaps beer or kapfo would be in order. A shot of skee?" The angel sniffed. "You've already imbibed a bit of skee, I think. Better to eat the fruit of the same tree. Your digestion will thank you."

The angel tapped his long, lacquered fingernails against the slender palm of his hand. A stout handmaid dashed into the reception chamber with the dispatch of an athlete. "Dote, bring the lieutenant a shot of skee. And d'ka for me." He sighed deeply. "I'm all undone by that beastly consecration."

"Yes, milord." The handmaid fled and returned with the refreshments before Regim could even think to protest and decline.

Regim refused the shot glass she proffered, but the handmaid set it on a side table next to the couch. In another moment, he found himself reaching for the glass, found himself drinking. The angel's skee was smooth and thick and rich, far superior to what he carried in his pocket flask. *Well, of course, what did you expect?*

"Now then," said the angel, smacking his lips over his

d'ka. ''Why do you think I know this impure person you mentioned?''

''I am Lieutenant Regim Deuceman naitre Secundus—''

''I can see that from your badge.''

''Yes. I entered into sacred sharelock with Prefect Clere Twine on the night of the Big Shock.'' He briefly made the sign of the Imperial star over his chest. ''Councillor Twine is my father-in-lock.''

The angel's eyes widened. ''May Pan preserve Prefect Twine for Eternity.'' With disingenuous courtesy, ''That will bode well for your career, lieutenant.''

''Then you've heard what happened at the temple that night?''

''Everyone in Pangaea heard or invoked Imperial sharemind with a local crier. I'm terribly sorry, truly I am. I had no idea you were Clere Twine's sharer. As you well know, I can sympathize. But I still don't see what that has to do with me.''

Regim studied the angel's thin pale face. *Traitor, puny parlous traitor.* ''Two impure criminals known as Heaven's Devils attempted to abduct Clere. I intercepted them. We fought, and they killed her. One of them mentioned your name as if he knew you.''

The angel's mouth dropped open. It didn't seem possible he could become more pale, but he visibly blanched. *''What?''*

''That's right. Horan Zehar, one of the most wanted criminals in Pangaea, suggested that you dreamed of the Orb of Eternity because you're a collaborator with the impure cause.''

The angel struggled to his feet, pace. ''But that's outrageous. Absurd! I've never heard of this Zehar person, or seen this orb you keep carping about.'' He added, ''I'm famous, of course. Everyone in Pangaea thinks they know me.''

No, you can't hide your depravity from me. I'll roust it out of you, one way or another.

"No doubt," Regim said. "But there's more. The strumpet who appeared in your dream is Horan Zehar's daughter, Salit, herself a Heaven's Devil and a vicious murderer. She gutted Clere, right before my eyes."

Keen satisfaction at the angel's gasp, his anguish. Tears slid down the gaunt cheeks, and he collapsed back into the chair. Good. Good. The angel should suffer as Regim had suffered. As Regim suffered still. Would suffer for Eternity.

"I . . . am . . . so . . . sorry."

"Yes." Regim's voice quavered. "So, milord. Did any impure person approach you before you dreamed the dream?"

"Of course not. And I never go out into the mundanity."

"So you said." Regim thought. "Did anything unusual occur before or during the dream?"

"Well, I was audited by an acolyte-auditor from the Temple of the Mind of the World. Annoying, yes, but hardly unusual."

Regim couldn't resist a barb. "Why," he said, "does Milord Lucyd require auditing?"

The aetherist drew himself up indignantly. "I'm sure I don't know. Why don't you ask the Cardinal yourself? I'd be most interested in Her Holiness's answer."

"And you've had no contact with Heaven's Devils?"

Lucyd's eyes flashed with fury. "Why would I? Hasn't Vigilance determined it was the Heaven's Devils who massacred my beloved Danti?"

"We believe so."

"You *believe*? You don't know this for a fact?"

"No. Unfortunately, we can only speculate."

Vigilance could do no more than deduce from the evidence. Regim had entered into purity sharemind with the official observers who had stood in the garden every three spans. Observers were low magister pures but their subpure possessed extraordinary visual and aural faculties and the capability of ceaselessly focusing their perceptual faculties for incredible lengths of time. Invoking magister sharemind he'd seen and heard what the observers had as if with his own eyes and ears. The exquisite gardens, the lovely slender angels drifting among the roses. Danti herself, the unforgettable face of five thousand dreams.

And then the ripple of shadows behind the south fountain, at the north periphery. Two observers had spied shimmers among the branches of the pital trees. Four small explosions had flared at the corners of the garden and a noxious gas known as cherry laurel had infused the air. Two observers had fainted. The remaining observers had heard an ominous hissing sound as a thousand devil stars flashed through the air, flicked out their startips, and whirled through the angels. Literally *through* them, slicing torsos in half, hacking off limbs, separating heads from necks in decapitations so swift the deed was done before the bodyguards could commence their alarm.

"The official observers never actually saw the perpetrators," Regim said dryly. "We believe they were Devils because the criminals deployed devil stars."

"Devil stars?"

"A multibladed semisentient knife. Deploying it requires considerable expertise. I myself have never been able to throw one. Heaven's Devils are the only clan among the impure that are known to manufacture and deploy them. But there may be others. Hell's Teeth are suspected, as well."

Lucyd heaved a ragged sigh. His handmaid rushed to his side with a silk fan, stirring a breeze over the ivory-white cheeks. "Then we have a common interest in annihilating these Heaven's Devils, lieutenant, don't you agree?"

"So it would seem."

Was there a hint of smugness, of slyness, in the aetherist's expression? A glimmer of relief? An intimation he'd concealed something? Had deceived, and reveled in the deception?

"You're excused, lieutenant," the angel said. "I must dream."

. . .

"You harassed an angel of the highest subpure in public, Lieutenant Deuceman, and caused him great distress at his sharer's consecration," said the Chief Commander of Vigilance. "Your entire squad witnessed your inexcusable behavior."

Regim stood at attention before her high bench in her cavernous private offices on the top story of Vigilance Authority. A massive magister pure with a tremendous halo of blue-white hair, the Chief Commander's expression, always stern, rivaled the thunderclouds churning overhead. Her voice, always astringent, crackled with menace more sharp than the lightning bolts crackling across the sky.

Beside her sat Councillor Claren Twine, Advisor on Impure Activities to the High Council. Regim dared not catch the eye of his forbidding father-in-lock, dared not give the slightest hint that he sought to exploit any connection with his family-in-lock in a confrontation with his superior. Councillor Twine would renounce him, Regim had no doubt. And he would find himself in worse trouble than he already was.

The summer deluge pummeled the tiled roof, sounding more like iron barbs than raindrops. Regim's soaked cloak and uniform had begun to stink of sour wet linen, sweat, his festering infections. His anger clouded around him in a miasma.

The Chief Commander has gone soft on the impure, Clere Twine had told him the day they met. *The Chief Commander needs to be brought before the Chamber of Justice.* He quickly glanced up at the Chief Commander and just as quickly averted his eyes. *Careful. She'll see your contempt, your accusation.*

"I"—Regim bit back the "merely" he wanted to add, felt justified in adding—"I requested that Milord Lucyd disembark from his windship, Chief Commander, according to the wishes of the Highest Councillor and the Supreme Memorializer of the pyramid.'' He sincerely hoped the mintstick he'd chewed before this summons concealed the stench of skee on his breath. ''They requested that Milord Lucyd stand beside them for the consecration. I defer to angels, of course, but I report to magisters. I was attempting to fulfill my Imperial duty.''

''Harassed the angel in full view of a mob of buckwheat threshers and roadbuilders, as well. Do you have any notion how damaging such behavior is to a drud's understanding of purity protocol? Vigilance enforces protocol. Vigilance does not violate it.'' Regim began to protest but the Chief Commander held up her hand. ''That's not all, lieutenant. That's not the worst of it. We know you tracked down milord's private residence, trespassed on his property, and lay in wait for him. Our observers aboard the escort craft saw you. I entered into sharemind with the observers,'' the Chief Commander added. ''Despite the poor visibility, *I* saw you. I'm convinced it was you, sir.''

''Chief Commander, Milord Lucyd granted me an interview. I''—bit back the ''merely'' again—''I waited for him at his residence and was duly admitted to the grounds by his majordomo.''

''Not according to Milord Lucyd,'' the Chief Commander said acidly. ''According to milord, you improperly exercised your vigilance sharemind to force the majordomo to admit you to the garden. Regretfully, milord was compelled to whip the majordomo for contradicting his express orders. Milord feels very badly. And milord believes you've abused your vigilance sharemind.''

Dear Pan! Had the aetherist communicated so swiftly with the Chief Commander? Favor at the High Council? Obviously, from the appearance of Councillor Twine at this summons. Favor at Vigilance, too.

''I didn't mean to improperly—''

''One moment, my son-in-lock,'' Councillor Twine said. How much he resembled his deceased daughter. The blond hair threaded with grey, the tall, angular physique. The pale, slightly crossed blue eyes that regarded him down the length of the distinctive prominent nose. The councillor drew on a bacco cheroot. He'd had a growth removed from the inside of his throat and spoke in a whisper that managed to reverberate throughout the Chief Commander's chambers. Fondly, to the Chief Commander, "Perhaps we should inquire why my son-in-lock has acted so improperly, dear Gwenda."

Dear Gwenda?

Regim waited, anxiety and anticipation thrumming in his blood.

Councillor Twine stood, descended from the bench, and paced to and fro before Regim. "After all, he's a vigile with an outstanding record of service and obedience. And the sacred sharer of my dearly beloved late daughter." Now Councillor Twine caught his eye and addressed Regim directly. "My son-in-lock, why have you pursued Milord Lucyd in this uncouth manner?"

Regim dropped to his knees, offering his submission, conceding to his lower status. He presented himself several head-lengths below the councillor, instead of towering over the elder magister if he'd been standing. "I have reason to believe Milord Lucyd has commenced a collaboration with the Heaven's Devils to taint the Mind of the World."

The Chief Commander exhaled sharply. "Milord Lucyd is one of Pangaea's most eminent citizens. Do you realize what you're saying, lieutenant? That would amount to a crime of the most heinous dimensions against the Imperium. That's an outrageous slur, a slander, a blasphemy, and by claiming it, you commit a crime, as well."

"Patience, Gwenda," said Councillor Twine. "My beloved Clere—Regim's beloved Clere—was slain by Heaven's Devils. The lieutenant was grievously wounded attempting to defend her. *Those* are heinous crimes against the Imperium. Let's hear what my son-in-lock has to say."

The councillor gazed into Regim's eyes, blue into blue,

and a twinkle of complicity hidden deep in his autocratic facade surfaced for a moment.

His father-in-lock; sympathetic? As the lower subpure and inferior sharer in his sharelock with Clere, Regim had moved his possessions into his assigned quarters at the Twine family compound, an intimidating fortress of grey stone at the crest of Majestic Heights. Since the night of Clere's murder, though, he had neither dined nor conversed with anyone of the Twine family, and all the handmaids, averting their eyes, had been pledged to a vow of silence. Staff memorializers from the Pyramid of Perpetuities had cheerfully bustled about, preparing the household for Clere's consecration to the Eternal. But the family had gone into seclusion and private mourning.

Especially Councillor Claren Twine. He'd neither sought out Regim to express his condolences nor sent a message setting forth what he now expected of his son-in-lock. Regim, expecting either or both, had spent long, lonely evenings in his new quarters, alternately plunged into rage and grief or numbing his physical pain with quantities of skee.

Encouraged by that twinkle now, Regim reprised the struggle in the duct that night, the inconclusive yet provocative interview with Lucyd. "If you dreamed Milord Lucyd's dream on the morning of the Big Shock, you would have seen how Milady Danti changed into Salit Zehar. You would have seen the Orb of Eternity and the oracle of Darkness."

The Chief Commander snorted. "One could very well interpret the aetherist's dream as an extraordinarily prescient warning. Of the Big Shock. Of the tragedy at the temple. Perhaps both. If Milord Lucyd is a collaborator, surely he wouldn't announce it in a dream in the Mind of the World."

"And surely you would never concede, Gwenda, that an impure abomination like the Orb of Eternity actually possesses the power of prescience," Councillor Twine said coolly.

The Chief Commander blanched. "Of course not, Claren. I'm suggesting the angel himself may possess prescience. Some do."

"But the angel denies he's ever seen an orb before," Regim blurted out. "Why would he employ the orb's image, then, to express his warning?"

"Lieutenant!" barked the Chief Commander.

He bowed his head, bit his lip. "Forgive me. I spoke out of turn."

"No, I have to agree that the angel's dream casts suspicion directly on the angel," said Councillor Twine. "Milord Lucyd ought to be investigated. Place him under surveillance, Chief Commander."

The Chief Commander scribbled a note. "Very well," she said reluctantly. "That still doesn't give the lieutenant permission to act at his own whim." To Regim, "Why haven't you reported all this to Colonel Dikson?"

"We lieutenants have an unpleasant name for the colonel, Chief Commander, which I do not wish to repeat in these chambers. A name that suggests how well—or poorly—the colonel administers the impure matters under his jurisdiction."

"Colonel Dikson is my personal appointee," the Chief Commander snapped.

Gone soft on the impure . . .

"With all due respect, and given my sincere personal interest, Chief Commander, I thought I might make some preliminary investigations myself without the standard procedures Vigilance employs that so often alert our quarry of our intentions. Naturally," Regim added, "I intended to report any significant findings to the colonel. I'd hoped I might assist in any official action."

"That is insubordination, Lieutenant Deuceman," said the Chief Commander.

"You may stand, my son-in-lock," said Councillor Twine. He turned on his heel as Regim rose and rejoined the Chief Commander at her bench.

The two distinguished magisters lowered their heads and conferred, the Chief Commander highly agitated, Regim's father-in-lock composed and earnest. Regim stood at attention, eyes averted. He dared not attempt sharemind with his father-in-lock, though he knew now that Claren was sympathetic. His worry was the Chief Commander. She was a canny magister and a superior vigile subpure, the scope of her apprehension broader than Regim's. She would discern any sharemind they attempted in her presence and enter as well.

The distinguished heads lifted, parted. The whispered conference was over.

Regim clenched his teeth, wincing at the pain. *What have I done? By fulfilling my Imperial duty have I ruined myself?* There'd be a reprimand, of course. Perhaps even a demotion. Would the Chief Commander bring official charges of protocol violation and abuse of vigilance sharemind?

The Chief Commander glared down at him, displeasure clenching every muscle in her massive face. "As your highest superior, Lieutenant Deuceman, I hereby inform you that you are promoted to lieutenant captain in recognition of your obedience to the higher obligations of your Imperial duty. You are relieved of all standard surveillance duties and assigned to investigation of the impure."

"Lieutenant captain?" Regim whispered, astounded. His first mother hadn't made lieutenant till she was fifty-five. Neither his father nor his second mother had ever risen above the rank of walkabout vigile. He swiftly controlled his shock—his glee!

No, why should he be surprised? Higher rank, greater power—*these are everything you deserve, Regim.* Investigation of the impure? He could think of nothing else he cared to devote his life to. He'd been handed an official license to hunt Salit Zehar. To torture and finally kill her.

He summoned the proper humility and saluted smartly. "Thank you, Chief Commander."

"And as your highest superior's superior, Lieutenant

Captain Regim," Councillor Twine said impassively, "I hereby inform you that you are to report directly to me."

The Chief Commander needs to be brought before the Chamber of Justice. . . .

Regim saw a brief flicker of a hooded eyelid.

The councillor winked.

Muck pooled on the broken cobblestones of Jugglers Lane. Clumps of ash as foul as excrement sluiced to the edges of the fissure still gaping in the middle of the lane and slid in. This was all that was left of the Bawdy Harridan: muck and soot consigned by the summer rain to the open sewer foaming in the cleft of the lane.

Regim picked his way, placing the metal tip of his body support on the soiled cobblestones with extreme caution. He'd slipped more than once on the rain-slick streets that day.

Somewhere drums beat a tattoo in the quarter, pipes shrilled, a cymbalon strummed. The denizens of Jugglers Lane had taken the Big Shock and summer rain with equanimity. Regim frowned, perplexed and displeased at the sound of such gaiety amid the filth and ruin and inclement weather. He disliked the insistent beat, the shrill ebullience.

How could the Imperium harness the irrepressible exuberance of the lower purities? Did the Imperium truly rule them? What did it mean to rule? That proximity and purity protocol were to be observed at the end of a security club? Or were the dreams of the angels an enforcement tool, as well? *If that's so, then the contamination of Lucyd's dream is a heinous crime, indeed.* If only Clere were here, they could discuss everything.

"Hai, vigile. Ain't seen you around here in a while."

The saloonkeep of the Harridan vigorously assisted the rain's work with a shovel and broom. Ergeo grinned. His sharer, a porcine creature whose fleshy jowls always looked bruised, glared at him. "Once we clear away this ash heap, we'll rebuild her again, don't you worry. We'll have her on her feet in no time. If our Imperium knows no end, neither does our Harridan.''

Stupid creature. Well, the Imperium required vast numbers of pures and subpures fit and willing for labor and serving. And content with their pures. *Content among the pures and subpures is the backbone of the Imperium,* this was the first lesson Regim had learned at Vigilance Academy. Stupidity was necessary, then, if sometimes inconvenient.

Ergeo shoved his face up to Regim's. He stank of teq and sweat and qut. ''I'd say the Imperium *can't* last without our Harridan, eh? I'd say the Imperium needs our Harridan's drink to go on. What do you say to that, vigile?'' The proprietor slapped him on the back in a comradely way.

Regim flinched and ducked away from the vile touch. Bile stained his throat. A throb recommenced in his wounds through the thickness of soporifics and skee. At any other time of his life, he would have slammed his security club in the saloonkeep's suety gut for daring to touch a vigile and a superior pure. As a walkabout, he would never have tolerated such behavior from subjects in his territory. His command of the streets had demanded dominance and distance from all the pures and subpures, except the angels.

And at any other time of his life, he would have slammed the saloonkeep's drunken consciousness with vigilance sharemind. He shuddered now, recalling his days as a walkabout. He'd often cast his vigilance sharemind over mobs of unruly druds or servs. He'd always felt soiled afterward, as if clods of excrement had struck him in the face.

Now he could wield neither his security club nor his vigilance sharemind. *So weak. So weary. So much pain.* The conference with the Chief Commander had exhausted him. He could only ignore the saloonkeep's raucous laughter and stumble away as swiftly as he was able. *I won't forget, you poxy serv.* The muck, the stink, the drumbeat, the steady rain—he had to get out of the street, had to sit, before he swooned.

How he *loathed* this debility!

Oddly, as if through no volition of his own, Regim found himself standing before the Salon of Shame. He hesitated, then rapped with the tip of his body support on the rose-pink door. Mout the handmaid genuflected and beckoned him within.

"Tahliq," he rasped, exercising his prerogative.

"You're soaked to the skin," Tahliq cried as he hobbled into the foyer. "My sweet, my sweet. Get out of that wet cloak at once. Let me help you, my darling. Permit me to serve you."

Clere's silent condemnation—*you would let a drud sub-pure touch your magister's body?*—stung in his ears.

Tahliq wore scarlet silk today, her mounds of flesh, her prominent nipples, visible through the fragile draperies. She'd coiled her hair atop her head in a gleaming bronze crown.

He should be repulsed. He should revile her. Yet he did not. Desire stabbed him at the sight of her in a way the sight of Clere had never done. It was shameful, disgraceful, the lowest urge of a beast.

And yet here he was, as if he were iron, she a magnet.

Her touch was so familiar, comforting and tender, as the erotician eased him out of his wet cloak. He permitted Tahliq's touch the way he'd always permitted her ministrations, bestial anticipation rising in his loins.

But he had entered into sacred sharelock, still wore the diamond-shaped chips in his hands. Clere may have died, but their sharelock lasted for all Eternity. That's what the priestess had said, but what did it mean? What was he supposed to do? He reached into the intimacy of sharer's sharemind, searching for her, beseeching her Eternal Essence to come to him.

Silence. Nothing. The priestess had warned him. He nearly wept with frustration and grief.

"Dear Afrodite, what is this body support?" Tahliq said in an appalled whisper. She stared at him, her huge dark eyes darting over him. His movements throughout the day had torn open his wounds, soaking his bandages, staining his uniform. "Come, take it off, take these clothes off, too, and get into the bath. At once, my Regim."

"The bath? No, no . . ."

"My sweet, at once! We must soak off these foul stains and cleanse you. I have herbs that will help. What the devil have your damn physicians done to you?"

He permitted her to lead him to her bath, an enormous tub of beaten copper the color of her sleek skin. Her handmaids scurried for washcloths, soaps, and towels, and served him his favorite honeyed meatbits speared with splinters of teak. Tahliq mulled over a row of crystal jars filled with variegated powders.

As hot water cascaded from the spigots, he winced and swallowed skee from his flask. "Is this water from the Rancid Flats Reservoir?" he asked uneasily.

She smiled, tossed a handful of crushed blue leaves into the bath. "My darling, I've got special arrangements with the watermaster for Jugglers Lane. You needn't fear any impurity."

Impurity. Through his haze of pain and intoxication, suddenly Regim remembered. *Impurity.* Tahliq had possessed an Orb of Eternity. Tahliq had entertained a mysterious visitor who'd vanished at his arrival. Vanished the way Heaven's Devils did in plain view of Vigilance authorities. The way Salit Zehar had vanished that night.

Impurity.

He would have leapt to his feet if he'd had the strength, spit out the honeyed meatbit the handmaid had fed him. Arrested her and her handmaids. No hesitating this time.

But the pain and the skee and the infernal blue leaves she'd dumped in the bathwater enervated him as thoroughly as if he'd become a helpless cripple. His legs, his muscles, felt like quicksand. He couldn't command his lips and tongue to spit out the meatbit. Poison. Had the drud witch poisoned him? Helpless rage staggered through his blood.

He and Clere had kept the date and time of their sharelock under strictest security, to be announced to the criers only after the ceremony was completed. The lower pures, let alone the impure, could have had no knowledge of when and where the ceremony was to take place.

"*You*, Tahliq," he whispered. "I told *you* I was entering into sacred sharelock that night."

FACET 9

Sun: An angel or a devil.
The sun nourishes or scorches vegetation.
The action is enthusiasm.
The forbearance is wrath.

The Orb of Eternity

Commentaries:

Councillor Sausal: We have contemplated the Essence of reality and the illusion of duality. Next, the abstract shapes of mathematics and geometry.

Next we contemplate the natural features and phenomena of the world and how they stand in proximity to Pan.

As Pan is ever-present, penetrating the highest clouds and the deepest rocks, so our sun that fosters life always shines. Yet now the sun shines in our eyes, then shines upon the torrents of the world.

So, too, the Imperium governs public life, influences private life, and appears in dreams. But only Pan lives within one's Essence.

Therefore the prudent person must cultivate faith, but beware of fanaticism.

Guttersage (usu. considered vulgar): A fool who labors beneath the sun all day becomes as golden as sunlight.

A fool who could labor beneath the sun all day and all night would burn into a cinder.

*Our City of Atlan, the periphery of Northwest Marketplace,
Rancid Flats. Jugglers Lane, the Salon of Shame:*

"And I wept till my eyes ran dry when I heard what happened at the temple that night," Tahliq said. "And then I wept some more. One of the worst atrocities the foes have ever committed against the Imperium. I'm sorry, my sweet, truly I am."

"Are you, Tahliq?" Regim raised his brilliant blue eyes and glared at her. Such malice in those eyes! "Or perhaps you're glad."

"Glad! Why would I be glad?"

"You'd started singing Milady Danti's theme to me—"

"A pretty melody—"

"—and I told you to stop, that it was useless and impossible. And then you wept when I told you I was entering into sharelock that evening with Clere Twine—"

"—wept with joy. For you. For her—"

"You wept with sorrow that you and I can never share. Will never share."

That day he'd been solicitous, even sympathetic. Passionate! He'd kissed her again on the casting carpet, kneeling before her on the library floor. And she'd dared hope, as she'd always hoped, that he'd return to her pleasure couch again. He was, after all, a lusty young vigile entering into sharelock with an ugly stick thirty-two years his senior. An autocratic woman of a much higher subpure.

And for what? Pannish love? Political gain?

As the lower subpure, he would have had to respect Clere Twine's prerogative. Bend to her will. To her protocol. The Twine family could afford to hire caretakers for their children, but Clere could have demanded that he give up his career at Vigilance to caretake them himself. He would have had to learn the language of deference, the postures of submission.

I wonder how my fine arrogant Regim would have liked his place as Clere Twine's inferior sharer?

Now his tone was mean. Worse than mean. Vicious.

Annoyed, Tahliq sat back on her heels at the side of her capacious copper bathtub, swept aside her scarlet silk, and planted her hands on her hips. Her hips, usually so abundant and firm, felt slack, flaccid, almost scrawny. She'd been off her feed for days. She couldn't bear the smell of her usual morning feast of roast rock hen and apple wine. Her courses were due today, and now this outburst from the only bedmate she'd ever truly loved?

He didn't seem likely to desire indulgence in the shameful urge. Good. She would have accommodated him, as always, but not gladly. She'd inserted a sponge into her pleasure passage to absorb the flow of her courses, and her belly felt swollen and achy.

She'd felt uneasy since he'd burst through her rose-pink door, trailing the stink of trouble. Since he'd arrived, seething with his pain and his pique, the shadows cast by her magmalamps at this storm-soaked noon had shimmered strangely. Erratic shadows. Familiar shadows. Where had she seen these shadows before? Summer rain hammered her rooftop in uneven tattoos.

Wasn't that just like Regim, sniping at her like a nasty little boy, and at just the moment when she succored him sweetly. He'd arrived without warning or a prior assignation. Had she ordered her handmaids to turn him away? Had she refused to see him?

Of course not. She never refused Regim, though she was late for the Festival of Motherwine on Sanguine. It had been twenty-two seasons since the Grand Mistress of the Bloody Fishes Sect had lain upon her pleasure couch, and Tahliq had glimpsed, with her allpure sharemind, the secrets of the atlantium miners, their strange sect, and the Door to Sanguine.

She'd had her courses that morning, too. And at every full moon, Tahliq had pressed between her brows the simulated protocol chip of the Imperial Atlantium Mining Consortium and met the sect's smugglers. They'd always designated the place for their clandestine rendezvous the previous day by a message slipped into her morning delivery of wine or sometimes among the pastries.

She had no intention of missing her rendezvous that day.

Still, when she'd laid eyes upon Regim, his suffering face, his soiled clothes, she'd set aside all preparations for her departure.

Set aside everything for him.

Yes, she'd wept with sorrow when he'd told her of his impending sharelock with Clere Twine. Yes, she'd wept with glee when she'd heard Clere Twine had been executed. Ha! and ha! Cruelty was as cruelty did. Regim, coming to bed her every three days over nine full seasons. They couldn't share? They didn't share? With her allpure sharemind she'd proven—to herself, if not to him—they *could* share Pannish love, the utter intimacy of sharelock, and more. Even without his knowledge of her allpure sharemind, he shared his thoughts, his feelings, his passion, his time. His fine strong body.

Perhaps she'd kept her presence *too* quiet when they entered into her allpure sharemind. She'd concealed herself completely from him, while encompassing his entire consciousness. *Is the sharemind I possess when I lie with a patron more powerful than that of a magister's, then?* How much of his wrath would she provoke if she revealed her deception now?

He was the higher pure. He held the power to shape relations between them, shape them differently—if he'd chosen. As the lower pure, she could offer nothing but her body, her loyalty, her love. And had no other choice, no other recourse under purity protocol.

The Imperium would have frowned on their union. The temple might have forbidden their sharelock. All Pangaea would disapprove, and make life difficult for both of them.

But he could have chosen.

Instead he'd chosen to spurn her. Denied all she'd tenderly, constantly nurtured between them. Abandoned the truth of his own heart, the unity they'd always felt together, in the name of sacred sharelock and his Imperial duty.

Gotten his comeuppance, had her fine arrogant Regim. And sooner than Tahliq could have ever envisioned. She recalled her foreboding after the Big Shock, her certainty, *Something else will happen. Something terrible.* That day she'd thought she'd sensed his announcement of his impending sharelock. His renunciation of her, a dismissal with a ring of finality. Now she knew her foreboding had presaged a far grimmer event. Her casting of the orb for Horan Zehar had confirmed it. Regim had been ravaged by the terrorism against him. It was terrible to see.

Yet cruelty is as cruelty does, she thought and smiled her sardonic smile.

Tahliq sorrowed a little for Clere Twine. The prefect had suffered the worst way anyone can. But all her life Clere Twine had enjoyed the privileges of the magister purity. She'd finagled Regim's Pannish love. She'd earned a reputation as the most notorious prefect of Our Sacred City, preaching purges and purgatories at every storm season, finding an impure under every bed, an impurity in every thought other than her own. She'd been the feared ally of her fearsome father. Feared and hated by many among the pures and subpures, from angels to druds. Many had disapproved of her harassment of the impure, who—Tahliq and others thought—mostly deserved pity. Many had not been unhappy to learn Clere Twine would never advance to the High Council one day.

Ha! and ha! So the foes had struck down Clere Twine as Tahliq knew they would one day, and *much* sooner than later. Who was truly sorry? The Twine family, of course. Regim Deuceman? Anyone would think so. Yet there he reclined in her bathtub, no more than a handful of days after the tragedy of his lifetime. A handful of days since he'd renounced her and reduced her to tears.

It will be quite some time, she decided, *before I shed tears over this man again.*

She took up a washcloth to rinse his shoulders, and her uneasiness returned. There! What was *that*? A dart of darkness, an unaccountable rustling. "Mout! There's a palm beetle in the corner of the bath chamber. Kill it at once."

"Yes, my dame." The handmaid lumbered away for a handnet and pincers.

Why did his beautiful blue eyes glint with ugly suspicion? With hatred? At her, at *her*? "I don't understand this sudden foul mood, my sweet. I know you're in pain—"

"Who did you tell about my sharelock ceremony, Tahliq?"

"Who did I *tell*— Why, no one!"

He studied her, his jaw muscles clenching, unclenching. She could hear the grinding of his teeth. "How do you know about what happened that night?"

"The criers, of course. They ran from street corner to street corner, with the Imperial sharemind. Rumors spread like wildfire that night. It was the talk of Jugglers Lane. Of all Atlan." She added, "At a prefect and a vigile's sharelock ceremony, of all things."

He nodded, missing her sarcasm, and relaxed a little. "That's what Milord Lucyd said, too." Curiosity stole over his face. "What did the criers say about me, exactly?"

Always worrying about what others thought of him, that was Regim. Yet he persisted in his heedless ways. Tahliq said tartly, "That Clere Twine and her new sharer were viciously attacked by the Heaven's Devils just after they'd entered into sharelock. Of course I knew they meant you, my sweet, even if they didn't say so."

He struggled to sit up, the herb-strewn bathwater splashing, his handsome golden face twisted with torment despite her efforts to soothe him.

Now what?

"The criers didn't identify me by name? Didn't mention my new rank, my new family-in-lock?"

"Well, no, my sweet. I'm certain the Twine family wished to protect your privacy, and commanded the criers not to mention you by name. The Twine family possesses that kind of power.''

''How would you know what kind of power the Twine family possesses?''

''Everyone knows about the Twines. Such suspicions, my sweet! In Milady Faro's dream of the assault on the temple—''

''There's a *dream* in the Mind of the World?''

''Well, of course! You should dream more often, Regim. The dream depicts so well the bravery of the councillors and prefects. And the vigiles, they were so brave, especially the one who slew the Heaven's Devil. It's quite thrilling!''

''Tahliq,'' he said impatiently. ''I was *there. I'm* the vigile who slew the Devil.''

''Oh. Um.'' Tahliq studied him skeptically. Could it be true this battered man lying naked in her bathtub was actually the vigile who slew the Devil in the most popular dream in the Mind of the World? But of course. It *had* been his sharelock ceremony. She shuddered at his stained bandages. Still, it was hard to believe.

Sometimes the dreams of the angels seem more real than reality.

''In any case,'' she added, ''Milady Faro didn't cast in the dream the terrible harm the foes did to you, my poor Regim.'' The bathwater had finally loosened his bandages. She gently pulled them away and gasped.

Deep purple punctures, festering abrasions, blackening flesh marred his muscular chest, his flat abdomen, his sturdy thigh. Scarlet threads of infection traced down the length of his leg, up his arm, through his biceps.

Her mouth parched. She could scarcely swallow. Whispered, ''Oh, my darling. We must treat you at once.'' She reached for her jar of crimson chihli, poured out a handful of the potent astringent into the bathwater. ''This will sting, but that means it's cleansing the wounds.''

He lashed out, caught her wrist in two massive fingers,

bent her hand back. "More of your drud sorceries? I think not, Tahliq."

"Yes, yes. You'll lose your leg if we don't purge the infection as soon as possible. Dear Afrodite," she murmured. She'd never seen such ugly wounds. "A devil star did this?"

"And how do you know what sort of wounds devil stars inflict?"

"You told me all about them yourself, Regim. On the day Milady Danti died."

"Yes. I suppose I did." He released her wrist and brooded as she scattered crimson chihli powder into his bathwater. He glanced sidelong at her, keen suspicion glinting in his eyes again.

She sighed. *And now what?* He was impossible today.

" '*One* of the worst atrocities'? Isn't that what you said? What did you mean by that?"

"Well, my sweet." She gently scrubbed his shoulder blades, running her hands down the sculptural column of his spine. How his body delighted her. Yet despite the hot water and fragrant herbs, he still stank of his anger and illness. She ran the spigots again. "There's Milady Danti and the angels, of course. Not that your tragedy is any less," she added as he whipped around to glare at her again.

He was a keg of firepowder, waiting to explode. "What did you do the night of my sharelock, Tahliq?"

"You know very well what I do every night."

His frown deepened. She'd never discussed her other patrons with him. "Who was here with you that afternoon? Just as I entered."

"But there was no one."

"There was, and you know it, Tahliq."

"*There was no one.*" She stood, signaled Mout. "As you plainly saw for yourself."

"No! Someone was here. And someone vanished. The way Heaven's Devils do." He tried to stand again, could not. The anodyne in the blue bay leaves was doing its work. That, and his skee, and the soporific spice she'd flavored the honeyed meatbits with, would keep this vigorous young vigile on his bum for at least an hour.

"You're mistaken, my Regim. Sadly, I've got to go. Mout, fetch Dame Marik." She snapped her fingers at the handmaid. "Regim, my healer will assist you with your bath and dress those wounds with fresh bandages. Mout?"

Be quick, girl. She shot a command in drud sharemind to the stupid creature, apprehending in turn Mout's plodding acquiescence. *How awful to enter into sharemind with a drud of such limited intelligence. What a waste purity sharemind can be.*

The handmaid scurried away, heading for the healer's lodge two blocks away on Iberian Avenue.

Regim heaved back against the tub, splashing water everywhere. "Oh, no. I don't want your drud healer."

"She's very good, my sweet. Marik probably knows more about devil star wounds than your physicians at Secundus Infirmary." Tahliq brushed the golden curls off his fevered forehead with soft, cool fingertips.

"I'll not have a drud touch me." Knowing full well she was a drud pure. Cruel Regim.

"As it happens," she said airily, "my healer is the sacred sharer of a fine walkabout vigile. Officer Bower. Perhaps you know him?"

He started at that. "How could a drud healer enter into sharelock with a magister subpure?"

Pointedly, voice dripping with acid, "Bower applied for an Imperial exemption. Oh, he was denied, but he appealed to the temple and signed all the natalry disclaimers. You do know there are exemption procedures, don't you, Regim? Didn't they teach you that at Vigilance Academy?"

He scowled. "A vigile could never be satisfied with a drud healer."

"It seems Bower couldn't be satisfied *without* Marik. Oh, they had to submit to compatibility testing and a faith evaluation, naturally, but Marik knew she and Bower would match just fine. They installed sharelock chips, and everything. Marik says that with the chips they achieve full sharers' sharemind, and the discrepancy between their purity sharemind has just about disappeared.''

''Impossible. Can't be done.''

''But it can. And has. They enter into each other completely.'' *As I enter you, my Regim.*

He started again. Had he apprehended her? Then he shook his head, scandalized. ''How could a vigile permit his progeny to grow in a drud natalry? His sons and daughters would all turn out to be druds, street healers or worse, without any possibility—''

''Wrong again, my sweet. Bower obtained permission to beget and grow his and Marik's unborn in Secundus Natalry. They'll have the best of any magister pure. You see, Bower loves Marik in a thousand different ways. Of course, they're bedmates, too. Neither Marik nor her sharer ever patronize eroticians. They're much too preoccupied with each other.''

He continued to glare at her, but she could see the simmer of guilt in his eyes. *So he would have returned to my couch even if Clere Twine had lived. How would he have concealed my fees from her, I wonder?*

''And now Marik enjoys all the benefits of magister *and* drud purities. She can touch and speak first to just about anyone, defer when she wishes, and never offends anyone's protocol.''

''Sounds promiscuous. Sounds like just the sort of aberration the Imperium shouldn't permit.''

''Works well for a healer. I daresay you'll be glad when she heals these wounds and relieves your pain.''

''Your healer is one in a million,'' Regim grudgingly conceded.

''She certainly is. She's the best healer I've ever met. Marik heals every pure and subpure, except the angels, and everyone knows angels never need healing. I'd never send anyone unworthy of you, my darling.''

Tahliq stood. Her knees ached from kneeling beside the bathtub while she tended him. *It will be quite some time,* she decided again, *before I kneel for this man again.*

"Tahliq, you are not to leave," he warned.

"I must go, my sweet. I'm late."

She took out her jewel box, chose ruby rings and gold bracelets studded with more rubies. She stood before the massive mirror in her bath chamber and preened, smiling at her reflection, ignoring Regim's avid eyes. She pressed the simulated protocol chip into her forehead and swiftly concealed it from him with a headband of scarlet silk. She furled a cloak of heavy scarlet suede around her shoulders. What else? Scarlet suede boots that laced up to her knees? Absolutely. It would be bitter cold on Sanguine. She popped a mintstick into her mouth to soothe her uneasy stomach. She strode out the bath chamber door without a glance back.

"Tahliq!" Regim called after her, his voice hoarse with desperation. "What were you doing with an Orb of Eternity that afternoon?"

She paused. "With what?"

He tried to lift himself from the bath, failed. "I saw it move. Then disappear."

"My sweet, you *are* seeing things. You ought to go easy on the skee."

"You'd better tell me, Tahliq."

She turned, then, and fluttered her long eyelashes. "Why, my darling, what the devil is an Orb of Eternity? And how do *you* know about orbs?"

Money changed hands between the Bloody Fishes smuggler and the Doorkeeper while Tahliq waited beneath a wide-brimmed rainshade. They stood behind the weather-beaten stable sheltering the Doors, then hastily stepped inside.

Tahliq slipped in behind the two women. Both were short hirsute atlantium miner subpures with muscular shoulders and genuine protocol chips twinkling in their foreheads between the dark slits of their eyes.

This was the moment of danger, when security officers of Imperial Atlantium Mining Consortium could intercept her. If they did, they'd search her and discover that her protocol chip wasn't genuine. "What will they do if they discover me?" she'd asked the Grand Mistress when, twenty-two seasons ago, the eminent atlantium miner had proposed that she preside at the Festival of Motherwine. The Grand Mistress had patted her shoulder. "We lost our last Blessed Vessel to the consortium's wrath. But don't worry," she'd added cheerfully. "We've learned our lesson. We won't let them discover you."

Tahliq shivered. She'd witnessed the consortium's security officers flog a drayer to death for bolting at the Door's threshold. She'd shivered with a deeper chill when twenty-two seasons ago the Grand Mistress had told Tahliq the rumors were true—the Imperium possessed the means to go to the moon and Sanguine. It was true—settlements and industries eked out an existence on the other worlds, atlantium mining on Sanguine, waste disposal on the moon. It was true—for nearly a century the Imperium and the consortiums managing the industries had kept the Doors, the settlements, the industries, an Imperial Secret.

How many protocol chips had bound how many minds? How many floggings? How many people had discovered the Secret and shouldn't have? How many had disappeared?

"Do you know how to keep a secret?" the Grand Mistress had asked her.

Tahliq certainly did.

Now the Doorkeeper grinned and said, "This way, my dame. Watch your step, but step quickly."

She waved Tahliq into the queue.

After the trek through the sultry storm from Jugglers Lane, winding here and there on the bucolic paths of the

Iapetus Plains, Tahliq still felt uneasy. So uneasy. If Regim had brought restless shadows with him, she'd carried those shadows with her when she'd left the Salon of Shame.

The Door to Sanguine loomed before her as lofty as two tall prefects standing one atop the other, as broad as five hefty vigiles standing shoulder to shoulder. Lintel, jambs, and threshold of petrified oak had been set into concrete stained a deep turquoise blue. It resembled nothing so much as an ancient Iapetus stablegate of gigantic proportions.

It was in a defunct steedstable south of Magestic Heights amid the golden buckwheat fields of the Iapetus Plains that both Doors had been discovered. The stable, a ramshackle structure built in times lost to antiquity, had been slated for demolition to make way for an Imperial roadway. Storytellers among the atlantium miners still told the Tale of the Roadbuilder Who Stepped on Sanguine, the amusing version in Sanguinese nurturies, the bawdy version in taverns.

Tahliq had no doubt that the abrupt change in scenery when the hapless roadbuilder had stumbled through the Door from verdant rolling fields to barren red Sanguinese mountains would have been enough to cause the most stalwart man to loosen his bowels in shock.

The second Door opened to the moon. Smaller but no less efficacious, this Door had been discovered shortly after the first by a methodical search, rather than the accidental bumbling of a roadbuilder.

"After they discovered the Doors and what they did, where they led, and what lay on the other side," the Grand Mistress had said twenty-two seasons ago, "the High Council authorized the consortiums. Then the dear old supers conscripted suitable subpures of laborers."

Like all the miners, the Grand Mistress had worked her whole life on Sanguine and was sharelocked with another miner. When it came to the bestial urge, though, her preference ran to men. She'd indulged her shame only when on a rare leave on Pangaea, and only with licensed eroticians. Tahliq had been pleased to furnish her with Qon Qinto naitre Quintus, a handsome and skillful erotician who often split fees with Tahliq. The Grand Mistress so seldom saw men, she'd been shy around Qon Qinto. Tahliq had lain with them both, their cheerful assistant.

After he'd gone, Tahliq had rubbed oil onto the Grand Mistress's shoulders, entering softly, quietly into her allpure sharemind—and the astonishing Secret had tumbled into their mutual consciousness.

"The consortiums installed protocol chips so we cannot speak of the Doors to anyone who doesn't speak of them first. Well, that rules out just about everyone 'cept our supers and their supers, doesn't it? Yet you spoke first, Dame Tahliq. I don't know how you know, but now that you've spoken, I can speak, too."

Tahliq had kept her silence. Oh yes, she could keep secrets.

"Is it really true," the Grand Mistress had ventured, "that you've still got your courses? Have you ever heard of the Festival of Motherwine?"

Jingle of bridles, tramp of boots, groans and curses of drayers and drivers. Flash of brass, flare of magmalamps, wink of protocol chips in foreheads. Ceaseless commerce marched through the Door. At the threshold, the heady mix of hot Pangaean mist and Sanguinese frost formed a dense alkaline fog that squeezed a sneeze out of Tahliq.

"Hai, move your ass!"

"Get up, poxy drud."

"Bog you, chum!"

"Tah, I'll flog your butt."

No beasts pulled the handcarts lumbering over the threshold. No beast had yet been bridled that could withstand the shock of stepping through the Door. Huge muscular drayers did the job, many of them wearing blinders as well as protocol chips. Tahliq spied loads of dried meat and leathered fruit, bacco cheroots, great jars of water, beer, and wine, great crystal globes misty with dense Pangaean air, and dozens of rawhide boots.

Other handcarts bore tremendous blocks of speckled granite, bound for monuments under Imperial construction. One was a foolish Obelisk of Eternity, which the wind whittled away even as the builders attempted to raise it. The other was a controversial Face of Pan, which the carvers had fancifully rendered as a sphinx in homage to all drud pures and which unknown Sanguinese persons secretly defaced every night.

Six barrows rattled past her from the other side of the Door, stacked with opalescent atlantium bars bound for Imperial mints and jewelers' vaults in Central Atlan.

Tahliq did what she always did whenever she was about to step over the Fold in the threshold of the Door—touched the tip of her fifth finger to the top knuckle of her second, made the hexagram of Afrodite over her breast, and held her breath.

A crack in the threshold no wider than the smallest joint of her fifth finger, black beyond black, deep beyond deep, the Fold never failed to propel a knife blade of dread down her spine. A breeze, freezing cold, emanated from its awful depths, and a metallic smell like a well plunging into another world.

That's why no beast could be persuaded to cross the threshold. Why no beasts in the ancient stable had ever stumbled through the Doors. That's why drayers bound in bridles and harnesses, mind-bound with protocol chips, whipped by hard-eyed drivers, pulled the wagons and carts and sledges. Only human beings could suspend common sense and the will to survive in the face of the unknown.

The Orb of Eternity, Tahliq knew, intimated such heresies with each facet. One kaligraph, one symbol—but with divergent outcomes. You had to take responsibility. You had to choose. Councillor Sausal's commentaries hinted at that. The quips of tavern wits celebrated the conundrum of choice.

The High Council doesn't want people to realize that even a Pangaean can make a choice. The purities are the purities, and the Imperium lasts without end. The natalries conquer impurity, Vigilance conquers the foes, Ground Control conquers earthshocks, Eternity conquers death— that's what the High Council wants us to believe. But the Imperium cannot conquer our human will—if we only realize it.

The queue surged forward. Tahliq wrapped her cloak more tightly around her shoulders.

"That's the way, Dame Tahliq," the Doorkeeper said with a toothless smile. "Bundle up. That's a lot o' space to step over." A wizened miner whose many long decades in the deep mine shafts had earned her the respite of staffing the Door, the Doorkeeper closed and opened one of her furry nostrils in the Sanguinese equivalent of a wink.

"A lot of space? Whatever do you mean?"

"Why, the Fold's all the space 'twixt here and there. 'Twas in times lost to antiquity. *Some*body knew how to fold space. Like that pleat in your gown." The Doorkeeper winced when her protocol chip pulsed. "Careful, there's a floorboard comin' loose. Don't stumble, my dame."

Tahliq stepped over the floorboard in question. "Why don't you repair it?"

"Ooh, we daren't tinker with the Doors for fear we'll bollix something up." She lowered her voice. "And then we won't get no more atlantium from Sanguine. And the moon? She'll just be a pretty light in the night, not a place to dump the city's waste."

"Would the miners and streetsweepers perish?"

"That they would. Wouldn't last long on permafrost and dust, eh? Couldn't breathe the air for very long, neither."

"Why doesn't the Imperium simply build another Door?"

The Doorkeeper closed and opened her furry nostril again. "Would if they could. Ha! But they can't."

"But if the Imperium owns the Doors—"

Lower whisper. "That's why the Doors is a Secret, dearie." The Doorkeeper tapped the chip in her forehead.

In her many decades, she'd undoubtedly spoken traitorous words that even the protocol chip couldn't censor. "The High Council won't admit no one in all Pangaea knows how to repair them Doors. Let alone replace 'em."

"Then who built the Doors in the first place?"

"The High Council says the angels did. But if that were so, the angels would know how to rig up another Door, now, wouldn't they? No, 'twas someone not of the Imperium, I say. 'Twas Pan, and none other."

Tahliq shook her head. *Some*one had built the Doors, and it wasn't the Eternal Essence. An Ancient One? A comrade of the One who'd fashioned Orbs of Eternity? She recalled the huge almond-shaped eyes, the silvery blue skin, the face that fleetingly appeared whenever she held an orb in the palms of her hands for a casting.

And kept her silence.

The Imperium has its Secrets, but so do I. How many others among us?

She swallowed her trepidation, stepped over the Fold—loose floorboard and all—and through the threshold. She caught her breath. The thin, frigid air of the red planet struck her like a blow. She closed her eyes to ward off the moment of vertigo. Even after twenty-two seasons, she'd never become fully accustomed to the precipitous change from verdant plains to barren red mountains. The Doorkeeper on the Sanguinese side steadied her shoulder.

She blinked back the harsh sunlight radiating out of the vault of deep indigo-blue studded with fierce stars. The blazing orange disk of the sun appeared considerably smaller in the dark Sanguinese sky.

She strode away from the Door, clutching her cape, and trudged up the wind-blasted path to the Tycho Docks. As promised, the dilapidated little side-wheeler awaited her, bobbing on the viscous, metallic-colored water. She boarded and stood in the cabin, warming herself before the captain's potbelly stove. After a lurching ferry ride up

Arago Canal that did little to alleviate her nausea, she disembarked at Port di Mare Australe.

Camp di Mare Australe, the main settlement on Sanguine, lay before her.

A throng bedecked in their festival best, helmet-lamps
ablaze, greeted her at the dock, shrieking and gesticulating
at the sight of her. All the scrappy miners serving on Sanguine were females, heavily shaped drud subpures with
stubby legs, knees like dinner plates, long muscular arms,
and tiny deft hands suited for sifting ore. Three grinning
miners met her, scarlet-cheeked, clad in the peaked caps of
the Bloody Fishes Sect, already deeply inebriated. They
gleefully escorted her from dock to camp.

Massive granite outbuildings huddled low on the terra-
cotta-colored dust, protecting entrances to the mine shafts
and living chambers belowground from the harsh
Sanguinese wind. Laden with granulated ice crystals, the
wind unceasingly gnawed at the granite, the mountains,
anything unfortunate enough to find itself aboveground for
very long. Construction crews conscripted by the consortium always bustled about, raising new outbuildings over
the ruins of the old. The ruins might have been less than a
season old but appeared as pocked and worn as if they'd
stood since times lost to antiquity.

Tahliq and her escorts stepped into an ore cart waiting in
the sheltered entrance to a mine shaft. She sat, and her
gleeful escorts strapped her in. Whooping and swaying,
they descended the switchbacked track two leagues down to
the festival hall. Tahliq clutched her belly and chewed three
more mintsticks.

"Blessed Vessel! Blessed Vessel!"

The shout poured forth from two thousand throats as
Tahliq entered the low-domed festival hall. Ecstatic miners
capered and leapt, swirling skirts of vermilion and fuchsia.
Variegated subpure pennants and family flags festooned the
walls, the only cheerful place on all Sanguine. Bacco
smoke choked the air, but Tahliq didn't mind. The Festival

of Motherwine amounted to the one pleasure most miners would ever enjoy in their short, arduous lives on Sanguine. She beamed with pride, honored and privileged to preside as the Blessed Vessel. Her purse bulged with a thousand new ores.

" 'Tis hazardous labor, atlantium mining," the Grand Mistress had told her twenty-two seasons ago. She'd marveled over the blood-soaked sponge Tahliq had shown her that night when they lingered on the pleasure couch. "And Sanguine, she's a harsh world. We can waste no muscle or flesh." Quintus Natalry harvested each miner at her age of ripeness and stored her Imperial materia in Natalry Bank, pending her sharelock one day. By long tradition and the requirements of their off-world labor, the miners were also purified. "They take it all," the Grand Mistress had said with a sigh. "Our birthpods, our blood chambers, everything. Ah, well. It's not as if we need 'em." She'd made the sign of the Imperial star and then the hexagram. "May Pan and Afrodite preserve Natalry Bank."

Now Tahliq climbed the altar steps, ascending to the podium, and greeted the Grand Mistress. Slowly, deliberately, reveling in the hoots and exhortations, Tahliq removed her cape, her boots, her gown. How she adored unclothing herself before this enthusiastic audience! She reveled in the stares of admiration and envy.

"I am the Eternal female," Tahliq said in the cult's invocation. "I am She who has never changed."

A mob of young miners in the front row jostled each other and pointed, openmouthed, shrieking with astonishment.

"I am She who once bore the unborn in this belly. She who expelled the unborn through these hips. She who fed the unborn with these breasts."

"We welcome thee, Blessed Vessel!" said the Grand Mistress.

Tahliq mounted the sacred dais—a broad-backed leviathan carved of red-speckled granite—and lay back amid rich quilts of plum-red suede. She spread her knees—ec-static shouts rang out—and permitted the Grand Mistress to tug and remove the sponge in her.

She closed her eyes and smiled. Now the Grand Mistress would display the blood-soaked fetish to the cheering masses. She would squeeze drops of Tahliq's motherblood into a great vat of thick red wine. Now Fish cultists who stood around the vat would dip their ladles into the blood-infused wine and distribute thimble-sized cups among the frenzied devotees.

"Thus this motherwine of the Blessed Vessel, whom we revere—" the Grand Mistress intoned.

"Blessed Living Vessel!" shouted the crowd.

"—is the sacred wine of Afrodite drunk by the un-born—"

"Wine, wine, wine!"

"As we drink the blessed motherwine, so Afrodite will bless our materia and make it fruitful. We drink as our unborn will one day drink the motherwine of the natalry. We beseech Afrodite to bless and preserve our unborn, who will generate and grow and emerge—"

"There's no blood!" someone cried out.

A thousand miners screamed.

Tahliq sat up, horrified. She seized the sponge from the Grand Mistress's fingertips.

An anxious hush fell over the crowd.

It was true! The sponge remained pristine, pure white, without the slightest trace of her courses. Tahliq's stomach clenched. Sickness rose in her throat. Would she become nauseous in front of two thousand devotees? She pressed her fingertips into the base of her throat.

"I'm sorry," she whispered to the Grand Mistress. "My courses must be . . . late."

The Grand Mistress looked aghast. "How can that be, my dame?"

"I don't know. It's never happened before."

She shuddered, aghast herself. She knew very well the

risk and expense the Bloody Fishes undertook to smuggle her here. The consortium would be shocked and outraged to discover that the Grand Mistress, a long-trusted and obedient laborer, participated in the sect. Who knew what punishment would await her, if the festival were ever discovered?

And now I've failed them.

"Please forgive me, I beg you, Grand Mistress," she whispered.

Shadows below the dais rippled strangely the way heat rises off the pavement in shimmering mirages. Yet there was no heat, only the bitter Sanguinese cold. *Again, those shadows.* She abruptly recalled the same shadows in her dallying chamber the last time she'd seen Horan Zehar on the day of the Big Shock. Recalled Regim's accusation, *Someone was there. And someone vanished.* Apprehension thrummed through her nerves.

She seized her gown and boots and cape, hastily drew the garments on. Shivers wracked her body. Her teeth chattered in her jaw. "Take me away, at once."

Her three escorts, no longer grinning, their peaked caps askew, caught her by her arms as she stumbled off the dais and assisted her down the steep steps of the altar. They cleaved a path through the restive throng, jostling stunned celebrants out of Tahliq's way. Fisticuffs broke out as she passed. Her escorts shielded her.

"This way, my dame," they murmured and took her to a dark sleeping chamber lit by a lone, sputtering magmalamp nearly out of fuel. How like Sanguine. Perpetually plundered, perpetually impoverished, and nearly out of fuel. And forced to go on.

They left her there, alone. Far above, the Sanguinese wind boomed. She lay back on the bed, a narrow cot about as comfortable as a slab of bare rock, and caught her breath. Caught her breath again. The imported Pangaean air that bolstered the camp's atmosphere belowground was so thin today. She sucked at it, struggling to breathe.

"Dear Afrodite, what's wrong with me?" she whispered to herself, huddling beneath flimsy blankets in the freezing darkness.

"You know exactly what's wrong, erotician," came a mocking, sibilant voice. "You've got plenty of forbidden books in your library that spell out exactly what bestial begetting is all about."

"What's that?" Tahliq jolted up, seized the lamp, and brandished it like a battering rod. "Who's there?" She frantically searched the shadows, heart hammering in her breast.

Suddenly a female stood before her as if she'd unfolded from the shadows themselves. A very young woman with a slight figure, brightly blemished cheeks, glittering mismatched black eyes. She'd drawn curliques of black facepaint around those awful eyes, black spirals on her forehead, the tip of her bony chin. Her bald head gleamed in the dim light, ridges stitching across her skull, little domes of bone extruding here and there. A tunic and leggings of black sacking clung to her scrawny limbs.

Impure.

She grinned, sly and calculating. "I know what's wrong with you, Dame Tahliq, and so do you. You won't bleed again for these idiotic miners till the Imperium harvests you and scrapes away the unborn that's growing inside you."

That mocking voice. That lopsided smirk. "Who the devil are you?"

"I'm a Devil, all right. Call me Salit. Salit Zehar."

"Salit *Zehar*?"

Tahliq's nerves snapped. If this scrawny girl was of the same clan, she was dangerous, as dangerous as Horan Zehar. Perhaps more so, since she burned with insolent youth and Horan, for all his reprehensibility, was a mature man who knew the consequences of his actions.

Erratic shadows, shimmering.

A small explosion went off in her head. "I don't know how exactly, but you've been following me, haven't you, little girl? All the way from the Salon of Shame. I want to know why."

The girl shrugged, bit a hangnail from her thumb. Devil stars, loosely folded, dangled from her belt, and a dagger, and odd-shaped metal balls bristling with spikes. She wore the same sort of black cloak Horan Zehar wore, a cloak that rippled around her from shoulders to ankles as if stirred by a breeze.

The air in the sleeping chamber was as still as a tomb.

"All right, let's try this. How is it you know me?"

"I know you buy qut from Horan Zehar. I'm taking over his purveyance. From now on, I'll be delivering the wares and collecting your money."

"Will you now? Horan Zehar may have something to say about that."

"Horan Zehar has nothing more to say about anything. Horan Zehar is dead. He died in the waterduct behind the Temple of Sacred Sharelock on the night of the Big Shock." The girl's lower lip quivered, but she transformed her look of naked grief into an extravagant sneer. "He was my father."

"Your father!" He might have disgusted and terrified her, still the qut purveyor had had his purpose. *Horan Zehar, dead. And a Heaven's Devil died beside Clere Twine in the waterduct, that's what Milady Faro's dream depicted. Could it be . . . ?* "I'm sorry," Tahliq murmured politely. "How difficult for you and your mother."

"My mother is dead, too. I'm . . . all alone."

Fear skittered down Tahliq's spine, yet she regained her self-possession. *Horan Zehar's daughter, my, my.* She'd had no quarrel with Horan, or any foe. She was the lowest pure and most despised subpure in all Pangaea. And sometimes the outrageous acts of the foes—the execution of Clere Twine, for instance—secretly pleased her.

Tahliq smiled her sardonic smile. This impure girl was an orphan standing before her, not a seasoned terrorist. Her grief plain on her youthful face, despite her attempt to conceal it. Tahliq found her heart reaching out for this snarling, sneering young girl the way she left out meat scraps for the vicious little wild sphinxes that lived in Jugglers Lane. She had a soft spot for anything young and wild and lonely.

The girl shrugged again, but she eyed Tahliq's smile. "You'd better submit to Imperial harvesting like a good drud, my dame."

Tahliq shook her head in disbelief. "I cannot possibly be with child. All my patrons are pures. They've all been harvested by the natalries."

"Harvested, but not all purified like these pathetic atlantium miners. You yourself have never been purified, isn't that so, Dame Tahliq? You still have your courses." Salit Zehar grinned and chanted in a mocking singsong, "I know who the father is."

FACET 10

Moon: A devil or an angel.
The moon illuminates or obscures the night.
The action is nurturing.
The forbearance is smothering.

The Orb of Eternity

Commentaries:

Councillor Sausal: As Pan is ever hidden, concealed within darkness and below the torrents, so the moon that waxes and wanes may light our way at night or may abandon us to starlight.

So, too, the Imperium seeks out that which is concealed and reveals it.

Therefore the prudent person should serve the needs and desires of higher pures, subpures, and superiors but beware of oppressing lower pures, subpures, and inferiors.

Guttersage (usu. considered vulgar): An academe reading late at night in the library reads in peace and quiet.

A fool traveling late at night on the road travels in peril of bandits and murderers.

Our Imperial Planet of Sanguine, Camp di Mare Australe. The Grand Mistress's sleeping chamber:

Salit smirked at her clever taunt. What sport to torment the erotician! Look how she brandished a lamp as if a flimsy ceramic rod dripping with imported magma could possibly save her should she, Salit Zehar, Heaven's Devil extraordinaire, decide to execute her.

Execute the erotician without mercy or purpose. Or with a purpose: to prove that the Heaven's Devils—that *she*—had infiltrated yet another Imperial Secret.

The Door to Sanguine.

Perhaps she'd gut the erotician the way she'd gutted Clere Twine, with a devil star flung at close range. Perhaps she'd use her bare hands, clapping her palms with such force over the erotician's ears that her eardrums would shatter and her brains splatter out. Perhaps she'd give her a second smile below her chin, the one that went from ear to ear, courtesy of a knife blade.

Stink of blood and excrement, ululation of pain . . .

Terrible memories assailed her. Her father—her mentor, her idol, the only nurturer she'd ever known—writhing in his death throes, filthy ductwater purling around him.

The Twine she-butcher, gah, how Salit despised the prefect. But to see her flayed open like a slaughtered beast, to witness blood and entrails and excrement spilling through the water, devastation wrought by her own hands . . .

No! Farewell tears and grief!

She drew herself up, thrust the memories away. She must *not* indulge in pity, for herself or anyone else. Must *not* be a weakling and a coward. Truly, she was mastering her lessons more quickly than ever, now that she was all alone.

On Penetration of the Enemy Camp, Technique One: Opportune timing includes when the enemy is setting up camp, meals, arrival after a tedious journey, after an accident, festivals, during storms and moonless nights, and any other time when the necessities of life distract from vigilance.

The erotician lowered the lamp and leaned forward, keen intelligence suddenly sparkling in her big dark eyes. "And who do you think the father is, little girl? Not that I concede I'm with child."

Salit started at the sparkle of intelligence, the erotician's nonchalance facing a foe terrorist. Most drud subpures possessed as few wits and fewer nerves than a beast in the field. With wild drud subpures Horan Zehar had taught her the elementary ways to kill. *This licensed erotician—and a wealthy, successful one, at that—is no ordinary drud. She is a woman to be reckoned with.*

But that was her father's dead voice clamoring in her ears. Salit stamped her foot. "Stop calling me 'little girl.' "

"Stop acting like one."

"I'm not!"

"You are." The erotician tossed the lamp onto a side table and rose, swirling her cape and gown. "Barging in here while I'm hiding in shame after I've failed miserably before two thousand Bloody Fishes. Atlantium miners, the poor wretches, who adore me. Who need me. How dare you."

"I didn't mean to—" Salit cringed before the erotician's indignation.

"Yes, you meant to. Popping out of thin air, that's what you did. I suppose you think you're clever. Following me all day—and I still want to know why. This is no time or place for a qut delivery, if it's true you're taking over Horan's purveyance. You haven't brought my usual package, have you?"

"N-no."

"I thought not." The erotician studied her shrewdly. "And even if you had, I'd refuse to take it. Do you really expect me to lug around a fullweight of qut in my festival cape and gown?" She haughtily brushed Sanguinese dust off the garments in question.

Salit found herself fidgeting. Gut the erotician, that's what she should do. What a glory! Imagine the hubbub when the Bloody Fishes found her corpse. Yet the erotician's huge dark eyes shimmered with . . . Gah, Salit didn't know what the erotician's eyes shimmered with, but her expression suddenly shamed Salit. The way no one else but her father had ever shamed her for not behaving as well as she should. She shuffled her feet. "I-I guess not. I-I'm sorry."

"That's better. How old are you, Salit Zehar?" the erotician asked, her voice suddenly soft.

"S-sixteen." How had *she* suddenly become the one on the run, the one being questioned? Disdainful, Salit hawked and spit on the floor. *That's what I think of you, erotician.* The chameleon cloak swayed out of the way of the spittle. A tickle of pain pattered down her spine. *Poxy cloak! I'll make it obey me.* But a familiar sting of fear followed the pain. *Will I ever command the cloak? It . . . doesn't like me.* "Sixteen and a half in the autumn turning, not that you care. And I've already got my own chameleon cloak."

"Chameleon cloak?"

"This!" Swirled the cloak proudly.

"Is *that* what it's called?"

"Sure. Also the cloak of changes and the cloak of secrecy." Another swirl. "Some call it the shadow cloak."

"So many mysterious names for the same thing. Why is a little cloak called all these things?"

Salit started to blurt out exactly what the cloak did, then bit her tongue. *Tricking me. She's tricking me into telling my secrets.* "The cloak permits me to come and go as I please." Smirk. How clever of her to hint about a secret without really telling it.

The erotician nodded slowly. "I see. Or perhaps I should say I *don't* see."

"Yeah." Clever of the erotician to understand. "The cloak was my father's. He left it to me . . . just before he died."

"I remember that cloak well. I remember *him* well. It must be hard for you, Salit. With your mother gone, too? Losing one's father is always difficult."

"Nah, he was a beast to me." *That* wasn't true at all, but

she felt better saying it. Why was she chattering on like this? Why was the erotician being so *nice*? Seducing her, that's why, the way the erotician seduced everyone. Didn't care what pure or subpure or even that she was impure. Seduced every living thing, any way she could. Salit summoned rage, but ended up simpering, "It's none of your business, anyway."

The erotician laughed, a high little tinkle like the ringing of a chime. "Somehow I don't believe you, the way you say that. Listen, Salit. I've been doing business with your father since before you were born. I'm old enough to be your mother—"

Salit flinched at the word, and the grief she always felt when she thought about her mother welled up. *Farewell tears and grief!* Could not bear any more grief.

"—though, of course, I'm not." The erotician was shrewdly studying her again. "Let's return to my first question. Your father and I had our differences. About the Imperium, the purities, proximity, protocol, who doesn't? But there was no bad blood between me and Horan Zehar. He always delivered on time, and I always paid my accounts in full. You do know that, don't you, Salit?"

She shrugged. "Yeah."

"Good. Then why are you following me?"

"Well . . ." She shuffled again. Wanted to tell *some*-one. So alone, now that her father was dead. Wasn't sure, though, she should trust *any*one with her secrets. Began cautiously, "Well, I was shopping in Marketplace, see"— she had been shoplifting baubles—"and I happened to see the vigile"—she'd been lying in wait for the golden-haired beast—"coming out of Vigilance Authority. I followed him to your salon. And then I followed you here."

"That's a description, not an explanation. Why me?"

Unnerving, this erotician. Salit cocked her head, listening to the wind booming far above them. She'd seen the erotician so many times—in the flickering light of Horan

Zehar's mnemons—that she felt as if she knew her. In truth, she'd come to admire the erotician's spunk.

But confronting the erotician face-to-face brought out her shyness and her snarls in equal measure, and she couldn't confess to her admiration. *Why?* She shrugged. "The impure have always heard rumors that the Imperium knows how to go to Sanguine and the moon. We never knew if the rumors were true."

"No one among the purities knows, either, except the consortiums and their laborers, and they wear protocol chips to bind their minds. I suppose the High Council knows as well. Perhaps, though, not all the councillors know. The ones from newer families, for instance." The erotician rubbed her chin thoughtfully. "The Doors were discovered a century ago, after all. And magisters love their secrets."

Salit nodded. "No one knew how it could possibly be done."

"You do now."

"Thanks to you, Dame Tahliq. Doors, of all things! Do you suppose it's true? All the space"—she still gasped at the notion—"between Pangaea and the little red star twinkling high in the night sky is . . . *folded*?"

"Sometimes asking how and why is pointless," the erotician said dryly. "Sometimes the best thing to ask is, *How can I profit from this?*"

Salit grinned. That was *just* the sort of advice Horan Zehar would dispense, with the same sardonic smile. She took out and lit a cheroot with a flick of her flint. "Perhaps I can purvey qut here, you know? These pitiful miners look like they could use more pleasure in their lives. Tell you what. I'll discount your next wares by fifteen percent if you'll introduce me to the Grand Mistress. Perhaps she can arrange to smuggle me through the Door."

"I've no doubt the Grand Mistress can smuggle anything. Make it twenty percent off all my wares henceforth, and we have a deal." At Salit's shrug, the erotician said,

"Done." She lay back on the bed and stretched languorously, as if inviting Salit's admiration of her remarkable body. But her lively eyes glinted again.

"So, my little Salit. You've answered why me, more or less. Now I want to know why the vigile? He's very handsome, I know, but quite the arrogant proximicist. His injuries have brought out the worst in him. I doubt he gives money to impure girls on the street."

"He's the vigile who m-murdered my father on the night of Clere Twine's assassination. At the Temple of Sacred Sharelock. I was there. I saw it with my own eyes."

To Salit's astonishment, the erotician sprang from the bed and embraced her. Stroked her bald head tenderly, smoothing the grain of the stubble just right, so the caress felt comforting and pleasurable. Not like someone grinding sand against her scraped scalp. To Salit's further astonishment, she found herself sobbing.

The erotician murmured, "I know, I know. Poor little girl."

Only Asif had ever embraced her when he'd found her that terrible night in the waterduct. A clumsy boy's embrace, arousing and slightly embarrassing. They'd made their way through the chaos in Marketplace to the pipeline, but Habash Qaled hadn't been waiting for them. Fiery-eyed vigiles had marched through every subterranean route and trampled the tentsites, rounding up any impure foolish enough to tarry.

Blackblood Cavern had been deserted. Asif had gone with her to her father's tentsite, helped her toss money, food, a pack of cheroots, and a change of stockings into her knapsack. They'd taken her father's corpse to a fire still raging in Rancid Flats and committed him to the flames. Salit hadn't wanted to leave any chance that Vigilance would find his body and display him like a trophy in Allpure Square.

She'd stood, numb and tearless, Asif's arm around her shoulders, as the conflagration consumed Horan Zehar.

How small he'd been. How finely made. She'd seen a peculiar gout of flame and a plume of smoke rise up from his chest. If it was true one's Essence ascended to Eternity, she knew her father had entered there and waged his war anew against the Imperium.

Then she'd insisted they split up, against Asif's protests. She'd vowed to rendezvous with him when Vigilance's wrath had cooled. If the vigiles would take her and execute her, they would do it that night, and she hadn't wanted to place Asif in jeopardy.

She'd taken a new path her father had shown her, a service alley that threaded through observation facilities installed by Ground Control beneath the coast. She'd set up a new little tentsite of her own and hidden there for days, secret and secluded.

The erotician's embrace was something far different than Asif's. Salit stood stock-still, stiff in the nurturing caress. Had she fallen into a vat of goose feathers? Was she smothering?

No, she wished she could climb into the erotician's lap like a child and listen to a nurtury tale. How lonely she'd been! She was about to brag about her execution of the she-butcher Clere Twine, then bit her tongue. "The vigile has vowed to kill me for . . . witnessing what I saw. I've returned a vow to resist the vigile and avenge my father. I shall harass him, then one day, when the time is right, I shall kill him. I'm sorry, my dame. I know you lust for him. He's the one, of course."

"What?"

"The one who seeded the unborn growing inside your body."

"Regim!" The erotician sat heavily on the bed, as if suddenly her legs couldn't hold her. "And just how do you know this, my little Salit?"

"The cloak's got a pocket."

She'd been standing by the shock-damaged Obelisk of Eternity at the periphery of Allpure Square, trying to force the cloak to simulate the bustle of northwest Marketplace during the afternoon. Solid, static surfaces like the wall of the waterduct had been easy, but she'd had a world of trouble with lively, variegated backgrounds. The drud quadrant had teemed with drayers, dust, and dung. As she'd concentrated on camouflaging herself amid a passing gang of ragpickers, she'd inadvertently yanked the pocket open.

She stared in horror as the tiny pitch-black abyss yawned open opposite her heart. Suddenly a flat little square made of white light slipped out. The square of light hovered before her eyes, then filled with images and emitted sounds. She'd seen the bald head of a baby emerging from a straining portal of muscle and blood. She'd heard a woman's screams and groans.

Salit. Name her Salit, my Horan. Oh, I'm lost! Good-bye, my bonded one.

Salit had been so stunned by the mnemon of her own birth that she'd taken off the cloak and hidden in her tentsite, chastened, grief-stricken, and astounded. She'd dared ask no one for guidance on how to employ the pocket. She'd feared news of her acquisition would find its way to the Dark Ones, and they'd send a proxy to appropriate her prized possession. After a day, she'd cautiously donned the cloak again and opened the pocket.

"My father had a way of recording events and things he'd seen in this pocket. I've seen the record of the time he visited you in your library. The vigile had visited you, too, didn't he? The afternoon before his sharelock ceremony. My father saw and heard . . . everything. *And* he was with the vigile and Clere Twine in a preparatory chamber in the temple before their sharelock ceremony. He saw and heard everything there, too. The vigile's subpure," she added, blushing furiously, "permits its men to retain custody of their seed till they enter into sharelock. The vigile said it's their custom."

"I see." The erotician's eyes were wide in the magmalight. "Dear Afrodite! I had no notion magister subpures allowed such things. They're so fanatic about their purity.''

"The Twine she-butcher wanted him for bedding, too, but let me tell you, he didn't want her.'' Ardently, still grateful for the erotician's embrace, "He wanted you.''

"Thank you for your account, Salit.'' The erotician rose from the bed with a dignified flourish and straightened her gown. She blotted a tear from the corner of her eye, though perhaps she was only wiping away a bit of grit.

"How is it you still have your courses? Why didn't your natalry purify you?''

The erotician laughed, bitterness in her tone. "I'm paid well to remain the Eternal female who once grew the unborn inside her bestial body. The Bloody Fishes pay me very well to preside at their festival. Anyway, there's usually no danger when I perform my Imperial duty. I've got cleansing teas.'' She rubbed her chin again. "Ha! and ha! I'd always thought magisters purified themselves.''

Salit nodded, pondering her answer. "My father had a record of the time you cast the Orb of Eternity for him. You cast the facet for Darkness. Dame Tahliq, is it true the orb foretells?''

"Sometimes the orb foretells. Sometimes it does more than foretell. The orb doesn't exist in time and space the way we do.''

Salit pondered that answer, too. She'd heard many strange things about orbs. She'd lacked the patience to study the intricate facets and decipher their complex meanings. Had never dared roll an orb for fear the thing would hex her. She'd heard plenty of stories of hexings. She carried her contraband on the thong around her neck the way she carried her devil stars and dagger on her belt—as dangerous and valuable tools. "Is Darkness a prophecy of death? Did my father know this?''

The erotician considered her question, then nodded gravely. "Yes. Yes, I believe your father knew he was going to die. Knew that the orb foretold. Knew more, perhaps.''

"And still he went to the temple." Now Salit touched a fingertip to the corner of her own eye.

"You know," the erotician said, "you'd look much prettier with a bit of hair on your noggin. Stop by the salon, and I'll give you a jug of my nettle soap. It's very effective for lice."

"I'm not troubled by lice," Salit said indignantly. "I'm troubled by Vigilance Authority."

"What could Vigilance Authority possibly want with a little girl like you?"

I executed the Twine she-beast! Bit her tongue again. The erotician, her new . . . friend, might fear and revile her, if she knew the truth. "Because I'm impure. Just because I'm impure."

The erotician nodded, sympathy in her eyes. "I understand. I'll go summon the Grand Mistress for you now."

The erotician strode to the sleeping chamber door and paused, her hand poised on the doorknob. "Tell me, little Salit. What happened to the Orb of Eternity your father brought to my library that afternoon? I never did find it, though I plainly saw it roll beneath my settee."

Salit stroked the contraband strung around her neck on the leather cord, huge orbs sparkling in the magmalight, four of them now. She'd discovered the fourth orb where her father had stashed it in another pocket, an ordinary pocket meant for carrying things. Horan Zehar would never have abandoned his orb. "Dame Tahliq, I can't tell you *all* my secrets."

Salit crept back through the Door to Pangaea behind a handcart groaning with bars of atlantium.

Ho! The stuff was mined on Sanguine, then. Yet another Secret revealed. The moon was a different matter, from the look of the handcarts coming and going through the second Door. Piles of offal disappeared through that Door, and only weary streetsweepers and their sledges returned.

The way to other worlds had been no idle rumor, yet even Horan Zehar had never discovered the means or the location of the Doors. Salit carefully recalled the circuitous route the erotician had taken from the weaving factory where she'd met the Sanguinese smugglers. The Doors, now that Salit knew how to find them, courtesy of Dame Tahliq, presented fine opportunities for ambush and armed robbery.

What luck! What a phenomenal find! How would her father advise her? *Keep this Secret all to yourself, my darling. It's much too valuable to share, except as it may profit you.*

Yes. Horan Zehar had kept his own secrets from the Heaven's Devils. Kept secrets even from her. She suddenly understood why. *What other power do the impure possess but the secrets they may know?*

Thick opalescent bars of the precious lavender metal gleamed a handbreadth away beneath their security net. Should she try to slip a bar out? Her hands were small and thin and agile. No, the net would probably seize her hands, sound an alarm, or both. Another time, after she'd found and studied her father's mnemon on how to infiltrate security nets.

She hadn't yet found that particular square of light. She had no idea how her father had organized the mnemons. *Secrets and secrets. So those were the strange little lights he studied late at night when he thought I was sleeping.* She had no idea how to find a particular subject she wanted. She simply pulled mnemons out at random, viewed and listened to all they contained, and stuffed them back into the pocket. She had no doubt Horan would have expounded at length about security nets and recorded his views on the subject. She would have to keep searching.

She crept between the two lumbering drayers pushing the handcart, easily evading the mining consortium's security officers, thuggish low subpure magisters who stood watch at the Door. She wasn't sure which stank worse, the drayers or the magisters.

On Penetration of the Enemy Camp, Technique Two: Opportune entry includes the opposite side of a busy kitchen, the druds' entrance, empty guest chambers, embalmers' quarters, back doors and windows, latrines, waterducts, sewage ducts, and any place especially unpleasant.

The cart rattled out of the stable and down Iapetus Boulevard, heading north toward Central Atlan. She gratefully gulped fresh air and considered what to steal for dinner. She'd been so preoccupied prowling after people, she hadn't eaten a thing all day.

Suddenly a hand clamped over her shoulder, violently yanked her backward out of the entourage, whipped her around, and shoved her into the towering buckwheat stalks bordering the road.

An arrogant rasp, assured of commanding and being obeyed. "Got you now, you chit." Another hand clawed at the clasp of her cloak, thrust the cloak wide open.

Exposed, vulnerable, the cloak's camouflaging scattered.

The turbid Pangaean air clogged her throat after the cold, arid air of Sanguine. Her eyes misted over, her sinuses congested, and she sneezed violently. She squirmed away, but another set of hands seized her other arm, pinning her in the buckwheat stalks.

She blinked away tears and glanced, horrified, at the man at her side.

A gangly young impure man.

"Asif, my comrade! What in hell are you *doing*?"

"Shut up, Salit," he muttered.

"He's obeying what's commanded of him, unlike you, Salit," rasped Habash Qaled. A grizzled little woman with bloodred eyes and half a dozen greasy little grey braids sprouting from her skull, the notorious poisoner stood beside her, gripping the edge of the chameleon cloak in a gnarled hand. Habash wasn't a Heaven's Devil, but of the Hell's Teeth clan, and she'd gone on many a blooding with

Horan. "You'll come with us. The Dark Ones want to have a word with you."

"I've got nothing to say to the Dark Ones," Salit said contemptuously. No emissary from the Dark Ones had sought out her lonely little tentsite to comfort her in her grief. The Dark Ones hadn't given two clucks about the murder of their best assassin. Or his bereaved daughter and the young assassin of the Twine she-butcher. Salit had expected honor, accolades, perhaps a reward.

But there had been nothing.

"Yes, well, they've got something to say to you, chit," Habash said impassively and shoved her shoulder, hustling her through the field.

"Boy, are you in trouble," Asif whispered in her ear.

"Go fall in a swamp." Salit pouted. "How did you track me down?"

"We've been following you all day, Salit. We didn't want to risk tangling with the vigilance posted at the stable-door. We've been sweating for hours in the damn field, waiting for you to come back out of the poxy stable. What's in that place, anyway?"

"That's for me to know, and you to find out," she said smugly. "But how did you see me? I've been camouflaged in the cloak all day."

"Salit," Asif whispered in an exasperated tone, "you're as plain as spit. Right now you look as if you've been dipped in red dust. You think you're camouflaged?"

She glanced down and cursed. The cloak swirling around her had remained the terra-cotta color of Sanguinese soil.

Pox, pox, pox! The chameleon cloak hadn't re-camouflaged when she stepped through the Door. It was true, her eyes had misted over, she couldn't see, and her thoughts had scattered hither and yon over all that had transpired on Sanguine. Then her vision had cleared, but the cloak hadn't responded. And what about Asif's insinuation that he and Habash had followed her, seen her, all day? Salit frowned. She'd concealed herself from the erotician well enough. Had the cloak's camouflagings been that inept to the eyes of her fellow foes?

Was it possible to punish the cloak?

Infuriated, she wrested her arm out of Asif's grip. "How stupid of me to think you might care a little for me."

"I care very much for you, my comrade," he said grimly.

"Then how can you do this to me?"

His eyes met hers and wrenched away. "The Dark Ones have commanded me."

Water cascaded down the walls in the Cavern of Reckoning, where the Dark Ones presided over matters of the impure. Water seemed thicker in these depths, cold and slow and viscous. Gurgling curtains sheeted across the black-granite facade. Droplets slid off stalactites and plunked in a steady rhythm into ebony pools gathered around stalagmites.

Salit stood upon the Platform of Reckoning. The aged wood bore dark, suspicious-looking mottles and what could only be bloodstains. A hooded whipmaster and phlegmatic torturer stood to one side.

Her escorts had blindfolded her and led her down into the deep secret spaces the impure inhabited. Asif was gentle, Habash peremptory, as they pulled her this way, pushed her that. A knot of resentment curled around Salit's heart. Why should Asif, her senior by only a few years and not nearly her match in blooding, have been permitted knowledge of the route to the Cavern of Reckoning, and she had been denied? The summer heat swiftly dissipated as they descended, the air growing colder and colder with each step till it was nearly as cold as Sanguine. But a damp, dank cold. The dripping cold of Pangaea.

Salit shivered.

To hell with the Dark Ones. They owe me a debt for my father's death, not the other way around. But beneath the blindfold, impersonally escorted by two people she thought she knew—and one of whom she was sure she loved—she'd suddenly begun to feel afraid.

Now freed of the blindfold, she searched the darkness for a friendly face. Magmalamps flickered, casting icy luminescence on the cascades, the pools. Shadows shifted around her in the flickering darkness. She heard murmurs. People had gathered here, a tremendous congregation. Who were they? Why had they come to witness this confrontation?

Looming before her upon a bench so high she had to lift her chin and crane her neck to regard them, sat the Dark Ones—five figures cloaked in roiling black miasmas. Only their misshapen eyes were visible in the darkness, mandorlas of shimmering amber fire.

Certain chosen women and men among the oldest and most powerful of the impure knew who the Dark Ones were. Where their tentsites lay. How they functioned in the world outside the Cavern of Reckoning. What clan they belonged to.

Imperial Vigilance assumed the opposite: that every person of the impure knew who they were, these architects of the holy war against the Imperium, or had their suspicions. Throughout her childhood Salit had suspected one person or another—a neighbor, the woman who tended her, an elder comrade. Even that her father had been a Dark One. Vigiles periodically swept through impure tentsites and cavedwellings and detained children and adults for interrogation. The detainees would emerge from these interrogations with burns and whiplashes, stubs of knuckles, an empty eye socket. Salit had never been detained, but she'd heard the rumors, had seen the maimed survivors.

The first question the interrogators always asked was, "Who are the Dark Ones?"

The Dark Ones presided before her now, gazing down with their blazing eyes. Her knees quaked so violently she could barely stand. She clasped her icy hands behind her back.

"Salit Zehar," came the first voice, a guttural whisper that reverberated throughout the cavern. The voice sounded as if the speaker had had a growth removed from the inside of his throat. "Your father Horan Zehar thought you too immature and impetuous to possess your own chameleon cloak. Even he did not trust you with one."

"Dark One, he told me that *you* doubted me."

"He convinced *us* of his doubt. Once you master the cloak, you may become invisible even to the eyes and ears of the impure. Even *we* may not be able to command you."

May not be able to command me? Shock tingled down her spine. *Really?*

"Yet now you possess a cloak," the whisper continued. "Now you gad about our tentsites and on the streets of Atlan, behaving in whatever careless way you please. You take preposterous risks, for a Heaven's Devil who has not yet mastered her cloak. So! We will take custody of the chameleon cloak, Salit, till you've reached the age of eighteen."

She flared with anger. "My father gave the cloak to me with his own hand during his death throes. 'Tis mine by right of free inheritance and succession."

The five shrouded heads huddled together amid a torrent of whispers. The congregation gathered around her murmured.

A second voice, as gravelly and rough as a skee drinker's, boomed from the Dark Ones' high bench. "It's true we oppose the Imperium's seizure of half of all inheritances among the purities, especially since this wealth is used mainly to support the evil technology of the natalries. By the right of free inheritance, we will permit you to keep your father's cloak. But, Salit Zehar, we demand your absolute submission and obedience to our command. Will you give us your word?"

Ho! She'd gladly give her word—and submit to no one.

"I will obey, Dark Ones," she said sarcastically and

crossed her forefinger over her thumb in the secret sign of
liars.

The whip stung her across her shoulder in less than an
instant, and she collapsed, falling heavily to her knees. The
cloak surged over her protectively, but Habash Qaled
stepped forward and seized the hem, preventing the fabric
from closing. Salit ground her teeth, bit back her cry of
pain. *I won't give you the satisfaction!*

But tears sprang to her eyes.

She heard murmurs of protest in the congregation. Someone said, "She *is* Horan Zehar's daughter."

Asif gently took her by the waist, helped her to her feet.
She glanced at him through the scrim of tears. Defiant, his
love for her plain on his face, he scowled up at the Dark
Ones and stepped between her and the whipmaster, shielding her. "I protest this punishment of my brave comrade.
You'll have to whip me before I'll permit you to punish her
again."

"Asif, my comrade," she whispered, "I'll never forget
this."

"Step aside, Asif Zehest" came the resounding whisper.
But Asif stood and planted his hands on Salit's shoulders.

Her courage burgeoned as the murmurs supporting her
grew louder. She wiped away her tears and gazed up at the
Dark Ones again.

"My father, Horan Zehar, the most brilliant assassin in
all Pangaea, gave his life for the cause of the impure. I, his
daughter and only age sixteen, have slain the she-butcher
Clere Twine with my own hands. Yet you castigate me in
this humiliating manner. You confer no honor upon my father, grant me no sympathy—"

"Silence, girl," said a third voice, sonorous yet dis-
tinctly female. "Horan Zehar failed. *You* failed."

Salit gasped, stammered, "But he g-gave his l-life—"

"He was not supposed to die," sibilated a fourth voice
like the hissing of a serpent. "And *you,* my girl, were not

supposed to take the life of Dame Clere Twine. She was to be brought here, to us. To be disposed of as we saw fit.''

Salit nearly spat in disgust. ''And the vigile was not supposed to have surprised us. Our escape with the prisoner was supposed to have been guaranteed by the Heaven's Devils and Hell's Teeth in the Sanctum. Why don't you ask our comrades in the temple why they failed to stop the vigile?''

''We have, bold girl. You'll find the head of one and the liver of another buzzing with flies on the Wall of Humiliation.''

Salit closed her eyes. A wave of vertigo rippling through her. She'd only seen it once, the bloodstained brick wall on the outskirts of the Iapetus Plains where the clans among the foes nailed ears, fingers, hands, heads, feet—trophies of the holy war against the Imperium. Drud and serv youths, sometimes even magisters, came and ogled the wall—or pointed with outrage to a limb or entrails that might have been hacked from kin who had disappeared.

Her stomach plummeted to her feet. Was her stomach, her head next? She'd had no notion she and her father had failed so miserably. And she'd thought they'd become champions among the foes! She could not speak.

''So, Salit Zehar,'' came the fifth voice, a kindly one, gently quavering like the voice of a solicitous elder. ''Do you understand a little better what your standing is before us?''

She squeezed her eyes shut, leaned against Asif. She nodded, sincerely contrite.

''Good. We command you to cease tormenting Lieutenant Regim Deuceman. Yes, we've been watching you. And we're aware of your oath of vengeance.''

She glanced accusingly at Asif, but he returned her glance and shook his head. *The eyes and ears of the impure are everywhere.*

''He slew my father, Dark One,'' she protested in a small

voice. "Don't the Dark Ones swear eternal vengeance against the Imperium and its butchers?"

"The Dark Ones will decide how the vigile is to be disposed of. Salit"—the kindly elder's voice grew confiding, sympathetic—"we recognize your natural grief. We recognize that your father was your only close kin, and that you have no mother. We recognize, too, you were placed in a terrible, unanticipated situation. Mistakes may occur on a blooding. It certainly isn't the first time. *And* we recognize your tender years. Do you understand, Salit?"

"Yes, Dark One."

"But these things do not justify your vendetta. The vigile is not yours to take. We have called these witnesses to observe this proceeding because they know you, they see you in the world every day. We have no Vigilance Authority. We have only each other to enforce the mandates of the Dark Ones. Once again, do you understand, Salit?"

"Yes, Dark One," she whispered. But the knot of rebellion burned like a cookstone in her breast, a stone that would not cool despite the cold water of censure. She was a Heaven's Devil. Heir to Horan Zehar's chameleon cloak and mnemon pocket and all the pocket contained. Heir to the precarious freedom of the impure.

"One more question, Salit Zehar," came the first thunderous whisper. "We want to know how you infiltrated the Mind of the World and contaminated Milord Lucyd's dream."

She stared up, amazed, at the five shrouded figures. *They* didn't know?

So my father kept secrets from the purities, the High Council, our clan, me—and from the Dark Ones.

She said honestly, "Dark One, I've got no idea."

They released her in southwest Marketplace as a fresh squall blew in curtains of feverish rain. Fancyfree Lane, the magister quadrant. Elegant concessions, glittering jewels, strolling musicians in swooping rain hats. Nude glamourists posed on street corners, living statues streaming with rain. Rain cascaded from the angels' mezzanine floating over her head.

Vigiles prowled everywhere.

Salit turned to Asif to thank him again and invite him to tip a jar of beer with her at her secret tentsite. But as soon as they released her, he and Habash disappeared down the service alley behind a perfumery shop, leaving her to fend for herself.

Alone.

So. My beloved comrade submits and obeys.

Sometimes she thought less of the Dark Ones than she thought of the High Council.

If the Dark Ones had sent spies to surveil her, they knew full well she hadn't mastered the chameleon cloak's capabilities in an environment like Marketplace, let alone the southwest quadrant. And knew full well an impure girl in southwest Marketplace would be as conspicuous as a naked plower painted scarlet. They meant to teach her a lesson.

She had learned her lesson, all right. *No one, not even the Dark Ones, will ever push me around.*

"Hai! You there! Impure wench," a commanding voice called out. A squad of vigiles turned, thumping the tips of their security clubs into the palms of their gigantic, meaty hands. "You don't belong here."

No, I don't!

Salit swiftly backed away into the throng of merchants and buyers out to trade despite the inclement weather. Crashed into the hull of a private windship bearing an irate angel descending from the mezzanine. Jostled against caretakers, their protocol chips winking between their brows, shepherding a brood of bratty prefect clovens.

She dodged out of the splashing path of a massive logging wagon pulled by four humpbacked drayers. From their unswerving course, the drayers were bound for the construction crews repairing the Obelisk of Eternity. She trotted after the wagon, seized the end of a log, and swung aboard.

The wagon transported her across the magister quadrant. She clasped the cloak tightly around her, drew the hood over her head, but the fabric remained dead black.

She hopped off the logging wagon at Allpure Square and ducked behind a streetsweepers' sledge loaded with steaming offal. The streetsweepers had parked the sledge and set the brake. They made their way across the square and headed into the northeast quadrant, brooms and bins in hand, hooded cloaks concealing their features so as not to offend any higher pures among the tourists gawking at the famous obelisk.

Salit caught and stilled her frantic breath.

It was no boast when she'd told Tahliq she was wanted by Vigilance Authority. Her likeness appeared on every wanted poster in Central Atlan. In all Pangaea, for all she knew. Were her shaved head and black facepaint sufficient disguise? Perhaps not, if her distinctive face loomed large in the Mind of the World for all who dreamed to examine and study.

How did you infiltrate the Mind of the World?

Good question!

The streetsweepers returned and flung heaps of offal onto the sledge. Rumor said the impure loved the smell of filth, ate filth, slept on beds of filth, but it wasn't true. Salit gagged. Her tentsite might have been threadbare, but it was immaculately clean and spare as a bleached bone.

The streetsweepers' sledge ground forward.

She darted straight across Allpure Square in the direction the streetsweepers had come from, ducked past the security monitor guarding the gate into northeast quadrant, dashed through the crowd of sturdy servs. She looked around. She spied a stairway leading up to a gigantic storehouse constructed of granite blocks. Beneath the stairway, the shelter of a dark alcove beckoned. She darted inside and squatted on her heels.

The long day had flown away. The sky perceptibly darkened above the relentless thunderheads that now intermittently spilled summer rain.

She pulled the cloak apart and gingerly opened the mnemon pocket, her thoughts scrambling. With one eye peeled on a street where an impure girl wasn't supposed to be and one eye on the pocket, she said, "I want to see Horan's thoughts on infiltration of the Mind of the World."

I want to see. Give to me. Let me see. No command she'd attempted so far had produced more than random results from the impudent pocket. She tapped out a cheroot and lit up while she waited for the pocket to respond. Stubbed the cheroot out again and waved away the trail of smoke when a squad of scowling vigiles trooped past, their huge heads swinging to and fro, keen eyes gleaming. Surveilling, always surveilling.

A mnemon fluttered out of the pocket at last, feather-thin, glowing bright white, and flung itself into frisky loop-the-loops. Cursing, she seized the mnemon between thumb and forefinger before the blasted thing gave her away. She studied the images scurrying across the luminescent surface.

A gigantic storehouse constructed of granite blocks. A stairway, an alcove beneath it. On the marble transom, a block engraving—

QUARTIUS NATALRY

Salit glanced out and up, and saw the same engraving above her, carved in relief. *What? Now* what was the mnemon pocket doing? Showing her images of where she actually was? What good would *that* do her? She ought to fling the poxy cloak away, toss it *and* its pocket onto the streetsweepers' sledge for all the good it had done her.

The mnemon flickered, and she saw her father stealing up the same stairway, slipping past the security monitors, creeping through blank-walled corridors within. What an oppressive place! She saw hordes of uniformed serv sub-pures shuffling down the bleak corridors, their dispirited eyes cast down. She saw rows and rows of bubbling tanks packed with the curled pink forms of the unborn like so many boiled shrimp in brine. How exposed these unborn were in their Imperial tanks. So unlike Salit, who'd been carried, unseen and unmonitored, within the flesh belly of her mother.

A stark, well-lit room appeared on the mnemon, and her father's voice whispered, "The laboratory, Quartius Natalry. Dubban Quartermain, midwife-natalist, works here and in other laboratories throughout the natalries. Uses a viewglass. His debt to me? Two hundred and twenty ores, long overdue. No prospects, no family money, no ambition, no sharer. Not even a bedmate he can touch for extra cash, despite the fact he's a handsome lad. Completely lacking in vanity. Not a criminal bone in his body, but a quick temper and an indiscriminate appetite for qut. He'll take any qual-ity, anytime, anywhere. Self-destructive, maybe. Nursing a secret sorrow. Difficult situation. Viewglass might be worth appropriating. Might fetch a hundred ores alone on the shadow market, but who besides the Alchemist knows how to use one? And what for? So what does our fine Dubban do *with* the viewglass? Whatever it is, may be worth much more. Extreme security around laboratories in all natalries. More so for entrances to Primus and Secundus Natalries. Other natalries may be fairly easily penetrated, though. Ask . . ."

On Penetration of the Enemy Camp, Technique Three: Opportune weaknesses include stupidity, laziness, fearful-ness, excessive bravado, short temper, gambling debts, illness, delicate constitution, deafness, blindness, drunken-ness, any type of addiction, and any other frailty of human-ity.

And before the mnemon flickered out, Salit saw bold swarthy features, thick black hair tied back with a thong. The sinewy shoulders of a handsome young man.

FACET 11

Comet: A genius or a lunatic.
The comet comes once in a lifetime.
The action is inspiration.
The forbearance is insanity.

The Orb of Eternity

Commentaries:

Councillor Sausal: Pan may appear as a sudden brilliance like the comet glimpsed in times lost to antiquity. Some believed the comet was the harbinger of apocalypse. Some revered it for its beauty. When the comet left the skies, those who revered it and those who reviled it each formed sects devoted to its return.

The comet has never been seen again.

So, too, the Imperium once knew the Ancient Ones. But the Ancient Ones are gone.

Therefore the prudent person should respect revelation if revelation comes. But beware of seeking that which cannot be compelled to appear. Beware of idolizing that which cannot be compelled to stay.

Guttersage (usu. considered vulgar): Genius is the little sister of lunacy.

Our City of Atlan, the periphery of northeast Marketplace. The Imperial Natalries, Quartius Natalry:

"Damn!" Dubban shouted as the monster stepped out of the lavatory wall. His voice echoed throughout the empty stalls. "What the hell?"

"Playing with your nightstick again, huh, midwife?" it—*she*—said, grinning the lopsided grimace of an impure. "That all you use it for? Pissing?"

He hastily pulled up his leggings as it—*she*—stood there, smirking. "Where'd you come from? How'd you get in here? What are you *doing* in here?"

"Enjoying the view."

That taunting voice. Those misshapen mismatched black eyes. That strange swirling cloak—dripping with rainwater. But it wasn't Horan Zehar.

It—*she*—was a girl!

"You're in the wrong lav, sweetie," he stammered. "You want the facilities across the hall."

"Nuh-uh, I don't. You Dubban Quartermain?"

"Who wants to know?"

He'd been standing before the urinal, meditatively emptying his bladder. Waldo had docked his wages but hadn't sacked him or decreased his hours, so he didn't qualify for Imperial labor relief. He would have taken the relief in an eyeblink. It would have been great! The stipend would have amounted to less than his full wage, but a little more than the docked wage, and he could have lounged around the temporary shelter, drinking beer, keeping out of the rain, touching one of the randy stonecrafters for a quid of qut. Maybe he'd try his hand at knucklebones or pokey. Maybe he'd take up wagering on athletes. Who knows, maybe Fortuna, goddess of luck, would finally smile on him and he'd win a pile of money. He'd pay off the qut purveyor, once and for all, and never owe money to anyone ever again.

Instead, finding himself betwixt and between had left him brooding, melancholy, simmering with agitation. Plagued with doubts and impure thoughts.

If the Imperium says the Apocalyptists' prophecies are false, does that mean Inim won't seize those with impure

*thoughts and fling them into Eternal Torment? Does that
mean that respecting proximity and observing purity protocol and fulfilling one's Imperial duties don't matter anymore?*

His thoughts had become more and more impure with
each squall blowing overhead, dumping tepid rain on the
megalopolis and on his face.

*What do I owe Pan if Inim isn't real and nothing you do
in this life—pure or impure—condemns you to Eternal Torment? What can the Imperium do?*

Plenty, as it turned out.

Since the Big Shock, vigiles had relentlessly marched
down every boulevard and alley, especially in Rancid Flats,
harassing the lower purities and enforcing security. Shortly
after midnight on the Revel of the Summer Buckwheat Harvest, his old chums Soral and Natch, both skilled machin-
ists, had gotten into drunken fisticuffs with a gang of
Imperial mechanics. Hardly an unusual event for a minor
festival night. But this time the lot of them had ended up on
their buttocks in Quartius Jail for a hundred and twenty
days. Ten days for disturbing the peace, thirty days for assault and battery, eighty days for protocol violations.

Eighty days for protocol violations!

Their subpures were so evenly matched, Dubban thought
the rowdies all ought to enter into sharelock and do their
face-pounding in the privacy of their own shack.

Natch, a born womanizer, would have guffawed at such
an Imperially proper suggestion, but Dubban hadn't dared
visit the jail and share the quip with his chum. The protocol
charge was obviously bogus. Meaning Vigilance wanted to
teach the rowdies a lesson. Once Vigilance had it in for
you, you couldn't do anything pure. He didn't need to be
associated with servs like that. Plus, he'd heard a rumor
that Soral had resisted arrest and now his left ankle boasted
a bloody stump. Soral had always pedaled his grinder with
his dexterous left foot when he'd fabricated ratchets and
pawls for firebolts and threshers.

What the Imperium gives, the Imperium takes away.

The incident had sobered him. Dubban recalled how, in the aftermath of the Big Shock, he'd tried to strike Garth twice. He could have been charged with assault, possibly battery. The spectacular attack by the Heaven's Devils on the Temple of Sharelock had only fueled the new hysteria. Heightened vigilance, fear of foe attacks, the rains, the mud, bone-rattling aftershocks, damage still unrepaired from the Big Shock. It seemed that everyone had been driven into a foul temper, acute frustration, and perpetual anxiety.

Dubban supposed he'd gotten off easy. He hadn't been charged or arrested for assault.

But he didn't feel easy. By day he'd had to work for a wage that barely paid for a carton of cod and wouldn't pay for a jar of beer *or* a quid of qut. Garth had taken new pleasure in taunting him. It was all he could do not to smash the twit's teeth down his throat. Resa had flaunted Romana. Waldo had harangued him every chance he got.

And by night, after his long hours at the natalries, Dubban had donated the sweat of his brow to reconstructing his neighbors' hovels destroyed by the Big Shock. The Imperium couldn't spare construction workers under Imperial contract to repair the temples, ducts, and roads. He and his neighbors couldn't afford to hire the remaining independent contractors. The cheery new slogan, heartily endorsed by the Prefecture of Atlan, was, "Do It Yourself!"

They hadn't much choice.

His head throbbed. His back ached. His stomach rumbled, and he wasn't sleeping well.

He had no idea when Horan Zehar would pay him another visit. He hadn't seen the qut purveyor since the day of the Big Shock, but that didn't mean Horan hadn't seen him. Who knew when the qut purveyor would swoop down upon him again? Who knew what Horan Zehar would demand?

You will do whatever I say.

Dubban was beat.

He could have left Atlan. He could have returned to his parents' household in the Far Reaches. Bandular had sent a sack of cakies and a message that the family's rambling shack had survived the Big Shock. Loosened hearthstones, cracked windowpanes, but otherwise unscathed and fine. His four closest brothers and their sharers had done just that—returned home from Andea and gotten local work permits. His fifth brother had returned home, too, and was courting the daughter of one of Bandular's assistants. But there was still plenty of room for Dubban.

At night, when the babbling serv shareminds of the megalopolis quieted and he could concentrate, he'd found and entered into mutual consciousness with his parents and brothers for the first time in a long time. He'd enjoyed the sharemind well enough. But as the youngest and most inferior family member, he'd been completely apprehended by all of them and in turn had apprehended less than anyone else. The sensation of being swallowed whole, yet of being denied the fullness of the others, irritated and depressed him. As usual.

His mother had offered to secure a work permit for him, too. He'd be welcome at the Far Reaches natalries, after his labors in prestigious Atlan.

Return home? Take work as a midwife-natalist at the outlying natalries? Natalries his mother effectively commanded, but in which officially she could only and always assume the humble role of a midwife?

The thought filled him with wistful longing—and revulsion.

Despite the arguments over whose turn it was to wash the clothes and tantrums over who'd eaten the last corn fritter, the old resentments and the lack of privacy, he'd loved family life. He always knew exactly where he stood. If a super sassed him or a bedmate left him or his debts were mounting, he'd always find a sympathetic ear, a pat on the back, a bowl of hot chowder, an ore slipped into his pocket. Bandular employed a dozen serv assistants, several of whom had dark-haired, dark-eyed daughters of proximate subpures and similar age who would have loved to see him in the Far Reaches again.

In the heart of the megalopolis, surrounded by so many people of different pures and subpures, he'd felt so alone.

But every time he thought of leaving Atlan, he thought of the lovely woman with hair like autumn leaves. The way she'd looked at him. The way he'd felt . . . a *connection* with her, despite all the odds against it. Pannish love? The ancient shame? He didn't know what to call it. He only knew he'd never see her again if he left Atlan.

Yet if he stayed, and if he ever saw her again, he could never approach her. *Enter into sharelock with the purity of Pannish love and with desire.* But, *Never mingle what belongs to one purity with another.*

Two curved horns of his dilemma—more sharp than before. He wasn't sure what he believed about proximity anymore.

Hopeless.

Impossible.

But how could he leave Atlan?

Bandular and Kendi loved him unconditionally, he knew. But devout Pannists that they were, especially his mother, they strictly observed the rules of proximity and protocol. No, he'd rather live alone in his rented hovel than live as the lowest member of his family. Forever the inferior bound to serve and submit to his superiors, however much they loved him.

It was bad enough, the destiny of a midwife-natalist.

In the end, practicality won out. Someone might seize his hovelsite on Misty Alley. It was a choice site, too, despite the bad water, frequent muggery, incessant noise, and uneasy mingling of serv subpures and druds. His walk to the natalry took less than ten minutes, sober or qutted out. In any case, his hovel would never get rebuilt if he didn't stay to claim his share of daub and wattle and his neighbors' donated labor.

He stayed.

He stared now at the cheeky impure girl. She smirked and kept her silence, as if waiting for him to recognize her first. He'd never seen her before in his life. And then he gasped. He *did* recognize her, despite her black facepaint and shaved head. How could he *not* recognize her?

She was the grotesque girl in Milord Lucyd's terrible dream!

He repeated angrily, "Who wants to know?"

"You may call me Salit, Dubban Quartermain."

"How do you know who I am? I've seen you, Salit, in the Mind of the World, but I've never known your name, or whether you were real. Till now. How did you find me? Why did you find me?"

"How? You're quite the creature of habit, Dubban. You're easy to find. Always in the laboratory on this floor, on this day, at this time. Why? I want the money you owe me and I want it now." She fluttered her weedy eyelashes in a repulsive approximation of coquetry.

"Owe *you*? I don't owe you anything. I owe that poxy qut purveyor, Horan—"

"That poxy qut purveyor was my father. The money you owed him is money you owe me. Cough it up, or I'll make you sorrier than my father ever did, Dubban Quartermain."

She lunged at him, pulled a dagger, seized his shoulder. Pressed the blade to his throat.

Dubban stared, stunned, disbelieving. In another moment, he could believe it only too well. He closed his eyes, remembering Horan Zehar. Of course. The resemblance was striking, her clawlike grip exactly the same. She stood so close he could smell her, surprisingly mundane scents of bacco and female sweat, undercut—he could swear—with the sweet reek of disease. Or perhaps she only wore an unpleasant cologne. How could he know? He held his breath, unwilling to contract infection from her.

Her blade teased his throat, a thin line of pain. His pulse pounded beneath it.

But just because she was Horan Zehar's daughter didn't mean he should meekly hand over money to her, dagger or no. What if she was estranged from her father and acting independently? What if the qut purveyor touched him for the same debt tomorrow?

He shook his head slightly, as much as he dared. "I've got exactly two bits in my pocket, so slitting my throat won't get you your money, sweetie. And I won't be chiseled, no matter what. You bring along your father to vouch for you, and then I'll pay you."

"You've got some nerve, for a midwife." But she released the pressure of the dagger and backed away.

He squinted at her. She was so hideous, he winced.

Her face twisted. "My father is dead. He was murdered by a vigile at the Temple of Sacred Sharelock on the night of the Big Shock. Did you hear about the atrocity?" At his nod, "Then you'll have to believe me, Dubban Quartermain, because I was there."

He nodded again, the truth of her words plain on her ghastly face. Terror gnawed at him. He'd always suspected Horan Zehar of being one of the foes. But a Heaven's Devil? He eyed the girl. *She must be one, too!* Then the rumors were true. Heaven's Devils could become invisible, could appear in one place and reappear someplace else leagues away, in less than an instant.

How else had she stepped out of the wall in the lavatory of Quartius Natalry? Her cloak dripped with rainwater. Clearly, she'd been outside only a moment ago. The natalries were Imperial facilities. Security surrounded them. Security she'd circumvented with ease.

Why hadn't Vigilance rounded up the foes, imprisoned them, punished them?

Because the foes possessed powers beyond the Imperium.

That's why.

He took a deep breath. *I'm standing face-to-face with a Heaven's Devil.*

She was very young, small, and sickly. Half-crippled in the way Horan Zehar had seemed crippled, but Dubban knew better. He kneaded his shoulder where he still ached from the qut purveyor's last beating. *Don't assume this frail girl is harmless, or that you could overpower her if you needed to. You don't know what she may be capable of.*

The line across his throat still burned.

She flung her cloak wider, deliberately displaying the weapons dangling from her belt. He examined her more carefully. She wore four enormous Orbs of Eternity strung on a leather thong around her neck. He averted his eyes from the orbs and their evil influence. She was armed to her teeth. Were those folded metal triangles dangling from her belt the notorious devil stars? The weapon that had sliced Milady Danti and the angels into a thousand pieces? Had murdered Clere Twine?

Her smirk returned at his terrified expression. She twirled her dagger through her fingers, enjoying his distress.

"My father left his qut purveyancing and his cloak to me. So, now, midwife, you *do* owe me."

"But I haven't got it," he whispered. "You can beat me if you want to. Go ahead, slit my throat. I haven't got it. You can't squeeze blood from dust. My wages have been docked, my family hasn't got two bits to rub together—"

"Gah, you say the same tiresome things every time. Can't you invent a new excuse?"

He stared, speechless. *How does she know?*

"Let's try something different." She idly rested her gnarled hand on one of her devil stars and circled him, gazing at him in her appraising way. "How about this? I want to kill every magister unborn in the natalries. How would I go about doing that? Poison the motherblood you feed them? Poison the tanks you store them in? Tell me, show me, and I'll cancel your debt in full."

His hands began to shake, his heart palpitate. He'd never heard of such an atrocity in his life. Couldn't have imagined it himself in five thousand years. She proposed to strike at the core of his Imperial duty. The foundation of the Imperium itself.

He nearly laughed out loud. How long and horribly would Vigilance torture him for even speaking with a Heaven's Devil who proposed treachery beyond imagining?

"No, no, Salit, I can't show you that." He desperately cast about for a lie. "I'm just a midwife-natalist. Serv pure. I'm much too low to get inside Secundus Natalry. That's where the magister unborns are grown, you see."

That wasn't true at all, of course. He and the midwife-natalists were the only subpure among the natalries who could touch ephemeral filth like pruned threads, abandoned birthsacks, and soiled amniotic fluid. With his skill at manipulating the miniscule pruners beneath the view-glasses, Dubban was routinely given access permits to enter higher pure natalries on assigned days.

It was the physician-natalists and priest- and priestess-natalists who were restricted among the five natalries. Lower subpures—those with unattractive variances, poor academic performance, or from families who had lost their wealth, for instance—were relegated to Quartius and Quintus Natalries. Those of brilliant, especially talented, or distinguished subpures enjoyed labor at Secundus or Primus. And it wasn't unknown for bribes to change hands among the middle pures.

But this impure girl wouldn't know any of that. She was removed from the intricacies of proximity and purity protocol. For that matter, most midwives he knew and many of the physicians, priests, and priestesses ran into trouble now and then with protocol.

"You couldn't enter those natalries, either," he continued as she pouted and played with her dagger. "The security is airtight! And, anyway, I couldn't tell you where to go or what to do." He bit his lip as she regarded him steadily with her terrible black eyes. Did he sound convincing? "To, um, do what you propose to do." He laughed nervously.

"Gah, you pures! Led around by the nose like oxen on a tether. You mean you've never even tried to enter Secundus?"

"No! I've got no business with magister unborns."

"Till now, midwife." She smirked. Her large, crooked teeth overlapped and gapped by turns, and had been ground to points as sharp and deadly as feline fangs. Or perhaps she'd been born that way.

Born. This creature had been seeded and grown inside a living human body. Had never had the threads of disease and disfigurement pruned from her birthpod. Had torn her way out of that living body and emerged—like this.

Bile rose in his throat at the very notion.

Think, Dubban! Think quickly!

"Listen, Salit, even if you and I *could* enter Secundus Natalry, even if we *could* get past security—"

"I can get past any security, anytime, anywhere." She thrust her painted chin at him, defying him to contradict her.

"Yes, well, even if we could, you couldn't possibly poison all the unborns. Each unborn has its own gestation tank. The ges tank is carefully sealed. Each unborn is fed through its own yolk stalk. It would be impossible for anyone to poison them all. A whole new generation would emerge before you'd even finished the first row."

"But at least I'd have culled the first row. And then there'd be the next row. And next row after that. Listen, and listen well, Dubban Quartermain. 'Tis the sacred duty of the Heaven's Devils to destroy the purities. Understand? Destruction of the purities will be your liberation." She barked with laughter. "You ought to feel proud to assist me."

Dubban kneaded his aching forehead.

She was insane.

But it isn't at all impossible, what she rants about. She could do exactly what she proposes. The unborn are nourished through a separate yolk stalk, yes, but each yolk stalk

connects to the Feed. Poison the Feed, and she could poison
every ges tank in every natalry. Exterminate an entire gen-
eration of Pangaeans of every purity in an eyeblink.

He gazed at her, sick to his heart. "I can't do it, Salit."

She gazed back, unplacated, contemptuous. "There must
be something else you can do to tide me over, then. And
don't get any ideas that something less'll satisfy your debt,
midwife." Her lopsided lips pulled into a rictus of amusement. "My father was interested in what you do in your
boring old laboratory. With the viewglass. So tell me."

"Oh! The viewglass! Well," he said slowly, pondering
why Horan Zehar would have been interested in thread
pruning. Questions tumbled through his mind. Suddenly he
realized, *Could it be? A way out? At least for now.*

Few Pangaeans had more than a vague idea of what the
midwives did in the laboratories. Rumors about the
natalries ran rampant among all the pures. Dubban had
heard more than a few ceramists and glaziers in the taverns
where he drank wonder loudly whether midwife-natalists
turned out more ceramists and glaziers from Quartius
Natalry not because of their lineage but because that's what
the Imperium ordered them to do.

The wonderments of tavern rowdies amounted only to
simplistic suspicions, of course. Anyone voicing such slurs
in front of a vigile could expect to wind up in the clang.

Still, Dubban had seen a lot in four years. He'd wondered
about the threads himself.

Now hope rose up like a bubble.

"I look through my viewglass—that's an instrument that
makes really tiny things visible." His collar felt tight
around his throat. He loosened it with his usual jittery ges-
ture. "I look at birthpods that have been seeded or sparked
into clovens. Each birthpod is a bundle of threads, like a
ball of yarn, only very, very tiny, and much more tangled.
Most of the threads are good threads, but there are always a
few bad ones. Threads that contain disease, and I do my
best—"

He abruptly stopped at her frown. Did she have any notion how diseased she appeared to his eyes? Why mention
to this lunatic Devil girl that, even with all his skill, sometimes he slipped and pruned bits of threads the physicians
hadn't marked? That sometimes he'd erred on the side of
caution and cut less? Or that some of his fellow midwife-
natalists were too timid to cut much of anything at all?

He said simply, "I cut out the bad threads. The threads
of disease."

"Disease," she said in the same savoring tone another
girl might have said *chocolate*. "And what do you do with
these disease threads?"

"I deliver them to the orderlies, who destroy them."
When her face lit up, he added, "The threads are very
dangerous."

He'd never told so many lies in one day!

"But you could smuggle out these threads before they're
destroyed?"

"I suppose I could. And then you could do with them
what you like. Maybe," he suggested slyly, "you've got
people among the impure who could use them to make
poison."

The Devil girl clapped her hands with delight. "Oh, yes!
My father's intuition was right. These threads could be
worth a fortune. And strike a blow against the Imperium.
You must contrive to get some threads to me at once." At
his ready nod, "Maybe you're not such a tethered ox after
all, Dubban Quartermain." She slapped him on the shoulder and slipped him a quid of qut. "No charge. Enjoy."

"Thanks."

Relief flooded him more powerfully than a quid of qut.
He'd bought himself time and a joke on Salit Zehar. By
themselves, pruned from the birthpods, the threads were as
harmless as a spent birthsack or soiled amniotic fluid.
Whether they contained disease and disfigurement—or
some other peculiarity or feature of the unborn—pruned

threads were worthless filth. Disposable garbage. Pruned threads couldn't harm anything.

At least, that's what the physicians said.

"It's about time you got back, Dub," Nita said, her purr of a voice strained and impatient. "We need you to help raise the roof on my hovel tonight before the blasted rains start up again."

Dubban wearily closed the tent flap of the temporary shelter, dragged his feet to his pallet, and collapsed on the straw with his soaked cloak and clogs on.

A swaybacked tent of dirty grey canvas, latrine dug in back, cookpots and cookstones beneath the awning in front, the shelter billeted thirty shareless people, plus two families with three sharers and three youngsters apiece. All had been Dubban's neighbors, serv subpures in close proximity, their hovels crammed together on the western quarterblock of Misty Alley. Now, instead of living a handbreadth away with daub-and-wattle walls between them, they lived a handbreadth away with only the odor of unwashed bodies and neighborly enmity between them.

Dubban avoided the nasty sharemind flickering open and shut among them. The effort rewarded him with a perpetual headache.

The straw was cold and fresh. The stalks pricked his skin through his clothes. How he regretted that his old pallet had burned in the conflagration which had destroyed his hovel after the Big Shock. He regretted its loss more than hovel itself and his other paltry belongings. He'd slept on that pallet three whole seasons before the straw had finally broken in, becoming pliant from the weight of his body and fragrant with the scent of Romana and his other bedmates.

He supposed he shouldn't complain. Atlan Prefecture had supplied the bedding by emergency decree, together with daub and wattle, lumber, other construction supplies, cookpots, and ten fullweights of buckwheat.

Do it yourself!

Or remain without a home.

He found it impossible to get a good night's sleep on the fresh straw. Every way he lay, the stiff stalks poked at him and crackled.

"My back is gimpy," he fibbed. His back *was* gimpy, but mostly he felt as worn as a rag from the confrontation with Salit Zehar.

She'd left the way she'd arrived—drawn up her hood, drawn the cloak across her breast, fastened the clasp, stepped back—and vanished. The still dank air in the lavatory had shimmered strangely. He'd thought he heard footsteps. Had she left an evil spirit behind to haunt him? To watch him? The sound had frightened him so thoroughly he'd sprinted for the door, slapped it open, and dashed all the way back to the laboratory.

"You're a quiet one tonight," Nita said. "Have a shot of skee and up and at it, chum. The sooner we get mine up, the sooner we'll get yours."

She pressed a cup into his hand and sat on the edge of his pallet, smiling persuasively. Her brown eyes sparkled mischievously at her innuendo. Crewing with an Imperial Archipelago Fisheries skiff had agreed with pretty Nita. The physical labor had nicely shaped every one of her muscles, the fresh air given her a ruddy glow.

Desire surged through him at her close presence—her smile, her eyes, her voice, the scent of her sweat, the musky oil she wore in her bobbed brown hair. How he longed to become closer to Nita. Longed to share her bed, maybe more. She was just the sort of woman with whom he might have properly entered into sharelock. A serv pure, of a subpure nearly equal to his own, from a respectable happy family, as sunny as a spring day, and very, very desirable.

But Nita had shared her bed for five long seasons with Rando, another fisher with quick fists, a quicker temper, and little respect for proximity. Or Nita. Dubban had seen Rando at Serpent Sect raves, snuggling up to a crude young roadbuilder whenever the boy drove in from Andea. Nita didn't bed with anyone else, at least as far as Dubban could see. He'd often found himself watching her closely and listening to the rumors.

Rumor said she and Rando would enter into sacred sharelock soon. *Terrible. A fine woman like her deserves better.* She ought to know her intended bedded a lower pure, but Dubban didn't think it was his place to tell her. She'd never shown anything other than friendly interest.

Till now.

"You only want me for my purity," he teased and drained the cup of skee.

"Dear me, no! I only want you for your body," she teased back.

"Sweet, strong Nita," he murmured and took her rugged hand, running his fingertips over thick calluses in her palm. Her hands were more brawny than his.

He and his neighbors staying at the shelter had drawn lots. Whose hovel on the quarterblock would be rebuilt first and in what order? Let Pan and destiny choose, as Pan and destiny chose everything. His hovel had been twenty-first on the list. Since the Big Shock, they'd managed to erect four new hovels before the summer rains came. Construction on Nita's hovel, the fifth, had slowed to a crawl, and the rain had ruined the first roof they'd tried to raise.

At this rate, he'd be living in the damn tent till the autumn turning.

"You two look cosy," came Rando's rasping baritone and the astringent stink of his cheap bacco. "I think I'll take care of that."

He seized Nita's arm and lifted her off Dubban's pallet into a proprietary embrace, his eyes fixed balefully on Dubban. "You coming, Dub? We've got a roof to raise."

"And some other things, too," Nita murmured, nuzzling Rando's neck.

Dubban rubbed his eyes, annoyed. Had she only been toying with him? His arousal ached; he willed it to subside.

"No, you know? I've knocked my back out every night since the Big Shock. I've raised four roofs for the likes of you." He surprised himself even more than Nita and Rando with his rebellion. "Tonight I'm going to rave."

"Do you want to die?" shouted the High Pythoness into the amplifier on the dais at Stompsalot Cavern.

"I want to die!" shouted three thousand Serpent Sect devotees.

Dubban stuffed his forefingers in his ears. *This* was why he hated raves, grimacing against the din. *Why did I come here tonight?* But the cultists' frenzy stirred his blood, lifting him out of his melancholy and exhaustion.

"Do you want to emerge again?" the High Pythoness screamed. She thrashed six bejeweled arms over her head and around her torso in a vertiginous blur.

Dubban was certain the arms were part of her costume, but rumor whispered the High Pythoness was a freak. That she'd been bred that way in an Andean natalry and the arms were real.

A lurid rumor, ridiculous. He worked in the natalries. He ought to know. No physician could splice four extra arms into the threads of a birthpod. Who would want to commit such an atrocity?

Still, he shivered to look at her.

"I want to emerge again!" the cultists shrieked.

"Then first you must enter the Sacred Serpent!" The High Pythoness had sheathed herself in a variegated leather bodysuit. She undulated, sinuous and sinister. She opened her mouth and extruded an astonishing length of flicking scarlet tongue.

"Enter the Sacred Serpent!"

"And shed your skin—"

"Shed my skin! Shed my sins!"

"—and go forth from the coils—"

"From the coils, from the coils—"

"—and only then, will you emerge again—"

"Emerge, emerge!"

"—emerge again to live forever till Eternity!"

Music pulsed and blared. Drums throbbed, zitars wailed, flutes shrilled in wanton arpeggios. Magmalamps flared on and off and on, releasing trembling globes of orange-and-scarlet light. The globes exploded, spraying luminous streamers that sizzled and arced across the cavern, and winked out, plunging the place into dizzying darkness, only to be illuminated again. Bacco smoke, the narcotic scent of raptureroot, spicy pondplum incense infused the air and hung about in redolent bluish clouds.

"Would you like to die tonight?" murmured sect priests and priestesses, serpents writhing around their foreheads and through their hair as they mingled in the mob. "Only five ores. Would you like to die tonight?"

A sect vendor meandered through the crowd, bearing aloft a fragrant tray. "Two bits for flatbread, three bits for tato chips, four bits for a chocolate cakie, five bits for a codstick. Exact change, if you please."

Another vendor shouted, "Beer, kapfo, skee, bacco! Beer, kapfo, skee, bacco!"

And two young impures, their misshapen faces painted with black spirals and glyphs, crept through the crowd. Now they concealed themselves in a shadowed corner, now they confronted cultists, murmuring, "Qut, raptureroot, nopaine. Qut, raptureroot, nopaine."

Dubban scrutinized the impures. He saw no weapons dangling from their belts. *Only purveyors of raptureroot. Not terrorists like Salit Zehar.* Still, he gave them a wide berth.

Cultists leapt and pirouetted and capered, clad in tightly laced bodysuits of gaudy leather. Most were short stocky serv subpures with swarthy faces, dark hair, and strong cal-lused hands destined for skilled manual labor, though sev-eral subpures of tall, skinny monument builders with straw-

colored hair and long, protruding noses giggled and flirted
with each other.

"Hai, Dub, what a surprise. We thought you didn't want
to rave anymore. Did you decide you wanted to bed some
real women, after all? Outside of sacred, sacred
sharelock?"

A gale of giggles. Dubban turned. Romana and Resa in
full cult regalia, defiant, glittery-eyed, and deeply drunk.
Their huge breasts, hips and buttocks fairly burst out of
imitation serpentskin bodysuits, their limbs entwined
around each other.

A strange gritty feeling entwined around his heart.
Romana. Romana with Resa. Yet why should he feel disappointed? He would never enter into sharelock with either
woman. He didn't *love* either one. He ought to wish them
well if they'd decided to enter into sharelock with each
other. Did he want to bed one or the other, or both? Desire
still coiled in his loins, the aftermath of his tête-à-tête with
Nita. They both smiled invitingly. He wondered what the
two of them together might be like.

No.

He didn't want to relieve his bestial urge with a woman,
let alone two, who'd left him feeling dead inside. Degraded.

He forced a smile. "You both look preoccupied with
each other, lovely ladies. May your joy last tonight and
forever."

The two astonished women thanked him and grasped at
him with fluttering hands, but he pushed past them through
the crowd to the sacrificial altar. Priests laboriously raised a
wooden scaffold and secured it. Priestesses brought wide
deep brass bowls and laid them upon the altar.

"I think I'd like to emerge tonight," he told a priestess.

"You *think*?" she teased him, baring her qut-stained
teeth in an insinuating smile.

"I *want* to emerge. Yes, I do."

On this day when he'd agreed to commit a crime against
the Imperium, he needed absolution.

That's why he had come here tonight. Maybe the disease threads were worthless and harmless, but thievery was thievery. Collaboration with a Heaven's Devil, collaboration. He'd always been a reasonably good citizen. He'd observed proximity and purity protocol, taken his Imperial duties seriously, even if he'd wanted to punch Garth in the teeth and exchanged glances with a higher pure woman.

Impure thoughts are only thoughts. The romance of rebellion, a quickening of the blood. But impure deeds? Traitorous deeds?

What terrible step had he taken? What criminal road was he about to travel down?

He wasn't proud of his illicit bargain with Salit Zehar.

And all because of his hunger for qut, a greasy little bundle of bitter herb that plunged him into a fleeting oblivion and gave him a splitting headache in the morning.

He hated it!

As he hated the emergence ceremony. He'd sworn he'd never participate in a Serpent Sect rave again.

Yet now, tonight, he needed to emerge.

"I don't have five ores on me, but I do have this." He proffered the quid of qut Salit had given him. "I don't want it anymore. It's worth more than five ores, I'm sure."

"Done," the priestess said and slid the quid into her mouth. "Strip down, honey."

Dubban removed his clothes and handed them to her. She threaded the string of an identification tag through a button-hole, tied a corresponding tag around his wrist.

"Stand over there with the others for the sacrifice and the bloodbath. You'll enter the Sacred Serpent there, and emerge over there. Someone will be waiting with your clothes. Got it? Good." She reached up and brushed a strand of hair from his forehead, pointedly looked him up and down, and winked. "May you live forever, honey."

He nodded and hurried to the foot of the altar, anxiety beating in his chest. He had never been ashamed of his physique, had usually wandered unclothed through his parents' house without a qualm, but he felt uneasy striding naked through this crowd. This was the moment of danger. If Vigilance Authority intended to raid the rave and arrest everyone, vigiles would also be striding through the crowd—now, before the sacrifice could take place. He cautiously surveyed the frenzied cultists, ran his eyes over the crowd again, but saw no sign of vigiles lurking about. No vigilance sharemind crackled through his consciousness.

Chanting began.

Drummers commenced a hypnotic beat.

Three priests led in a bovine drud, a drayer or plower from the look of her brawny shoulders and sturdy thighs, her loins wound round with a strip of burlap rag. She babbled and giggled, plainly disoriented, her idiot's face slick with oil and sweat. Dubban wondered where the priests had kidnapped her.

Her hands were bound behind her with garlanded rope.

The priests brandished sticks of burning raptureroot in her face, exhorting her to breathe deeply. They led her to the altar and bade her lie down, which she did, clumsily climbing up and collapsing on her back. A priest bound her ankles with more of the garlanded rope, and handed the end of the rope to a priest perched on a ladder next to the scaffold. The priest on the ladder secured the rope to a winch atop the arm of the scaffold, and hastily descended.

All three priests seized the long wooden handle of the crank attached to the winch and vigorously turned it. The drud was hoisted up by her ankles till she hung from the crossbar of the scaffold, the mounds of her massive breasts sagging down to her chin.

The drud's intoxicated expression suffused with terror and confusion. She rolled her eyes and opened them so wide Dubban could see the whites all around her irises. She convulsed, struggling to loosen her bonds. In a guttural accent Dubban could barely understand, she entreated the crowd.

Bile collected in his throat at the awful sight, at the knowledge of what was to happen.

Better her than me.

He flinched at the cruelty of his thought. He pitied druds and serv subpures lower than his own, as was proper under purity protocol. Keen pity, since he knew as the youngest member of his family what ceaseless inferiority felt like.

But the pounding drums, the wailing zitars, the chanting, unleashed darkness inside him. Could he step away from this abomination? Withdraw his participation, denounce the sect?

Whether he stayed or left wouldn't save the drud now.

Cultists danced violently, swooping, leaping, whirling. Cultists gathered around the altar to watch. Some solemn, some laughing, some mocking. Some openly weeping. A serv sharemind rose up, reverberating with excruciating emotions.

The drud began to keen, a low moaning that crescendoed into a rending scream.

The High Pythoness approached the altar, gazed down at Dubban and five other supplicants. She chanted, "Will you enter the coils tonight?"

"I shall enter the coils tonight!" *Don't think about the drud, don't think about her.* Dubban bobbed to the drumbeat, feeling the frenzy grip him.

The High Pythoness climbed onto the altar, stood next to the struggling drud. She brandished a long, curved gleaming saber, while her other arms writhed like agitated serpents. She intoned—

I am Spawn of the Primeval Flood,
I am that which Emerged from the Waters,
I am the Speaker of What Has Been and What Will Be;
I extend Everywhere.
I bend round Myself, I enter my own Coils,
I am what Comes Forth from my own Mouth.
I copulate with the World,

And eat Her Blood
That you may Emerge
And live Forever!

A swift flash, and the drud's neck gaped open from ear to ear. The crowd howled. The priests hurried to catch the surging blood in the large brass bowls.

A priest bearing a brimming bowl approached Dubban and bade him kneel. "Close your eyes tightly, or this will sting and blind you," the priest shouted in his ear, and then, "Go forth through the coils, and emerge." The priest poured the entire bowlful of the drud's blood on Dubban's head and shoulders, drenching him.

Dubban closed his eyes as tightly as he could. Hot, thick fluid slid over his skin, the jism of death. His eyes burned anyway, the blood seeping through his eyelids. He nearly retched from the stink—raw flesh, hot metal, rank sweetness—life opened into death. Two priests took his hands, lifted him to his feet, and guided him to the gigantic mummified python. They helped him kneel again and then he entered the python through an aperture in its tail, wriggling on his belly as serpents do.

Pitch-black inside. With hands and feet, he propelled himself through the python's coils, pushing with his toes, pulling with his palms.

Sweat surged out of his pores, mingling with the sacrificial blood. His eyes stung so fiercely he feared he really would go blind. With every reckless motion he made, the python squeezed him tighter and tighter till he thought he might suffocate.

Is the serpent alive, after all?

If he slowed or rested, would the python clamp around him in a death grip? The thought of entrapment, of suffocation panicked him. His breath blew out of his lungs in painful gasps. He wriggled violently forward. *Faster, faster, get out!*

He heard the cultists outside shrieking, "Emerge! Emerge! Or die!"

In the suffocating darkness with the stink of blood on him, his thoughts twisted desperately to his life, his family, this day, his bargain with the Devil girl, and what he must do. The bitterness and futility of his existence in Pangaea. His inescapable distance from proximity to Pan. His hopes and desires that so frustrated and oppressed him, and would not leave him alone. The lovely woman, unreachable, unattainable.

And he realized this *was* his absolution, his salvation, his gift. That he *did* still hope, *did* still desire. *Did* still believe he might attain the unattainable. That if he lost his hopes and desires, he would truly be lost forever, dead and forgotten. That his hopes and desires, his impossible belief propelled him through each wearisome day, even as he propelled himself now through the coils of the Sacred Serpent.

Single-minded purpose overcame him, and he calmed his movements. He began to move slowly, smoothly, powerfully. Almost instantly the python loosened its constriction.

A strange peace invaded him, and a fierce new conviction—

I will become more than my destiny, reach beyond my birthright. I will find my sacred sharer. I will win her love and evoke her desire, whatever her pure. I will defy the Imperium, proximity, purity protocol, and all the strictures of sharelock, if I have to. I will generate the progeny I envision—three fine daughters and three fine sons. And my children will know the name of Dubban Quartermain. In some far future, in the world without end, they will tell how a midwife-natalist lived, labored, and loved in old Pangaea. How he refused to relinquish his dreams.

He saw a blazing light and a fence of fangs as long as his arm. He'd reached the python's yawning mouth. He struggled to his knees, then stood, and staggered out along the length of a huge serpentine tongue. A gleeful flock greeted him. Two laughing priests doused him with buckets of warm milk, washing the sacrificial blood away.

And a figure stood before him, impossibly lovely.

Impossibly *there*.

He swiped blood and milk out of his stinging eyes and stared.

She stepped up to him, the woman with wavy hair the color of autumn leaves. Shadows pooled beneath her cheekbones. Her gold-green eyes glittered. Her full lips curved in her exquisite smile. She wore a close-fitting tunic of emerald-colored silk that clung to her breasts and slender waist.

She proffered the pile of his clothes and a white summer rose.

She said, "May you live forever."

FACET 12

Clouds: Gathering or dispersal.
Clouds signify uncertainty.
Roll the Orb twice to complete the oracle.
The action is fulfilling potential.
The forbearance is idle speculation.

The Orb of Eternity

Commentaries:

Councillor Sausal: The atmosphere surrounding Pangaea is ever-present, yet the clouds are ever ephemeral, dispersing with the wind. Thus clouds must be regarded with a special ambivalence in the order by which all things of the world stand in proximity to Pan.

So, too, the Imperium is beset with the uncertainty of storms, earthshocks, and impurity.

Therefore, when beset by ambivalence, the prudent person will be permitted to prevail upon the oracle twice: first for the proper direction, and second for the proper time.

Guttersage (usu. considered vulgar): The answer, fool, is blowin' in the clouds. The answer is blowin' in the clouds.

Gondwana Peninsula, Gondwana Valley, at the southern border of Greater Atlan. Stompsalot Cavern:

"Thank you, milady," the bold swarthy boy stammered and reached for the sweet little heap of his rumpled clothes. With a mockingly gracious bow, Plaia presented them, relishing his reverent tone, the blush that stained his cheekbones.

Serv pure. Lower. Inferior.
Contaminated. Tainted. Filthy, even, to her touch.
Forbidden.

Her fingertips brushed his. The sensation of heat seared all the way up her arms. His hands trembled. She wondered if hers did. She had no idea. She'd never touched a serv in her life.

Cultists all around them shrieked, "Emerge! Emerge! Emerge!"

The boy bowed in return. "The Sacred Serpent has brought me a miracle. A living goddess."

He stared at Plaia as if she were a statue cast of atlantium with gemstones for eyes. No one had ever gazed at her with such adoration—and tenderness. And desire. He revealed his shameful urge more nakedly than he revealed his splendid body.

Amid the blasting music and the throb of drums—and for the first time in her life—Plaia found herself moved beyond speech.

How very strange! Plaia the Plaything, struck dumb?

"May you live forever, too," he continued, becoming more assured as he registered her answering fascination. She hadn't dismissed him, recoiled from him, or even cared much about protocol, at the moment. He was panting from the exertion of the emergence ordeal, his bronze skin glossy with sweat. "May you find the sacred sharer who will join with you for all Eternity."

He noticed Julretta, then, scowling at Plaia's side, disapproval, jealousy, and covetousness conspicuous on her plain little face, her hands balled into angry fists. And wild-haired Paven, grinning madly, bobbing to the drums, his fists beating imaginary drumsticks to the relentless rhythm.

Pain and longing spasmed across the boy's bold features, like the first time Plaia had seen him in southeast Marketplace.

''That sharer will be a very fortunate person,'' he added, aiming a wistful smile at Julretta. A doubtful look at Paven, who with his blue-green finery and effeminate stature exuded an academe's sophistication.

Julretta whipped her eyes away, disdainfully refusing to return the boy's smile. Paven shrugged and seized the elbow of a voluptuous serv girl, spinning her into a jig.

Plaia found her voice again at last. ''Yes, my sharer will, when I finally decide to tie the knot.'' She'd never spoken two personal words to a serv pure, or many formal words except in the course of daily protocol. And even then, she usually never spoke at all with the gardeners who cultivated the vineyards around her fathers' villa or the maintenance keepers who kept order among the vast lampworks and waterworks at Sausal Academy.

Did the boy assume Julretta was her sharer? Paven, their escort? She'd disabuse him of that notion, straightaway.

''It may be difficult to know if, or when, or where, I'll ever find Pannish love with a person of my pure, proximate subpure, and suitable family.'' Such formal words! In a rush, ''But I'll always share my bed with a man.''

She heard Julretta gasp at her audacious words, Paven guffaw. She astonished herself, saying such words to a serv.

She'd recognized him the moment she'd seen him standing at the foot of the altar. The sacrifice had been appalling, of course, but she couldn't dwell upon the protections of drud pures just then. She'd bribed the sect priestess for his clothes, bought a rose from a vendor, elbowed her way to the mouth of the Sacred Serpent.

And waited for him.

The boy blushed again, scarlet spreading down his neck to his chest. Lust leapt into his eyes, not to mention his groin. Plaia half concealed her delighted smile behind the palm of her hand. His voice, that was it. How she resonated to his voice! It rumbled through her, a silky baritone that made his gracious words rendered in a foreign serv accent all the more delectable. Where was he from? Siluria? Laurentia? The Far Reaches?

He was even more handsome close at hand than far away. She suddenly loathed the strictures of proximity. How much had she been denied? *It's not fair.* She'd never thought of the order of things as fair or unfair; they simply were. *The way the Imperium says the world must be.* Now she wondered if proximity *was* a natural law, purity protocol the resultant necessity. Destiny a divine force, forever unavoidable. The will of Pan, inexorable.

She took her fill of looking at him—such shoulders! such thighs! ahem!—as he fumbled with his clothes.

"This is awful, Plaia," Julretta complained in her ear. "He's a ductdigger. Don't make a fool of yourself."

"What a proximicist you are," Plaia scolded her. Thought *Serves you right* when Julretta winced at her disparaging tone. Everyone in Pangaea, down to ductdiggers, might have been a proximicist, but good Pannists treated lower pures, subpures, and inferiors with pity and compassion, not contempt. Or they were supposed to. Julretta was nothing if not a good Pannist.

Had Plaia thought that way, too? No, not possible. Not with this boy standing an arm's length away. "They're all ductdiggers, Julretta. Actually, they're all servs. We're the only academes in the whole damn place."

Paven, never one for propriety, twirled with his serv wench across the dance floor.

Suddenly a current of agitation rippled through the crowd. The musicians abandoned their instruments amid a clatter of cymbals and jangling chords. The globes of orange-and-scarlet light flared, then disappeared, plunging the cavern into smoke-choked darkness.

A scream, "It's the foes!" and lamps sharply illuminated the cavern's entrance twenty paces away from where Plaia stood. She heard a *crack!* like a bullwhip and a tumult

of voices. "It's the Heaven's Devils!" Fear stunned her.
She'd glimpsed a couple of scrawny impure boys peddling
narcotics, but they'd faded in and out of the crowd, as wary
as feral beasts. *That's how they operate. You don't see them
till they strike.* She glanced at Julretta, saw the young
woman's mouth yawn open with terror. Paven embraced
the voluptuous serv, both of them blinking, dazed, in the
harsh blue-white light at the entrance to the cavern.

The boy shouted in her ear. "It's not the foes. It's *not* the
foes."

A squad of enormous vigiles strode into the cavern,
smashing security clubs into stumbling dancers. Vigilance
sharemind whipped into Plaia's consciousness, as sharp as
a volley of needles.

A monotonic voice boomed, "Where is the drud? You're
all under arrest for protocol violations. You're all under
arrest as accessories to a blood sacrifice."

Two vigiles swung their glittering eyes toward Paven,
wrested him away from the serv girl, snatched him up as if
he were a child's doll. He flew into the air, limbs flailing.
Two other vigiles snared him and trussed him with security
leashes.

Plaia heard one vigile drone, "What are you doing here,
fine sir? Middle pure, aren't you? You've got no business at
a serv rave. State your name, pure, subpure, and security
number. You're under arrest for proximity violations."

Plaia stood, aghast, rooted to the spot. What to do?
Where to go?

"You're in danger!" the boy shouted in her ear. "May I
take your hand? Will you come with me?"

She nodded. He seized her hand. She reached for
Julretta, who clung to her other hand and tagged after her
and the boy.

The boy darted through the frenzied crowd, leading them
to the Sacred Serpent's mouth, the lolling tongue drenched
with blood and spilled milk. Plaia nearly gagged at the
stench, but the boy beckoned her and Julretta inside. They

crept into the serpent's throat and knelt, concealing themselves in the shadows of the huge curved fangs.

The boy crept in after them, dropped the bundle of his clothes, and knelt behind Plaia, tense and watchful. He tugged on the serpent's upper jaw, closing the mouth more tightly. She could smell his male scent, sense his protectiveness toward her, toward Julretta. Sharemind might have even flickered between them, but Plaia dared not exercise her prerogative. The vigiles might apprehend their sharemind. She leaned back and felt him kneeling behind her. The air felt like fire between them. *Forbidden. Filthy. Low.* She accidentally brushed against him when she shifted her weight on her knees.

It was as if she'd let the arrow fly from a crossbow.

Compulsively she turned around and embraced him, kneeling with her thigh between his knees, her hands resting lightly on his lean waist. She pressed her forehead against his cheek and closed her eyes.

He tentatively circled his arms around her shoulders.

They waited, barely breathing, within the fence of fangs.

"Plaia, don't," Julretta whispered. "It's tainted—"

"Shut up, Julree," Plaia whispered back harshly. "The vigiles will hear you."

She'd enjoyed tangling with Julretta's devotion less and less since the Big Shock, though she still respected and admired the young woman tremendously. Thankfully the riftsite expedition had ended. Gunther had permitted the resonance team to go aboveground late that afternoon and go home. The team—weary, traumatized, badly in need of hot baths and proper beds—had reported back to the academy, field data in hand, their aggregate sharemind of the experience dispersed equally among the teammates for analysis. They'd commenced the wearisome task of organizing their proof for Ground Control.

During the team's absence, the debate over preventing earthshocks had taken an ugly, disturbing turn. Farber and Helden, the main proselytizers of Tivern's shell theory two

decades ago and senior proctors with considerable influence at Ground Control, had published a particularly vicious article attacking their erstwhile mentor. Tivern—they
wrote—an unstable woman, had treated the unstable zones
as if they could be coddled into behaving properly. "Perhaps the cure for skee addiction includes listening to sym-
phonies, but we should beware of extrapolating personal
difficulties to difficulties of global importance."

If instability was the question—they declared—control
was the answer. If capriciousness caused untold damage,
discipline must be imposed. Further cracking of the world
shell must be halted and eliminated, the rifts stabilized and
permanently sealed.

The rousing conclusion?

"As Pan is the creative Essence of the universe that en-
dures for all Eternity, so must Pangaea endure, the planetary embodiment of the divine and physical foundation of
the Imperium."

Plaia had shaken her head at the analogies Farber and
Helden had drawn between the landmass and Pan. Rift
movements were observable phenomena, not the workings
of Inim's demons in the babe's fable her father had told her
years ago. Casting scientific inquiry as a spiritual quest
didn't help discover the truth. Even Ribba and Julretta, who
ought to have known better, had begun employing quasi-
mystical terminology.

Plaia had kept her silence.

And the solution?

"The perpetuity of the Imperium must be ensured with
forceful action," Farber and Helden advised. They advo-
cated a new program of force-flooding of the rifts with
enormous volumes of seawater.

Plaia had been incensed at the ad hominem attack on her
beloved mentor. Of course Tivern had viewed the planet as
if it might be coddled. Tivern had believed the planet was a
living being. Rumors ran rampant that the academy would
shut down resonance theory and application within the sea-

son. She'd been terrified her mastery was in jeopardy and applied herself with desperate vigor to organizing the expedition's proof.

The notion of force-flooding rubbed her the wrong way. But she wasn't quite sure why.

And Gunther? Plaia wasn't sure if good ol' Gunther knew she'd fucked Donson ten steps away from his bedroll, but their argument and her angry rejection had been more than enough to estrange them. At the academy he would only nod, aloof and solemn, when they'd pass in the halls. No conferences, no tutorials, no debates about theory. He hadn't called upon her at her fathers' villa. She noticed he'd removed the super's protocol chip from his forehead. She hadn't confronted his sharemind at all.

She'd sighed with relief. He had relinquished his petition to tie the knot with her, apparently, and she hadn't been burdened with the unpleasant chore of telling a higher subpure their relationship was over.

Julretta had been another matter. The hot summer storms had driven her affections into a disturbing fever pitch. She'd attached herself to Plaia at the academy, called upon her evenings after class, regularly stayed too late at her fathers' villa, fabricating excuses to spend the night. And spent nights, curled up at the foot of Plaia's bed like a pet sphinx. She'd brought flowers, books, a silk scarf that must have cost the young woman half her weekly stipend.

Plaia had wearied of always finding Julree's adoring gaze fixed upon her. Had Plaia encouraged the young woman too enthusiastically? She was beginning to feel as confined by Julretta's devotion as she'd felt incarcerated by Gunther's intentions.

But this boy. This boy, the boy of her forbidden fantasies.

Frenzied cultists scattered before the vigiles' onslaught, some scrambling into the shadows or disappearing into side exits, some caught like wriggling fish in security leashes. The sect priestesses and priests had vanished. The High Pythoness, the corpse of the sacrificial drud, too. The sect's inner sanctum had evaded Vigilance before, Plaia had no doubt. Took the cultists' money and didn't give a damn what happened to them when vigiles came calling.

"May I speak?" the boy whispered in her ear.

"Yes."

"I know an exit through the kitchen in back. When the vigiles assemble the arrestees, I'll take you there." He exhaled through his teeth, his breath hot on her cheek. "May I ask why you came here tonight? You, uh, don't belong here."

"I don't know." She laughed softly. Then, "I came looking for you."

He caught his breath, then slowly exhaled with a murmur of wonder. At last, "I'm sorry this has been an ordeal for you. I'm sorry," he added, "about your other friend."

Abruptly Plaia planted her hands on his shoulders and shoved him back on the serpent's tongue. He submitted to her bidding and quietly lay prone. "You've been through an ordeal, too," she whispered and knelt over him. "Permit me to serve you."

"Please," the boy begged her. "A fine lady like you shouldn't kneel before me."

"A lady like me wants to do a lot more than kneel before you," she said, smiling at him.

And despite the *crack!* of whiplashes and the vigiles' sharp commands as they arrested the cultists they'd caught, in spite of Julretta's outraged whispers and her own palpitating heart, Plaia set about relieving the boy of his distress.

"I cannot *believe* it," Julretta complained all the way from Gondwana Valley to Central Atlan. "Poor Paven is dragged off in leashes. Did you hear that dreadful vigile? For proximity violations! Who knows what will happen to him now."

"He'll be all right. Paven is part cat. He always lands on his feet."

"Don't be so sure. No one trifles with Vigilance these days. I'm still shaking all over. There we are, hiding like criminals, Vigilance is arresting the roadbuilders, and you decide to blow him. I cannot *believe* it."

"I thought you said they were ductdiggers."

"Don't be an idiot. I *knew* we shouldn't have gone to a cult rave. We almost got *arrested*. We could've gotten *flogged*. I *knew* we shouldn't have listened to that barkeep at Abandon All Hope. 'Ever hear of the Serpent Sect?' he says with that stupid wink of his. Of course you and Paven *had* to go. I'll never, *ever,* go with you to such a disgusting event again. All those servs. Ugh!"

"His name is Dubban Quartermain," Plaia said dreamily and licked her lips, savoring the taste of him lingering in her mouth. "Do you suppose he goes to raves often?" Remembering his fingers threaded through her hair. The way he'd whispered, "My goddess! My goddess!"

Any other time she would have been heaving into a sickbag as the public windship jolted and dipped through the storm. Creaky, filthy with litter, obscenities scrawled everywhere, the windship was the only transport service from an impoverished sector like Gondwana Valley to Central Atlan. Rain lashed down from the midnight sky, the tempest raged with renewed fury, but Plaia scarcely felt anything except a warm glow.

"Isn't he magnificent? I've never seen a man like that among our pure. Or our subpures. He's blessed."

"You ought to be ashamed of yourself. Why don't you just go fuck an ox?"

Plaia widened her eyes and dropped her jaw. "Do you really think he's as well endowed as an ox, Julree?"

"You're disgusting, Plaia." The young woman huddled into the corner of the bench. "Get away from me. You're horrid."

"Maybe you just don't like men as much as I do."

Julretta glared, a frisson of acknowledgment in her dark little eyes. "He's not a man, he's a serv. I can't *believe* they performed a blood sacrifice. That pathetic drud! Isn't Vigilance supposed to assert its presence and protect druds from atrocities?''

"Vigilance did assert its presence, you may recall.''

"Vigilance was a little too late. We could've gotten arrested *and* flogged *and* thrown in the clang for a long, *long* time. Accessories to a blood sacrifice! And *then* where would our masteries be?''

"The sacrifice *was* horrid. How do you suppose Vigilance can protect druds like that? She looked like a plower, poor thing.''

"Don't change the subject. You know how filthy it is to mingle with lower purities. I don't know how some people get exemptions to sharelock with lower pures.''

"There you go. They do. All the time.''

"Not all the time, Plaia. Hardly ever. And only if the higher pure's family doesn't die of humiliation first. And only if each natalry approves. And only if there's compatibility, matching physicality, intelligence, sharemind potential, none of which could possibly be likely between a high and low pure.''

"The bloody requirements go on and on,'' Plaia agreed.

"Don't be so blasé. I heard a rumor the High Council is repealing the exemption. It's too bestial. It's tricky enough between higher and lower just among subpures, let alone pures.''

Julretta bit her lip so violently Plaia feared she'd bleed. Poor little Julree. Higher and lower just among subpures had been one of two reasons Plaia had rejected her sharelock bid. In a voice trembling with suppressed rage, "Your fathers would be shocked and appalled, Plaia.''

"Yes, but my fathers will never find out, will they? Unless *you* decide to tell them. I think,'' she said coolly, "you'd better go home to your family instead of spending the night with me again.''

"But, Plaia—''

"No, go home. You bore me, Julretta.''

The young woman burst into tears and beseeched her forgiveness, but Plaia was implacable. When the windship touched down at the Pleasant Valley junction, she disembarked and refused to allow Julretta to join her.

"Go home," she commanded as if to a lost puppy.

What a confounding night!

She was still shaking, too.

She trudged down the well-lit block of Creek Street to her fathers' villa, leaning into the wind. Everyone complained about the summer storms, the inconvenience, snarled traffic, possibility of floods, but Plaia loved the rain. Summer storms cleansed the air of grit and smoke, the streets of offal and debris, and the wind smelled sweet and freshly laundered. Hot mist ghosted up from the cascading creek, whirling away with each new gust.

Dubban Quartermain. He'd offered his name—improper under purity protocol since she hadn't asked. She hadn't offered her name in return.

They'd parted rather more familiar but no better acquainted.

Why hadn't she given him her name? Why hadn't she asked where he lived, what his subpure was, where he labored? If she could come over tomorrow night for an hour in his bed? Why had she permitted Julretta to hustle her away? Why hadn't she turned back, found a secluded sward amid the rocky outcropping, and stayed with him a while?

She could have. Between the two of them, she possessed the prerogative.

But a higher pure's prerogative was meant to facilitate the interstices of commerce, the unavoidable necessary intermingling of lives in the megalopolis. As she trudged through the storm, fundamental school teachings resounded in her mind like the labored wheeze of her protocol teacher. *Angels need drayers to haul buckwheat from Iapetus Plains, just as drayers need angels to dream. Purity sharemind facilitates protocol and enforces protocol, as well. Preroga-*

*tive ensures proximity is respected while enabling unequals
to interact.*

On and bloody on! Her prerogative was not permitted, of
course, that she might satiate her shame with a serv pure.

Forbidden fruit? His impressive endowments? His demeanor, sweet and bold, deferent and defiant? So unlike
anyone of her pure or subpure!

Or something else, something she was blind to, and pro-
foundly wanted to see?

Julretta was right. She should feel ashamed. It had been
bestial, self-indulgent, outrageous. She *did* feel ashamed.
And soiled. And satiated. And thrilled. She recalled her
bold boy over and over, and cursed her timidity. Plaia the
Plaything, a repressed proximicist? Was she so bound by
the Imperium's strictures she couldn't even tell him her
name?

Apparently.

She would never see him again.

The thought nearly made her weep.

I'm going insane. She didn't need another stone wall to
beat her head against. Defending resonance theory and application against vicious detractors like Farber and
Helden—she had her battles to fight. She didn't need to
challenge proximity, purity protocol, and all Pangaean society just because she thought she might love a young man.

A stranger. A serv.

Did he go to raves often?

She shook with illogical laughter.

Her fathers' villa loomed ahead, a sprawling single-story
structure of pink stucco, brass security gates, ancient ivy
eroding the terra-cotta tile roof. The tremendous buttresses
of wrought iron they'd installed after the earthshock
twenty-six years ago to reinforce the villa's north side had
withstood time, smaller earthshocks, and the Big Shock
admirably well.

The Big Shock had emanated several leagues away, deep
in the primary fissure of Appalacia Rift. The shock twenty-

six years ago had issued from a small tributary fissure angling south from Sausal Coast, a fissure that lay directly below Pleasant Valley. That was the reason, Plaia realized, why her fathers' villa had nearly collapsed when she was a child but had withstood the Big Shock with few consequences. The precise location where the shell of rock became disharmonious, destabilized, suffered the greatest damage.

Ground Control had done an admirable job of monitoring disharmony in the rifts, but disharmony vibrated and dispersed along the length and breadth of a fissure and its tributaries. Even with the five predictors, no one could specify *precisely* where destabilization would occur.

Plaia had seen plenty of rift maps, the ominous webwork of cracks deep beneath tranquil valleys, grassy hills, sea-splashed coasts. *Someone should chart where each emanation occurs. Is it random? Is there a pattern? What would the pattern tell us about the nature of the landmass and how it's moving?*

Magmalamps sizzled in the storm, casting intermittent shafts of wan light across the topiaries and tossing pital trees.

"There you are, at last, dear child," cried Trenton as she straggled in the door, soaked to the skin from the rain. "Let me get you a towel. Let me dry your beautiful hair."

Gentle, sweet Trenton. Her second father took her drenched cloak from her shoulders and rushed away to the linen closet.

"We've been waiting for you all night, our daughter," said Cairn sternly. Tight-lipped tyrant, that was her first father.

"Well, here I am, my fathers. Goodness! Look at the time." She braced herself. "You ought to be in bed. Why are you waiting up for me?"

Her fathers—two balding academes with identical owlish eyeglasses set upon their long pale faces, somber dark blue scholars' robes rustling around their tall, slender physiques, sharelock chips winking in their hands—plainly had something on their minds. And it wasn't the perils and pleasures of her evening.

She was in no mood. She yawned extravagantly. "My fathers, I'm six winks away from sleep myself. And I've got a morning class. Can't this wait till the morrow?"

"Dear child," said Trenton, rushing back from the linen closet and proffering a plush white towel. "We might as well get this over. As your parents we've been tendered an offer for your Imperial materia. We've decided to grant our approval submitting you into sharelock with Gunther Triadius."

She laughed without mirth, disbelieving. "Are you joking?"

"I'm afraid not."

"But . . . don't be absurd!"

"We're hardly being absurd, our daughter," Cairn said. "The Imperium anticipates expanding the staffs at Sausal Academy and the Bureau of Ground Control. You should be happy. Your progeny will be assured of excellent positions, if their attributes manifest well and they fulfill their Imperial duties. The expansion will have much to do with Gunther's labors in earthshock prevention."

"*Gunther's* labors."

"In twenty years," Cairn continued in his oblivious way, "the Imperium will need intelligent, well-bred young academes with scientific predilections. Even a streak of impetuousness here or there will be welcome. It's time you face your Imperial duty, Plaia."

"But . . . I have no Pannish love for Gunther. I don't even *like* him anymore."

"We believe Gunther will be a good sharer for you," Cairn said. "He has declared his Pannish love for you. He's confided in us that you've been compatible bedmates—"

"I cannot *stand* Gunther in bed, my fathers." Panic gripped her throat. All the tiresome legalities of one's natalry account flashed before her weary eyes. "If you're so keen on my Imperial duty, approve of my sharelock with Julretta. I don't care if she's five years younger and a slightly lower subpure. I prefer to be the superior sharer. Julretta longs for a family. She adores me." When her fathers continued to shake their heads, "Naturally, we'd be honored to accept your Imperial materia for seeding hers. I've chosen two of her uncles to seed mine."

"That's very considerate of you, dear child. Of course we'd be honored, too, wouldn't we, Cairn?" Trenton said. "But it's out of the question."

"I'd rather sharelock with Julretta and endure her small faults than bed one *moment* with Gunther."

"—and we think Gunther's feelings about you are important, our daughter," Cairn plodded on as if he'd heard nothing. "You know we've always opposed that young woman. Her subpure's much too low for you—"

"She's from respectable clerics and librarians. The same as *you*"—she glared at Trenton—"my father."

"You can feel Pannish love for a higher subpure as easily as for someone lower," Cairn said. "In any case, we've never wanted you to enter into sharelock with someone who would drive you to eroticians. You've made your predilections plain enough. Our daughter," he added sternly, "we only want your happiness."

Cairn wrinkled his long nose and frowned deeply. Her first father had always disapproved of eroticians. The only extreme political position Cairn Triadana naitre Tertius had ever taken in his life was to support the eradication of Imperially licensed eroticians. The proposed legislation had been tabled before the High Council since times lost to antiquity. The council might have banned the Orb of Eternity—amid considerable contempt and scant compliance among her colleagues, Plaia had noticed, despite the threat of punishment. But eroticians would never be banned.

Not till the Imperium eradicates desire—however shameful, bestial, forbidden—and channels every yearning of the human Essence into piety toward Pan, labor for the Impe-

*rium, and sacred sharelock to guarantee the next genera-
tion.*

For the first time, she despised eroticians. She could bed
an erotician, if she wanted to. That was only a purchased
carnal act that had nothing to do with generation of the
family or perpetuation of her purity. The exchange of
money, the guarantee of services rendered, clarified the nature of the exchange to participants and society alike.

But the Imperium censured her, drove her into hiding
like a criminal, would *arrest* her, if out of the ancient
shame, out of a simple longing that had little to do with
Pannish love or Imperial duty, she dared consort with a
lower pure.

Like her bold young man. The memory of the first time
they had exchanged glances across the quadrant, the way a
vigile had swiped at him with a dagger and a security club,
filled her with rage.

She paced across the reception chamber. At last, meanly,
"What about you, my fathers? Your families permitted you
two fine fellows to enter into sharelock."

"Now, Plaia, dear child," pleaded Trenton, "your father
and I have an ideal sharelock. Neither of us has ever patronized eroticians."

"Oh, I see. Once again Pannish love conquers shame,
and the Imperium lasts without end," she said acidly. Her
fathers had indulged most of her whims, but the private
living chamber they shared had been off-limits to her and
her sisters. She had no notion whether Cairn and Trenton
slept in one bed or two.

"Plaia!" Cairn said sharply. "Watch your language."

Trenton gestured placatingly at them both. "Now, our
dear daughter, all children believe their parents never share
anything more than Pannish love." Sly smile and a wink.
"But we do."

She would have laughed out loud at her father's genteel
bawdiness if she hadn't been outraged and terrified. She
cast about for another protest. "Gunther's wage won't pay

for a caretaker when this new family is generated. And I'm still ten classes away from my mastery." She stared at them, wild-eyed. "Who's going to serve as the caretaker?"

It didn't take her long to figure out who.

"Our daughter, your subpure is lower than Gunther's. Your status at the academy, too," Cairn said.

"He's twelve years older. I don't want to enter into sharelock with an older man. It's unnatural!"

Cairn rattled on, "You don't earn a wage. You live off our stipend, in our villa. After all this time, you haven't even earned your degree."

The old sting, the long-standing accusations. "I'm *only* ten classes away."

"You might decide to change your mastery again," Cairn said pointedly.

"I won't change my mastery, I promise. But I'll never finish if I'm forced to caretake a brood of Gunther's brats. I don't *have* to. I don't *want* to!" She struggled for breath, lowered her voice. "I believe in resonance. I do. And I really, *really* want to finish my fucking degree."

Trenton said, "Child, watch your language with your father."

"That's enough, our daughter," Cairn said. He sniffed imperiously. "Are you drunk again? You look disheveled. Where have you been tonight?"

"I'm thirty years old. I don't need to account for myself to you."

"You do while you're living in our home and taking our stipend."

Trenton pawed at Cairn's shoulder appeasingly. "Dear child, get some sleep or you'll miss your class tomorrow morning." He bent and tenderly kissed her cheek.

Was that a haunted glimmer? A tear in her second father's eye? Or only his customary resignation? Trenton had served as caretaker to her and her three sisters. He'd been a wonderful caretaker, kind and understanding, the one they'd run to when Cairn had been harsh. Always quick with praise, gentle with criticism, a fountain of wisdom and practical advice.

She'd never known if Trenton had become their caretaker because he'd wanted to or because his subpure had been slightly lower than Cairn's and Cairn, exercising his prerogative, hadn't wished to caretake. *That's why sharers wear sharelock chips and enter into the intimacy of sharers' sharemind. It makes protocol more palatable between unequals who have to live together.*

"I'm not through discussing this, my fathers."

"Done is done," Cairn said. "There's nothing more to say."

Trenton added, "Gunther has made more sacrifices for you than you know, dear child. He's acquired respectable savings on that academe's wage you speak so disparagingly of—"

"Sure, he's stingy!"

"—and he's shrewdly managed the inheritance from one of his mothers."

"A *pondplum* paddy? That takes shrewdness."

"Perhaps you forget, our daughter," Cairn said, "that your father and I, and the Imperium, have an interest in your materia."

"Which is kept in the bank to devote as I see fit."

"To devote, ultimately, as the Imperium sees fit. The Imperium has freed the purities from the ancient barbarity of growing the unborn in the body," Cairn said, ponderously repeating the Imperial propaganda. "The Imperium is the final arbiter of generating a family."

"I'm not dead or incompetent yet."

Her fathers exchanged a glance that froze her blood.

"Gunther has expressed some concern," Trenton said gently, "about your competency."

"And we *are* legally supporting you," Cairn added. "We pay the taxes."

As if she didn't know. Her father's implication sunk in. Her fathers *could* act as her proxy in directing the use of her materia. She exhaled with frustration. "So you're going to toss me in the river because I don't earn my own wage yet? Because I don't pay my own *taxes*?"

"You have no one to blame but yourself," Cairn said.

"Such promise," Trenton murmured.

Cairn said, "Gunther formally applied to the temple and Tertius Natalry. He's observed all the proper procedures for arranging a sharelock in preparation of a begetting."

"I'm sure."

"Now, dear child," Trenton said. His softly insistent voice suddenly infuriated her. Her gentle second father was colluding in this travesty, too! "He's tendered a bid to seed five of your birthpods for the first generation. The natalry is delighted."

"His bid has been approved, accepted, and blessed," Cairn added dryly. "He's offered a very generous begetting fee. Which we'll hold in trust on your behalf till the first generation emerges since you refuse to take responsibility for yourself."

The momentousness of their decision suddenly descended on her. "Damn," she muttered and kneaded her forehead with a trembling hand. "Gunther can't force me into sharelock against my will. *You* can't force me. I'm over the age of ripeness. I have the right of refusal. I have my choice!"

"My, my, you modern young people with your dissolute ways," Cairn said, with a disapproving cluck of his tongue. He had *I told you so* written all over his face. "You do *not* have a choice. You have your Imperial duty. Our daughter, we've set the date."

"Bastard." Plaia refused to look at Gunther's smirking face when he sat down next to her in the library.

Julretta, Donson, and Ribba, seated at a long oak reading table, kept their eyes resolutely trained on their books and databoards. Rain pelted the rosette portals set between the tops of soaring stacks. Between the hazy luminescence of magmalamps and the pallid sunlight filtering through the portals, the library remained steeped in morning shadows.

"Now, that's hardly proper protocol, my pretty pet." Gunther reached for her hand.

She stood and took the chair across the table, ensconcing herself between Donson and Ribba. "You'll never touch me again as long as I live."

Gunther feigned anguish, his brow knit, eyes slicked with contrition. Then abandoned his pose and chuckled indulgently, as if she were an unruly child. "You're fetching when you're angry, but your anger will pass into nothing, as all inferior things do. You'll change your mind once the priestess-facilitators and their surgeons embed the sharelock chips."

"I'd rather die than wear sharelock chips with you."

"You'll live a long, long time, my Plaia, and our happiness will live for Eternity."

"I'd rather live with a Heaven's Devil."

Flash of his anger at that. He straightened his heavy proctor's tunic with a peremptory snap. "You act as if you're beholden to no one, but you're wrong. You didn't learn your lessons very well in fundamental school, did you? You owe your life to the Imperium."

"My life is my own."

"I don't think so. The Imperium needs academes. I've bid on the rights to your Imperial materia. I've submitted a begetting fee. Our lives will be joined as one. I'm so looking forward to it."

"My fathers informed me last night of your treachery. I'm appealing your bid. I reject your fee."

"Do you, indeed? Your fathers have approved of me and accepted the fee on your behalf."

"I don't give a damn what my fathers did behind my back."

He pursed his lips in a moue of censure. "You'll have to

give a damn while your fathers still have legal custody of you."

"I'm putting an end to that."

"How? You'd have to move out of their house, relinquish your habitation privileges *and* your stipend to terminate their legal custody."

"I started searching for a room first thing this morning." She'd also put aside a little money from one of her doting grandmothers, but that wasn't Gunther's business.

Gunther tossed back his head and guffawed. Misshapen yellow teeth lined his gums, she suddenly noticed, studded with metal slugs. Decayed, crooked teeth? His dull yellow quiff curled around his widening pate. Balding? How impure!

"Now where," he said, "would a gentle child like you find fit lodgings without your family stipend? You'll have to rent a hovel in Rancid Flats next door to a bricklayer. How could you possibly live on your own, my pretty pet?"

"As of this morning, I am."

"I forbid it!" Gunther slammed the palm of his hand on the table. The sharp report echoed throughout the library. Her colleagues at the table flinched. Everyone else in the library murmured and stared. Plaia silently congratulated herself for not moving one single muscle. What a fine demonstration of his domination. What a beast! Julretta had been right.

"Yes, I can," she said calmly. "You've changed, Gun. I almost used to like you."

"You'll be sharing my bed when I want you there before the end of the season," Gunther said in an even voice. "Naturally, I'll expect your complete obedience as my inferior sharer. Oh, and by the way. The academy is expelling you."

That got to her. *"What?"*

He smiled, pleased at her dismay. "I'm afraid I was compelled to make the recommendation. Let me see. I believe your measurements of the Tivern grooves at Appalacia Rift were appallingly inaccurate.''

"They were not. Anyway, *you* said it didn't really matter.''

"Of course it matters. Tracking the movements of the rifts is essential in determining how we're going to stabilize the shell. And you have no talent whatsoever for producing resonance.''

That stung. "Tivern said I'm the best cymbalist—''

"Tivern was a drunk and a slut without a sharer to settle her down and remind her of her Imperial duties. I'm not surprised you sought out her proctorship. I also understand you wrote a nasty letter to my colleagues Farber and Helden—''

"Your colleagues deserved it, after the rubbish they published about Tiv.''

"—criticizing their theory of force-flooding. 'Insane,' I believe is the word you used.''

"Force-flooding *is* insane! Think about it. I haven't been able to think of anything else since I first read about the proposal, and now I know why. How *could* Farber propose such a harebrained application when she knows damn well excess substream water in the rifts *correlates* with major earthshock activity?''

"Oh, Pan,'' Julretta whispered and rolled her eyes at Plaia. *I didn't think of that. You're right.*

"It's a moot point,'' Gunther snapped. "You're out of here.''

But she saw the flicker of acknowledgment in his eyes. And a tinge of sadness. Would he miss discussing theory with her? Miss entering into the exuberant purity sharemind they'd shared, when she'd been willing?

Too bad.

"Hardly moot, and I'm not gone yet, Gunther. You force seawater into a rift that isn't just bouncing, but moving, moving laterally and moving down, moving in ways we don't understand, force enough water to so-called 'seal it permanently,' impeding that lateral movement, and you could *cause* an earthshock of such magnitude it would make the Big Shock look like a child shaking a rattle.''

She felt the shudder of alarm in sharemind with her colleagues. Julretta and Donson stared at her, wide-eyed. Ribba averted her gaze, a peculiar expression flitting across her brazen features. Priestess subpures imbued Ribba's materia. She wore a look of perpetual rapture even after three cups of caf at eight in the morning.

Gunther shook his head, smoothed his yellow quiff over his pate. ''You see? You're very bright, Plaia, but you've become misguided. You've lost your way. I'm sorry, but you sound hysterical, and it's all because you were drinking wine when you measured the Tivern grooves. I'm sorry if my lack of attentiveness to your needs lately has played a part. But, my darling, I assure you I'll make it up to you.'' He smiled, the picture of condescending benevolence. ''In any case, I'm glad you have children on your mind.''

She could have wrung his thick neck. *Stay calm if it kills you.* A public show of temper would be just what he'd like. Witnesses at every table, darting covert glances. Coolly, ''I have allies who will support my contributions to earthshock prevention and my talent at resonance.''

''We shall see.'' He stood, stalked away. Stopped in his tracks, turned, and shook his finger at Donson. ''And you. You fuck her again, and I'll have Vigilance arrest you for alienation of intended sharelock.''

When Gunther turned away Donson waggled his fingers in a mocking farewell, but visibly blanched. ''It was fun, Plaia,'' he said nervously and diligently returned to his studies.

''Splendid, Plaia,'' Julretta whispered. ''You've only insulted the most promising proctor at Sausal Academy.''

''*I've* insulted *him*?''

''Rumor says Ground Control is going to give him a permanency.''

"Oh, fine. We'll find ourselves forever under his thumb."

"You look terrible this morning, Plaia," Julretta said tartly. "I haven't seen Paven anywhere. Have you?"

She shook her head, too dejected to speak.

"I'm really worried about him," Julretta rattled on. "I can't see Paven in jail. And his family lost their money. If there's a bond—"

"I'll go over to Tertius Jail at noon, all right?" Plaia scraped her fingers through her hair. "I'll pay Paven's bond myself. Will that make you happy, Julretta?" She winced with guilt. After her exhilarating encounter with her bold boy and the terrible confrontation with her fathers, she hadn't given Paven a second thought. *Gunther has expressed concern about your competency,* Trenton had said. "Dear Pan," she whispered. "Gunther is setting me up."

"Oh, Plaia," Julretta said in her complaining tone. "I know how you feel about Gunther. I can't stand him, either. But I implore you, put common sense before your feelings. Maybe you could be a little nicer. He wouldn't have his own sharer-to-be expelled from the academy. He's proud of you."

"Don't be so sure. He's going to need a caretaker more than a fellow academe. I should have listened to you, Julree. I should never have bedded him."

"Too late now." Her small, plain face was taut with tension, the whites of her eyes veined with red, her eyelids swollen. She looked as if she'd wept all night. Plaia winced again at how cruelly she'd treated her closest colleague. Julretta stared down at her databoard dancing with kaligraphs. "Is it really true, then? He's formally applied for your hand? And your fathers gave custodial approval?"

"I'll appeal," she said dryly at Julretta's muffled gasp. "Like I told Gunther." His name tasted bitter on her tongue. "Listen to me. That's not the worst of it. Did you hear how he's currying favor with Farber and Helden? 'My colleagues'? I think he's going soft on resonance. Maybe our last field data weren't compelling enough. Or the team's sharemind of how the shock subsided after we projected resonance has blurred. I was afraid of that. Remember how we all danced jigs and whooped it up just a little too soon?'' She mulled over her copy of the neatly organized proof. "Our timing was all off. Maybe someone at Ground Control wanted it that way."

Julretta frowned. "Well, Plaia, resonance doesn't physically stabilize the rifts, it only harmonizes them and lessens the shock—sometimes. If all the rifts need is cooling of the basement magma and bolstering of unstable crust structure, force-flooding makes a great deal of sense."

Donson whispered, "I have to agree, Plaia. Maybe there isn't *enough* water in the rifts when a shock strikes. Maybe water would *cushion*—"

"Spare me the feather bed of rock, Donson." Plaia lowered her voice to a whisper. "Force-flooding the rifts, or any other application to seal them permanently, is only sensible if we assume Pangaea is one big shell that has remained the same and *will* remain the same except for cooling and hardening. Stabilizing, becoming static. Becoming dead. What if that's not the nature of the landmass at all?"

Julretta knitted her brow, her eyes clouded with confusion. "Did you *really* measure lateral movement of the south side of Appalacia? Four whole lengths?"

"Don't insult me. I've had enough insults for one day."

"But Gunther has a point. Where can the landmass move *to*? It's like saying Pan is somewhere else when Pan is everywhere."

"It is *not* like saying Pan is somewhere else, Julretta. I'm saying the south side of Appalacia Rift moved laterally four lengths. But your question's valid. Where *is* it moving to? That's not a metaphysical question. It's a scientific one."

Julretta studied her gravely. "All right, let's suppose you've got evidence the rift moved. Let's suppose the landmass is sliding over the inner core and that stimulates magma to seep through the rifts, causing volcanic activity, bounce, and the resultant shocks. That's all the more reason to seal the rifts. Then the shell can slide around all it wants to! That won't affect the surface any more than the spinning of the planet on its axis flings people off into space.''

''And what if our concept of the landmass is incomplete? Too simplistic? Or all wrong? What if the landmass isn't one big static thing, but active? What if it isn't bouncing *or* sliding as a whole, it's moving in some places but not others? What if the rifts *relieve* tension when there's movement? Sealing them could create tension *worse* than the present disharmonies, and cause the rifts to *really* explode.'' Plaia laughed caustically. ''Talk about the end of the world.''

''Plaia, the world's not going to end. Just like Pan and the Imperium are never going to—''

''Open your fucking eyes, Julretta.'' Ribba bent her mass of brown curls and impassive face over the text she was studying, and whispered out of the corner of her mouth. ''Resonance theory is *based* on disparate movement of the shell.''

''What?'' Plaia and Julretta exclaimed at the same time. ''Ssh!'' hissed a librarian.

Plaia shrank from the annoyed stares. ''Rib, resonance is based on this foolhardy fixation with bounce when we should be worrying about lateral movement. Where it's happening, in what direction, and why.''

''Nope. Tiv started revising bounce theory a long time ago, Plaia. Goons like Farber and Helden and even higher muckety-mucks at our fine academy suppressed her later data. I ought to know. I bedded her three whole glorious seasons before she died.'' Ribba added, ''I despise good ol' Gunther, but I suppose I can't blame him. You want to be the one to tell the High Council that Pangaea is moving and changing in ways we don't understand and there isn't much we can do about it except play 'Oh, Darkest Night' on a cymbalon?''

"I can't take this anymore," Donson muttered. But he didn't move.

Shock shuddered through Plaia. And a jolt of sorrow. It was still hard to believe Tivern was dead. "But Rib, she never breathed a word of this when I studied under her. It was all about bounce."

"Oh, I've no doubt Ground Control had placed her under a gag order by then. She wouldn't even say very much in bed. It's a wonder they permitted her to continue to teach at all, let alone go out into the field. I guess they were still hoping she'd discover something that would work. She went to Andea to measure the Tivern grooves. I would bet my last bit that she predicted magma was going to blow there. And because of lateral movement, not bounce."

"So she suicided," Donson said.

"No!" Ribba whispered. "Tiv placed her career and her life on the line, but she would never have gotten herself trapped in a rift during an eruption she knew was going to blow sky-high. She took risks, but she wasn't stupid. *Or* suicidal."

Plaia whispered, "Then . . . someone arranged for her to be in the rift when it blew?"

Julretta gasped.

Ribba only clamped her eyes and her lips shut, her face a mask of sorrow.

They all sat in silence, horrified and grief-stricken.

Here's to you, Tiv, Plaia thought bitterly. "Let's find out who did it and bring murder charges."

"Don't you think I've wanted to?" Ribba said. "The moment I started asking questions, I began receiving failing grades on all my tests and papers. And not just from one proctor. From all of them. Not to mention my apartment was burgled. A wagon hit and killed my dog. Three of my bills somehow got lost in our Imperial mail, and creditors came knocking at my door. All during the same half season."

Apprehension needled down Plaia's spine. "Why didn't you tell me, Rib?"

"And get you involved, too?"

"We're all involved now."

"Leave it alone, Plaia," Julretta pleaded.

Plaia's temper flared. "I won't leave it alone. Tiv must have written up the data supporting her latest theories. She was obsessive about documentation."

"Her family took custody of her files after she died. Probably sold them to Ground Control. No, I wasn't invited to her consecration, either," Ribba said ruefully. "I've never seen her later data, Plaia."

"If she knew she was in danger, wouldn't she have hidden it? Hidden it where *we* could find it, so we could carry on her work?"

Ribba snapped her fingers. "Yes! I know she loved me. And she was very fond of you, too, Plaia."

Plaia gazed into Ribba's eyes and they entered into sharemind, trading memories of Tivern. Her sweep of silver hair, her deep voice percolating with laughter, her grey eyes, her bodysuits of blue velvet, her bone-and-silver bracelets. Her graceful fingers dancing over her flute, peeling an orange, cracking an egg, scooping out the albumen with her thumb . . .

Ribba snapped her fingers again. "Egg!"

"Huh?" Plaia and Julretta said together.

"Ssh!" hissed the librarian.

"It became her favorite word toward the end. One of her funny little obsessions in our last days together. 'Consider the egg,' she'd say. I didn't know what the hell she meant, other than she was hungry. Or lusty. That was Tiv," she said with a wistful sigh. "Always hungry." Ribba closed her text, yawned, rubbed her eyes, stretched. "You know? I think I'm going to wander through the east stacks, just for fun. I've got a sudden hankering for eggs. Watch your back."

She stood, shouldered her rucksack, and set off at a leisurely pace, disappearing into the darkness of the east stacks.

"Coming?" Plaia murmured to Donson and Julretta.

"Beauties before the beast," Donson muttered. "I don't want good ol' Gunther sending Vigilance to arrest me for walking next to you."

"Let's split up," Plaia agreed.

Julretta strolled into the south stacks, Plaia headed north. She climbed the stairs to the second story. She suddenly became aware that her heart throbbed with trepidation. The stacks were deserted, musty-smelling, and very dark this rainy morning, some of the corridors lit only by a tiny column of tenebrous light angling down from a portal in the wall. She found a shortcut she knew that would take her to the east stacks.

She found Ribba seated cross-legged on the floor in, of all places, the section marked *Cuisine of the Provinces and Food Preparation,* pulling out two dusty texts and a scroll off a bottom shelf stuffed haphazardly with books and papers.

"Is it—?"

"She was nuts about omelettes."

"You're a genius, Rib."

"Thanks. I know."

Plaia sat, sneezed twice, and examined one of the texts. She chuckled. "*On the Nature of the Egg,* by Dame T. Driftwood. No wonder everyone says Tiv was off the edge."

She unrolled the scroll and found herself gazing at a map. Two views of the planet, side by side: the beautiful cluster that was the familiar archipelago of Pangaea in the left rendering, the barren torrents of Panthalassa Ocean in the right.

A hand gripped her shoulder. She started, but it was only Julretta, followed by a wide-eyed, pale Donson. They too sat on the floor, forming a tight little conspiratorial circle. A security monitor lurched through the "D" stack, mutter-

ing and cursing softly to herself. The acrid smell of skee
wafted into Plaia's face as the monitor passed. They all
held their breaths and ducked down, striving to become
stillness itself. The monitor vanished down the corridor.
Outside, the wind moaned. Rain beat on the portal above
them.

*I never realized resonance theory could be . . . danger-
ous. Can Gunther really influence the academy to expel
me? After all I've contributed, all I've committed to?*

Anger surged through Plaia so fiercely her hands shook.
And then cool calculation. *Be a little nicer,* wise Julretta
had said. Perhaps. Perhaps she shouldn't challenge Gunther's bid to enter into sharelock. Perhaps she should enter
willingly. Secure his official support of resonance theory
and application on the flat of her back. Was he really going
to earn a permanency with Ground Control?

Could she do it? Eroticians bedded for money, but that
was the destiny of their subpure. She'd bedded so many of
her own subpure for lust, for sport. For no reason at all.

Now she had a reason.

Gunther and his virtues. Sixth—

A wave of nausea rose in her throat at the thought of
lying with Gunther again. With sharelock chips installed in
her hands, the utter intimacy of sharers' sharemind the
chips conferred. Gunther commanding the prerogative between them. Demanding her obedience. She shuddered at
the thought of submitting to him.

And what about her bold swarthy boy? If destiny should
bring him back to her, he'd truly be forbidden. Forever
banished from her touch.

"Plaia, look," Ribba whispered, pointing to kaligraphs
inked on the maps. "Tiv measured the magnetic angles of
inclination and declination in sedimentary rocks of a known
age. Here. And here. Discrepancies in the angles theoretically trace ancient movements in the bedrock and indicate
the path of future movement. She called it magnetic

wander. She extrapolated magnetic wander curves for each province of the archipelago.''

Plaia studied the kaligraphs, arrows pointing here and there, meticulously inked in Tivern's hand. ''The Appalacia wander curve is extrapolated to . . . the northwest. The northwest, Rib!''

''Yeah. Your measurements of the south side were appalling, all right, honey.''

''And the wander curve of Andea is . . . southwest, sort of. And both of those extrapolations are different from the Far Reaches, Siluria, *and* Cordilleran.'' She glanced at Ribba. ''Now I'm *really* confused.''

Ribba nodded sympathetically and reverently smoothed her fingers over her mentor's texts. She opened at random to a page. ''Look. Tiv wrote, 'The shell isn't the shell.' She was always saying weird shit like that.''

''Why doesn't Ground Control just admit the shell is moving in ways we don't understand?'' Julretta said, exasperated, wrinkling her forehead. ''And let us get on with solving the problem?''

Plaia reached out and smoothed the young woman's brow. ''Because the Imperium will never admit the world could change, my little Julree.''

Donson nodded, his thin face somber. ''If the Imperium were to admit that, what else might change?'' Distracted, meditative, he withdrew the Orb of Eternity from his jacket pocket.

''Put that thing away,'' Julretta whispered, fear bright in her eyes. ''You really want to get us in trouble?''

''No, go ahead, Donson,'' Plaia said. ''I'm not afraid.''

Donson nodded and gazed at the orb. ''Only three seasons ago anyone who could afford an orb could buy one. The academy offered a course in orb studies. Councillor Sausal himself investigated orbs for years. All the commentaries we read in fundamental school were originally appended to the facets and their oracles.''

''I thought the orb was of impure origin,'' Plaia said.

Julretta shook her head. "Sausal never completely endorsed that theory. He believed the orb offered insights into Pannist philosophy. Remember I told you, Plaia? I took the last course."

. "Now orbs are outlawed, orbrolls forbidden," Donson said. "And Sausal, after all his piety and promulgation of Imperial morals, banished from the High Council. No one has seen him since. And you know why?"

"Why, Donson?" Plaia said.

"Because Sausal knew each oracle talks about change, the contradictions and oppositions embodied in everything." Donson's cheeks were flushed. His eyes glittered. "Even Pan."

Plaia took the orb from Donson, examining the facet of exquisitely rendered Clouds. "Julree, I granted you the two rolls of the orb I'd won at Appalacia Rift that morning."

"But they're yours—"

"No, no. I won a considerable number of ores, didn't I, Donson?"

He grinned devilishly. "You ravished us all that morning, sweet Plaia."

"Please." Plaia pressed the orb into the young woman's hand. "I forced you to go to the rave with me last night, and then I abused you terribly, didn't I, child? Consider this my way of making it up to you. I give my two rolls to you. Two more chances at destiny, isn't that what you said?"

Julretta blushed deep scarlet but her eyes shone with renewed ardor.

Plaia pulled a jumble of money out of her pocket. "I've got five ores and seven bits. Thirty to one on Clouds as the ruling facet."

Ribba searched her rucksack. "I'll call. Five ores on the Spider, fifteen to one on ruling facet, fifteen to one once removed."

Donson and Julretta each pulled five ores from their pockets and placed their wagers. Julretta cupped the orb in her hands, jiggled it, and flung it to the floor.

Plaia expected a crashing noise, but the orb landed on the hardwood floor without a sound and silently circumnavigated their little circle. The orb skittered round once, twice, then came to rest precisely in front of Julretta.

Plaia examined the facet. Two eyes, lids shut. The tiny glyphs danced and shimmered.

"Facet 29," Ribba whispered. "Closed Eyes. Death."

"No, no, Closed Eyes means Resting," Julretta whispered indignantly. "Closed Eyes means Sleep. We're all still exhausted from the riftsite expedition. The facet is advising us to get some rest."

"Closed Eyes," Ribba said, "portends Death." She hastily shut Tivern's texts, rolled up the map, and shoved everything in the shelfspace behind a tome on omelette recipes.

"Wait a minute, Rib," Plaia said. "I'll check out the whole set. I'm still in good standing."

"And alert Gunther and Farber and Helden that Tiv's last texts and a map exist right under their noses? Not a good idea. I bet the librarians catalogued 'em and shelved 'em without knowing what they are. Let's keep it that way."

Plaia laid her hand across Ribba's. "Then let's take them."

"You mean steal them?"

"Appropriate. That's a nicer word. I have a feeling they're not safe here in any case."

"Don't even think about it, Plaia," Donson said. "They're riddled with security codes. You'd never get past the door. And then you really will get expelled from the academy."

Plaia snorted. She'd never given much of a damn about anything. Now everything she'd worked for, everything she'd believed in, was crumbling before her eyes. "Roll the orb again, Julree. You've got a second chance, isn't that so?"

The young woman gingerly picked up the orb a second time, shook it, and released it as if it were a hot cookstone.

The orb noiselessly spun past their feet again, just once this time, and wobbled to a halt before Julretta.

The wind outside lifted, moaned. A cold gust blew through the portal, circled them like an invisible presence, and blasted against Julretta. Her dark hair streamed wildly back from her face, her clothes tossed around her limbs, papers on the shelf behind her spun up into a diminutive whirlwind around her.

"Plaia," she whispered, her teeth chattering. "Plaia, help me!"

Plaia seized her icy hands, and the gust departed. The whirling papers abruptly fell to the floor. All was still again.

"Facet 29," she said. "Closed Eyes. Closed Eyes again! What does it mean?"

"It means trouble, that's what it means." Donson plucked the orb from the floor, shoved it into his pocket. He staggered to his feet. "I never saw you here," he muttered. He strode away into the shadowed corridor.

Ribba rubbed her forehead, ran her fingers through the curly brown corkscrews of her hair. "We're doomed, Plaia. Resonance theory is doomed. *That's* what it means. Gunther will defect, Farber and Helden will prevail, and Ground Control will force-flood the rifts. Who knows what will happen to Pangaea, then? To us all?"

"Then we must account for the magma eruption at Andea, and the lateral movement in Appalacia Rift," Plaia said. "We must produce more proof. We must make predictions based on the magnetic wander curves, way ahead of the five predictors, and document our predictions."

Julretta shook her head and hugged her ribs. "Perhaps we should give it up, Plaia. We're up against Gunther, the academy, Ground Control, the High Council. The Imperium!"

Ribba muttered, "Julretta's right. We'll ruin our careers. It's too hard, Plaia."

And she knew then that she had found something to

which she could commit a lifetime. Something more than the pleasures and tastes and fancies of the moment.

Something worthy.

Something in very close proximity to Pan.

Plaia said, "I'll *never* give up."

III

RIFT

FACET 13

Rain: Watering or deluge.
The pauper receives an inheritance.
The action is investment.
The forbearance is gambling.

The Orb of Eternity

Commentaries:

Councillor Sausal: Pan manifests in glorious abundance like the summer rains nourish all living things of the world. Yet an overabundance of rain may produce floods that drown plowers and rot the harvest.

So, too, the Imperium takes pride in the abundance of the purities and encourages investment in worthy concerns.

Therefore the prudent person who receives an abundance should cultivate that abundance for the future and refrain from indulgence on pleasures of the moment.

But beware the plower's complacency when first rains fall. Beware of those who covet another's abundance.

Guttersage (usu. considered vulgar): The tax collector takes half of every fool's inheritance.

The gamemaster, the barkeep, and the erotician take the other half.

Hercynian Sea, northeast of Sausal Bay. The Floating Towers of Hercyn, Tower of the Jade-Eyed Sprite:

Steam surged out of the restless waves, staining the sea grape-green with submarine heat. At the vortex of the vent, the water boiled as magma spewed from the ocean floor. Fiery orange-red mingled with green and turquoise in a spectacular display of fire and water. Above the waves, steam roiled in colossal wraiths, infusing the humid morning air with the reek of sulfur and demons.

"Yes, that's what I'm respectfully telling you. To say an eruption is imminent is an understatement, Milady Faro," Plaia pleaded and dabbed at her forehead with a kerchief. "We implore you to evacuate while you've got the chance."

Her head swam with fatigue, her stomach clenched. Her neck ached from sleeping on a hard bench. The Tertius Ferry had departed from the Port of Atlan at midnight, jammed with tourists, and not a single berth had been available. She'd sat cheek by jowl with a quartet of rowdy acolyte-auditors, trying to doze as they'd dealt endless hands of pokey and guzzled the same number of jugs of teq. Ahead and behind sailed four ferries bearing tourists of the other purities. The angels' ferry looked deserted. The druds' ferry overflowed. Sails billowing, side-wheels churning, brawny rowers bending over their oars, the ferries had sped through the sea. Still, the journey had taken nearly eight hours, and at dawn the waves had been turbulent.

Were angels capable of gratitude? Not from the look of the angel reclining before her.

Plaia wished she could pluck at her tunic, the turquoise blue linen of an academe, lift the sticky cloth plastered to her breasts, waft some air onto her skin, and breathe. She wished she could dispense with her tunic altogether. Since the Tertius Ferry had touched port, she'd observed that no one vacationing at the Floating Towers possessed the slightest reticence about nudity. She'd spied sun-browned breasts and buttocks of every shape and size on the balconies and decks of every purity's towers.

But the eminent aetherist Milady Faro Ahmen naitre Primus regarded Plaia and her entourage with such cool condescension, she didn't dare relax her formal pose of obeisance. Let alone go native and disrobe.

Julretta echoed softly, "We implore you, milady."

Ribba added in her brass, cheeky way, "We've shipped all the way out here at our own behest and our own expense, milady. Consider yourself fortunate we give a damn."

"Ssh," Plaia whispered to her colleague, but secretly smiled at Ribba's irrepressible insolence.

It was true, the reclusive aetherist ought to have been grateful for their warning. And ought to have been alarmed. The situation demanded swift and decisive action. After observing the magma flume with her own eyes, steam filtering up past the windows of Faro's reception chamber, Plaia shifted uncomfortably. She'd coaxed Julretta and Ribba into accompanying her, excited by the prospect of visiting the towers, which none of them had seen before.

Now she didn't want to stay one moment longer than she needed to.

It's going to blow.

She would have sent Milady Faro a message, but didn't trust the Imperial mail service. Since her expulsion, her correspondence had been intercepted twice, and those had only been letters that her grandmothers on the Cordilleran Coast had received ripped open and crudely resealed. *So here we are, standing on top of a disaster about to happen, and the angel doesn't care.*

She and her two devoted colleagues had taken more and more risks after stealing Tivern's map and texts from Sausal Academy Library. Taking the first risk led naturally to the second. Perhaps the dire-faced social obedience teachers in fundamental school had been right. Once you took that step down the road to ruin, you slid the rest of the way.

If Milady Faro cared nothing for herself and her hand-maids, at least she ought exercise responsibility toward the tourists. Tens of thousands flocked to the Floating Towers for the glorious seafood, the succulent waterfruit, the inspiring views, the famous Hercynian Vent with its enigmatic steam and multicolored boiling waters. Druds scrimped and saved half a lifetime to spend a scant quarter season at the place.

Carved of crystal, poised on buoyant pavilions, the towers scintillated like colossal jewels against the pink-and-turquoise skies. Fifteen public towers in all, three reserved exclusively for each purity, the sixteenth the private domain of the famous aetherist. Meticulously faceted and polished daily to a high shine, the towers were perfectly transparent. Occupants preserved privacy or dispensed with it by drawing shut or open sateen draperies the traditional colors of each purity.

All Pangaea should be so pretty, Plaia thought, gazing at the lovely arrangement. Terra-cotta and stone grey for the drud towers. Orange-yellow and bright copper for servs. Brilliant blue-green and rich bronze for the middle purities. The magisters' towers solemn in indigo blue and silver, the angels' resplendent in Imperial purple and gold. As if the purities, the strictures of proximity, the tribulations of protocol, that which was permitted or forbidden, were just a scheme for decorating the sea.

The twenty-story towers housed hotels, concessions, gaming chambers, ceremonial chambers, dancehalls, feast-halls, saloons, tailors, gemstone purveyors, a temple of sacred sharelock in each. The only tower that permitted mingling of purities was a drud tower entirely leased to eroticians—five hundred salons of every price and preference imaginable. The shameful urge saturated the air as wetly as the humidity.

The aetherist's universal fame rendered Milady Faro's

personal tower a tourist draw in itself. Draperies forming a
backdrop of shimmering gold had been cleverly painted and
arranged to form the Face of Pan wrapped around the cylin-
drical structure.

Plaia waited impatiently for Faro's reply. Jittery anxiety
permeated her and her colleagues' sharemind, giving her a
throbbing headache and a ringing in her ears. She wondered
how the angel apprehended them, or if Faro had deigned to
enter their sharemind at all. Plaia had never entered into the
most powerful sharemind with the highest pure. She had no
idea if the anxiety emanated from the angel or was simply
the overwrought state of their mutual consciousness.

The aetherist had declined to speak directly with
academe subpures, but had appeared at their requested audience with her proxy. Etiolated, emaciated, the aetherist
appeared as if sculpted of bone, translucent skin layered on
as a tissue-thin afterthought. Wispy white hair had been
gathered in a coil wound around her high forehead. She
reclined on a chaise longue upholstered in pythonskin in-
cised with kaligraphs of the Final Battle of Atlan. Faro lay
completely nude but, unlike her sun-browned tourists, her
skin was marmoreal, with a suggestion of sickness.
Whiplashed atlantium-and-gold jewelry set with jade
cabochons encircled her neck, wrists, waist, knees, ankles.
Her eyes were a shocking shade of jade green, but might
have been enhanced with eye dye.

Handmaids as burly as bodyguard subpures bore atlantium crucifixes upon which a dozen trained white swans
had been bound at the neck and feet. The swans ceaselessly
beat their wings, producing a breeze over the aetherist and
the susurration of feathers flapping. A tiny exquisite female
sphinx with the same wispy white hair of her mistress
perched at the foot of the chaise longue and obsessively
groomed her coiffure with a diminutive silver haircomb.

That sphinx. Where have I seen it before?

Plaia had never encountered an angel as close as ten
steps away, let alone an aetherist as renowned, rich, and

powerful as Milady Faro. It was impossible to speculate
Faro's age. She seemed as flawless as an infant, as ancient
as time, perfectly preserved and halfway moribund. Beautiful? Of course the angel was beautiful, the way the Obelisk
of Eternity was beautiful. Glacial, passionless, inspiring
nothing warmer than stunned awe.

*No wonder there are so few of them. How do they culti-
vate intimacy among themselves long enough to feel Pannish love, enter into sharelock, and generate a family? Does
Milord Lucyd resemble this remote, bizarre person? Had
Milady Danti?*

And *this* was the aetherist who cast dreams of bloody
battles and desperate conquest, insidious betrayal and violent insurrection, mayhem and torture and cruelty in every
form and deviation. Gunther had preferred Faro's dreams.
"They satisfy my cruel streak," he'd once told her, only
half-joking.

Plaia hoped her expression didn't betray disgust or disre-
spect. She never dreamed Milady Faro's dreams. She'd
never wanted to.

Faro murmured to the proxy again. The proxy, a grim
and icy-eyed person, was an angel pure by the look of his
pallor and emaciation, his permission to speak directly with
Milady Faro and sometimes—Plaia noticed—even to speak
first. But obviously a much lower subpure than the aetherist,
upon whom he doted with overweening solicitude. He did
not touch her or stand within touching distance.

The proxy said, "Why do you believe an eruption is
imminent? Magma has flowed from the vent for over two
hundred years. We earn a very fine income selling fuel for
lamps."

"We have assembled evidence, milady," Plaia said, ad-
dressing her remarks to the aetherist. Every now and then
the aetherist darted those emerald eyes at her. "We've got
instruments that measure movement in the deep rocks. The
movement suggests that the bedrock is exerting severe pres-

sure on the substrata of magma feeding the vent. Haven't you felt the tremors?''

"We always feel tremors," the proxy said. " 'Tis part of the rapture of sojourning at the Floating Towers.''

Plaia expelled a frustrated breath. "Yes. Well. We measure other features, too, of the air and the water. Magnetic properties of different layers of sediment. Idiosyncratic behavior among beasts who are sensitives.'' She brandished her databoard. "The main thing is we've got an accurate map showing how the landmasses and waterways of the world archipelago fit together. And how," she took a deep breath, "the archipelago is changing.''

The aetherist smiled, inclined her heavy head, and permitted a titter to traverse her bony throat. She recovered her composure and leaned impassively toward the proxy, whispering harshly.

The proxy said with deep suspicion, "Are you Apocalyptists, then?''

"No!" Plaia answered at once. The query amounted to an accusation. The High Council had just declared the prophecies promulgated a millennium ago not merely false and impure, but a new brand of heresy. Anyone who dared deny the Imperium could control and prevent earthshocks was liable to find the tip of her tongue sliced off by a Vigilance blade. "It is exactly because we wish to preserve the Imperium—and preserve *your* lives—that we come here with this warning.''

"Well, then," the proxy said. "The archipelago has lasted since times lost to antiquity. Why should it suddenly change now?''

"That's just it!" Julretta burst out. "The world hasn't *suddenly* changed. It's always changing, sometimes slowly, sometimes suddenly. Milady Faro, you of all the angels should understand. You dream of the discord that grew among the Ancient Ones and the spectacular battles that changed the face of the Imperium—''

"In times lost to antiquity," the proxy snapped.

"Hush, Julree," Plaia murmured. "It won't help."

Faro murmured and the proxy said, "We are unclear about your credentials, Mistress Plaia. Did you say you and your colleagues are consultants with Imperial Ground Control?"

The three academes exchanged wary glances. Exhortations—*Careful! Be bold! Silence! Say anything! Lie!*—darted through their sharemind. If the angel apprehended their dismay, there was nothing Plaia could do about it.

"We are known to certain consultants at Ground Control," Ribba said cagily.

"You are proctors at Sausal Academy, then?" the proxy said.

Plaia hesitated. How far had her ill repute traveled? Would a wealthy reclusive angel dwelling in the luxurious and remote Floating Towers have heard or cared? She was only a disgraced young academe who'd been expelled from Sausal Academy at the autumn turning.

Gunther had been true to his treacherous word. A solemn crier had come to her fathers' villa the next dawn after their altercation in the library. She hadn't found a room to let yet. Cairn had coldly summoned her from her childhood bed. The crier had presented the academy's sharemind, a formal demand for an expulsion hearing. Her fathers had retired to their private quarters, refusing her entreaties to see them. Finally she'd realized they had no intention of aiding her or appearing as her witnesses. *Money. They took Gunther's money. They want to force me to enter into sharelock with him.*

She'd never been so shaken in her life. She'd vowed never to speak to her fathers again, packed a few possessions, and left the villa.

She'd gone alone, clad in a ceremonial suit, to the gilt-and-ebony judgment chamber in which she'd once been joyfully admitted to her mastery program. Farber, a skeletal crone, and Helden, an equally skeletal curmudgeon, sat upon the podium with Gunther, the dean, and all her proctors from all her unfinished masteries. Everyone except Tivern, of course.

They'd submitted briefs denouncing her. Farber had brandished her offending letter. None of her allies had appeared. The interrogation had been lengthy and brutal. For a man who expected her to live harmoniously with him as his sharer, Gunther had viciously attacked her, her competency, her sanity. He wanted to wear her down, strip her of whatever small power she might still possess. Perhaps he expected the sharelock chips to bind her mind to him, if he himself never could.

If she'd once considered entering into sharelock with him out of expediency, he'd killed that consideration forever. She'd freely offered her outrage and contempt in sharemind, felt his mutual consciousness hovering around her like a miasma. As the final insult, he'd exercised his loathsome prerogative and declined to enter into mutual consciousness with her.

And then it was over. She'd cleared out her locker, turned in her security codes. Donson had passed her in the halls with stony, blank eyes as if he'd never known her, let alone bedded her.

She gazed at the angel and her proxy, the inquiry about her credentials hovering between them. She hated falsehood. After all her beddings and entanglements of the heart, she'd never lied to anyone. Yet what she had to say to Milady Faro affected the lives of thirty-five thousand people touring the Floating Towers. If a small fabrication conferred the credibility she needed, she ought to dispense with moral qualms.

Say we're proctors, damn it, and be done with it, whispered through her sharemind. Julretta, probably. Gentle-spoken Julree had taken up cursing after living with Ribba and Plaia. Plaia no longer cared what Faro apprehended of their sharemind.

"Proctors at the academy. Sort of," Plaia rasped. *Yes* stuck in her throat.

"We are academes," Julretta added dryly.

"We can see that. What exactly are your degrees and your positions?" the proxy persisted, wrinkling his brow. Murmured to Faro, "Dear me, they're not with Ground Control, after all, milady."

"I am, ah, pursuing an independent mastery," Plaia said diffidently, "and my two colleagues are pursuing their masteries in resonance theory and application."

"Pursuing masteries," the proxy murmured to Faro. "Only pursuing masteries."

Faro raised the silver crescent moons of her eyebrows in an expression of consummate disdain and gestured dismissively. At once the handmaids scurried forward and lifted the chaise longue, taking care not to touch the angel's body. They bore aetherist and sphinx away from the reception chamber without further ceremony or even a polite farewell.

The proxy watched Faro go, then turned back to Plaia, yearning plain on his emaciated face. "Mistresses, on my own behalf, I do thank you for your concern. I'm certain you mean well. But the boiling sea is very beautiful, you see. 'Tis quite an attraction for the tourists and yields us an excellent income. We cannot possibly close the towers and send everyone away. We cannot possibly evacuate. This is our home. This is our paradise. Our passion."

Plaia nodded and said sadly, "Well, we tried."

They'd sailed all the way to the mouth of Sausal Bay, five and a half hours through turbulent surf, when they heard the explosion, a roar gentled by the vast distance. They could actually see fiery gouts of magma like festival streamers, high in the turquoise sky.

"If that ain't conclusive proof, honey, I'm a Heaven's Devil," Ribba quipped as the trio tipped beer and lunched on flatbreads and hard-boiled eggs in their rented hovel on Tomfoolery Lane. "You really called it. You're starting to scare me." She picked up her flute, blew a shrill arpeggio. "Damn it, Plaia. Our resonance isn't the same without you and your cymbals."

An inarticulate shout outside, the roar of the surf pounding against their walls. Tomfoolery Lane lay southeast of Marketplace, on a gentle rise. Plaia had chosen it for the modest elevation. This sector of Rancid Flats stood knee-deep in seawater and raw sewage, but the flood wasn't nearly as high as in the low-lying northwest sectors. Plaia remembered considering that when they'd leased the place. *It's not Majestic Heights, but we won't drown if there's another Big Shock.*

"I agree, Plaia," Julretta said and tenderly massaged Plaia's shoulders. "Let's go to Ground Control. Let's go over Gunther's head. Let's beg them on our knees. Now, before they force-flood Andea Rift and it may be too late."

"No." Plaia shook her head and sipped the frothy brew. She pulled off the academe's tunic, donned the rough copper cotton of a serv. "Rib, you're right, the beer's doing wonders for my seasickness. What a ride!"

Tertius Ferry had bucked all the way back to the Port of Atlan, but they'd gotten a good head start, and the ferry had outrun the waves flung up by the Hercynian eruption. By the time the first gigantic tidal wave struck the Sausal Coast, they'd sandbagged the hovel all around and battened down the door and the two small windows.

Have we come to accept the unacceptable? Or have we transcended what was once unacceptable in the name of survival?

"Plaia," Julretta said in her complaining tone, "this is the most persuasive proof I've ever seen."

"So we'll document it and stash it in my safe box. With all this rift movement and magmatic activity, it's a perfect time for a field trip to the Bog."

"Julretta," Ribba said warningly, "she's talking us into

something again." She set down the flute and rubbed her eyes. "I'm *tired.* I want to *sleep.*"

"Just listen, this is no time for sleep," Plaia said with a wry grin. "Tiv was fascinated with the Ouachita floodplain, Rib, you know that. It's not too far. I want to see it, too."

"But, Plaia—" Julretta said.

She held up her hand, belched loudly. "Listen—oh, that felt good—listen to me. The Hercynian eruption suggests that Appalacia Rift and Atlan are in a world of trouble. The bedrock's moving north and pressing down, all right. Who knows what Appalacia will do next? But that doesn't help our argument for Andea. Ouachita is the largest significant geological feature due north of the rift. When is Ground Control planning on force-flooding there?"

"Gunther says by the winter turning," Ribba said, lighting a raptureroot. "Says they're boring the well shafts and excavating canals right now. The bastard."

"Do you mind?" Julretta said indignantly, coughing when Ribba let loose a dense blue cloud of narcotic smoke.

"Hai, settles my seasickness," Ribba said with a naughty grin. Another surge of surf slapped against the hovel wall. "Want a draw, Plaia?"

She shook her head, waved the root away, frowning over the copy they'd drawn of Tivern's map. She'd stashed the original map in her safe box at her treasury. She'd reserved the box under the whimsical codename, Mistress Egghead. *Here's to you, Tiv.* The bored treasury clerk had taken her fee and a small jar of d'ka without recording her security number.

"Privacy, you know," she'd said with a bat of her eyelashes.

"A scarce commodity in our Imperium, isn't it?" the clerk had replied with a wink. Short and slender, with deep brown eyes and chestnut hair, the clerk was just the sort of lower middle pure she might have invited out for a shot of skee—once. How strange! Plaia the Plaything, disinterested in a casual dalliance with an attractive man?

"The winter turning?" she said now. "Then we've got a little time. Look here. All this disparate movement. Appalacia to the northwest. Hercynian Vent, or what's left of it, tends to establish the south side of the rift is pressing into the magmatic core. Pressing *down*."

Julretta groaned and shook her head. " 'Tends to establish'? Since when have you become so conservative, Plaia?"

"Since I got my butt kicked out of the academy." She returned to Tiv's map. "Andea moving to the southwest? The magma eruption that incinerated Tiv suggests a similar type of movement—lateral and down, bearing pressure against the magmatic core. By the way, I'm beginning to think Farber and Helden had something to do with luring Tiv into the observation chamber right before the magma blew."

"For Pan's sake, Plaia," Julretta complained.

"Yeah?" Ribba said, eagerly leaning forward.

"Yeah. At my expulsion hearing, I presented evidence of the Andea eruption as support for Tiv's theories and her proctorship with me. I said, 'Tivern decided to investigate Andea,' and Farber—"

"—the old witch," Ribba muttered.

"—and the old witch jumped down my throat. She said, 'Tivern didn't decide anything. *We* ordered Tivern there.' Couldn't give up her precious prerogative long enough to cover up. Well! Helden shut her up, right away. Of course, the observers' sharemind of my hearing is sealed. But *I* still apprehend it. They can't take *that* away till they take away *my* sharemind."

"*If* they can," Ribba said.

"Yeah, *if*," Plaia said. "Or maybe *when*."

"It's too awful," Julretta whispered.

"Look. The Andea eruption doesn't help us much as proof if Ground Control denies it ever happened. So. If Tiv's extrapolations of the magnetic wander curves are right, then Pangaea somehow is . . . *spreading*. Spreading *apart.* It looks to me as if the Gondwana landmass is actually pushing against the south side of Andea Rift.''

"If that's true, only idiots would advocate forcing more matter into a rift that's being squeezed tighter," Ribba said.

"Ahem. We're talking about Ground Control, Rib. If Gondwana is spreading to the south, I predict that salinity in the floodplain will be intensified from seawater percolating up through the substrata." Plaia brandished Volume II of *On the Nature of the Egg.* "Tiv documented salinity in the floodplain ten seasons ago. I'd never been sure why— before. My colleagues, she suspected the spreading phenomenon back then. But who would believe her?''

"One big shell could never behave like that," Ribba observed.

"That's for sure! We've got to update the salinity data. Julree, where's the sal-meter? We're going to need it.''

Julretta exhaled with frustration, but went to fetch the salinometer she'd carted home from the academy at Plaia's behest. Gunther hadn't a clue how the instrument worked. A simple, deliberate loosening of the rotary selector switch passed as a malfunction, which Julretta had dutifully volunteered to fix in her spare time.

As for Tivern's texts and map—as Donson had predicted—those treasures had security codes embedded all over them. Ribba had been pleased to toss a lit match into an overflowing wastebin in the library's lav. How the security monitors had shrieked at every exit! Everyone had gathered up belongings and books and fled, helter-skelter. Ribba had carried out one text in her rucksack, Plaia had carried out the other in an armload of books, and Julretta had shoved the rolled-up map down her leggings.

"Say, maybe we'll find new magmaflows out on the floodplain," Ribba said, as if she were chattering about a long-anticipated gift on her emergence day. She exhaled another cloud of intoxicating smoke.

"Wouldn't *that* be fine! But let's not taint our scientific observations with preconceptions," Plaia said with a smile.

"Remember, we're going to present this evidence to Ground Control magisters more difficult to impress than good ol' Gunther."

The prospect of witnessing another active magmaflow sent a palpable chill down her spine. *Closed Eyes, the Orb of Eternity had foretold in the library. Death, foretold twice. Foretold for whom?* She heard a shout, discerned a rustling of consciousness. In the lane outside their door, a crier projected an Imperial sharemind about a "disturbance" in the Hercynian Sea, which was the cause of the giant waves pummeling the Sausal Coast. The crier was noticeably silent about the Floating Towers. The devastation must have been spectacular.

A needle of sorrow pierced Plaia's triumph. Milady Faro might have been insufferable and her dreams repulsive, but her crystal towers had been fabulous works of art.

And her pet sphinx an innocent soul.

A tiny white-haired sphinx, blinking enigmatically. Her fathers' distraught faces, Gunther's frown, a fiery spray of magma.

She'd seen this vision, these images before—when?

The first time I touched an Orb of Eternity. At Appalacia, in the observation chamber, on the morning of the Big Shock.

Foreboding stung her. Did the orb truly foretell, then? But more than merely foretelling. The orb had shown her moments when she could choose—this path or that. Had she made responsible choices? She wasn't sure. And every time she'd chosen, how had her choices changed her future?

Donson's voice whispered in her memory, *Each facet talks about change, the contradictions and oppositions embodied in everything.*

Even Pan.

Does one's will affect fate?

Or is that illusion, and there is only destiny. Are the purities the purities, does the Imperium go on without end,

*does the world remain as ordained by Pan, like the priests
and priestesses say?*

*But I have chosen. Perhaps not always wisely, but I've
chosen.*

"Too bad we didn't place wagers on the eruption at the
towers' gaming tables," Plaia said sardonically. "We'd be
rich now."

"Now, honey, that's a terrible thing to say," Ribba said.
Milady Faro had definitely rubbed Ribba the wrong way. "I
mean, how could we collect?"

"You're both terrible," Julretta said, returning with the
sal-meter cradled in her arms. "Remember the white-haired
sphinx, Plaia? With the silver comb?"

"How can she remember something she's never seen
before?" Ribba demanded.

"Yes, I do, Julree," Plaia quietly replied. To Ribba,
"Never mind. It was in Appalacia Rift. You didn't notice."

"Huh!" Ribba said, nonplussed, but she shrugged. "Did
you notice how many times Milady Faro's proxy mentioned
money? 'It earns us a very fine income.' "

"I don't have enough fingers on my two hands to count,
and that was a *very* brief interview," Plaia said.

"And I thought angels were so rich, money meant nothing to them," Ribba said. "Silly me."

Plaia had never thought much about money, for good or
for ill, till she'd left her fathers' villa and rejected Gunther's bid for her hand in sharelock. The natalries bled
money. The Imperium devoured money. The exchange of
value touched every hand, every hunger, every movement.

Every choice.

How heedless and credulous she'd been, believing the
hard realities of the Imperium would never affect her.

After the expulsion hearing, Julretta and Ribba had both
declared they'd resign from resonance in protest, but Plaia
had insisted they continue with their masteries. Continue to
smile sweetly at Gunther and find out everything they

could. "Be my eyes and ears at the academy," Plaia urged her colleagues.

"But what about Paven?" Julretta had cried. No one had seen their rambunctious sable-haired colleague since the night of the Serpent Sect rave, and his mother and fathers had refused to speak with Plaia when she'd called upon their villa to inquire about him.

Plaia and her two colleagues had gone down to Our Sacred City's Detainment Center for the Tertius with as much money as they could scrape together for Paven's bond. The surly jailer had informed them no one by Paven's name or description had ever been committed there. Plaia had argued, Ribba had shouted, Julretta had wept, but the jailer had been adamant, finally threatening to incarcerate *them*.

Ribba's rooms had been burgled again when they'd returned, distraught and exhausted.

"Paven's disappeared," Julretta moaned.

That was when Plaia had insisted she and her two colleagues no longer study and drink together before the eyes of the world, but conceal their association behind the walls of the hovel they rented on Tomfoolery Lane. They signed false names on the lease.

One night they'd dirked their forefingers, mingled their blood, and vowed an oath of allegiance to the truth of Pangaea. They'd drafted a joint will leaving to each other the half of their Imperial materia stored in Natalry Bank remaining after taxes if any of them died.

They'd signed the will in their blood.

"This goes beyond any one of us," Plaia declared.

Julretta whispered, "This is our destiny."

"What else did I have to do with the rest of my life?" Ribba said with a chuckle.

Now Ribba stubbed out her raptureroot. "Landmass spread is still a pretty wild theory, Plaia. I mean, so a fragment of the landmass presses down against the magma core at a rift 'cause it's bumping against the other side. *Then* what? Where *can* it go after that? At your expulsion hear-

ing, didn't Gunther hit you up one side of your head and
down the other for such a crazy idea?''

"Sure was fun.'' She plucked a boiled egg from the
lunch tray. "Know what Tiv's aphorism is, the whole
thing? Are you listening?'' She cleared her throat. '' 'Consider the egg. When is the shell not the shell?' '' She rolled
the boiled egg in the palms of her hands. '' 'Now eat it.' ''

"Sounds bestial,'' Julretta complained.

Ribba winked.

Plaia tapped the egg on the tabletop till the entire shell
was thoroughly riddled with cracks, then gently squeezed
the egg. Fragments of eggshell overlapped each other, some
edges pushing beneath other edges. When one sizeable
piece of shell pushed deeply beneath another, the entire
piece popped off.

"The shell isn't the shell,'' she whispered. She peeled
off the rest of the shell and devoured the egg in three bites.

"Damn, child. You really do scare me sometimes, you
know that?'' Ribba seized a handful of raptureroots and
stuffed them in her pocket. "Listen. A former bedmate of
mine is a gatekeeper at the Great Wall. Strictly bean counting, honey, which I always thought was so low pure of her.
She had a chance to audit dreams in the Mind of the World.
Acolyte-auditors and priestesses crawling all over that family. Ah, but Yvette said she hates sharemind. Would rather
run around in the jungle and get fresh air.''

"I know exactly how she feels.'' Plaia rolled up the map.
"Pack that sal-meter, Julree.''

"How are we going to get out of here without flooding
our place?'' Julretta said doubtfully.

"Up and out the trapdoor in the roof.''

"That's what trapdoors are for, honey,'' Ribba said.

"Oh, fine. And how are we going to get to the Wall
without getting soaked?''

Plaia grinned. "We're not. We're going to get soaked.
Rib? Bring your voicebox. Speak of everything you see.''

She gathered her reddish gold curls into a slipshod mass

at the top of her head and wound a thong around it, grimacing at herself in the tiny mirror on their wall. When she lived with her fathers she'd patronized the beauticians' salons every new moon for the latest coiffure, a manicure, and a body waxing. How much money had she squandered on inconsequential things? She pulled on a high-crowned fisher's cap, concealing her hair. How she wished now she'd set aside that money.

The price of rebellion.

And how far had she'd fallen since she'd last seen Dubban Quartermain? She ruefully chewed off the broken nail on her thumb. Would he still think her a goddess in serv togs? Heart hammering in her breast, she'd gone to Our Sacred City Hall and looked him up in the serv registry. But since the flats had burned after the Big Shock, and so many had relocated or left the megalopolis, Atlan Prefecture had deemed the old registry obsolete and discarded it, pending a new census.

Every time she ventured out into the teeming alleys and lanes of Rancid Flats she'd searched for him.

But what would her prerogative amount to now? What would the protocol be between them? What good could come of forbidden love when her world was shattering?

"This former bedmate," Plaia said. "Will she let us in?"

"She'll take us through the Wall without a qualm. Yvette's got full access to Gate Five. And an appetite for raptureroot." Ribba tapped her pocket meaningfully.

Plaia said, "What are former bedmates for?"

They'd shared three raptureroots and considerable hilarity by the time they spotted their first bogbeasts.

"You slut!"

"Tah, not me. I've been searching for my sacred sharer my whole entire life."

"In Tivern's bed?"

"Well . . ."

"How many devotees who would jump off a roof for her did Tiv have, anyway?"

"Are you sure this is going to be all right?" Plaia anxiously asked the gatekeeper.

"As right as pondplum pie," Yvette said and winked for maybe the fiftieth time. The former bedmates Ribba had. Plaia was relieved to see modest Julretta was smiling and enjoying their highly illegal excursion.

Plaia had once seen the outer periphery of the Great Wall on a field trip during fundamental school, but she'd never driven through one of the gates. Who had? Sequestered from the megalopolis, the Bog was forbidden to the generality of pures and subpures as both an Imperially protected preserve and a hazardous wilderness. The tunnel went on and on, soaring archways, decorative caryatids, masonry so beautifully brickworked she found it difficult to believe the Wall was two millennia old and never meant for anyone's eyes.

And the Bog, dear Pan, the Bog!

Seated next to Yvette in her rover, speeding over the river of mud that passed for a maintenance pathway, her colleagues and their cheerful escort bantering and flirting, the drayers sweating and grunting in their harnesses, Plaia had to prop up her open jaw with her fist or risk snaring gnats in her teeth.

"To think I was always afraid of the Bog," she said to Yvette who nodded and laughed. "To think I never even *wanted* to see this, because I'd always been taught it was an evil, dangerous place."

"It's a dangerous place, all right," Yvette said and whipped the drayers again.

Plaia filled her eyes.

Rampage of vegetation.

Stupendous mountains jutting across the southern horizon.

Steaming excremental mud reeking of fertility.

Those were seed ferns the brilliant color of emeralds and palm fans towering eight stories high, the lush fronds forming a canopy of living lace. Those were dragonflies the size of Imperial hunting hawks flitting through the jungle of ferns. Those were flesh-flowers, lewd pink petals jawlike and fanged, yawning open in carnivorous bowls the size of bathtubs. Those were pondplums as big as gameballs, roses the size of feast tables, lianas like necklaces for a titan.

Little lizards whizzed overhead on multicolored wings. Birds as tall as a man, sporting tremendous plumed topknots and tails, galloped gracefully across the mud. A basilisk slithered down to a jungle pool to drink. A herd of steeds as petite as pet sphinxes galloped by, and a feral sphinx the size of an ox crept out of the dripping jungle to laze in the interlude of autumn sunshine.

A herd of lizards sloshed through the muck, their long, swooping necks bobbing, each beast the size of thirty wagons. A porcine beast that could have swallowed ten swine, and boasted three horns the length of sabers on its forehead, shuffled past, grunting and farting.

"Oh," Plaia whispered. Julretta squeezed her hand.

There, a manticore, his humanoid face framed in a halo of golden fur, his goatish form crouching upon four clawed aquiline feet. There, slipping into the jungle pool, a maremaid, her soaked mane trailing down her sensuous spine, equine buttocks twitching. And there, a python as thick as a waterduct, the face of a beautiful woman poised on its neck, unwound from the rhizome of a giant fern and sinuously descended to drink from the pool, lapping green water with a darting pink tongue.

To preserve this for Eternity!

Plaia finally understood the Imperium's obsession with perpetuity. If only the world in all its fullness and glory could last forever.

Plaia said urgently, "Yvette, we need to take a salinity reading in the Ouachita floodplain."

"Tell me where."

"As far west as you can take us and bring us back again before nightfall. Have you seen any new magmaflows seeping from the swampbeds? Are any beasts dying in greater numbers than the usual mortality rate?" Plaia hesitated. "Is it really dangerous out here at night?"

By way of her answer, Yvette whipped the drayers pulling the rover and swiftly took them to the nearest edge of the Ouachita floodplain.

A vast expanse of verdant wetlands and steaming swamps, the floodplain stretched to the horizon. Out in midplain, perhaps three leagues away, Plaia saw the oozing sepia waters interlaced with lazy curls of red-hot magma. Closer to their vantage point, the molten rock had crusted over in lacy black interstices.

Magma. Magma in the middle of the Bog. In the middle of a major landmass. Where there is no known rift.

Yvette fed the drayers lardsticks as Plaia and her two colleagues nervously disembarked from the rover. Julretta pushed her leggings over her knees and waded into the shallow water. She dipped in the feed of the salinometer, commenced the drip, and took readings as soon as they registered. Ribba wandered along the swampy periphery, sinking ankle-deep in mud, speaking in a hushed whisper into her voicebox.

Plaia waded in after Julretta.

The bugs were horrendous.

But the bugs couldn't compare to the stench of death.

Plaia thought of the oracle the Orb of Eternity had given them in the library: *Closed Eyes. Death.*

The place was a waterlogged graveyard. The dead lay everywhere, gape-mouthed corpses, pearlescent rot gleaming in the sunlight, flesh melting off bones. Submerged carrion eaters had gnawed their fill till they too swelled with the killing salt, burst open, and died.

"Damn," Plaia murmured and pinched her nostrils shut, trying not to retch. Unwilling yet compelled to witness this desecration, she shuffled through the shallow, mud-laced

water, examining the corpses. "*Way* too much salt, don't
you think, Julree?"

Her boot toe connected with a clutch of rotting eggs. Up
they bobbed out of the brine, speckled brown, thick-shelled
ovules the size of handballs. She gently worried at them
with her toe, frowning.

Which was worse, this grim spectacle or what they'd
witnessed in the morning from afar? The sudden annihila-
tion of the Floating Towers, a jewel in the crown of the
Imperium? Or this slow torture of a disintegrating primordial world, new life stillborn, the steady carnage of change?

Change. Everything the Imperium opposes.

"Never again will we see beasts like this," Plaia whispered, wading out of the muck. She felt ill, exhausted,
hopeless.

"It's getting a little late," Yvette called in an uneasy
voice. "I suggest we get the hell out of here."

Was foreboding floating in their sharemind? Had a
shadow fallen across the autumn sun? Had the wind lifted
fallen leaves into a little whirlwind, the way an invisible
presence had lifted papers in the library after the orbroll?

Plaia would never know.

She only knew that's when the beast galloped out of the
jungle, a brawny dragon with brindled olive skin and a
vicious set of teeth bared in its long jaws. Standing upright
on powerful hind legs, little forelegs curled against its
chest, the dragon charged at Julretta as she waded ankle-
deep in the muck. She bent over her sal-meter, touching the
rotting eggs Plaia had stirred up, as intent as a curious
child. Julretta glanced up at the sound of splashing water,
smiled back at Plaia, gaily waved.

"Julree!" Plaia cried. "Get out!"

She wanted to shield or defend her colleague, the one
person she'd ever seriously considered as a sharer. But terror and her own instinct to survive propelled her to the edge
of the jungle. She sprinted to a giant fern, scrambled up the

huge frond, and perched there with a terrified Yvette and the four bawling drayers.

Julretta turned toward Plaia's voice, her plain little face a mask of horror as the dragon leapt. Its huge curved fangs ripped off one arm, then the other, sank deep into the nape of her neck, and neatly beheaded her. Julretta poised for a moment, blood gouting from her neck and her shoulder sockets, before her stunned corpse collapsed into the muck.

"Oh, Julree," Plaia moaned. "I'm sorry if I was ever cruel to you. Little love, I'm so sorry."

"Shut up," Yvette whispered, then shouted. "Ribba! Oh, fuck!"

Ribba turned from her meander along the shore and dropped her voicebox, shrieking furiously at the sight of Julretta, the dragon ripping off chunks of flesh from her corpse. Ribba had always been quick and far too foolishly bold, and now she galloped into the water, leapt on the dragon's back, riding it like a steed, kicking and punching at it wildly.

"Rib! Rib!" Plaia screamed. "It's no use! Jul's dead. Come back! Come up here! Now!"

The dragon swiveled around at the sound of Plaia's voice. Its jaws jerked over its shoulder and snapped off Ribba's left hand at the wrist.

Plaia heard a *thunk*.

The dragon dropped like a flung stone, an Imperial arrow quivering clear through its snarling face. Ribba fell with it, still clinging to its back. Plaia scrambled down the giant fern, splashed through the muck—*not fast enough, not fast enough*—and scooped up her colleague, flinging Ribba over her shoulder though the woman weighed two stone more. Staggering, falling to her knees and getting up again, she carried Ribba back to the muddy shore, her breath snagging so painfully she thought her lungs would burst.

Wide-eyed with disbelief, too stunned to scream or weep, Ribba clutched her dismembered wrist, bright blood pulsing from the stump in rhythm to her heartbeat.

"Rib, Rib, honey," Plaia moaned and tore off her belt, strapping it round Ribba's arm in a makeshift tourniquet.

"We've got to help Julree," Ribba sobbed. "We've got to help Julree."

"We can't," Plaia said in anguish. "Oh, Rib, we just can't. The oracle came true."

She heard the whirring of wings, saw a shadow cross the sun, and a Vigilance surveillance windship descended, landing on the wetlands between jungle and floodplain. A squad of uniformed vigiles leapt out of the hatch, bearing crossbows and firebolts, and dashed to the dragon. They surrounded the beast, weapons trained, and kicked at the beast's corpse with their boots.

A vigile-physician with a medical bag sprinted to Plaia's side.

"They're my colleagues," Plaia cried, reason abandoning her at last. "Oh Pan, oh Pan, they're my *sisters*."

"I'm going to need *you* to stay calm," the vigile-physician said. She whipped out bandages, a syringe and needle, thrust the needle into Ribba's shoulder. "Peace and calm," she murmured in Ribba's ear. "It's a bit of nopaine." To Plaia, "She'll be all right, but there's nothing"—grimacing at Julretta's corpse, which the other vigiles gingerly lifted from the muck—"nothing I can do for your other sister."

"Thank Pan, you've come," Plaia cried. "Dear Pan, thank you, thank you."

Her gratitude choked in her throat.

A huge golden-haired vigile laboriously disembarked from the craft, leaning heavily on two muscular, hard-eyed bodyguards, turquoise-blue protocol chips winking between their brows. The bodyguards fit beneath the vigile's arms and assisted him as he walked.

Plaia blinked up at him.

The vigile's left leg had been amputated at the hip, his legging pinned up at the knee. He was handsome, or once had been, but now his face was bloated and sallow. One corner of his frowning mouth perpetually twitched. His brows knit together in a deep scowl. He methodically scanned the scene before him, finally fixing his gaze upon her.

She recoiled. His brilliant blue eyes reflected some horror he'd witnessed that had never ceased haunting him, and a depthless sorrow. And rage. And cruelty.

She embraced Ribba tightly. The vigile terrified her.

"State your name, pure and subpure, and security number," he said in an exhausted drawl. "You're under arrest."

FACET 14

Lightning: Sudden illumination or catastrophe.
The vigile's sword may hew the foe's chains or cut off
her head.
The action is insight.
The forbearance is confusion.

The Orb of Eternity

Commentaries:

Councillor Sausal: Know that Pan, in all Its glory,
has Its terrible aspect, too. Apprehension of Pan in Its
terrible aspect may confer precipitous enlightenment,
but is fraught with peril.

Apprehension of Pan in Its terrible aspect is the
province of the priestess, just as apprehension of a
foe is the province of the vigile.

So, too, there are times when the Imperium must
carry out swift justice.

Therefore when lightning strikes, the prudent person should seek shelter, but watch for fires to light
the cookstones.

Guttersage (usu. considered vulgar): Lightning illuminates the fool's path, but only for a moment.

Then lightning strikes the fool dead.

*Our Imperial Botanical & Wildlife Preserve of Pangaea
("the Bog"), northwest periphery of the Ouachita floodplain:*

"You're trespassing on Imperial property," Regim informed the weeping women. "Consider yourselves fortunate my ship was passing by on Vigilance business and a Wall vigile spied your vehicle as you were departing. The beast would have devoured you all. And *you,*" he said to the cowering gatekeeper and her team of terrified drayers, "are in a world of trouble. You ought to be severely reprimanded and summarily dismissed for flouting your Imperial duty in such a flagrant and irresponsible manner." When she babbled apologies and begged for mercy, he added, "I will see to it myself."

No angels or magisters these women, but lower pures. He cracked his vigilance sharemind over them like a whip, simultaneously discerning their fear, asserting his authority, and registering their submission.

At least they won't be trouble. He'd seen worse out in the Bog. He loathed this place, with its strange stinking gases and stranger beasts, the dead ones rotting in the muck. The liquid stone boiled up out of the basin of the floodplain like red-hot porridge from a neglected cookpot. The filthy conditions had worsened considerably since he'd last seen the place as a walkabout only seasons ago. It was disgusting, disgraceful. He could well understand why the Imperium had chosen to sequester the Bog behind the Great Wall.

Look at the dragon. Creatures like that ought to be exterminated. They were useless and dangerous, a menace to the Imperium.

Why would any sane person seek out this forsaken place? These women didn't *look* drunk or foolish with qut. He stooped, briefly sniffed the gatekeeper's breath, recoiling from her low female odors. She smelled of narcotics, all right, had probably smoked raptureroot.

He stared contemptuously as the pretty woman sobbed, her face streaked with tears and mud, her clothes filthy, her hands smeared with blood. She tenderly cradled her injured companion as if they were sisters or bedmates while his vigile-physician bandaged the companion's amputated wrist and administered a second needle of nopaine.

In the face of the carnage, he finally winced.

Amputated . . .

The pain. The aching. And worse than the pain, the tingling like gnats crawling over my . . . over where my leg used to be. Crawling and biting and I can't scratch or swat them or shoo them away. Sometimes the ache is like fire, spasms of fire.

He'd given up expecting relief from the physicians at Secundus Infirmary. Tahliq's stinging red powder, her soothing blue leaves, her healer Marik's poultices, had done more for his wounds than those incompetents' druggery. But he could not bring himself to return—quivering with pain, weak as a child—to the Salon of Shame or the drud healer. Marik, the sharer of a vigile? Still he could not bring himself to submit to her drud sympathy, her drud touch.

And his flesh had turned black and blacker still.

His physicians had explained that the devil stars had poison and filth on their tips, poison that was killing his flesh even as he lived. And the poison, the dying flesh, would kill him, too, they'd explained as they'd amputated his leg . . .

The Wall. That first time he'd entered into deep sharemind with Clere had been at the Wall. At the drud village of Al-Muud.

The sharelock chips throbbed in his hands. The priestess-facilitator had warned him, but he reached again, reached automatically, into the utter intimacy of sharers' sharemind. *Clere! My beloved Clere. Where are you? If only I knew how to find your Essence in the Eternal. I can sense you, I can feel you, oh, Clere, we didn't have long enough, not nearly long enough.*

And then he discerned a whisper, a sigh, the slightest susurration, *My darling Regim* . . .

Yes! He'd been hearing her, hearing her for some time, so far away at first. Yet he knew it. *She,* Clere Twine, of all the great magisters that had ever lived on Pangaea, would not abandon her sacred sharer. *She* could pierce the veil of Eternity just as she'd accomplished everything in her life— with single-minded purpose, tenacity, purity of spirit, and ruthless ambition.

The whisper sent a shiver of pure elation through him, and courage. And hope. He bore down on the bodyguards' muscular shoulders beneath his arms and pulled himself up with new determination.

"Bag that body. You, Officer Wartek and Lieutenant Dr. Prussard. Take these women to Atlan and book them," he brusquely told his squad. "You may take my ship. Take the injured woman to her purity's hospital. Contact their families, all of them. If their families have the money, they may pay the bond and take custody. Otherwise throw these fine ladies in their purity's jail." He amended, "Except the gatekeeper's drayers. They'll come with me. I'm appropriating the rover, too. The rest of you will come with me. I have that Vigilance business at Al-Muud to attend to."

She puzzled Regim, the distraught little woman with her disheveled mop of reddish gold curls. She was very voluptuous, he couldn't help but notice, and very pretty despite her crude serv clothes and filthy hygiene. Her small hands were as well wrought as those of a scribe but as ill tended as those of a dishwasher. She wore no sharelock chips. Pretty, then, perhaps, but in a low pure sort of way.

Not a decadent drud of the erotician subpure like Tahliq. No, he didn't think so despite her bestial femaleness. In any case, a pampered creature like Tahliq would rather submit to a flogging in Marketplace than root about in this muck. And certainly not the elegant, highborn sophisticate Clere Twine had been—who would have gladly rooted about in the muck if there had been a compelling Imperial purpose. He didn't think she was a serv, despite her clothes. Neither serv nor any other sort of drud. Her coloring and stature were too refined, too variant. One of the vast middle purities, he decided, though he had no idea what her subpure might be.

Typically it was drunken serv subpures, fishers or falconers, tough rowdies who craved danger, disdained cults, and stole into the Bog for a lark. He'd once apprehended a teq-drenched gang of female firefighters who'd contrived to scale the Wall. They'd behaved so violently toward his squad he'd been compelled to thrash them in order to take them into custody, and received a broken nose and two bitten fingers for his trouble. Sometimes equally drunken drud subpures, window washers or buckwheat threshers too stupid to realize how dangerous the Bog could be, managed to stumble through the long tunnels beneath the Wall and evade the lackadaisical gatekeepers.

Now he noticed the equipment the women had brought with them—databoards, some kind of meter, a voicebox bobbing in the bloodstained shallows. *Now, that's a first. Academes? Who the hell are these women, anyway?*

"Approach that woman," he commanded the bodyguards. They bore him swiftly to her as she tearfully tendered her name—"Plaia Triadana"—pure and subpure, and security number to his officer. *An academe, then. Very good, Regim, your judgment is astute.* He stood over her, methodically examining her at closer range.

She recoiled, her golden green eyes wide with terror. But her full-lipped mouth was grim with resolution, her tiny hands balled into enraged fists.

"What are you doing here, Plaia Triadana?" he said.

"Research," she spat out. "Extremely important research, sir. Certainly nothing illegal."

"You're trespassing."

"Fine! Issue a citation and let me and my colleague go. I must protest this treatment—"

"You'll be quiet."

She stammered into silence, but her fury and grief blazed through his vigilance sharemind. *A kinder tone will solicit her information more effectively, my Regim.*

Clere! Clere?

The tantalizing whisper faded away, and he closed his eyes for a moment, shuddering with gratitude. *Clere.* He assumed a kinder tone, wrestled his lips into a sympathetic smile. "Research. I see. What sort of research, Plaia? On whose behalf? And what are these instruments?"

She glanced at him warily, but she was traumatized by the dragon's attack, her companion's demise, her other companion's maiming. He could see the desperation in her eyes. The need to justify, to explain why a woman's life and another woman's irrevocable pain had been worth it.

"That's a sal-meter, um, a salinometer," she began. "We're conducting earthshock research to be submitted to Ground Control, sir. This floodplain, this . . . part of the landmass. It isn't bouncing. It's spreading. The whole configuration of the landmass is *changing*! Spreading south, and breaking apart! That's why the beasts are dying." She gesticulated frantically with her hands. "Saltwater is percolating through the substrata from the Panthalassa Ocean and poisoning the fresh water the bogbeasts are accustomed to. Don't you see? Blocking the spread to the south would create tremendous tension, far more than exists now. That's why Ground Control *mustn't* force-flood Andea Rift. It would be a disaster of unbelievable—"

"Wait, wait." He placed his huge hand over her two tiny ones and held them firmly, even though he loathed touching a lower pure. "I'm not certain I understand. Plaia, did I hear you say you believe Pangaea is changing? The very ground on which the Imperium has existed and will exist for all Eternity is breaking apart?"

"Belief, sir, has nothing to do with it. And I'm sorry, I know it's too terrible to contemplate, but we must face the *facts* so that we *can* do something—"

"And Our Imperial Bureau of Ground Control subscribes to this heresy, as well?"

"No, no, the bureau *refuses* to acknowledge the facts, to understand, to *see,* and the proctors at Sausal Academy

persist in misinforming key people who could make a difference—''

"You say this heresy is *not* the official position of
Ground Control?"

"Well, of course not. That's the point! We've *got* to present proof before they commence this *insane* policy of force-
flooding—"

Regim flung her hands away. "Officer Wartek? Book this
one for Apocalypticism, too."

Al-Muud: a sullen village of a million drud pures and subpures. Grey-thatched domes of low hovels spread over the
scoured hillocks. "Like a layer of dust," Clere had said
with a laugh on that blessed day when Regim first met her.
Dust that had been swept up against the baseboard of the
Great Wall and had settled, undisturbed, since times lost to
antiquity.

Her metaphor had been perfect. Al-Muud was a filthy
place, not only because of the crude hovels. The impure
lived here, too. Who knew how many.

Regim consulted his databoard. The Devil girl had clan
here. Clan—Regim wouldn't dignify as *family* these people
spewed out of bodies connected to other bodies and other
bodies still sheerly through the haphazard consequences of
the bestial act. His informant, Rota, was a half-pure bastard
of a disgraced cleric who'd been allowed by her subpure to
retain her courses and repaid that allowance by begetting
with an impure thief.

*A shining example of why all women of all the purities
ought to be purified when they're harvested by the natalry.
Except perhaps women of quality like you, Clere.* Yet he'd
remained uneasy even about Clere, haunted by the memory
of her virginal blood on the couch. That she might have
been carrying his child before she died. That the Devil girl
might have slain two lives, not just one.

Heavy-breasted, gap-toothed, as dim-witted as a drayer,

Rota had been only too pleased to take Regim's look-see money and report that Salit Zehar had departed from Atlan, bound for Al-Muud. Bound for distant clanfolk, the Devil girl was apparently both destitute and sentimental in equal measure, and likely to touch the druds for money. Rota said the Devil girl had shaved her head, wore the black facepaint of impure raptureroot dealers, affected a shivering black cloak like the one her father had worn.

Of course. I saw Horan Zehar give his cloak to the girl. And I will know her ugly face anywhere. There is no disguise she can assume that will conceal her from my eyes. There is no place she can hide.

"Hai, get up, you druds," called the vigile driving the rover and timidly flipped the whip over the sweating drayers, who trotted no faster.

Regim discerned the anxiety rippling through the sharemind of his squad. No one was happy about entering this vast village of plowers and basketweavers and streetsweepers without the security of their windship. The vigiles' Imperial uniforms, their shiny-bright crossbows and daggers and firebolts, only rendered them more conspicuous targets to covert foes.

"Find Lane One Thousand Seventy-eight, Hovel Two Thousand Three," he told the driver as he stood behind her on the rover's cargo bed. The vigile wasn't trained for driving drayers. Well, Regim would excuse her fumbling this first time. After which he'd expect her to whip the drayers bloody.

He settled heavily on the bodyguards and leaned back against the side of the rover. The bodyguards adjusted their weapons and leaned back with him. Fierce clean-smelling servs, they evinced complete devotion to his security and keen intuition about his every need. They ought to, with those protocol chips in their foreheads. He didn't even bother dominating sharemind with them. They should know exactly what he wanted. They usually did.

The vehicle careened down the uneven cobblestones, pitching over potholes washed out by the summer rains.

The Imperium had tamed these labyrinthine lanes long ago, meticulously identifying the streets and numbering each parcel and hovel. A never-ending task as challenging in this outlying village as in Our Sacred City. Each season a village planner of a competent magister subpure directed teams of surveyors and signpainters throughout the lanes, refreshing the identification markers and subdividing parcel numbers where three new, tiny hovels had sprung up on the former site of one.

And there. Dread prickled across Regim's skin as he spied tents of charcoal-black sacking, tent flaps stirring in the breeze. Sometimes interspersed among the hovels in small clusters, sometimes segregated in one great smudge at the end of a lane—the tentsites of the impure.

He wasn't accustomed to the sight. The impure were much more visible here than in Central Atlan, where the great waterducts and catacombs and caverns beneath the megalopolis afforded their concealment.

The druds of Al-Muud tolerated the impure among them with simple-minded equanimity. The impure begged from them, stole from them, vandalized what small property the druds owned. Threatened their elderly with muggery, their children with worse. And still the druds acquiesced to the impures' blatant presence. "Kindness is as Kindness Does," proclaimed the kaligraphs on the village banner.

Proof positive of the low morality and lower intelligence of the drud purity.

"Lieutenant captain," the driver called over her shoulder to him as she struggled to rein the drayers in. "We approach the address."

The rover halted before the targeted hovel. Regim and his squad disembarked, automatically drawing their crossbows and daggers. One of his officers carried an inferno bolt of cherry laurel vapors. He ordered her to draw the bolt as a horde of hard-eyed druds silently drifted out of the alleys and surrounded the vigiles, watching them.

Regim methodically scanned the parcel, ordered his bodyguards to stoop as he bent down and picked up a green-glazed jar from a crockery display set out at the curb.

This hovel, according to Rota, housed a family of jarmakers who fashioned their wares on their own premises, apart from the vast Al-Muud jar factory. Which immediately made the jarmakers suspect in Regim's eyes. *Supervision of the purities is the security of the Imperium,* this was the second lesson Regim had learned at Vigilance Academy. The Imperium frowned upon small independent endeavors and taxed and regulated them more severely than the Imperial bureaus, academies dependent upon Imperial funding, or the enormous conglomerates and consortiums that had organized commerce since times lost to antiquity. Even the angels in their marble cloudscrapers were subject to Imperial supervision—the acolyte-auditors at the Temple of the Mind of the World made sure of that.

Not just jarmakers, then, but independent jarmakers very far removed from proximity to Pan. Yet jars were in great demand among all the purities for beer and honey and preserved fruit. Independent production of jars with a bit of craftwork to them, a kaligraph carved around the lid, for instance, could easily command a fine price. Regim smoothed his fingertip over the rich green glaze. As ephemeral as jars were, jars were everywhere to be seen, an object bought and sold and stored on a shelf, not like the services of Regim's pure and subpure.

The services of magisters were crucial to the Imperium. They carried out the mandates of the law so that perpetuity was ensured. *Yet a lifetime of services vanishes once the life is over. As Clere's life is over and now there is nothing but her name, a footnote in history, to show for all her sacrifices and services.*

Regim scowled. Why should this little green jar endure while his beloved Clere had vanished from the world? He

flung the jar to the cobblestones, shattering it. The gathered
druds murmured and jostled each other.

"Go home, all of you," Regim said. "Go about your
business and begone."

"What be yer business here, off'cer?" an old woman
asked, her boldness as prominent as her buckwheat
thresher's cheekbones.

Not all lower pures are properly obedient or submissive,
Clere had told him, *especially in the more barbarous regions.*

"No business of yours, dame. Begone, or I'll arrest you
all for loitering."

As the druds grudgingly dispersed, returning to the lanes
from which they'd drifted, it struck Regim that these independent jarmakers were prosperous, tucked away in their
hovel on Lane One Thousand Seventy-Eight. *Prosperity
among the lower purities,* Clere had said, *leads to one
thing—subversion.* To collaboration with discontents
against the Imperium. He'd heartily agreed.

Regim peered more closely. Yes, the low conical frontroom and flat roof of the outbuilding beyond were studded
with ventilation and smoke pipes, indicating the structure's
subterranean depths, the firepits and cookpits and wastepits.
Superstitious as all druds were, someone of this family had
set *ch'i ch'i* upon every eave—tiny dragons and birds of
prey carved of tourmaline and other semiprecious stones
meant to ward off evil spirits.

Drud, yet prosperous. Very prosperous, indeed.

Who knew how deep those depths plunged, or how
deeply they delved into the secret spaces of the impure?
Perhaps the black tents amounted only to slight evidence of
the impure presence, the way scum on the surface of a pond
is a film, a scrim, a fractional indication of leagues-thick
putrefaction festering in the depths. A thousand suspicions
sprang to his mind. Perhaps the impure enjoyed subterranean burrows and ducts here, after all.

Regim saw no black tents anywhere near Hovel Two Thousand Three.

"Surround the parcel," he ordered, exhausted, aching, his voice slurring. "You, Frit, Wrener, Spor, and Baen, come with me." When his nerves became taut and his blood quickened in anticipation, pain pulsed in his hip socket and in . . . the place where his leg had been. He rapped smartly on the knobby wooden door, bearing his Imperial search permission. "In the name of Pan and the Imperium, open up."

A wizened little grey-skinned man whose head barely reached Regim's waist cracked open the door, eyed Regim and his squad, peered at the permission, and admitted them without protest. The hovel was so cramped and low Regim and the squad had to kneel, crawl like beasts across the straw-strewn floor, through a narrow raised passage, and down into the subterranean living and fabrication chambers. The bodyguards knelt beneath Regim, awkwardly assisting his progress. In the hexagonally shaped fabrication chamber he could stand upright if he crooked his neck and slightly bent his knee. His leg trembled.

How I **loathe** *this debility!*

"I'm looking for an impure girl named Salit Zehar," he told the jarmaker in Al-Muud drud dialect. *Very good, my Regim,* filtered through his sharers' sharemind. Clere had been impressed he knew so many subpure dialects, including the quaint tongue of Al-Muud. *Thank you, my Clere,* and the rage, the grief throbbed again in his chest. He withdrew an ink rendering on linen paper that a scribe had made of the Heaven's Devil girl. The scribe had never seen the girl herself. He'd invoked Imperial sharemind and studied her image in Milord Lucyd's confounding dream. "This girl."

"No impure here," the jarmaker said, barely glancing at the rendering. He made the sign of the Imperial star over his chest, gestured deferentially to his busy fabrication chamber. "We good jarmakers, sir. Not impure."

A flock of grey-skinned children crouched before pottery wheels, their dexterous little fingers fashioning jars with astonishing speed and skill. Racks of unfired jars lined three of the six walls, racks of fired jars lined the rest. Massive blocks of raw clay had been stacked everywhere. A trio of white-haired, grey-skinned women shoveled red-hot cookstones into half a dozen cavernous kilns or withdrew platters of freshly fired jars.

The vigiles searched among the wares and shook their heads.

"Nothing improper here, lieutenant captain," Officer Spor said.

"I'll be the judge of that," Regim snapped and examined the industrious children through narrowed eyes. There—was that a purple gleam, a crystalline curve at a girl's slender throat? "Officer Spor, seize that child and bring her to me. What's she wearing?"

But the girl's deft fingers must have been quicker than Regim's trained eye. When Spor brought her, eyes averted, arms limp at her sides, and lifted her shirt over her head, Regim saw only the curves of a well-fed young torso, a string of green-glazed beads lying against immature breasts.

Regim directed his bodyguards to her pottery wheel, seized the jar she'd been forming, tore the soft clay open. Nothing. He flung the ruined jar to the floor, scrutinized the other children, who averted their terrified eyes and stared down at their wheels.

One trembling child slid her eyes to a corner behind a rack of fired jars, the merest flicker of eyelids, but Regim noticed at once—evidence of the jarmaker's monstrous guilt and collusion.

He hobbled to the rack, seized it, sent rack and greenware crashing to the floor. "There," he said to his officers. "There's a passage behind there."

" 'Tis ash-trap for the kilns, sir," the jarmaker pleaded. "I beg you, please, 'tis only ash-trap."

The vigiles tore past him, tore at wall and floor. Spor found the little loop of leather that lifted the trapdoor. Regim seized a torch and descended into hot, sooty darkness. The low ceiling compelled him and his bodyguards to kneel again and proceed at a crawl. The crawl space was thick with hot ashes that rose in a choking cloud with their laborious passage. The kilns blazed a handbreadth above Regim's head, scorching his golden hair, but he would not falter. *This filthy space is just the sort of place where the impure would skulk about. They love filth and darkness and hellishness.*

And there. There! A furtive movement ahead in the darkness, and then a flash of light as another trapdoor at the far end of the ash-trap flipped open and shut, plunging him back into choking darkness.

"I see something," he shouted over his shoulder to his officers. "Faster," he growled at his bodyguards, who hurtled him toward the trapdoor.

And then he was standing upright, he was flinging back the trapdoor, he was scrabbling out on one leg while his bodyguards pushed him up with frenzied hands.

He pulled himself out, heaving for air, onto a dusty yard twenty strides distant from the jarmaker's hovel.

He saw them running.

A tiny, grey-skinned woman whose lurching gait and uneven legs, the left considerably shorter than the right, branded her with impure blood. And next to her—holding hands with her—a scrawny figure clad in black sacking, her black cloak streaming around her. No bald head or grotesque facepaint could conceal her identity.

Cut out her womb first, my Regim, Clere whispered in his sharemind, *so Salit Zehar knows she can never get with child, if she should live. Then cut out her eyes, her breasts, her liver, her evil heart.*

He drew his dagger, somehow sprinted after the pair on his hands and one leg, leaving the heaving bodyguards behind. The Devil girl turned to face him, her black eyes glinting, and furiously shook and swatted at the draperies of her cloak, sending soot swirling around her. She hissed something to her weeping companion, who reluctantly hesitated, then loped away, losing herself in the twisting lanes.

"Monster," Regim said, sobbing, and seized her slim gnarled wrists in one hand before she could seize her weapons. He swiped at her belly with the dagger but she leapt back. The soiled cloak shivered like a dog shaking water off its fur. The cloak closed around her limbs and body, the charcoal black fading, fibrillating to the mottled olive blades of parched grass, and then in another vertiginous moment—

—she vanished.

But bone and sinew and filthy skin—he still held her wrists, felt her writhing in his grip.

My Regim, she's still there, she's still **there,** *you just cannot* **see** *her.*

He struggled to understand as he struggled with the flailing invisible presence in his grip, and terror swept over him so intensely his bowels loosened. *If I let go of her wrists, she can seize a devil star from her belt and fling it at me before I can see what she's doing. Fling it at close range . . .*

His officers pounded up behind him, their eyes wide, their faces blanched, and he snarled, "She's still *here,* you fools. Don't you see? Don't you *see*?"

The Devil girl yanked him forward and he fell heavily on his knee, cursing at the searing pain. How strong she was for such a tiny beast! He thrashed and rolled on the grass, gripping her wrists for dear life itself. If he released her, who knew what she might do?

"Seize her, *seize* her, you idiots!"

Officer Spor stood over him, her face contorted with fear and doubt. "Seize *who,* lieutenant captain?"

Her doubt, the terrified skepticism plain on the faces of his squad shocked him so mightily he inadvertently released his grip on the Devil girl's wrists. He cringed, crouched, wrapping one arm around his face, one arm around his torso, protecting his vital organs from a flung devil star or dagger.

Nothing. He felt nothing but sweat pouring down his forehead, his neck. Felt the hot autumn wind. After a moment, he glanced up and saw a shimmer, a dark silvery glimmer wafting away like a wraith down the labyrinthine lanes.

The Devil girl was gone.

Oh, my Regim, you let her get away.

And through the magister sharemind of his squad prickled thornier thoughts, *Our lieutenant captain is in pain. What was our lieutenant captain doing? Our lieutenant captain was wrestling with nothing. Nothing! Our lieutenant captain is becoming . . . unbalanced. Unhinged. Deranged . . . Our lieutenant captain is in pain. . . .*

His bodyguards heaved him to his feet, somberly tidied his uniform, swept off the ashes, and blotted his face with crisp cotton handkerchiefs.

He faced his squad, filled with fury. "Salit Zehar was in my grasp, and you did nothing to capture her."

"Lieutenant captain," murmured Spor, "we apologize, but we saw nothing to capture."

He stared stonily at his squad's anguished faces. "You're all blind. The cloaks the Heaven's Devils possess. They must cause the Devil to disappear, but the Devil is still *there.* Yes. Yes. Don't stare at me like a treeful of owls. The jarmaker *is* colluding with the impure. He has half-pure kin. I saw the woman." The neighbors had crept out of their hovels and lanes again, stood watching the vigiles. "Remove the jarmaker and his family from their hovel. All of them. Take them out onto the lane."

The squad hesitated, wary, glancing doubtfully among themselves, alarmed at his vehemence. Couldn't even conceal their insubordination, could they?

"I said remove them."

He directed his bodyguards to bear him to the front curb

of Hovel Two Thousand Three. *Tired, so tired, spasms of fire licking at . . . the place where my leg used to be.*

His squad rousted the jarmaker and his family from the depths of the hovel, lined them up.

"Have the traitors prostrate themselves before me," he told Officer Spor. "Have them extend their hands on the ground. And set aside the child who possesses an Orb of Eternity—no, no, they cannot deny it, *you* cannot deny it. Set aside her and the child who glanced at the ash-trap door." As his squad did as he bid, he announced to the glowering neighbors, "You druds want to know what our Imperial business is here? Our Imperial business is to root out the impure weeds that sprout among you in such abundance that you, too, have become contaminated by their malignancy."

"Please, sir, please," cried the old woman. Not so bold anymore. "Our neighbor Freken Benihm Zarh naitre Quintus is an excellent jarmaker. He is a good man with a devoted sharer and a fine family. Please, please—"

"A devoted sharer? Where is this sharer's devotion now that her family grovels before me? Where is she? *What* is she? Why won't she show her half-pure face? How is it this prosperous jarmaker harbors an impure foe wanted by the Imperium in the ash-trap below his fabrication chamber? How is it"—he glared down at the old woman—"that you don't even recognize the menace in your midst?"

She cowered, recoiled from him. The muttering crowd fell silent.

The half-pure did not come forward, well, of course. She was a conspirator, a collaborator, scum as filthy and evil as the impure chit who had begotten her.

The wizened jarmakers sobbed quietly, their slender hands extended before them, according to Regim's command.

Regim drew his long dagger. *Chop, chop, and chop, chop, and chop, chop.* He made his way down the row of the jarmaker's family, till their little dismembered hands lay like wilting blossoms on the dusty cobblestones. The villagers began to wail. There, it was done. Independent jarmakers no more unless they could learn to turn jars with their stumps. Independents they remained, still, refusing to cry out in pain as blood pulsed from their amputated wrists in rhythm to their heartbeats . . .

Amputated . . . The weeping women in the Bog, one companion amputated unto death, the other maimed as these jarmakers were maimed, as Regim had been grievously maimed . . .

To wreak the same type of damage that had been done him. It was more horrible for him than anyone in all Pangaea, couldn't these villagers comprehend that?

It's not enough. Teach them a lesson, my cherished Regim. A lesson they'll never forget.

He hobbled to the two tiny groveling children, the one who'd concealed an orb, the other with the glancing eyes. He drew his dagger, hefted it, flung it back, flung it forward—

—*one two, and one two,* he cleaved the children neck to buttocks. Their grey little bodies fell apart like hens split for the roasting spit, blood and entrails spilling across the cobblestones.

The wailing rose into a rending shriek. He ignored the sound, the howl of collaborators. He said to his officers, "Impale each half of these bodies on four stakes. Impale the hands on stakes, too, four to a stake will do. Plant the stakes before this jarmaker's hovel so that all Al-Muud will know the fate of impure collaborators."

His officers whispered, "Yes, lieutenant captain."

Early evening brought a violaceous sky and a cool breeze from the west. The drayers, jangling wearily in their traces, whiplashes oozing blood on their backs, trudged toward the deepening night on the long journey to Atlan.

Regim stood at his post behind the driver, his booted foot

resolutely set on the cargo bed of the rover. He shut out the cacophonous, nearly traitorous melee in his squad's sharemind. He'd done what he'd had to do.

A trace broke loose, and the drayer bawled, bucked. The other drayers shuddered in their traces. One hirsute female flung back her head and brayed, berating the vigiles, "Hai, hai, hai, poxy magisters—"

"What should I do, lieutenant captain?" said the wide-eyed, cowering driver.

And a promising vigile, too. There goes her promotion.

"Halt them, and get down there and reattach the traces, you nitwit."

"Yes, lieutenant captain."

As the vigile gingerly rebuckled the loose traces, the hub of a rear wheel tumbled off the rover, *clang clang clang* on the Imperial roadway.

Regim wearily dispatched another of his squad to re-mount the hub. What lazy wretches they were, this squad. Would he have to reprimand them all? Punish and demote them all?

The heap of their jackets the squad had discarded during the long, hot, jostling ride suddenly slid off the cargo bed, tumbling into the dust of the road.

As if the heap of jackets suddenly possessed an impetuous will of its own.

As if someone invisible had pushed it.

Regim scowled, commanded his bodyguards to carry him, and circumnavigated the rover, surveilling, surveilling.

Was there a shimmer? A dark glimmer? A disturbance among evening's lengthening shadows?

He would rip the Heaven's Devil apart with his bare hands. That she could torment him at her whim, unseen, terrified and enraged him.

But he could see nothing. Nothing but the fields and paddies and huddled stables stretching behind him and be-yond him to the horizon.

The traces broke again. Then the traces broke again. He

commanded the rover to stop. A wheel hub tumbled off. A wheel hub on the opposite side tumbled off. And again, twice, thrice, the load in the cargo bed spilled onto the road, soiling the vigiles' jackets, their waterskins, their food sacks.

Regim berated his squad, cursed the drayers, whipped them again and again with his own hand. Mishaps plagued them all the way back to Atlan.

As if, Clere's voice whispered in his sharers' sharemind, *a Devil was dogging you.*

"My son-in-lock, I'm deeply sorry to hear about this atrocity. And you didn't apprehend Salit Zehar, after all that effort? After the surveillance, the informant, the strategy? The surprise raid?"

Regim shook his head and suppressed a yawn. The return journey had taken all night. They'd arrived in Atlan at dawn. Exhausted, hazy from soporifics, Regim had been in dire need of sleep, but he'd reported at once to his father-in-lock. He'd found Claren Twine at breakfast, caf and bowls of fruit spread before him on the expansive dining table, a lit cheroot smoldering in an ashtray.

Now the councillor clasped his hands behind his back and clucked his tongue, reprovingly, but—Regim thought—sympathetically, too, as he paced across the grand living chamber of the Twine household.

At last! Regim had finally been invited to this, the chamber central to the Twines' family life, with its fabled rose marble pillars, the marble an exquisite antique from long depleted Silurian mines. Thick, hand-woven carpets of scarlet and cerulean blue the length of a gamefield lay beneath Regim's boots. Wafer-thin panes of cut atlantium set in every portal emitted only the most refined sunlight. And crystal, crystal everywhere, in the magmaliers, the sconces, the tabletops, the goblets. Frescoes winding around the high-domed ceiling depicted the Story of Pan and the Wor-

thy Magister in kaligraphs of atlantium purple, turquoise
blue, coral pink, and gold.

This was the most intimate moment Regim had yet
shared with the eminent Claren Twine, a moment he'd
dreamed of. And now it was tainted over this reckoning of
what he'd done in Al-Muud.

Never fear, my Regim, you fulfilled your Imperial duty.

Regim restrained a cough, the soot of the jarmaker's ash-
trap still trapped in his throat, the whimpers of the
jarmaker's family still trapped in his ears.

"My father-in-lock, the Devil girl and her kinswoman
fled."

"You pursued these impure creatures, of course."

"Diligently, but someone must have alerted them. Or
maybe the impure detected us as we entered the targeted
premises. I don't know, my father-in-lock. The ash-trap was
dark. I'm not as fleet as I was before becoming . . . dis-
abled."

"Of course." Claren Twine abruptly trained his pale blue
eyes on Regim. A gleam of sympathy twinkled, a comforting ray of sharemind. "Have you reported any of this to the
Chief Commander?"

"No, sir. You commanded me to report directly to you."

"Very good, my son-in-lock. Your obedience is exem-
plary."

"But I did employ a Vigilance windship with observers,
at least part of the way. And most of my squad witnessed
the incident at Al-Muud."

"Can't be helped. Don't concern yourself about your
squad. They'll obey you or lose their own two hands. Now,
you say there was something unusual about the girl's
cloak?"

Regim ran his hand over the aching scabs furrowing his
chest. "The Heaven's Devil possesses a cloak, my father-
in-lock. This cloak of hers . . . I witnessed when her father gave it to her, but I'd never realized precisely how it
functions. I did yesterday." Regim turned respectfully

toward his father-in-lock, maintaining a submissive posture, knowing full well Councillor Twine would commit into sharemind whatever he said and did. "The Devils do *not* disappear and reappear leagues away like rumor says."

"What do they do?" Councillor Twine said in his whisper that reverberated throughout the entire chamber.

"They . . . blend in, somehow. But they're still *there*." Regim stood unsteadily. The councillor had not wished their conversation to be overheard by the bodyguards. Regim had dismissed them. Handmaids had installed a new body support over his chest and given him a sculpted prosthesis that mimicked a leg and a foot tucked in his leggings, his boot. He felt as awkward as a babe learning to walk. "Maybe they stand very *still*. Maybe they stay in one place while we flail and thrash all around them. And then they take their leave, stealthily. As far as I can tell, they have no power of extraordinary locomotion like the rumors have always said."

Councillor Twine nodded, solemnly considering Regim's reconnaissance. "Fascinating. Well, you should know that I've secured the services of a spy in Milord Lucyd's household. If the angel collaborates with the impure, we shall discover it soon enough."

"Excellent. Thank you, my father-in-lock." Regim heaved a deep breath and said, "Sir. My beloved Clere came to me yesterday afternoon . . . in sharers' sharemind."

"Indeed? Is that so?" Claren stood before him, scrutinizing his face with an inexplicable expression.

"Yes, sir." Regim cautiously averted his eyes. Not everyone, even the most pious Pannist, believed fully in the Eternal. Or believed that one who had entered the Eternal could actually contact those who still suffered in the fleeting world. Who would wish to return to the Ephemeral after entering Eternity?

Would his father-in-lock, too, believe Regim had become unbalanced? Deranged?

You have been reunited with the Eternal Essence of your sacred sharer. You are not unbalanced, my Regim. You are blessed.

He dared to glance up. His father-in-lock was smiling.

"That's wonderful, my son-in-lock. Truly Pan preserves her for all Eternity. I think," Councillor Twine said, "it's time you generate a family with our beloved Clere."

FACET 15

Mountain: Lookout or barrier.

At the foot of the mountain, the plower looks up at the peak.

At the mountain's peak, the angel looks down at the whole valley.

The action is perspective.

The forbearance is dogma.

The Orb of Eternity

Commentaries:

Councillor Sausal: From the temple altar, the priestesses and priests describe the true nature of Pan to all the purities. Yet if Pan is both the center and everything that manifests from the center, then the true nature of Pan is that It encompasses infinite natures.

So, too, the Imperium is strong when the pures know and understand the law. The Imperium is invincible when the pures hold Pan dear within their Essence.

Therefore the prudent person should assiduously study the sacred teachings, but contemplate the meaning of Pan within one's own heart.

Guttersage (usu. considered vulgar): What you see depends upon where you stand.

Our City of Atlan, periphery of Northeast Marketplace. The Imperial Natalries, Secundus Natalry, the laboratory:

Apprehension pounded in Dubban's chest. Perspiration beaded his brow. He slid the empty dish next to the crystal sliver clipped beneath his viewglass. He'd just swiveled the left hand-lever so he could scrape the bad threads he'd cut into the dish when Waldo burst into the laboratory, shouting like a madman.

"Who the hell is on duty here today?" Dubban's super dashed among the midwives who stood, quietly industrious, before their viewglasses on the high platforms.

Dubban slid the empty dish back among the begetting dishes containing seeded magister birthpods to be pruned today. An enumerator from the Security Number Administration had assigned security numbers to the pods that morning. The enumerator, an emaciated woman with squinting hazel eyes, had also painstakingly recorded the security numbers of the sharers who had contributed their materia to the pods and double-checked her databoard. Standard procedure. By the time the unborns had developed arms, their security number chips would be manufactured and ready for installation by inductor-surgeons from the administration. Dubban didn't know who made the chips or how and exactly what the little blue mole contained. It wasn't his place, as a midwife-natalist, to know.

Still, he wondered. He remembered the loutish trio of inductors, their tray of spilled chips. He kept his wonderments to himself. Wondering was like drinking teq. The first shot made him sputter and cough, and tasted bad and good at the same time. Then the teq drenched him in its heady spell, and he wanted another shot, and another. After a while, he didn't sputter or care about the taste anymore.

Wondering hadn't made him heedless, though, the way teq did. Wondering had made him wary. He'd been wondering more and more lately, and thinking many impure thoughts. Sometimes he felt as if he'd burst from so many impure thoughts, like a child's tossball pumped too full of air.

If only he could tell someone. But he didn't dare.

The empty dish he'd stolen from the supply room didn't have a label with the security numbers of the sharers on it like the begetting dishes. But Waldo wasn't likely to notice that in the state he was in.

The natalry trembled. Another earthshock? Or was it only the quaking of his anxiety, now that he'd set about consummating his crime at the behest of the Heaven's Devil girl?

Small ceaseless earthshocks were not a product of his overwrought nerves, though. Atlan had rattled with them day and night. The criers had offered an Imperial sharemind of the disturbance at the famous pleasure towers on the boiling waters of the Hercynian Sea. The sharemind had depicted colorful sprays of magma set against the turquoise-blue waters. The disturbance was causing the small shocks, but Imperial Ground Control would soon restore peace and calm. That's what the criers said.

Apocalyptists' rumors, on the other hand, whispered in every cafe and tavern told a far different tale. The sinful Floating Towers, where the purities mingled too freely, had exploded in a burst of holy fire incurred by the wrath of Pan. And Inim had reached up with fiery claws and dragged anyone tainted with impurity into the molten agony of Eternal Torment.

Thirty-five thousand people were rumored to be missing.
Could the Apocalyptists be right, after all?

Dubban rankled at the thought. Just when he'd concluded that after committing his crime he would only have to worry about Imperial Vigilance—no mean feat—he had to wonder once more whether he should fear the wrath of Pan and the eternal fires of Inim.

He could deny collaborating with a Heaven's Devil to a Vigilance interrogator, deny striking a blow against the Imperium. But how could he ever atone for his sins before Pan?

For two days tremendous tidal waves had pummeled the Sausal waterfront and ravaged the boardwalk. Shippers had

sailed their vessels that hadn't yet been smashed to kindling
into inland harbors and soft-bottom swamps. He'd spied the
unusual sight of a great oceangoing ferry tethered in a
pondplum paddy. Atlan Prefecture had declared Antiquity
Park an Imperial disaster. All of Marketplace, Rancid Flats,
Pleasant Valley, even the northeastern buckwheat fields of
the Iapetus Plains, ran ankle-deep in tepid seawater infused
with raw sewage and rotting kelp. The stink was horrendous, securing potable water worse.

"You, Dubban," his super shouted. "Where in bloody
hell is the Superior Father, do you know? I've searched all
of Quartius for him. I can't find him anywhere!"

"Can't say that I do, supe," Dubban said, releasing both
hand-levers and the breath he hadn't realized he'd been
holding. He exhaled raggedly. Every moral homily his
mother had ever told him clanged in his ears like the tolling
of the Harbinger. *Thievery is thievery. Collaboration, collaboration.* He'd never been cut out for a life of crime.

He'd never been cut out to desire a higher pure woman,
either. *Never mingle what belongs to one purity . . .* No!
He stilled those moral homilies. Had no more use for his
mother's Pannist teachings when it came to purities and
what he was permitted or forbidden to desire. To love.

Was he impure and seditious to question the protocol
he'd been inculcated with his whole life?

Then I'm impure and seditious.

In fact Dubban *did* know where Father Doublet was at
the moment. Dubban had gone upstairs to the seventh floor
of Quartius Natalry in search of the empty dish. He'd last
seen Father Doublet in the supply room, embracing Garth.
But he wasn't about to tell Waldo. The Superior Father had
slipped him five ores for his silence. He fully intended to
keep his own counsel.

Once Dubban would have obediently reported the Father's forbidden fraternization while on duty, would have
refused the outrageous bribe. Would have trembled with
righteous indignation at how a middle-pure priest like Fa-

ther Doublet promiscuously violated proximity, and with a low, bumbling serv like Garth who engaged in illegal orb-rolls. Impurity upon impurity. An Imperial priest in Doublet's position—at a natalry, even Quartius Natalry—could find himself relieved of a testicle for such behavior.

But Dubban was a changed man. A man on fire. He knew exactly what he'd do with that five ores the moment he closed his fingers over the money.

He turned away from the viewglass and grinned at his super, hoping feigned friendliness would conceal the falsehood in his eyes. "What's the trouble, supe?"

"The *trouble* is the magisters have arrived for their Rite of Begetting and I can't find that damned Doublet anywhere. You!" Waldo stared at him, wild-eyed, perspiring heavily. "You'll have to preside in his stead."

"*Me?* No, no. I'm a midwife. I couldn't possibly—"

"You're tall enough. You've got that deep voice. That face. You'll pass this once. You can, and you will, chum."

Never cut out for a life of crime, perhaps, but Dubban had begun to understand the nature of criminality, the covert exchange of illicit value for illicit value. The power of overweening greed presented with sniveling need.

If he wasn't mistaken, his super had just flattered him. Had just acknowledged that his unique attributes were a cut above the ordinary midwife. A variance of his subpure, and not a bad variance, at that.

Well, well.

He pursed his lips, slowly untied the thong around his hair, smoothed back the long, raven-black strands, carefully retied the thong. "Waldo," he said. "Wouldn't your super collapse of a failed heart if she knew you'd sent a midwife to stand in for the Superior Father? These hands that touch filth, performing the holy Rite of Begetting?"

He extended them, pleased that his hands were as smooth and well tended as an angel's from midwifery and not chewed to bits from crewing on a fishing ship or grinding machine parts. If the lovely higher pure woman were ever to exercise her prerogative again, she would expect her man to touch her with genteel hands.

Waldo narrowed his eyes, disbelief plain on his swarthy face. Usually Dubban followed the super's orders without protest, even when the young man's temper flared. "Are you sassing me, you rowdy?"

"Just my low and filthy presence could contaminate Pan's miracle, you know that. You *and* the Superior Mother could get thrown in the clang. And each lose an eye for willfully failing to see your breach. Goodness me! What sacrilege!"

"Since when are you an expert on sacrilege?" But the super blanched.

The High Council, at the instigation of Councillor Twine, had announced new purity protocol. Lower pures were urged to report impure behavior or thoughts of higher pures, subpures, and superiors to a newly installed task force at Vigilance Authority. If the report proved true after a full investigation, the reporting person would be paid a considerable fee and conferred with other prerogatives. If the report proved false, though, the lower pure would be punished under traditional purity protocol. Punishments as terrible as tradition had always mandated, from the loss of an eye or tongue or finger to the loss of one's life.

Dubban wasn't afraid. What Waldo suggested amounted to an outrageous violation of protocol, not to mention natalry regulations. Not that Dubban cowered before protocol anymore. Or proximity. Or Imperial duty. Not even that he feared Eternal Torment anymore. No, he'd become exceedingly dutiful once he began to realize the advantages he might reap from diligent duty. Not in Eternal Bliss one day, but here and now—in his life on Pangaea.

He hadn't struck or threatened Garth or any other of his shiftmates for the rest of the summer season. He hadn't misbehaved in any way. He'd shown up on time for his shift, cheerful and qut-free, performed every task asked of

him, and gone home long after everyone else had quit for
the day.

And Waldo knew it. They both knew it.

Dubban shrugged, quietly suggested, "What's in it for
me?"

"What's in it—? Oh, I get it, I get it. You want your full
wage restored, eh? Why, you gimpy lug, you lamebrained
nitwit. I'll show you where you really belong. I'll teach you
to sass me—"

Cold smile. Dubban suddenly became aware he towered
over the super, he was younger by ten years, and probably
thrice as strong. If he wanted to, he could summon a vigile
and report Waldo right now. But he didn't do that. He casually flexed his fist as if considering the sculptural qualities
of his knuckles. "Well, yes, Waldo. My full wage restored
will do for a start."

"A start!" The super flinched violently.

Greed and need. Two sides of a coin.

"A start." Dubban's tentative embarkation upon a life of
crime had inspired a new boldness. "I want my full wage
restored. *And* I want another five ores an hour, if I'm to
fulfill the duties of the Superior Father, as well as those of
midwife. The Father earns ten times my wage, doesn't he?"

"Another five ores an hour! All right, all right. But just
this day, you piece of—"

"Another five ores till next season, when another five an
hour will do." Dubban doubtfully shook his head. "The
Father at a Rite of Begetting, no less. We could all get
thrown in the clang. I like having my eyes, y'know? I need
both of them to prune these threads."

Dubban hadn't been rotated to Secundus Natalry for laboratory duty since early summer. It was a lucky break.
Maybe luck *had* begun to smile upon him. And since the
Devil girl had evinced zealous interest in magister unborns,
he figured she'd be especially pleased that the smuggled
threads came from these, the seeded magister birthpods at

Secundus. Perhaps he could persuade her to cancel his debt in full.

He'd pondered what fabrication he would tell her as to how, exactly, he'd happened to get his hands on magister threads. How he regretted telling her he had no access to Secundus! Till he recalled exactly why he'd told the lie that day.

I thwarted a terrorist plot of staggering dimensions. I deserve a medal from the High Council.

But he could never tell anyone.

No, instead of effacing himself, he'd tell the Devil girl something grand and self-aggrandizing. Something that cast him in a heroic light—nefariously heroic, maybe, but heroic nonetheless. Not the act of a tethered ox. An act of small courage. *I bribed the orderly who transports filth from Secundus.* Or, *I stole the orderly's maintenance cart.* Better, better. The important thing about falsehood, he realized, is that one must keep one's lies consistent.

"Done," Waldo said. "Done, you rowdy. Take off that midwife's tunic, put this on. And trot yer arse over to the bank, quick!"

The super flung the ceremonial cape of forest-green velvet over Dubban's shoulders, shoved the green-velvet miter on his head. A high conical cap with a blunt, rounded crown, the miter, Dubban had always thought whenever he'd seen the Superior Father in his holy regalia, resembled nothing so much as the male instrument of the bestial urge.

Carolers had commenced the hymnals as Dubban dashed, cape flying, miter askew, into the begetting chambers on the top floor of Natalry Bank. The Superior Mother and her physician-natalists scurried about in the service chamber, more frantic than Waldo had been. The physicians bore bouquets of flowers, an enormous viewglass, two syringes, and bowls of sacred nectar.

Sacred nectar. This was simply the saline solution bolstered by nutrients and motherblood in which Dubban stored the seeded birthpods he tended, pending their transfer to sacks and tanks. Dubban smiled at this elevation in status of the ephemeral filth he discarded in the normal course of his midwifery chores.

"Rejoice, rejoice!" the carolers blared through their huge, fan-shaped mouths. "The miracle is nigh! An Essence joins us from on high—"

"Who in hell are *you*?" the Superior Mother demanded when he strode in the service door. A willowy, dark-haired woman of eminent priestess subpures, the Superior Mother had always reminded Dubban of his mother, stern yet compassionate, wise yet humble, dedicated to her Imperial duty but ready with a kind word. He'd always discreetly admired her, her vermilion veils spilling all around her like the petals of a rose.

Till now.

"You're not Doublet."

"Can't say that I am."

"Where in bloody hell is that twit? In a closet again with some doe-eyed boy?" She peered more closely at him, recoiled in horror. "You're one of the midwives! Is Waldo insane?" He shrugged, eager to concur with her assessment of his super and take his leave, but the Superior Mother seized his arm. "*Fuck* it. Both bloody families have arrived, *and* both sharers, and we haven't even heated up their doodles. Where are those dishes, doctor?" she shouted at a physician-natalist.

Dubban grinned at the Superior Mother's impertinent reference to Imperial materia, and materia of such important persons. He'd thought only insolent midwives called male seeds and female birthpods doodles.

"Such short notice," the physician-natalist replied in a complaining tone with which no midwife would dare address a priestess-natalist. "The vault hasn't sent up the dishes yet. We can only hope the materia has been pulled from the sharers' accounts."

Dubban raised his eyebrows at the physician's demeanor. Middle subpures like physicians and priests shifted in proximity to Pan with each season, depending on whether the latest High Council proclamation had declared the life of the ephemeral body or the life of the Eternal Essence more divine. Dubban was never quite sure which subpure was higher. He didn't try to ascertain that now and averted his eyes, breaching no protocol with either subpure.

The Superior Mother tore at her elaborate coiffure. "Idiots! I'm surrounded by idiots."

"Shall I retrieve the sharers' materia from the vault for you, Superior Mother?" Dubban said.

"Yes, you dolt. Go! *Go.*"

Greed and need. "I'm not exactly sure how—"

The Superior Mother snorted in exasperation, counted out five ores from her skirt pocket, dumped the money, a copper carrying rack, and a databoard dancing with kaligraphs into his hands. "Here are their security numbers, midwife. The clerks should have pulled the dishes out of the ice this morning. You tell Ping and Fen those doodles had better be thawed, or they'll all wind up streetsweepers. Get down to the vaults and back up here in ten moments, or I'll have your head. Here." She fumbled in her pocket again, retrieved and pressed a priest's protocol chip onto his forehead. "That'll clear you through security."

"Yes, Superior Mother. Thank you, Superior Mother," he murmured and dashed off, knowing exactly what he'd do with those five ores, too.

He knew an expeditious shortcut down to the vaults that a larcenous midwife had once shown him. Chort had been lifting medical supplies for the shadow market—nopaine, needles, astringent, that sort of thing—and asked Dubban if he'd wanted in on the scam. Of course Dubban had declined. At the time he'd believed obedience a higher virtue than supplementing his wage with petty thievery, though his wage barely fed and housed him. Then a physician-natalist had caught Chort with an orderly's cart chockablock with booty, and Dubban had never seen Chort again. Rumor whispered Chort had lost his right hand and foot to a Vigilance interrogator.

Dubban silently thanked the luckless thief for the tip about the shortcut. He vigorously pulled a service tray up its well shaft, yanked the tray above his head, gripped the rope and pulley, and precipitously descended three stories to Secundus Vault, swinging like a wild jungle drud on a vine.

That squandered less than a moment. He had nine and a half moments left.

He blew out a cloud of vapor as he stepped into the vault's freezing antechamber to find—no one behind the clerks' high padlocked booths. Ten impassive security monitors gazed at him with deadpan eyes. Between the natural furnace of his metabolism and the excitement of his new task, he wouldn't feel the polar chill for another five moments. He had no intention of waiting that long. He rang the bell and pounded on the booth. "Hai! Get your bums out here, you poxy clerks. We're begettin' upstairs."

The door to the vault swung open. A tremendous fog of frosty air spilled into the antechamber. Dubban glimpsed the endless racks inside the vault, the metal latticework frosted with ice, and countless little flat storage boxes meticulously labeled with security numbers that contained the harvested birthpods or seeds of magister pures.

A chill pierced him, not from the freezing temperature within the vault but from the sight of those endless racks, those countless boxes. Somewhere in the Tertius vault on the floor below this, the lovely woman's pods lay frozen. And in the Quartius vault on the floor below that, his seeds.

What power the Imperium wields over us—for the great gift of freeing the body from growing the unborn within. For the great gift of eliminating disease and deformity. And the purities submit to that power to reap the rewards of those gifts. But what price have we paid?

It was the most subversive thought he'd ever had. He swiftly thrust it from his mind.

Three rodentlike clerks with beady eyes and snouts to match scurried out of the vault, clutching teetering towers of tiny, lidded storage dishes in their spindly blue hands.

The first clerk carefully matched the two security numbers Dubban provided to two of the dishes. The second clerk cautiously rechecked the numbers twice. The third rechecked yet a third time, remarking, "Ooh, this 'un's been on ice for forty-odd years. In another fifty, the cream'll curdle an' we'll have to toss 'er."

"These thawed?"

"Yes, Superior Father, since dawn, when the begetting request flew in the door. But they're still cold. Say," the clerk called after him, "you ain't Father Doublet."

"Thank Pan," he agreed, marveling at how the natalries *could* be sabotaged by someone who knew how the whole system had been organized. He fitted the dishes into the carrying rack, took the stairs three steps at a time, and skidded into the service chamber with five moments to spare. "They're thawed but still cold," he informed the frenzied staff.

"Bless you. Bless you!" the Superior Mother shouted, seized the dishes from him, and practically flung them onto the Platform of Fertility.

The platform was a warming board as long as Dubban's two arms outstretched, fashioned of wafer-thin slices of emeralds heated and lit from below by simmering magmalamps installed in a hefty copper box. A physician-natalist poured a portion of warm sacred nectar into the storage dishes and artfully rearranged them on the platform, setting a dish on each side of the Bosom of Pan—a covered begetting dish of pale green crystal.

The Superior Mother straightened Dubban's cape and miter, smoothed beads of sweat off his brow with her thumb, reattached the priest's chip, spritzed him with a floral perfume, and finally smiled.

"What's your name, midwife?"

"Dubban Quartermain."

"I hereby anoint you, Superior Father Dubban. Father Dubban, you're about to beget a magister unborn. I've got the speeches." Her eyes widened in horror. "Shit! Can you read?" At his nod, she exhaled with relief. "Splendid. You only have to read yours and follow my movements. That's all that damned Doublet ever does."

"But they're magisters. What if they enter into sharemind with me?"

The Superior Mother blanched. "I'll enter, too, and say you've taken a vow of silence. Let's get this over with. Quickly."

They composed themselves, the Superior Mother gingerly took his hand in the ritual handclasp, and they and their entourage of physicians solemnly marched into the begetting chamber proper.

The chamber was sweltering, cookstones blazing in every corner, since the materia would not blend properly unless heated to the temperature inside a human body. Dubban blinked stinging perspiration out of his eyes and gazed at the tall, blond magister subpures crowding the chamber. Everyone was slicked with sweat, dark blossoms of perspiration sprouting in armpits and on breasts of their formal sateen costumes. Blue eyes, bright or pale, regarded him, some questioning his stature and coloring, some pleading for a fruitful begetting, others impassive.

At once their magister sharemind overwhelmed him with its power. He couldn't resist, but could only be compelled to enter, his consciousness completely apprehended. He felt as if a gigantic fist gripped him and squeezed. The booming of their vaster consciousness nearly deafened him. He wondered if the Superior Mother had tendered her explanation, but couldn't apprehend her individual consciousness at all amid the clamorous thoughts and gleaming images. He sincerely hoped these gigantic vigiles, prefects, and councillors wouldn't discern he was an impostor and murder him on the spot.

Dubban approached the front of the chamber where the sharers and their parents, clad in traditional green, stood for the Rite of Begetting.

The physicians set the Platform of Fertility upon the dais, positioned the huge viewglass over the Bosom of Pan, and distributed the bouquets among an array of carved-jade vases. More glorious bouquets of roses and lilies had been set around the chamber by the families, congesting the air with perfume and pollen.

Dubban suppressed a sneeze and stared.

One sharer was an enormous vigile with golden hair, his massive handsome face twitching with pain. He leaned heavily on a body support. Dubban noticed the stiff, unmoving line of the man's left leg. He hadn't lost an entire leg through a natal defect or an Imperial punishment. No, not a vigile of the magister purity about to beget among such company. He must have lost his leg in some grievous accident.

The other sharer was a dead woman.

Her preserved corpse, freshly clad in an emerald-green begetting gown, reclined in a translucent sarcophagus, her eyes comprised of ivory orbs and costly sapphires for the irises. Her family was obviously wealthy and a very high subpure. Dubban studied her face, then started. Was this the famous Prefect Clere Twine?

Dubban glanced again at the vigile, struck with deep sympathy and compassion for the suffering man. And was this Clere Twine's gallant sharer, then?

Dubban shuddered. *Horan Zehar was murdered by a vigile at the temple,* Salit Zehar had told him. And Clere Twine, according to Milady Faro's dream in the Mind of the World, had been slain by a Heaven's Devil.

He'd dreamed that dream at least three times.

And now he, Dubban Quartermain, collaborated with a Devil? The daughter of the same Devil who slew the prefect? A terrorist who had participated in the atrocity at the temple?

Dubban kneaded his forehead. What terrible thing was he about to do? How could he have agreed to bargain with Salit Zehar?

I'm averting a worse terrorism, he reminded himself for the thousandth time. *I deserve a medal, remember? She wanted to poison the very unborn you're about to beget. This unborn and all the rest in Secundus Natalry. No one wants the bad threads. Not these magisters. Not the natalry. Fulfill your bargain, erase your debt, and never deal with Heaven's Devils again.*

"Father Dubban," the Superior Mother whispered. "I know it's warm in here, but get hold of yourself. You begin." She thrust the speech into his clammy hands.

He cleared his throat and deepened his voice. "Hear ye, hear ye. All you who have gathered here today to witness this sacred begetting, by the grace of the Imperium. These sacred sharers"—he gestured at the maimed man and the dead woman—"have duly commissioned this begetting, which has been approved by Secundus Natalry, supremely blessed by Our Superior Mother"—she bowed—"and Our Superior Father"—he bowed—"and will be joyfully bestowed with the Imperial imprint of a security number after consummation of the miracle of Pan."

Spatter of applause. Several magisters began to weep.

The maimed vigile, flushed with excitement and the heat, suddenly gasped and clasped his chest. Dubban glanced up, horrified his speech had been faulty. The vigile's knee and prosthesis crumpled. The man began to collapse, but Dubban checked his impulse to reach out. Under protocol, before a whole room of magisters, he didn't dare touch the vigile unsolicited. "Help me," the vigile said in a strangled voice, exercising his prerogative. Dubban rushed forward and caught the man's broad shoulders. He saw dark scarlet stains surging through the vigile's green sateen tunic, heard voices gabbling all around him.

"—damned Heaven's Devils—"

"—wounds won't heal—"

"—*do* something, somebody, please!"

Three magisters stepped forward and seized the vigile by his shoulders and knees, lifting him off his feet.

"One moment, everyone," the Superior Mother called out brightly. "Our sacred sharer is overcome with the heat. We'll resume in a moment. Do help yourself to the refreshments in the banquet room to your left. Dubban," she said to him in a feverish whisper, "what can we do?"

She, the Superior Mother who presided at Rites of Begetting every day of the year, and all her physicians didn't know there was a supply room with medical kits five steps down the hall from this chamber?

A priestess-natalist asked a midwife what to do?

During initiation into the natalries, every midwife had been instructed and tested regarding the location of every supply room in every Imperial building—in case of an emergency.

Dubban pulled the ridiculous miter over his forehead, screwed up his face in feigned perplexity. "Well, uh, Superior Mother, I'm trying to think . . ."

The Superior Mother's eyes widened at his audacity. She yanked twenty more ores from her skirt pocket, shoved them into his hands. "You take care of this, midwife, or I *will* have your head."

"Your will is mine, Superior Mother."

Dubban directed the three magisters assisting the vigile and two of the attending physicians out of the begetting chamber and down the hall to the supply room. They entered and locked the door. Dubban scrabbled among the shelves, shoving aside jars of amnio and stacks of bandages. He pulled out a medical kit. Yes! Vials of nopaine, a needle and syringe to administer the anodyne, needles and thread for suturing, a bottle of potent astringent.

"Lift his tunic. Gently, gently, please," said one of the physician-natalists.

A magister, who from the resemblance of face and stature appeared to be the father of the vigile, lifted the injured man's stained tunic. Everyone gasped at the sight of the angry wounds, no longer fresh and still far from healed. One scabbed-over laceration had split open and drooled blood.

"You look strong, Superior Father," the physician said sarcastically, her revulsion at Dubban touching a magister pure plain on her face. The physician had invoked proper protocol, though, by inviting his touch. "Would you please hold him?"

Dubban grasped the vigile's muscular arms in his own and restrained them behind his broad back. The physician doused the laceration with astringent, then nopaine. The physician brandished the needle and thread and looked up at the vigile for permission.

"Proceed," the vigile gasped. "For Pan's sake, do it!"

The physician swiftly stitched the two ragged edges of skin with the needle and thread as if the man's chest were a patchwork quilt of inflamed flesh that needed mending.

The vigile's father held a silver flask to the man's pinched lips. Dubban smelled good skee. "There, there, our little Reg," the magister whispered tenderly. The vigile greedily drank.

Dubban released the vigile's arms and ran for a towel to blot the worst of the bloodstains from his tunic.

The vigile recovered himself. He stared at Dubban, the physicians, the magisters, his bright blue eyes fervent, as if committing their faces to memory. Whispered hoarsely, "My eternal thanks on this, the day of my first begetting. I won't forget any of you."

The magisters carried the vigile back to the begetting chamber, restored, refreshed, and cheerful. Applause thundered when they bore him in, smiling and waving. Shouts rang out, "Hear, hear, Regim!"

"For all Eternity will Regim live!"

"For all Eternity will Regim and Clere live!"

"Let us proceed with the miracle on this miraculous day," the Superior Mother cried.

The Superior Mother handed Dubban a syringe, took up the second syringe herself. They each extracted all the materia from the storage dishes with the syringes, Dubban from the maimed vigile's dish, the Superior Mother from the dead woman's dish. Together they pushed the plungers, spurting the liquid-borne contents into the tepid pool glistening in the Bosom of Pan. Someone among the families whooped indecently, followed by suppressed laughter and murmurs of "Hush!" The physician-natalists rushed forward and poured the rest of the sacred nectar into the green-crystal dish.

The Superior Mother peered through the viewglass at the mingled contents in the dish. "Damn," she muttered. "I can't see a thing. Father Doublet always did this part. Do you know how to focus a viewglass, midwife? And don't play the idiot again. You've taken every last ore I've got on me."

"Of course I know, Superior Mother." Dubban stepped up to the viewglass, expertly touched the knobs, and adjusted the focus the way he always did in the laboratories.

And he saw the miracle—the regal birthpod presiding in its sea of nectar surrounded by frenzied seeds, their tadpole tails wriggling madly. Some seeds assaulted the birthpod directly, some swam away, some chased their tails like dimwitted puppies. At last a vigorous seed broke through the birthpod's surface and gracefully dove inside like a swimmer diving into a forest pool.

All the other seeds battered haplessly against the pod, but no others succeeded in breaking the surface. Perhaps the skin of the birthpod had grown impervious to them.

One. It had taken only one.

"Ah," Dubban whispered, astounded at the sight and deeply moved. He'd seen many seeded birthpods in four years of midwifery, but he'd never seen this: the actual moment of begetting.

And an image of the lovely woman with hair like autumn leaves rose in his memory so powerfully she could have been kneeling before him again, here, in this chamber. One. Only one, the *right* one. That was all he needed.

All he needed. And everything.

He blushed, and guilt assailed him. This moment should have belonged to the maimed vigile, the sharer from whom the seeds had been harvested, from whose sacred sharer the birthpod had been harvested forty years ago. Not him, an impostor and a serv pure. He glanced up at the Superior Mother, mortified at having usurped the sacred moment from its rightful witness. Whispered, "It's done."

The Superior Mother smiled triumphantly, as if Dubban himself had facilitated the physical process. "You may step forward, Regim Deuceman. The power of Pan has manifested. Witness the miracle Our generous Sacred Imperium of Pangaea and Our skillful Superior Father have brought to you," she said in a ringing voice.

Dubban realized he'd done *just* the right thing. *Skillful?* But he hadn't done a thing. He breathed with relief that his presence hadn't impeded the power of Pan. Then he wondered, *If I did nothing to cause the begetting, how could I do anything to impede it?*

Enough! Enough wonderments for one day. But he wondered again—what his mother would say to that?

The maimed vigile stepped forward and stared through the viewglass for a long time. Tears cascaded down his tremendous cheekbones. Four memorializers from the Pyramid of Perpetuities carried the dead woman in her sarcophagus to the platform and leaned her preserved face over the viewglass as if she could see her birthpod seeded by her sacred sharer. A mimicker stood behind the sarcophagus, ready to pull the wires connected to the dead woman's jaw and deliver the speech her family had prepared, but the Superior Mother pressed her forefinger to her lips, signaling the mimicker to keep silent. The moment was too profound.

The vigile's father and mothers stepped forward to look and exclaim. Dubban gasped. Was that Councillor Claren Twine of the High Council? One of the most powerful pures in all Pangaea? Another quartet of memorializers bore the embalmed corpse of an old woman in a translucent sarcophagus and leaned that sarcophagus over the begetting dish, too.

Then each family member approached the Platform of Fertility, oohing and ahhing over the Imperial miracle transpiring before their eyes in the Bosom of Pan.

"Softly, gently," the physician-natalists whispered as the distinguished magisters jostled each other like unruly children for a better look. "Nothing is assured quite yet. We've yet to install the holy fruit into the birthsack and the gestation tank—"

"Best ges tank in Atlan," someone among the families shouted drunkenly.

"—but all should be well, by the grace of Pan," the physician-natalists murmured in their ritual affirmation. "All should be well for Regim and Clere's unborn."

The Superior Mother intoned in a stirring contralto—

I issue from the Bosom of Pan.
I come through You, Sacred Sharer and Sharer.
I am formed in the Nectar.
I emerge from the Blood.
I am shaped by my Ancestors,
I take Breath from the Imperium,
And all the Purities will welcome Me!

"Go on, get out of here, you rowdy," Waldo said over Dubban's shoulder. "And don't come back."

Dubban started, jostling the hand-levers, nearly cutting too far into a marked thread. He'd returned to Secundus laboratory to finish his pruning duties. He panted slightly, still winded from his sprint across the courtyard between the bank and the natalry, considerably wealthier than when

he'd left and intent on consummating his larceny for the
Devil girl.

"Damn it, supe. Don't do that. My hand almost
slipped." Dubban turned away from his viewglass. He'd
teased out the empty dish from the stack of begetting dishes
where he'd hidden it. *Steal the threads and be done with it.*
He pushed the dish back again. Nervous and skittish
enough at the interruption; now what did the super want?
And why was Waldo reprimanding him again when he'd
done everything he'd been asked to do? "I can't leave yet.
I'm not finished."

"Since when have you become the Obedient Midwife?"

"Just want my hours." He dropped the hand-levers with
a loud clatter. All he could think was, *How? How? How?*
"At my new wage, supe," he reminded Waldo.

"I'll credit ye with your hours. At your new wage."

"And since when have you become the Benevolent
Super?"

"I ain't no Benevolent Super, you rowdy. The Superior
Mother says you did the best damn job of begettin' she's
ever seen. Says there's a certain touch. Says you got that
touch. Says she can't believe a midwife could possibly perform a begettin'. But you done good."

The glitter in Waldo's little dark eyes was fear, Dubban
suddenly realized. Fear and deference toward that which is
superior, higher. Becoming closer to Pan.

Well, well.

"The Superior Mother says she told the magisters you're
from a high priest subpure out in Siluria. A subpure that's
especially fertile. Seems them magisters want you to preside at another begettin' of theirs. Seems they think you got
some kind of high variance even for a priest 'cause when
they entered into sharemind with you, they apprehended all
of you and couldn't apprehend nothin' more. Everybody's
buzzin' about it over at the bank. Seems the magisters think
you're some kind of holy man," Waldo rattled on in a
friendly way. *As if he's currying favor.* "Now, Father Dou-

blet, whoo. He may be out of a job. If that twit ever shows up, I'll have him finish your prunin'. Take the afternoon, Dub. Don't look so unhappy, man.''

The morrow. I'll try again on the morrow.

But Dubban didn't want his bargain with Salit Zehar hanging over his head till the morrow. Hanging over him like a sword of doom. He sprinted downstairs to the ground floor, ventured out onto the raised plaza behind Secundus Natalry where the cobblestones were more or less dry, bought a jar of beer from a vendor, and thought hard.

What would the lovely woman think of his terrible bargain? Would his living goddess revile him for what he'd agreed to do for Salit Zehar?

No. He'd make her understand.

He would become worthy of her. He would die trying to find her and win her, if he had to. He would do anything for her.

She'd shattered him, shattered every one of his mother's moral homilies, everything he'd ever thought possible for himself. That night, at the Serpent Sect rave, when his release had spasmed through him by her mercy, every vestige of the man he'd been had sloughed off.

Truly he'd emerged from the Sacred Serpent, wholly new.

He'd seized her shoulders, lifted her, searched her ecstatic face. He hadn't dared kiss her. "I'm Dubban Quartermain. Who are you? Where do you live? Where can I find you again?" He hadn't asked her pure and subpure, hadn't cared about that. His mother's voice had harangued him, *She's higher pure. She can touch you, if she desires, but you cannot touch her.*

He would have laid down his life for her at that moment. But most of all he'd wanted her to lie down with him, hidden in the mouth of the Sacred Serpent, and sweetly finish what she'd started.

The very notion of that, of his returning tenfold the pleasure and illumination she'd given him, had pierced him.

Spent though he was, he'd immediately stirred for her anew.

But she'd shaken her head, and her small dark friend had seized her from his arms. "Don't you touch her, serv," the friend had declared above the terrible din outside their hiding place. She'd glared at him, bestowing upon him the best approximation of the evil eye he'd ever seen. "You've got no place with her," the friend had informed him. "Take us to the back exit, at once, like you said you would. We've got to go before Vigilance arrests us," and forcibly dragged her through the fence of fangs.

He'd pulled on his leggings and taken them through the kitchen to the exit he knew. The tiny tunnel burrowed through several lengths of rock and spilled out into an outcropping half a league away from the main entrance to Stompsalot Cavern. A Vigilance surveillance craft had hovered above the main entrance, illuminating the entrance with bright lamplight. Vigiles had milled about, rounding up the arrestees.

He'd climbed out after her and her outraged friend, pointed in the direction of the public windship station they sought.

And then she and her friend had dashed away in the rain and the night.

If her sudden presence had been like the first sunrise of his life, her sudden departure had been a chasm yawning open at his feet. He'd considered following the two women, but he hadn't wanted to offend or frighten her or her protective friend. Outside the rave, no longer tainted by a proximity violation, the friend could have summoned a vigile and accused him of accosting them. And he would have spent the night in Quartius Jail or worse.

He'd let them go.

He regretted his reticence now. The man he'd been before would have shrugged and shaken his head at the wild ways of the megalopolis, where a high pure woman would risk contamination by willingly giving pleasure to a lower pure. He would have bought another quid of qut and raged at the futility of his life. So many people in the megalopolis. He'd never see her again.

But the newly emerged Dubban wouldn't let her go. Wouldn't let the hope of finding her again go. He'd made a solemn vow in the belly of the Sacred Serpent that night.

Defy the Imperium. Become worthy of her.

He'd set out to do just that.

He'd gone to Allpure Library and studied the practice of midwifery for the first time. He'd learned that the origin of the strange name of his subpure was a derivation of the designation women took when they entered into the sort of sharelock that existed before the natalries. He'd pondered over the tasks midwives had undertaken in times lost to antiquity. His mother had promised to tell him these shocking, barbarous things one day.

He'd found them out for himself.

The texts were frustratingly vague, but by cross-referencing to franker texts describing the behavior of beasts, he'd been able to deduce the meaning of terms like "birth chamber" and "pleasure passage." He'd studied the tasks physicians had undertaken, too, why they were deemed closer to Pan, and therefore higher pures than midwives. Though what midwives had undertaken in ancient times had often amounted, Dubban thought, to tasks of greater importance.

He'd raised his hovel on Misty Lane, demanding assistance from Nita and Rando. He'd spent extra ores on roof tiles of hard-cured clay that wouldn't catch fire in the next conflagration. He'd paved his dirt floor with more of the tiles and started tiling his daub-and-wattle walls. He'd discovered he had plenty of extra ores when he didn't squander everything he earned on qut and bedmates of the moment.

The ores he'd persuaded that day from pockets, free of Imperial taxes? Half he'd store in his treasury account, the first money he'd ever been able to amass in one place. The

other half he'd spend on a thick wool rug to warm his tile
floor and a bed, a real bed of feathers neatly stuffed in a
large cotton sack. Perhaps the tunic of copper-colored linen
for an ore that he'd tried on from the bin at the temporary
shelter, the one that flared over his shoulders and nipped
him closely at the waist. Rando had quipped, "You look
like a boy-chaser," but Nita had assured him, "You look
very handsome, Dub." If discord had arisen between fisher
and fisher, that was their trouble, not his.

And if it was utter foolishness to think *she'd* ever come
here, to Rancid Flats, to his hovel, to lie on his bed even for
one night—he didn't want to think about that.

Only that one night she would. She would.

Dubban tipped his jar of beer and surveyed northeast
Marketplace. Servs stepped up from the sopping street,
cursing and shaking out their sandals and clogs. From his
vantage point, he could see filthy water purling across cobblestones of the quadrant all the way to Allpure Square and
beyond, to the south and the west. Water respected no purity protocol.

Neither do earthshocks or magma eruptions.

He held that blasphemous thought in his mind, savoring
it the way he'd savor a pepper candy, eyes watering at the
spicy bite. Vigiles and prefects, physicians and priestesses,
midwives and orderlies—all would soak their shoes today.
No citizen of Atlan had escaped the disaster in the
Hercynian Sea. Except perhaps the angels, sequestered in
their cloudscrapers.

What of the self-aggrandizing lies he'd considered telling Salit Zehar? *I bribed the orderly who transports filth
from Secundus.* Or *I stole the orderly's maintenance cart.*

Hmm. And then *Yes!* If appropriating an empty storage
dish from the supply room, scraping pruned threads into the
dish, and slipping the dish from beneath the viewglass into
his pocket, all in front of Waldo's nose, had proven to be
nearly impossible—

—then stealing garbage from a drud orderly seemed a very sound strategy.

Dubban guzzled his beer, flung the jar into a wastebin, and ventured out onto the street.

He would not wait for the morrow.

"Hai, Yerba," Dubban called to the brawny orderly as she pushed her cart into the waste disposal chamber in the basement of Secundus Natalry. The chamber contained bins for discarded metal objects, paper, and cloth, and a huge incinerator leaping with flames. Since he'd been rotated to laboratory duty here, Dubban possessed an access permit to Secundus. Waldo had forgotten to appropriate his permit when he'd left. He could come and go from the natalry as he pleased for the entire day. "Wait a moment."

"Yeah?" Yerba turned, hopeful and wary, accustomed to bribery and abuse in equal measure. A wily creature, the orderly left a sprinkling of bacco ashes everywhere she went, could barely survive from one moment to the next without relighting a fresh cheroot. Yerba would feign deafness whenever anyone ordered her to do something she was disinclined to do.

"Got something for you, sweetie," Dubban said, mindful of all he knew about Yerba. He proffered the tin of cheroots and the paper box of seaberry cakies he'd bought in northeast Marketplace.

"Oh, my," the orderly said, fingering the treats. Her opaque eyes flew up at him, cloudy with suspicion. "What d'you want wit' me, midwife?"

How many physician-natalists had risked violating proximity and importuned upon this unfortunate creature to satisfy the bestial urge? Or the urge for cruelty? "Just want to help you out today, Yerba," he said kindly and pushed her cart up to the fiery maw of the incinerator.

Again, the suspicious eyes. "Why?"

"I've pledged to serve Pan today by serving a lower pure."

"Truly?"

"Truly."

The orderly's eyes filled with grateful tears. "Oh, mid-wife!"

"Go have a smoke and enjoy your cakies. I'll take care of this."

Again she said, "Truly?"

"Yes, yes. Truly. Go now."

He commenced tossing into the incinerator the sordid garbage the orderly handled—spent birthsacks, soiled fluids, discarded yolk stalks no longer necessary for feeding the unborn. The flames smoldered. The stench of burning human waste nearly made him retch.

A copper carrying rack held crystal slivers smeary with stale storage solution. Contaminated, Dubban knew, with the threads of disease.

May Pan and the woman I love forgive me for what I must do.

He withdrew a stack of glass dishes, carefully placed a sliver in each dish, snapped on the lid. He flung the rest of the slivers into the incinerator, watched as they crackled and burned. He slipped rack and dishes into a burlap sack, hoisted the sack over his shoulder.

And set out in search of the Devil.

Forthcoming in October 1999

PANGAEA: Book II
Imperium Afire

ABOUT THE AUTHOR

A Phi Beta Kappa scholar and a graduate of the University of Michigan Law School, Lisa Mason is the author of four previous novels: **Arachne** and **Cyberweb**, published by AvoNova, which are cyberpunk tales taking place in a future California; also, **Summer of Love** (a Philip K. Dick Award finalist) and **The Golden Nineties** (A *New York Times* Notable Book of the Year), published by Bantam Spectra, which are time travel tales.

Mason published her first short story, "Arachne," in *Omni* and has since published acclaimed short fiction in numerous publications and anthologies, including *Omni, Year's Best Fantasy and Horror, Full Spectrum, Asimov's Science Fiction Magazine, Magazine of Fantasy and Science Fiction, Universe, Unique, Transcendental Tales, Unter Die Haut, Immortal Unicorn, David Copperfield's Tales of the Impossible, Desire Burn, Fantastic Alice,* and *The Shimmering Door.* Her novels and short stories have been translated into French, German, Italian, Japanese, Portugese, Spanish, and Swedish. She optioned her 1989 *Omni* story, "Tomorrow's Child," to Universal Pictures. Mason lives in the San Francisco Bay area with her husband, the artist and jeweler Tom Robinson.

Readers who want to correspond with Lisa directly can reach her via e-mail at LisaSMason@aol.com.